*She was streetwise . . .*

He was conspicuously handsome and he displayed a fifty-dollar bill between two long white fingers. "We won't be long," he promised.

She decided he was safe.

He gripped her bare shoulders and swung her around so her body faced the light.

"You are the one," he said. "We escape this world together."

He kissed her temples, her eyes, her mouth, and a passion such as she'd never known began to build in her, hungry and demanding.

He moved his lips to her outstretched neck . . .

# SHATTERED GLASS

## ELAINE BERGSTROM

**J**

JOVE BOOKS, NEW YORK

SHATTERED GLASS

A Jove Book/published by arrangement with
the author

PRINTING HISTORY
Jove edition/July 1989

ISBN: 0-515-10055-2

PRINTED IN THE UNITED STATES OF AMERICA

10  9  8  7  6  5  4  3  2  1

*To Carl, Lenore and Kriista who lived without me for a while.*

*To Clemmie who looked the other way.*

*To Diane and Amy at Sherlock's who kept the coffee coming.*

*And to Ruthless who was one hell of a cat.*

"... 80 cathedrals and 500 churches of near cathedral size were started in France alone in the period 1170–1270; and many of these were almost finished within that period. It was an activity that is estimated to have taken up at least one third of what would now be called the Gross Domestic Product. It is a phenomenon that has never been explained and probably never will be. We can see only that something prompted people of all trades and classes to undertake a venture that resulted in workmanship and inspiration of a degree rarely equalled in the history of mankind...."

—from *Rose Windows* by Painton Cowen

# SHATTERED GLASS

# Prologue

## may 1955

SPIKED HEELS CLICKED on the sidewalk, the loudest sound on the lifeless, rainwashed streets. The girl traveled at a pace one step slower than a run, taking a circuitous route to the downtown bus station. Her ticket was waiting with her suitcase in a locker; one more hour of freedom and she'd be gone. Occasionally she risked a hasty glance beyond her reflection in dark windows to assure herself she was not being followed. As she walked, she prayed, an unconscious return to a religious childhood.

When she caught on to what she was doing, she giggled. "Everybody prays sometimes," Mama had screamed after her as she'd walked out of the house for good. *Well, Mama, you were right, and my time has come.* Giggling again, she merged her steps with the words of an irreverent litany: "Nevada . . . freedom . . . Nevada . . . Please, God . . . just this chance. . . . Please, God, don't let him know. . . . If he don't know I'm going, I'll be gone. . . . Please, God . . . just this once let *me* be the boss of my life."

So absorbed was she that she was startled when a lean man in black stepped out of the park gate and into the light of the solitary street lamp only a few yards in front of her. He motioned to her and she knew, in this place at this hour, precisely what he wanted.

Streetwise, she studied him and decided he was safe. Did she know this one? She didn't think so and she was sure she would remember him if they had met. Though she rarely no-

1

ticed men's looks, this one was conspicuously handsome and his bearing told anyone who cared to inquire that he was in charge here, now. She decided to skirt him cautiously—and then found herself walking over to him.

"I can't stop now. I gotta be somewhere in an hour."

He displayed a folded fifty-dollar bill between two long white fingers. "We won't be long."

Avarice flickered in her eyes. She considered the suddenness of his proposition, her wariness, her need for speed, and, again, the amount he offered. Avarice won. "Do you have a car?" she asked, glancing up and down the street.

"The park will suffice, and when we are finished, all you need do is tell me your destination and I will take you there." He took her arm and led her through the entrance and down a private path.

She detected some merriment in his voice. She liked that, and the accent as well, foreign and exotic. "My name's Angela." She accentuated her introduction with a seductive bounce and a wide smile. "What's yours?"

"Mine?" He paused as though he were trying to choose one name among a multitude of possibilities. "Charles," he said. Then repeated, more loudly, "Charles Austra." His mouth twisted in a smile as he grasped her arm more firmly and steered her toward the shadows. In a nearby clump of shrubbery, a drunk rolled over and went back to sleep.

"It's dangerous here," she said, glancing into dark places, half hoping to see a mugger lurking somewhere. An uneasy feeling began to gnaw at the streetwise part of her mind. This john was a mistake. There was no real reason to worry except that he gripped her arm too tightly, he looked at her too greedily, his desire—and she knew all about desire—was too detached.

"I love the night and the dark is so comfortable, don't you think?" His voice, low and musical, soothed her rising panic.

"But your suit," she protested. "It's really nice and it'll get all wet and grass-stained. If you got a car, we could—"

"Quiet!" he commanded, and his fingers squeezed even harder. She nearly cried out. He led her to a great clump of bushes a short distance off the path. They were mock orange, with a cloying fragrance that reeked too brazen for nature in the rain-soaked air.

His back was to the bushes, his face a pale mask in the weak light of a distant street lamp. When he released her, she would have bolted, but she had already been trapped by his dark magnetic beauty. "Shall I undress?" she asked with volatile calm.

"Your blouse." She complied with clumsy haste, forgetting all her charm, anxious only for this encounter to end.

"And your bra." She unsnapped it with shaking fingers. "Now the rest."

When she had finished, he gripped her bare shoulders and swung her around so her body faced the light. "Beautiful," he murmured. "I knew you would be. I have watched your desires. You are the one. We escape this world together."

She opened her mouth to make one final protest.

"Silence!" he ordered. His hands stroked her shoulders as his lips closed around one nipple, his tongue brushing until it hardened. He moved to the other, then back to the first, the sucking now followed by a light nip. It was no more than so many had done, yet her stomach fluttered in unfamiliar arousal, and a passion such as she had never known began to build in her, hungry and demanding. With one hand he grabbed her hair and pulled her face up to his while he forced the other between her thighs, seeking, then stroking. Perfectly—as she would herself. He kissed her temples, her eyes, her mouth, first lightly then fiercely, and moved his lips to her outstretched neck. Her fears, her needs, her life were forgotten as she shuddered in a fulfillment of glorious intensity. . . .

# Part
# One

Helen
*may 1955*

# Chapter One

## I

THE FRONT ARRIVED after the storm and cooled the hot and sticky air, making the evening as lovely as the day had been unbearable. Helen Wells sat on her uncle's porch, refreshed by the comfort of the night, calling and waving to an occasional friend who passed by.

She hoped the peace of this evening would never end, that the children would remain silent, that she could sit and wait. She was not certain what she expected. But she felt an expectation and it excited her.

The storm returned long enough to send down one final bolt of lightning. It knocked out the street lamps and made the inside lights flicker briefly. A hard rain fell for a few minutes, then it, too, was gone.

The final downpour so late in the evening forced most of the neighbors inside. Then they stayed in, so the street was empty. Only Helen on her covered porch remained to see the car, new and therefore unusual in that neighborhood, drive up and park in front of the empty duplex next door. A moving van followed close behind, and the occupants of both vehicles met on the dark sidewalk.

"You may begin unloading now. I'll open the doors for you." The man's tone was conversational yet firm, the tone of a person accustomed to giving orders and having them obeyed. Helen saw a slim figure walk up the steps, then a light switched on next door.

The movers were having difficulty unloading in the dark-

7

ness. One swore when a crate pinched his hand against the side of the van. "Couldn't this have waited until morning?" he complained. "No! He had to have this job done today. All the way from a penthouse in New York to this dive, and in the damned heat too!"

"Don't gripe," the other replied. "He paid us good money to move his stuff and if he wants to be out and then in again in one day, who can blame him. Moving is shit no matter how you plan it. What have you got to bitch about, anyway; you slept the whole trip. You act like you been on your feet for a week."

"That's how I feel. Maybe it's the flu coming on. Just my luck to be puking the whole drive back. Damned steps are probably slippery too." He looked up at the porch and added, "I can't even believe we're moving him in here. Dude'll fit in around here like a hangnail."

"I brought you a light." Both men started at the unexpected voice. "I don't want you to drop any of the crates," the man continued. "The contents are quite fragile."

Once they had light, the movers finished in less than an hour, and their client gave them each an additional ten dollars. They thanked him, puzzled by the bonus on top of the already generous payment.

"Thank *you*," he replied smoothly. "You have both been most helpful. Now, one final favor please?" He held out his car keys and an envelope. "If one of you would drive this back to the Hertz office on Lorain, you would save me some time tomorrow. It is on your way, yes?"

As the car and truck departed, the streetlights reappeared. Helen saw a man with broad shoulders, a slim waist accented by a belted French-style suit, and long-fingered hands. Aristocratic hands, her mother would have called them. Helen could not see his face under his wide-brimmed hat until, sensing he was being watched, her new neighbor looked up. His sharp features were chiseled by the light, and Helen inhaled audibly, for in that moment, she felt all of what life should be at nineteen. She could not determine his age but she knew that, even in full sunlight, he would have the darkest eyes and most handsome face she had ever seen.

They might have spoken, but a young voice called from the

house. Helen was immediately gone, gliding toward the door. Her neighbor heard distinctly the spongy sound of rubber wheels on the wood floor; the sound of a wheelchair.

# II

After fifteen years with the Cleveland police force, Dick Wells thought he was adept at ignoring the most brutal murders, the most grotesquely mutilated corpses. But nothing in his past prepared him for the apprehension that gripped him as he viewed the body of the prostitute killed the night before in one of the city's most beautiful—and violent—parks.

She lay naked, faceup in the bushes. Her lips were slightly open, and on them was the hint of a smile. Were it not for the gaping hole that had once been her neck, Dick would have sworn she was asleep, lost in a remarkable erotic dream.

What in the hell did she have to smile about? Dick wondered as he ran his fingers through his thick brown hair, crouching down to take a closer look at the wound.

"Kind of gets to ya, doesn't it?" a raspy voice said behind him. Sergeant Murray chuckled when he saw that he'd startled his superior. "Wonder why?"

Because people shouldn't look like that when they're murdered, Dick wanted to reply. It isn't natural. It isn't right. Instead he answered professionally, "She may have been killed in a more peaceful manner than we suppose. There is, first of all, the question of where. If it was here, there'd be more blood on the ground." He looked again at the wound on her neck. "Well, we'll see what Corey thinks. Is he on the way down from the lab?"

"An hour or so, he said."

Dick had stopped listening. He stared at the girl again, as if her expression should be able to answer all his questions.

"Want to talk to the bum?" Murray asked. When Dick nodded, the sergeant led the way to the park pavilion. "He didn't want to hang around the body, so we're serving him coffee. I promised him some breakfast and slipped him a few bucks so he can get plastered later. I can understand why he'd want to tie one on tonight."

The bum—warm, dry, but still shaking—sat at a table decorated with graffiti. "First thing I seen when I opened my eyes was her face smiling. No girl smiled like that at me for years. For a minute . . ." The bum's voice trailed off and he spilled some coffee on his stained pants. "Then I seen her neck."

"Last night," Wells said, prompting. "What did you see last night?"

"Nothin'. It was dark but I knew there was a guy and girl cuz they was talking. . . . No, I didn't see 'em. It was dark, like I said . . . yeah, I heard 'em a little bit. She asked who he was and he said Austrian or something. He sounded like a DP. . . . I dunno from where, Austria, I guess. . . . How the hell should I know the time, I don't own no watch. . . . The weather? Well, it was raining, then it stopped so I figured I'd stay where I was 'stead of moving someplace drier. . . . I heard 'em just after . . . then I went back to sleep. Next thing I knew, she was smiling at me." His hand slipped into his jacket pocket, then was quickly withdrawn. "That's all I know. Listen, can I go now?"

"Sure, sure. But first you have to take a trip downtown with Sergeant Murray and sign a statement, then make sure you leave an address where we can reach you if we need you again. You have some family, don't you?"

"My daughter, she lives in Lakewood. I call her sometimes. I'll give you the number. . . . No, I'll be sure to keep in touch. You think I don't want to know what did this? I'll call her a lot." He hesitated, then added with some dignity, "She's a nice girl. Things were never the same with us after her mom died."

Later the bum added Murray's five to the fifty he'd found in the girl's hand that morning. As he broke the large bill at a comfortable bar, he ignored the minute, meaningless symbols along one edge. He knew full well that if he turned the money in, he would never see it again.

# III

In her uncle's kitchen that morning, Helen lingered over a final cup of coffee while the children went outside to play. Her thoughts turned to her neighbor, and her blue eyes warmed as she remembered their brief encounter. She decided to send the children by later to invite him over . . . an invitation would be the neighborly thing to do.

Rationalizing like a schoolgirl, she chastised herself, though wasn't that after all what she was? The conflicting thoughts sobered her and all the might-have-beens threatened to cloud this sunny morning, when her cousin, Carol, burst in, ponytail flying.

"Go out on the porch and look at the house next door! It's prettier than church on Sunday! Close your eyes, I want to surprise you."

When Helen was allowed to look, she agreed. In every second-floor window of the graying, peeling duplex were magnificent designs in colored glass. The three in front appeared to be part of a set of changes of the seasons: a brilliant sunset reflected on snow, autumn leaves whipping in the wind, moonlight in a summer garden. Spring must be elsewhere, Helen thought, but when she looked out her dining-room window later, she saw instead a stylized Greek temple, its classic lines reflected in a deep blue pool.

"There's one with trees and a waterfall in the kitchen, and a pattern in dark red colors in the back bedroom," Carol informed her. "The windows above Swift Street are empty."

"He might have left those uncovered because the sun doesn't hit that side of the house and the colors wouldn't be so vivid," Helen said.

"He?" Carol asked with preteen interest.

"I saw a man move in last night. He's certainly been busy."

"Do you think he made those?"

"Perhaps he just owns them." Helen found it difficult to

move her eyes from the winter scene. "I wonder if he owns any more. Can you imagine how magnificent they must look from the inside if they're so lovely when we're only seeing the reflected light?"

"I want to see! Let's invite him over and then he'll have to invite us back." Carol leaned over the rail and motioned to her cousin Billy, who was standing on the sidewalk. "Let's do that now!"

"It was late when he moved in." Helen paused. "It was nearly eleven, and he must have been up for quite some time afterward. We had better..."

Carol watched her cousin walk up the steps to the front door of the house next door. "I think it's too late."

"Billy, not now!" Helen called.

"I already rang it, so I better wait," the boy called back.

They all waited. Helen prepared to apologize when the man appeared. Instead the door opened and Billy was motioned inside. A moment later he scurried back to them.

He glanced at Carol and whispered rapidly, "I shouldn't of done it. He was *really* mad. But he said he'd come over tonight. I think he was sleeping."

Next door, their new neighbor muttered an ancient and graphic curse regarding ravenous beasts and mischievous children, then returned to a low platform that served as his bed. He had placed it beneath the wine-colored window, and the morning light bathed the room in deep crimson, gold, and blood red. There was only a thick feather bed for a mattress and no sheets or covers, but he did not appear to notice. In a moment he was asleep.

# IV

It was another terrible afternoon, hot and sticky and endless, the black clouds over the lake tantalizing the city with the promise of rain. Helen's uncle called and said he would not be home for dinner, if at all that night. He made no complaints, gave no comments, and Helen knew he must be working on something important. Curious as to what the paper might report, she sent the children to Becker's Grocery with a quarter each for a soda and something extra for the *Cleveland Press*. Once they were gone, she drew a deep, cool bath.

It had not been easy, but she had finally learned to enter and exit the tub by herself so she could have privacy at one of those times she wished it most. Still, when she had achieved that success, she'd felt only a moment of triumph before her happiness twisted into something ugly, something crippled. She had ordered her congratulating parents out of the room and sat in the empty tub and cried for what seemed an eternity. When she had wheeled herself out of the bathroom, dry-eyed and composed, she'd never complained about her useless legs again.

Now, on this warm afternoon, refreshed and powdered, Helen remembered the anticipation of the night before. Humming an old ballad, she plaited her pale blond hair into two long braids and crisscrossed them over the top of her head. After slipping on a pastel sundress, she dabbed cologne behind her ears, found her sketch pad, and began to work. If she wanted any chance at even a partial scholarship for the fall term, she would need a more extensive portfolio by mid-July.

## V

Dick Wells sat in his office, typing furiously. There was an enormous amount of paperwork associated with a homicide, and while he usually hated to write reports, today he regarded the duty as a relief. Cold, precise words kept him from thinking about the smile on the face of that corpse. He thought again of the unusual personal fear this murder instilled in him; the wrongness of it, the—

"Got an hour or so, partner?" Bob Corey, Cleveland's forensic "specialist," strolled in.

Four keys jumbled together. "Christ, Cor! Can't you knock?"

"Never have." Corey plopped his thick body into a sagging

leather chair and chuckled. "My diagnosis is edgy, extremely edgy, so I can't wait to see what this report is going to do to you. You know, partner, I'm not ready to retire, but if I have to testify to any of this in a courtroom, I'll be laughed out of the coroner's office." He smacked the file down hard on Dick's desk, pulled a pack of cigarettes from his pocket, and, as usual, held them out.

Dick automatically reached for one, then pulled back his hand. "Gave them up," he said, then patted the file. "Do you want to editorialize, or just tell me what's in here?"

"You asked for it. I'll try to be brief, then fill in the editorial later.

"She was killed from loss of blood," Corey began, the cigarette smoke making his gravelly voice even hoarser. "She was killed on that spot; nobody moved her body there. There are two deep punctures in an artery on the right side of her neck. There is also one small but distinctive bruise on the left side of same, another on her right arm just above the elbow, and a number of small bites on her chest and breasts. She was not sexually assaulted. Because of the loss of blood, time of death is difficult to determine, but I would guess ten or eleven, give or take an hour."

"Nine-thirty is closer. What else have you got?"

"Plenty. Let me start by telling you what I think happened to her. She made a pickup and the two went into the park. She took off her clothes. Then, sometime during sexual foreplay, the killer applied pressure to her neck, knocking her out. While she was unconscious, he punctured her neck and through the holes drained the blood from her body. From her expression it must have been a painless send-off. Afterward he ripped out her throat."

"Sounds like a Friday night movie. On the other hand, we've seen stranger cases."

"I haven't. You see, the punctures may have been made by teeth. If that is true, the teeth resembled fangs and the blood may have been swallowed." He crossed his arms and grinned, a wordless, toothy comment. "And there's great odds that she was not killed by a person at all."

"Could she have been bitten by an animal while she was unconscious?"

"If you're thinking of that damned Doberman, you're miles

off. This critter was a lot more unusual. You see, our victim was an accommodating girl. Her john wanted to bite, so she bit him back. We found traces of the killer's blood in her mouth, and smeared across the side of her face. And a sample of the killer's saliva on her neck and breasts. I might have missed the saliva, except I got curious. In those spots where I found it, the blood had not dried. When I tested it, I discovered it contains an anticlotting chemical similar to that of some biting insects. As for the blood, it isn't human.

"It doesn't type or, rather, it types to anything. There's too many red cells, too many white, and too little plasma. Thick stuff. I suspect it isn't part of any known blood group, rare or otherwise. That's why I want permission to send a sample of it to the Blood Disease Research Center in Columbus for a complete workup. Their results might not help us solve the case, but it will be a first for the medical profession."

There was a long pause during which Dick looked out his window at his sun-drenched city, his brain racing. When he turned back, Corey saw a brief flash of anguish on his face and knew that this was Dick's adopted victim... the one troubling enough to keep his emotions miles away from all the rest. The feeling was shared. Though he dreaded the outcome, Corey loved this challenge. "Go ahead," Dick said, "but explain that they've got to keep their findings private until this case is solved. Maybe if we're lucky, they'll tell us your lab made a mistake."

Corey shook his head. "We didn't. All I expect is to learn a little more." He inhaled deeply on his cigarette, blowing out the smoke as he continued. "I haven't told you my favorite find. The weapon that was used to rip open that girl's throat resembled broad-tipped claws." He held up his hand. "Like fingers, Partner, this *is* the Friday night movie!"

Dick studied the section of the report dealing with the victim's wounds. "Cor, why do you think that... whatever killed that girl mutilated her body afterward?"

"Maybe he knows we won't tell the press the truth until after we catch him. In the meantime he's out there laughing at us."

"Could be, but when I looked at her neck, I thought of rage.... No, it's just this case getting to me."

Corey stubbed out his cigarette and stood. "Well, I'll leave you to contemplate my news."

"Not so fast, Dr. Corey." Dick slipped the reports into a legal envelope. "If your findings aren't chilling enough, try this: I want you to come with me now while I take this report to the chief."

Corey grimaced. "I knew you'd say that, Captain Wells. After all these years I find out I'm in the wrong calling. Damn it! I should have been a priest."

## Chapter Two

IN THE LATE afternoon the wind shifted, carrying in cooler air from the lake. On the porch, the children bounced up and down in the hammock and giggled until Billy and Alan closed their eyes. Carol covered them with a light blanket, then went inside, determined not to fall asleep. Her brother Alan was too young to appreciate art and Billy was an all-around moron, but she was not going to miss the opportunity to meet the new neighbor who owned the wonderful windows.

Both she and Helen made a pretense of watching television, hoping that someone would keep a promise he might not remember making.

It was after nine when they heard the knock. Carol rushed to open the lower door and was oddly silent as she led their visitor up the stairs. There was an awkward moment as two pairs of eyes fastened on his handsome face, but his eyes saw only Helen's.

And Helen was lost in them . . . in eyes that were so perfectly black that the pupils were distinguishable from the irises only by their greater depth. She found herself looking for her reflection there, certain that like Alice at the mirror, she could break through into another dimension. She knew in that moment not love, not passion, but rather obsession. She would go where he asked, do anything he asked, and gladly. And she waited.

But he made no requests. Instead he smiled—somewhat shyly, it seemed—and held out his hand. "How do you do. My name is Austra, Stephen Austra."

He pronounced this *Steffen*, and his English had a too-perfect enunciation, as if he had learned it as a second language. His voice was musically inflected, with an odd, lilting cadence.

Helen's arm felt as heavy as her legs but she found the will to raise it. "I'm so pleased you came. I'm Helen Wells." As she took his hand she panicked, as if in reaching for a familiar item she had touched instead something unknown and exotic. The feeling was too fleeting to analyze, but having grasped even this small part of him, she was oddly reluctant to let go.

Her cousin, however, would not be ignored. "I'm Carol Wells," she said, moving between them, "and I think your windows are the nicest thing I've seen in this..." She paused and sought a suitable word. "...wretched neighborhood."

"Wretched, is it? Tell me what makes it wretched."

"Everything." Carol rolled her eyes toward the ceiling and sighed with tremendous emphasis. "When you've been here a while, you'll understand."

He assumed an air of complete sincerity. "I certainly hope not, although I did request from the rental agent that my apartment not be on the ground floor in the eventuality that, as you say, this area is wretched. I wish to protect my art."

"Your windows are magnificent," Helen said. "Did you make them?"

"Yes." He paused, then added, "I am here to design and renovate windows at St. John's, but please, let that be our secret." He winked at Carol and she nodded agreeably.

"My uncle is on the Parish Council, so I understand. But don't your windows advertise that you're here."

"They are not noticeable from the street, and even if they were, I would put them there. I like to look at them."

He scanned the room and was surprised by what hung above the sofa. "That's a remarkable painting. Is the artist local?"

"Extremely. I did it two years ago." Helen spoke with hesitant pride.

"Ah! An artist for a neighbor. It will be so much like home!"

He went on to describe the Austra firm in Chavez, Portugal, then the more interesting places he'd visited in his work. He appeared interested in Carol's desire to become a doctor, and in Helen's decision to major in art when she began college in the fall. After Carol had fallen asleep, he coaxed Helen into showing him more of her work. "So many young artists begin by imitating others, yet your style seems your own from the beginning," he commented. He found two pieces that closely resembled those hanging above the sofa. "When did you paint these?"

"I was fifteen."

"But before, you must have worked a great deal, yes?"

She laughed. "I often receive compliments on my talent, but few people understand the years of work."

"How young did you begin?"

"I've always had some skill, but when I was twelve, painting suddenly eclipsed all else. I began to take care in planning my compositions and colors. When I had finished, I would look in amazement at what my hands had done, find the flaws, then begin another. Since then it is often difficult to concentrate on other things."

"When you have the capacity to create, you must be obsessed." He studied another group, then halted, marveling at the skill of her sole portrait. "Your parents?" he asked, noting the close resemblance of Helen to the woman in the picture. He caught Helen's curt nod and continued. "It is by far your best work. You must love them a great deal."

"Loved," she replied without emotion. "They died six months ago."

He recalled countless losses and, knowing the futility of words, silently expressed his compassion. From that soothing mental touch, she found the strength to continue.

"They were killed in an automobile accident. Afterward I had my family to lean on and keep me occupied. I watch Carol and her brother now, as my mother did after Aunt Mary died. Our parents bought this duplex together following the war. Now only my uncle is left. . . ." Her voice trailed off when, in a sudden rush of emotion, she exclaimed, "She was so young! He is so unfair!"

"Who?" he whispered, not trusting himself to take her hand.

"God. God is unfair. I go to church. I go through the motions of confession and communion but never have I admitted how I feel. I—" She stopped, stunned by her outburst, then pressed her lips together to keep them from trembling. When she could speak, she said softly, "I'm sorry. I didn't know."

"Nor did I. But the only wrong was to apologize."

His rebuke was so sad, she was certain he had experienced a similar grief. "Are your parents still living?" she asked.

"My mother died when I was born. My father is alive, though we have not seen each other for some years. He lives in Romania."

"And he cannot leave?" Helen asked, recalling how many of her grandmother's relations no longer wrote since the political walls had been raised around Hungary.

Stephen smiled inwardly. "Say, rather, that he prefers to live there. He has strong ties to his native soil."

They moved outside and continued earlier discussions of Europe and art. As they talked, the moon rose, making long shadows that gradually shortened until the porch became as bright as dawn. Somewhere in the house a clock struck one.

"Perhaps I should be going. It is late for you, yes?"

"Usually it would be," Helen admitted, "but not tonight." Stephen sat on the porch rail looking out at the treetops, his fair complexion, the sharp line of his jaw, the hollows under his high cheekbones accentuated by the colorless light. Chiaroscuro, Helen thought . . . so pale yet so perfectly one with the night. How candid, how much like her whole, too-forward self she felt as she told him, "I want you to know how much I have enjoyed this evening. I'm so pleased you moved next door."

"I am pleased as well." There was no mistaking the sincerity in his words.

A car pulled up in front of the house and Stephen glanced down at it. "Is this your uncle?"

"Yes. I'm surprised he came home at all."

"You said he was a policeman, yes?"

"Chief Detective, Homicide Unit . . . day shift, night shift, all shifts, especially in the summer." She added, "He will undoubtedly be in a terrible mood, so forgive him if he growls at you. The things he sees in his work sometimes affect him too much."

Dick Wells was hot, hungry, and beyond tired. In the past eighteen hours he had interviewed nearly that many friends, acquaintances, and "business associates" of the late Angela D'Amato. Other than the immediate family, which seemed decent and sadly unable to cope with the reality of this crime or their subsequent notoriety, all had been pitiful or disgusting. Bobby Rich had been particularly repulsive. The wiry pimp had pulled off his hat, turned his eyes upward, and laughed maliciously. "Too bad," he said. "That's for the record." He was still their best suspect, he and his damned killer dog, and they were checking his alibi. Dick knew it would be ironclad.

Now he wanted only a hot bath, two or three bologna and catsup sandwiches, and a few cold bottles of POC beer. Hell, he wanted to stay home, period, and push the swings for the kids and keep them safe by his presence from the "what-ifs" that crawled through the dark corners of his mind as he worked this case. So his first words when he walked through the unlocked door into the brightly lit house were less than pleasant. "Helen! What in the hell did I tell you about leaving this door open at night, and what's everybody doing up? Christ! It's one A.M.!"

"The only person up is me, Uncle, and we have a guest." Her voice, though sweet, reminded him of his late wife's. A smile, a kind word, and an undertone, though affectionate, that said "Shut up, you boor!"

Dick went into the kitchen and pried off the cap from the first of the bottles of beer he planned on consuming. He took a long swallow as he headed for the porch, fully prepared to send a giddy girlfriend packing. His rudeness in times of stress was habitual.

So Dick was confused as to whom Stephen was and what he was doing on the porch at one A.M. He turned to Helen and said gruffly, "I know it's Saturday, but this is a very inappropriate time for you to be entertaining a young man, Helen, so why don't I leave you both to say good night. And in the future—"

"Uncle Richard!" Helen cut him off, sounding like a typical American teenager.

It had been years since anyone had called Stephen "young man" in precisely that tone, and the absurdity of Wells's lecture, along with Helen's flushed face, was hilarious. As solemnly as he was able, he stood and faced Helen. "The hour is late and your uncle does naturally look to your well-being. We will be talking again, yes?"

Stifling a smile, he took her hand and raised it to his lips. As he bent forward a crimson teardrop on a gold chain fell out of his loose jade-green shirt, gleaming in the dim light. The unruly curls of coal-black hair fell down over his forehead, shading his eyes. Yet she felt the intensity of his gaze, could almost detect his perplexed look as he held her hand an instant too long. "Good night," he said, "and good night to you, sir." He nodded politely to a now-speechless Wells, turned, and left.

Dick sipped his beer and watched Stephen walk up the steps next door. "Why is it I feel like asking, 'Who was that masked man?'" he mumbled.

Helen, who had forgotten her anger, brushed the spot Stephen had kissed. "I don't know, Uncle," she replied absently, "but I like him very much. As you said, it is late. I'll go downstairs now. Good night."

The name. The accent. Dick couldn't help wondering. "Wait a minute, Helen. What time did he move in?"

"Late last night. He and the movers arrived around ten." When her uncle did not reply, she added, "He's the artist for St. John's."

Dick Wells's brief suspicion turned into embarrassment. "Listen, I'm sorry. I guess I was out of line before. Good night." As he watched the empty street he heard the low hum of Helen's wheelchair lift on the back stairway.

Stephen closed his door, leaned against the stair rail, and laughed with delight. The detective's remark, though not intended for his ears, had been the perfect final touch to a refreshing evening. If this was any preface to what the future held, America was going to be more enjoyable than he had ever imagined. Masked man! Wells had no way of knowing how appropriately that label suited him.

He congratulated himself on his decision to avoid hotel rooms on this trip. He had heard enough Mr. Austras, Monsieur Austras, and Señor Austras to last him another century or more. Young man, on the other hand, was unique.

How chagrined the young lady had been by that lecture, and his own response had been to feel briefly, but so pleasantly, the age he looked.

Ah, Helen. There lay talent, and the only sobering note in this whole evening. Normally he was repelled by infirmity, yet from the moment he touched her, he had felt an inexplicable attraction. This was not affection; he did not know her. It was not lust; lust could be ignored. It was, rather, a desire which, attacking unawares, had nearly destroyed his self-protective control, making him long to say the soft words he spoke so well; to caress her, to love her.

As he laid out the huge wooden tables that would cover most of the largest room of his second-floor apartment, he thought it might be best to avoid his neighbors altogether. But he wanted to determine the basis for her surprising allure, and it would be tragic to turn away from a friendship that had already given hints of becoming special.

*You're getting too human, Stephen, too rational. Trust your instincts.* And he settled down to work, pleasantly aware of where he would be for some part of tomorrow night.

# Chapter Three

## I

THE GOTHIC CHURCH of St. John's radiated the sweet smell of old incense, the rich tones of a dreary day diffused by gem-colored glass. As he walked past empty pews, Stephen sensed the echoes of its steeple bells, the murmur of whispered prayers. Looking up at the thirty-five-foot windows, crafted a century earlier, he contemplated the generations that had worshiped here and basked in its permanence, its enduring beauty, his own just pride.

Even from a distance his keen eyes could discern the faint cracks, the damaged leading, the cementing that must be replaced. Time, weather, and especially vandalism had marred these treasures, but once the restoration was complete, a layer of glass would be added to protect them from the elements and from the spite of man. That special glass, hard as the rocks from which it had been melted, had been his family's donation to this project.

Patrick O'Maera bustled with heavy feet down the center aisle. Accompanied by the rustling of cassock and jangling of rosary beads, he was a procession in himself . . . a huge Friar Tuck under a mane of graying red hair. He gave Stephen an enthusiastic handshake, then gestured at the surrounding glass.

"Beautiful, aren't they? A work of genius," he bellowed, "but of course you know all about them."

Thinking that the priest must chant a magnificent Pater

Noster, Stephen replied, "Austras made them, so an Austra should continue the work, yes?"

"Of course, of course, my son." He peered at Stephen in the deep, hued light. "Father Pascal's letter led me to believe you'd be older."

"I learned my art when I was quite young, and I am somewhat older than I look."

"Somewhat?" O'Maera misunderstood and thought he had given an unintended offense. "Ah, but age makes no difference when you have talent. I am given to understand that the Austras who crafted these windows were young also, and now these are national treasures. So thank God for the years you will have to create such beauty!"

The priest's voice boomed again so that Stephen, his ears sensitive to the smallest sounds, would have stepped back had O'Maera not rested one burly arm across his shoulders. "So many people have come to see our church, unusual people from all over the world, and I have relished meeting them all. But even more, I enjoy being the caretaker of this place. Sometimes, during the final benediction, I find myself looking past the congregation to the resurrected Christ in the center of that great rose window and I tell myself, 'Patrick O'Maera, when the Lord comes for you, you can say you're already in heaven.' Follow me now and I will show you the spaces for the new rectory windows. Then we'll surely have a glass of wine to celebrate your new additions to this wonderful church."

Still holding Stephen close to him, O'Maera continued as they walked. "In the rectory there's a file drawer full of proposals and letters, all clipped to negative responses. Then, when I'd almost stopped hoping, the foundations listened and the money flowed. For ten years I've labored and prayed for this day; now I am impatient for the summer to end. Ah, Stephen Austra, I am truly glad you are here."

Stephen declined the wine but did accept an offer of a game of chess. Within an hour he decided that the good father, for all his noise, would probably prove to be as pleasant a friend as he was an opponent over a chessboard. Besides, Patrick O'Maera had excellent taste in art.

## II

And time, which moved slowly for Stephen, acquired a frantic human pace as he began his second labor on the windows of St. John's.

Stephen made only three requests, and the first had to be granted before he would accept the commission. Under no circumstances were the church or foundation donors to announce that the work was in progress. Publicity, Stephen had written, would mean time spent giving interviews, answering questions from glass hobbyists, or protecting his methods. To this the Parish Council and donors had readily agreed. The congregation was told restoration would begin soon, and the scaffolding was in place only to remove damaged sections. In exchange, Stephen would work when the church was not in use. These irregular hours suited his habits perfectly.

The second, made after his arrival, was that the scaffolding be placed on all sides of the church, inside and out, immediately. "But there's only one of you, and you can't be in eight places at the same time," O'Maera had argued.

"And there are different hours of the day to do each section properly," Stephen replied. "The light must be at a certain level or I cannot work."

Nodding, O'Maera left to arrange the donation—certainly not the rental!—of the additional equipment.

From time to time O'Maera would gauge Stephen's progress but could determine no order to it save that Stephen only worked on the south windows on cloudy days or in the evenings. And he never saw Stephen check the outsides at all, but on some mornings whole sections were cleaned or marked for the repairs that were needed.

Stephen's final request was an informal one O'Maera found thoroughly puzzling. He could understand how, in the hellish summer heat, Stephen would want access to the rectory refrigerator. But all the lad ever put into it was some obscure brand of European mineral water of which he drank prodigious quantities.

O'Maera first believed this to be some sort of asceticism—a virtue he abhorred—but he was reluctant to discuss this directly with Stephen. On occasions when he had attempted to bring up personal matters, he had been rebuffed or pointedly ignored. Alone in the rectory, burdened with administrative duties while the other parish priests were vacationing, O'Maera relished Stephen's company during portions of his long, empty afternoons and did not wish to damage a tenuous friendship over what he hoped was a minor eccentricity.

So the priest approached the problem indirectly. Invitations to dinner were offered and politely declined. When he suggested that Stephen eat his lunches in the rectory kitchen, he was puzzled by the mirth he detected as the younger man shook his head.

O'Maera finally determined that Stephen must eat *sometime*. Though Stephen was unusually pale, no one possessing that much energy could be suffering from even a minor case of malnutrition. He therefore requested the retired nun who prepared his meals to make a few extras . . . particularly the cakes and pies that he, and certainly an energetic young man, could never refuse. Stephen accepted these with gracious thanks. An occasional portion reached the Wells household.

## III

When they worked together, as they often did, Helen sometimes discovered herself watching Stephen as if he were the subject of a portrait . . . one stroke here, another there, and the sharp line of his chin would be completed . . . here was the ideal shape for the hollows of his cheeks, and another, perfect for that classic Roman nose.

Studying her palette, searching for the correct tones for trees or earth or sky, the colors lived through Stephen . . . this ivory hue so perfect for his forehead and neck, that vivid black an ideal beginning for those dark and flashing eyes. Her creativity and the man had become inseparable.

Still there were times, often the best of times, when she would shudder at that unbidden memory of how she had been held on that table, her knees pressed tightly to her shoulders . . . how her sweat had covered the protective plastic gowns the doctors wore . . . and the way her nerves had danced molten pain as the needle hit the spinal cord, the unforgettable agony preceding the verdict that shattered her sense of self. A pernicious vision for this enchanting summer, yet easier than the other, of corpses and sudden madness.

Polio had taken Helen's legs, but her parents' deaths destroyed so much more. She became reclusive, confined (she lied to herself) by family obligations. Though she went out with friends, her few real dates had been disasters. They were with young men who remembered her as she had been, and so there were the awkward silences, the embarrassment, the pity. It had been worse somehow when they praised her strength, for she had but one strength: to accept the inevitable and ignore its injustice, as if she were some rare butterfly emerging from a cocoon into the dark chill of winter. Yet now rebellion grew.

From time to time she even considered arranging an appointment with her abandoned therapist. Then she would recall her past hysteria and decide not to test her newfound vitality. Not now. Later. Later, when he leaves. Later, when I am less busy.

And she was busy . . . wonderfully so! Her art became an escape, a solace, and finally her one approachable obsession as she responded to her new friend's encouragement and gentle direction.

Her portfolio was completed weeks ahead of schedule and she then created a series of delicately toned watercolors based on earlier sketches of wildflowers. When Stephen asked if he might buy two, she refused and presented them as a gift. In exchange, she received a gift of her own: a sculpture of flowers and branches beautifully wrought in pastel glass.

"It's lovely," she said, "but so much effort."

"Not so much for what you gave me. You must understand how talented you are."

She saw this was no polite praise. Her work had opened like the blooms she painted, becoming more vibrant, more graceful, more alive than she had imagined something from her mind and hands could ever be.

"Your career doesn't require an education," he told her one afternoon, then, to prove it, took five of her works to the Edel Gallery. Two were placed on display; one was sold within the week and the gallery requested the return of the rest.

"I suppose you'll have me doing a show next," she said happily as she looked down at the modest check for that first, and forever most important, sale.

"Not yet, but in two years if you work for it."

The following Friday they took a lengthly tour of the Cleveland Art Museum's modern collection, then visited some of the better private galleries. He left on his dark glasses and kept his attention on her or on the works surrounding them. Even so, she saw with a pleasant thrill, all eyes were on him, and if she was noticed at all, it was with envy.

He seemed unaware of the interest his presence caused as he pointed to various pieces. "This . . . this . . . even this. You can do better. It is merely a matter of desire and . . . practice." He'd nearly concluded with the word *time*, yet he sensed the future held little comfort for Helen.

How strong was she? Stephen dismissed this recurrent thought with the obvious conclusion: Not strong enough. So when hunger threatened control, he sought out—in convenient taverns, on crowded streets—thin girls, blond girls, girls with smoky eyes and delicate hands to hold in his way through lonely nights.

# IV

By the time school recessed for the summer, Dick had been thrust completely into the demanding role of parent. When he arrived home in the evening, Helen would often excuse herself and go down to her own apartment to work.

At first he was resentful that she did not take care of his children as before, but he quickly saw the meanness of that feeling and softened. He enjoyed seeing Helen so happy and, though far from a knowledgeable critic, even he detected the growing expertise in her work. An artist in the family . . . at last he believed it!

One Saturday afternoon when she was alone with her father, Carol requested they visit St. John's. After accepting a glass of lemonade from O'Maera, she walked to the church to watch Stephen work.

"Do I detect a crush?" the priest asked Dick.

"All of them," Dick replied, then laughed. "As my neighbor would say, 'There are sadder things, yes?' though if I were Stephen, I'd put more distance between myself and the younger members of the Wells tribe."

The priest looked at Dick with a flash of genuine concern.

"Don't take me wrong, Father, they're *mine*, but even I'd think twice before I'd take Carol to the symphony. Funny, though, she seemed to enjoy it as much as Helen did. She gets more like her mother every day."

As he drove home with Carol that afternoon, Dick reflected on his wife and the bittersweet changes his life had taken. Seven years ago, he'd been a sergeant on the night shift. Tall and broad-shouldered, he'd inherited his father's build and shrewd temper. As a result, he'd gotten a reputation on the force for cooling off the most dangerous situations merely by his presence.

Following one violent night, he'd come home to find Mary asleep at the kitchen table, her head resting beside their police radio. The next day, he sold the radio to someone at work and put in for a desk job. Even now he wished he'd made the move earlier, as if that change in his position could have postponed her death.

Dick's transfer came two weeks after her funeral and he immediately knew he'd made the right decision. Family responsibilities made him unreliable on the street, and he discovered that his real talent lay in administrative work. Promotion had been swift and, unlike Corey, he never missed those turbulent nights driving a squad.

# V

Stephen worked with an urgency acquired in a more barbaric past, when his fortunes had too often taken abrupt turns. As usual, he would have spent all of his afternoons and a good portion of his nights at St. John's, but this O'Maera refused to allow. Having watched the hellish pace Stephen set during the first three weeks, he admonished, "You need rest, laddie. Go out and do what other young people do . . . enjoy yourself!"

"But this *is* what I enjoy," Stephen called down from his platform well above the church floor, his protest colored with laughter. He pulled out one of the huge window sections from the south bank, laid it flat on the scaffolding, then covered the empty space with a sheet of plywood.

The priest leaned his bulky body against the back pew and fanned himself with the previous week's parish bulletin. When it was apparent Stephen had finished this immediate task, he continued, "You'll get dull if you keep up this pace. One-sided. That is, if you don't drop first. Just how how is it up there?"

"Enough! I surrender." Stephen wrapped one leg around a rope and slid easily down, letting go for the last ten feet and landing with a soft plop.

"Just like a cat. Ah, the wonders of youth!" And he barely sweats, O'Maera noted enviously as he pulled out a rumpled handkerchief and mopped his own dripping face.

"I need the church wagon tonight, Patrick."

"Windows, eh?" Stephen nodded. "Well, unless it's to be also used for picking up a lass, you'll not be gettin' it."

"Yer soundin' a bit more Irish than usual tonight, Patrick. And pray, what lass should I be a-pickin' up?"

"Oooh," crooned O'Maera, adopting a Barry Fitzgerald brogue. "Ye might be a-pickin' up that lovely lassie who lives next door to ye. Judging from how ye handled that

window, ye'll have no trouble a-pickin' her up a'tall." He
cackled at his play on words. "Seriously, she likes you very
much, I hear."

"I don't think that would be . . . appropriate."

Stephen's tone had grown rigid, and O'Maera reached the
obvious, wrong conclusion. "She's twice the girl—"

"And she is nineteen years old and utterly innocent! I outgrew chaste kisses some time ago!" His eyes narrowed as his
anger flared. "I am not one of your flock, Patrick. There are
things you should not presume."

Had Stephen not been a friend, O'Maera might have
melted in the heat of that anger. Instead he said stiffly, "Do
what you like. Take the car. The keys will be in the rectory
when you're ready to go."

# VI

With O'Maera's advice still echoing in his ears, Stephen
carried the windows to the church wagon and, in those few
steps, abandoned all ambitious thoughts. This was a luscious
evening, velvet-soft, with a shy sliver of a moon. And he felt
the pain, the hunger, and succumbed.

That night, within the distracting enclosure of the '47
Chevy, Stephen tasted again the intoxicating flavor of America.

He parked the car often, finally abandoning it to walk
among the multitude of sights, of sounds, of scents in the
enclaves of Germans, Poles, Czechs, Hungarians, and Ital-
ians. It had been less than a century since he'd traveled the
streets of this city, and the differences amazed him. Here was
America, growing and dynamic, with monuments ripped
down to make way for new heroes, new commemorations; the
buildings he remembered—some beautiful, some ugly—destroyed and replaced. Yet there were others that remained . . .
classic jewels of mansions and churches that had endured the
frenzied pace of New World time.

As the night assailed him, the press of the city, its lights and its people, closed in like street gangs, and he recalled vividly a wild, private place he was sure had not changed.

It was nearly two A.M., over two hours to dawn as he measured time, when he turned the wagon away from town and drove west toward the suburbs. Newer, cleaner, homogeneous, these did not appeal. But suddenly the road fell away on his left and he saw the narrow, deep gorge of the river valley. He followed the roadway that wound steeply down through sheltering trees and, a mile from the base of the hill, he turned off on a dirt road and parked. Slipping off his shoes, he walked barefoot, confident in the familiar dark, studying the pieces of sky that appeared through the trees.

These were the unchanging things . . . the same stars, the same moon . . . as immutable as he, as elemental. And it was the same night, rich and delicious, with waves of fog rolling down the valley from the lake, drowning the treetops in their frothy tide. Here the darkness was silent, predators and prey alike frozen, wondering. He knew what they were, both large and small, and detecting no human presence, he, the ultimate predator, rose and coupled with the night.

He stretched, in one instant demolishing the facade of centuries of civilization. Each sinewy muscle responded to the invitation, the hunt. He ran down fern-lined paths, across lonesome bridges, and the darkness warmed him and moved as he moved.

An hour passed, an eternity of release, when a four-point buck, astonished, broke and ran uphill toward protective civilization. At the edge of the woods, he was brought down, and his blood, dark and pulsing, nourished.

In a farmhouse on the edge of the valley, a couple engaged in their own primitive dance heard a shrill, penetrating cry. "What is it?" she asked, shivering in her lover's arms.

"Some animal in the night." And he held her closer and also wondered.

There had been another night like this countless years ago when he had been young, truly young, and he lay naked on frosty grass, his body glowing crystalline in the moonlight. He had turned and asked his father in a language that no longer existed, "Why did Mother choose me, knowing it would end her life?"

"Our women are given a wondrous gift," came the soft reply. "That of determining the hour of their death and, at the same instant, ensuring their own immortality."

And because he was innocent, he spoke the unspeakable. "What of us, if we wish to die."

"Do not ask," his father responded, "for there is only one way, and if you knew a love strong enough to give it to you, you would not welcome it."

The outside vendors at the West Side Market were arranging their stands, piling up hills of fresh fruit and vegetables in the colorless light of dawn, bantering in a multitude of native tongues. The dark-clad man walked among them, enjoying the pleasant sensation of half of Europe crowded into one small space. He stopped to make purchases only twice . . . once for a pair of aromatic Saville oranges and later for bunches of fresh thyme and coriander. He bought neither for food, but rather for the scents that reminded him so poignantly of home, of family.

# VII

It had been three weeks since the D'Amato murder. Dick had been considering moving the case down to second or even third priority on his list of the many horrible crimes of that summer when the call came in from North Olmsted. It was an interesting lead, so Dick picked up Corey and the two drove to the suburb together.

Their boots made sucking sounds in the spongy grass as they walked to the edge of the valley to view the remains of the huge buck.

"Did you see or hear anything last night?" Dick asked the couple who had found the carcass.

"We were busy"—the woman giggled—"but we heard it."

"And?"

"I don't know. A lynx maybe. Something like that."

"Dick, come and look at this." Corey was kneeling next to the buck's head, pointing to two punctures on the neck. "The blood is wet."

"So you think . . . ?"

"Damned right I do!" He looked keenly at the place where the lawn ended and the woods began and turned to see the couple edging closer, trying to eavesdrop on their conversation.

"Dick," he mumbled, "take these people to the house and come back alone."

"Hey!" Dick called, walking over to the pair. "Can we possibly get a cup of coffee? And then," he added as they walked toward the house, "I'll need to know the time you heard the noise and your names for our records and . . ."

Later, carrying a mug for Corey, Dick returned. "You always did have the eyes. What else did you find?"

Corey pointed to a footprint sunk in the mud. Without speaking, he walked down the side of the path and pointed to another print, that of a hand. Farther down there were two more footprints, then another hand. That was all—and more than enough!

"Jesus Christ!" Dick exclaimed, "those prints are at least twelve feet apart."

"Almost fifteen. And look here." Corey pointed to a bloody smear along the edge of a low-hanging leaf. "What do you think the Blood Disease Research Center will make of this?"

Dick didn't bother to answer. They both already knew.

While Corey collected his specimens, Dick walked farther down the steep hill into the muddy woods. After two near falls, he leaned against a tree and studied the area. It was difficult to believe that what had run down that buck on an uphill chase in the middle of the dark night was anything resembling a human being. But the facts were there—human hands, human feet, and alien blood. He knew how Corey felt about having to take his evidence into a courtroom. But Corey was a pathologist while Dick was still a cop, and with a cop's instinct he knew if this case was ever solved, it would end before an arrest was made. The anticipation astonished him.

Corey was packing his sample case into the trunk of the

squad car when Dick emerged from the trees. "Glad to see you," Corey called back. "Stay right where you are and we'll each grab an end of that carcass."

"You want it, huh?"

"Damn right I do!"

"Too bad. I was hoping we could say we went out for a steak."

"Well, didn't we? But I suspect we'll find it's a little on the dry side."

# VIII

O'Maera glanced furtively at the clock as he tried to follow the agenda of the Senior Citizens Outing, planned for the following Saturday. Little of what Mrs. Urban was explaining got past his wall of preoccupation, though he made a fine art of listening. Later he would rely on her notes, always meticulous, to inform him of details.

O'Maera had gone to church a little after one to apologize, and sincerely, for his meddling, and found it deserted. Where had Stephen gone? Why wasn't he here? Could he be that angry? *You're a foolish old man, Patrick*, he told himself. *Relax, it's not so important*.

But he remembered the artist's display of temper, and it was four-thirty and Stephen had not returned. As Mrs. Urban's voice droned on, O'Maera thought that at least he was in no danger of falling asleep on this formidable lady today.

At last he heard the car pull up, its potholed muffler giving it a distinctive sound. Catching his guest between sentences, he requested she excuse him a moment and rushed out of the room, leaving Mrs. Urban to gape after him in haughty astonishment.

Entering the church, O'Maera saw Stephen standing with his back to the door studying the diagrams of the north bank of windows. He paused, trying to collect his thoughts, and was about to walk forward when Stephen began to speak. "I would like to take advantage of your offer and arrange for assistants for a day or two. A quarter of the north bank and, from what I've seen, ten percent of the south should be taken down for repairs. On the other hand, the rose is finished. The scaffolding can come down tomorrow."

"Tomorrow?" O'Maera's voice was oddly subdued.

"Yes, tomorrow." Stephen turned and stared at his friend. "Patrick, is something wrong? I thought you would want it completed first."

"Oh, my son," the priest moaned, "for yesterday . . . I am so sorry."

Stephen walked toward him. "Is that all?" he asked doubtfully.

"You were so late."

Stephen's musical laughter echoed. "Patrick, I had a wonderful night!"

"Oh, laddie, I'm so glad!" O'Maera exclaimed and clapped Stephen on the shoulder in relief.

# Chapter Four

## I

BOBBY RICH ENJOYED the flats at night. If you wanted to talk business with somebody, there was no one around the warehouses to witness how the conversation would end, and the river water, cold and murky, could hide a multitude of inconveniences. He'd seen a B movie about ancient Rome and it had impressed him. Here was his Colosseum and he was Nero, his dog and his gun as Praetorian guards, obeying his orders for life or death. He didn't need this place any more than he did the girls he owned. He'd outgrown both but still used them the way wealthy politicians used poor family ties to keep their present in perspective.

He turned and smiled a wide, wolfish grin at the girl sitting silently beside him in the silver Lincoln, the nervous biting of her lower lip and the sweat sheening her light chocolate face both indications of her terrible fear. "Get out," he said, and made the thumbs-down gesture.

"Please, Bobby," she blurted, "I was scared when I talked to them, but now I'll do anything you want. I—"

"Get out." He opened his own door and pulled on the dog's leash. The huge Doberman growled and the girl felt its warm breath on her neck, heard the clicks of its nails on the leather upholstery.

He laughed as he noticed her eyes measuring the distance to the water. "Done any running lately, Linda? I'll give you to the count of five." His small eyes glinted in expectation. He liked to watch them run.

The girl pulled herself slowly out of the car, preparing to plead once more for her life. But the time for words ended when he said, "One."

She was smart enough to slip off her heels and, with one short cry of fear and rage, she bolted. Her feet were tender, the stones grated mercilessly. Behind her, Bobby said, "Two."

She saw nowhere to hide, no barrier to place between herself and death. There was only the river, distant as last night's dreams. She moved away from the glare of the headlights into the false comfort of darkness, hoping that somehow she would not fall.

"Three." She would never reach the water, and for the first time she considered a different destination. Her eyes darted, seeking a patrol car, a savior, a weapon. To her right she spied what might have been a length of pipe and veered off.

"Four." The dog's chain rattled as Bobby unhooked the leash. Her heart bruised her ribs as she summoned one final burst of speed.

"Kill." The Doberman's claws scratched on the gravel as it ran. She tripped and fell and for the first time screamed as, trying to scramble to her feet, she felt the dog's teeth close around her leg.

"Stay," a whisper commanded. When Linda dared to open her eyes, the dog was sitting quietly, looking obediently up at a man who seemed to have materialized out of the stones beneath her. She scrambled to her feet and turned to face the car in time to see Bobby pull his gun and begin walking toward them.

Her first impulse was to cringe behind the stranger, but she forced herself to remain bravely at his side. She began to offer some hurried explanation, but she looked at him—the set of his jaw and his cold, powerful eyes—and knew there was nothing she need tell.

"What the hell's the matter with you, you damned dog!" Bobby gave the Doberman a hard kick with a pointy toed shoe. Still it sat, waiting for a more important command. Bobby leveled his gun at the stranger who was, he decided, the source of his immediate problem. He preferred to use the dog—if the victim was pulled from the river, the cops were always in doubt whether a person had been involved in the death at all—but if the dog wouldn't obey, he'd risk the gun.

"Kill!" he commanded once more, with no success.

The stranger glanced at the girl, at her round, frightened child's eyes, and placed a protective arm over her shoulders. "That is your command?" he asked Rich, one raised brow the only indication this had been a question.

"Yeah, the fuckin' dog!" Bobby gave the order one last time.

# II

Linda's eyes focused first on the neon sign of a west-side diner. She knew this place—she had eaten in it many times—but not how she came to be there. The lack of memory left her curiously unconcerned. The identity of the man who had driven her there, and where he might be, were also unknown and inconsequential.

The station wagon in which she sat had seen newer days and there was a Bible in the backseat plus a few church bulletins, like those she remembered from when she had gone to Sunday services. As she moved to sit straighter, her feet, which had been resting on the car's seat, came into contact with the floor and she cried out in pain. What had happened to them? She could not remember...

The driver's door opened and a man she recognized from somewhere handed her a bag. "You're hungry," he said, giving her a reassuring pat on the leg.

So! She had been with men like this before; men who smoothed over their guilt by pretending to care. "Thank you," she replied, giving him a mechanical smile, then unwrapping the first hamburger with a kind of relief.

The smell assaulted her. She was ravenous and this was the king of all hamburgers. "Aren't you eating?" she mumbled between bites.

"I already have." One corner of his mouth twitched upward in a fleeting smile as he rubbed his chin with an index finger and considered her. "Well, Miss..."

"Linda, okay? The name's Linda."

"Well, Linda, I suggest you decide where you would like to go when you're finished."

"I don't handle that," she said, her tone suddenly all business. "You should have worked that out with . . . with . . ." With who? She had been about to say someone's name, but that wasn't right anymore, was it? Was it? The question echoed through the empty places in her mind.

"It's your decision now, Linda." There was no doubting it; not the way he said it.

"Take me home with you?"

He chuckled, more at himself than at her. He hadn't considered she might have no place to go.

## III

Patrick Joseph O'Maera muttered language not usually spoken by the religious as he tied his bathrobe and flipped on the rectory's porch light. Whoever was ringing his doorbell at three A.M. had better have an excellent excuse for doing so or he would be treated to a most unpriestly display of Irish temper—totally justified, of course. At this hour, the telephone brought the bad news; doorbells only brought drunks looking for an easy road to sobriety.

His ill temper turned to bewilderment as he opened the door to the end of its safety chain and saw Stephen with a barefoot girl in his arms. "Mother of God! What is this?" he exclaimed as he undid the lock.

Stephen gave him a look that said "Later," then placed the girl on the living-room sofa and flipped on the light. One glance at her feet sent O'Maera scurrying to the bathroom for whatever bandages and antiseptics he might be able to find.

As he cleaned and wrapped Linda's feet, he realized by her age, her clothing, and the reek of her perfume precisely what she must be. *A stray cat*, he thought, *dropped on my doorstep.*

He was angry but hid it for the girl's sake. As he picked

small pieces of glass and gravel out of her feet, he began to marvel at her endurance. By the time he had finished, his anger had vanished and in its place was a determined protectiveness. He would see that she was sent once more down the right path, for was she not also one of God's children? After finding her a blanket and pillow, O'Maera took Stephen to the rectory office.

Stephen had gambled on the priest's charitable heart and had won the toss. O'Maera did demand an explanation, and Stephen told him as much of the truth as he was able. He had found the girl, barefoot and hysterical, walking in the flats. With no place to take her, he had brought her here. "This is where stray lambs go, is it not?" he concluded.

"I'll take care of the lass, you damn fool!" O'Maera's wrath zeroed in on its intended victim. "But tell me, did it ever occur to you what sort of neighborhood you were strolling in? There's people down there who would cut your throat just for those leather boots you're wearing! Oooh!" He pounded his fist once on his desk in frustration and continued.

The lecture was educational. Stephen had not given any thought to the areas he roamed at night but, if he was going to be accepted here, and he relished the acceptance, he would have to follow some conventions. More sobering was the thought of what would occur if he were unexpectedly attacked. So he apologized for his foolishness and told the priest good night. As he walked home in the waxing light, he wondered less what the police would make of the corpse than what they would do with the dog, which was, after all, only an unfortunate, well-trained pawn.

Linda wandered in a dream world . . . a world where carnivores prowled, waiting for her to stumble as she ran, panicked, searching for memory. Pushed by unseen hands, she fell onto something soft and flowing and, as she rolled over, the Doberman rested his mammoth paws on her shoulders and stared at her with eyes fierce with the lust for blood. She fought, pushing away Bobby Rich, who leered obscenely at her, pleasuring in her struggles beneath him. "Kill," he snapped, and his face exploded into horror as parts of his flesh fell away, exposing the white skull beneath. When she could bear the sight no longer, she saw the face, cloudy except for the eyes, midnight eyes that brought forgetfulness. The dreamworld thickened and she fell into a deep, empty sleep.

In the morning, O'Maera tiptoed into the living room and in the dim light saw a small girl clutching a pillow to her chest, as a toddler would a cherished teddy bear. Her face possessed the innocence of all sleeping children, and O'Maera, sensing how close she had come to a tragic end, thanked his god for Stephen Austra.

While he fed his unexpected charge a hearty breakfast, O'Maera attempted to obtain information on her family, but for all she could or would tell him, she had no relations. He suggested she listen to the radio while he made a few phone calls, then winced as the sound of Buddy Holly filled the rectory. Before he could tell her to turn down the volume, the news came on. What was that about the flats? A dog, a dead man, a possible witness? By now he was standing beside Linda, the girl's expression indicating she preferred not to listen but felt compelled to.

"Do you know anything about this?" O'Maera questioned kindly.

"No . . . that is, I don't think so."

O'Maera recognized the truth. But inside her was a part that must remember. He felt his conscience prick him as he phoned the police so that, instead of talking to a stranger on the force, he asked for his friend, Dick Wells, knowing Dick would be gentle with Linda.

# IV

The news that Bobby Rich had reached a fitting end was the high point of Dick's day. The officer who first responded to the hysterical call from the tannery supervisor saw the mangled and partially devoured body in the center of a potholed parking lot in the middle of the flats. Standing protectively above the corpse was the dog, the magnificent Doberman that, after disobeying its old master, found its new one had abandoned him.

He was a good dog. He would serve who he could. No one was able to approach the body. The huge dog's snarls, his fierce predatory teeth, and, above all, the drops of crusting blood on his muzzle and paws kept horrified bystanders at a distance.

Police identified the victim immediately. They knew the car and the dog and Rich himself so well, they considered it only justice to try to capture the animal. But, when informed by headquarters that the dog would have to be destroyed anyway, the best marksman leveled his gun. As he took aim, the dog threw back his head and howled a wild, desolate plea to the one who would not return.

That afternoon, when the autopsy on Rich and the dissection of the dog were complete, Corey shed his brown-streaked lab coat, washed his hands, and marched upstairs to Dick's office. There, shooing out two beat cops, he sat and looked grim.

"Yes?" Dick asked, prepared to hear the worst.

"All I can say is . . . that dog deserved a better last meal than he got." With that, Corey's control broke, releasing the laughter.

"Too rich, huh?" Dick added, then laughed himself, less at the pun than with relief that the pimp had not died like Angela D'Amato.

"All rich, Dick, the dog was guilty as hell." When he was able to continue, Corey added, "Courteous of Rich to leave us this way. He's gone, the murderer is gone. . . ."

"Killer, Doc. Only people murder people."

"Picky, but I stand corrected. . . . The killer is gone and the paperwork will be minimal. Strange, though, that the dog would turn on Rich that way. There was no sign of disease in him. I suppose that unless we find our witness we'll never know what happened."

"We've got the main witness, I think. The pastor at my church called." He related the conversation, then concluded, "She may not remember anything about last night but I remember her. She was the only one of Rich's girls who would talk to me about Angela, and she said plenty. Any of it would have made Rich killing angry, assuming he found out."

The rest of Dick's day went steadily downhill. It began with Linda, who at first refused even to look at him. "You're not in any trouble," he said in exasperation. "We only need to know what happened to you."

Linda turned to O'Maera for support and, though the priest's expression seemed more implacable than the policeman's, he said, "You don't have to say anything, Linda. You're free to go."

Dick glowered at his pastor until he glanced back at Linda and saw that the girl had grown genuinely bewildered. "Go where?" she asked as O'Maera had expected.

"Home," he suggested firmly.

"I don't have one."

"Then go back where you've been staying," O'Maera persisted. "If you don't cooperate with us, you can't expect any help in return."

"I don't know," Linda said softly, then pleaded with both of them. "I'd tell you if I could, okay? But I can't. I don't know."

"Then start with what you *can* remember," Dick suggested. She looked so pitiful as she stared at him that he covered her hand with his, saddened by how small it felt against his palm. "You were a victim, Linda. There's no reason to be afraid of anything you might say. Try to remember why you were in the flats."

She took a long while to reply, then began by turning and pulling up the back of her pink angora sweater, revealing long dark bruises on her ribs. "I remember someone hitting me and saying I was gonna die, and we went somewhere and I ran." She covered her head with her arms as if to ward off an attack.

"Who drove you to the flats, Linda?"

She shook her head without looking up.

Dick laid Rich's photograph on the table in front of her. "Was it this man?"

She stared at it a long time before replying, then said only, "Maybe, I don't know."

Dick studied the wounds on the bottom of her feet and

noticed the teeth marks on one ankle. He knew the bite of a dog when he saw it, and the implication shocked him.

The girl acted as if someone had taken a damp cloth and erased selected sections of her memory so thoroughly that hardly a trace of the images remained. And someone—possibly some*thing*—had turned the dog away from Linda and straight to the throat of its master. Might that order have come from a more powerful killer . . . an intelligent predator?

*You're thinking crazy,* he told himself. Nonetheless, just before he left the rectory, he made a strange request in a deceptively businesslike voice. "Linda, would you please lift up your hair?" From what he could see, and he could see quite a bit with the cut of that sweater, there were no marks on her neck. Both relieved and disappointed, he walked to St. John's hoping that Stephen would be more help.

The church, silent and empty, reminded Wells of his years as an altar boy, when he'd walked down the deserted aisles to light the candles that would brighten this multicolored darkness. Unlike the other acolytes, he'd never felt fear in this glorious house of God, but rather a peaceful acceptance of the world. And those windows—those visions of paradise!—accented the heights, colored the depths, and spoke eloquently of the majesty that man, sanctified and purified, could obtain.

He approached the altar and, crossing himself, whispered personal, reflexive prayers for the soul of his wife and the future of his family, then turned toward the pews and called out softly, "Stephen?"

"Yes," came the immediate reply.

Dick whirled, but there was no one. In the darkness under the windows he could see nothing at all.

"The north bank," Stephen called, and Dick saw him, a black silhouette against the colored glass, sitting on the edge of the scaffolding thirty feet above him.

"I came to talk to you," Dick called in a voice so loud, it reverberated.

In response, Stephen grabbed the rope and began his descent. His bare feet plopped softly on the marble floor. "Forgive me, I would have spoken but I thought you came to pray. You wish to see me about Linda, yes?"

"I do." Dick grew uncomfortable. This was not his realm. It belonged to God and to Austra. "She must have had a pretty rough time last night. She doesn't remember anything."

Stephen sat on the front pew and slid his long legs out on the seat. "Perhaps that is for the best, yes?"

"Could be. I suppose you know the pimp she worked for was killed last night. She's our only witness—unless you saw something unusual."

"I'm not certain what would be considered unusual in that place, Richard, but I did not see anything out of the ordinary; except the girl, of course." This was a careful answer, carelessly spoken.

"Did you see a dog? A large Doberman?"

After an apparently thoughtful pause, Stephen replied, "Yes, I did. It was running. Perhaps it was chasing something."

"Did you notice a car? A silver Lincoln?"

"Yes. The doors were open and the lights were on, but it appeared empty." As Dick considered his next question, Stephen asked, "Is what happened to this man so important?"

"He was scum," Dick replied, "but the way he died was horrible. His dog turned on him. I'd like to know why."

"Perhaps the dog decided he was scum also."

This statement seemed less a question than a fact, and Dick wondered at his young friend's icy tone. "It's the best answer we've come up with. I hate mysteries, but I admit that this is one I can live with."

Stephen watched him, waiting patiently, but Dick couldn't think of anything else to ask. Instead, he commented, "It was good you were there, but in the future . . ."

Stephen sighed. "In the future I will be more cautious about where I wander. I have already made that promise to Patrick." He stretched, and in the dim light Dick had the fleeting illusion that Stephen's arms were longer than they should have been. "Have we finished? I would like to complete this section."

As Dick pulled out of the rectory lot, he remembered he had never asked his neighbor if he had seen the victim. He would have said something if he had, Dick concluded. After all, Stephen was right. How important was this?

# V

The discussion about dogs had been going on for half an hour before Dick walked into the cop shop. Originally started by Larson and Corey, it had spread to neighboring tables and now everyone was sharing their insights into the often inexplicable behavior of the canine species.

"Just the person we hoped to see," Corey called over. "Take a few minutes break, partner, and tell us if the girl knows what happened to Rich."

Dick filled his coffee mug and pulled up a chair. "She knows plenty, but she doesn't remember any of it. There's a dog bite on her ankle. The Doberman nearly had her."

"Too bad she can't tell you anything," Larson commented. "I've done a lot of moonlighting over at my uncle's kennel and we never heard of anything like what happened to Rich."

"Don't dogs get temperamental sometimes?" Corey grinned at his own understatement.

"Sure, they'll sometimes bite, especially the high-strung ones, but to kill and then eat their owners? Never. What's even stranger is that, after going crazy like that, the dog sits there and plays perfect pooch. If it weren't for Corey's autopsy, I wouldn't have believed it even after I saw it with my own eyes."

"You're the one who shot him, aren't you?" Dick asked.

"Yep, beautiful animal. Made me real sad."

"Did you find out anything afterward?"

"A night watchman heard the screams around one. He admits he played deaf. I couldn't find anybody else. I'm going to try to track down the dog's trainer tomorrow. Maybe he'll remember something odd about the dog's temperament."

Corey turned to Dick. "So the girl doesn't remember. You sure she's not faking it?"

"She's sincere." Dick described what Linda and Stephen had told him.

"What was your neighbor doing driving a colored street-

walker around the west side of Cleveland for two hours?"
Larson asked.

"He said she was hysterical and wouldn't go to the police.
He didn't want to drop her anywhere until she was lucid
enough to give a destination."

"Must have been quite an experience for him," Corey
commented.

"He seemed cool enough about it today," Dick said, then
concluded, "I suppose we'll never know what happened to
her."

"Why not call Bob Moore," Corey suggested. "He's had
some success using hypnotism to override hysterical amnesia.
He owes me one, as a matter of fact. Probably won't even
charge us."

"The girl's been through a lot. Don't you think we ought to
let this rest?"

"This isn't like you, partner," Corey replied with a concerned frown. "I'm surprised you're not in your office on the
phone right now."

Dick's temper snapped. "I'm here right now because you
asked me to sit down! Now, if you want to call up some
hokum shrink, go ahead—" He halted, puzzled by his outburst. "I'm sorry. I think I need a vacation this year."

Corey shook his head. "You need a vacation every year;
you just never take them." He paused, then continued. "Look,
Dick, like I said, Moore owes me one. Let me give him a call.
We've got to know what happened, right?"

For some inexplicable reason, Dick wanted to answer no.
"You're right. I'll call him, though; then I can explain how the
girl behaved when I talked to her."

Dick spent minutes studying his office phone before he
picked it up. He caught Moore just as the psychiatrist was
leaving for the day and explained what he needed in as general
a way as possible, underplaying any importance.

"Can it wait, Dick? I'm taking off for an eight-week workshop on Tuesday. It will be hard to fit her in before, but I have
plenty of openings afterward."

Murders—if this *was* a murder—didn't wait eight weeks.
You solved them fast or opportunities would slip out of your
hands, maybe forever. So Dick knew he should insist on an
immediate appointment for Linda but he wanted to agree that

it could wait. He wanted to agree so badly, that was what he did. They set an appointment for August sixteenth.

After the call, Dick wrote a few lines on Stephen's and Linda's statements and placed the report in the slim file that held the final troublesome remains of the pimp, Bobby Rich.

## Chapter Five

### I

PUNGENT SMELLS OF onion, garlic, and paprika drifted through the lower apartment as Helen prepared her grandmother's favorite meal. Carefully browning the chicken, mixing the dough for the *csipetke*, and soaking the green beans in the marinating mixture of salt, dill, and vinegar.

When the first form rushed past her from the back hall, she ignored it. When the second did the same, she only looked up. But when the first tried to slip by again, she took a good look. Alan was filthy . . . and what was that sound? She wheeled her chair into the living room in time to see Carol's head, topped with a short, shingled haircut (which, the girl had declared, made her "look more mature") disappear into the living-room floor.

Wheeling further into the room, Helen looked down at the now uncovered cold-air return that dropped six feet and, never connected, ended a short distance above the coal cellar's floor. "We found a secret passage but I didn't fit," Billy complained.

"How fortunate for you," Helen said sternly. Then she turned to a dust-covered Carol. "Look at you! And suppose you had gotten stuck?"

"I made sure I wouldn't," Carol replied. "I sent Alan first 'cause he's littler, and I tied a rope around him so he wouldn't fall."

"It was great!" Alan added with a huge smile. "You just push against the sides and walk down." He used the closet door frame to demonstrate.

51

Helen recalled how many times she had eyed that metal passage with the same idea and had to force herself to remain stern. "You have thirty minutes to wash and change, but first put this cover back on. Now get to it!"

She was interrupted again when Stephen entered carrying a grocery bag. "Patrick asked me to drop this off. He said it was from Sister St. Anne."

"That wonderful woman has rescued me again!" Helen spoke the sincere words with humorous emphasis. "My grandmother is coming for dinner and I had no time to prepare dessert." She pulled out a cake box containing a dobos torte, then a bottle of green Hungarian Rizling. "I don't think this came from Sister."

"From Patrick." Stephen sniffed. "You're having *csirke* paprikas, yes?"

"Yes. But if I don't get back to work, we won't have anything for the main course, either." She began dropping dough into the boiling water as she continued. "I forgot when I planned this dinner that today was registration at Reserve. Connie drove me over early this morning, and I had to spend twice as long checking to see if the classrooms would be accessible to me as I spent registering. There didn't seem to be any way to take more than thirteen credits. I wish I were still in braces. School would be so much easier."

"Still?" He tried to keep the question light, to hide the anger he felt at hearing her speak so carelessly of her slow self-destruction.

Helen did not look up as she replied. "I walked before my parents died. Just before." Her tone had hardened, ordering him not to pursue this, and he, not certain he could be kind, complied.

"Won't you stay for dinner?" she asked more brightly.

"No thank you, I've already eaten." This was, he recalled, the first time he'd ever had to say those words in this house.

"Then please stay and meet my grandmother. She's Hungarian and so pleased when she meets other Europeans."

"I will, thank you." Though he was incompetent in kitchens, he looked at what must have been confusion and felt compelled to ask, "Is there anything I can do to help you?"

"By all means." Helen stifled a laugh. "Go into the living room and make sure there is no longer a hole in the floor." As

Stephen looked quizzically in that direction, he heard a loud crash, followed by Carol muttering a thoroughly adult curse.

When Sylvia Ivani arrived at the house with Dick, she went immediately to her granddaughter. As she bent over to give Helen a hug, she noticed Stephen standing beside the wheelchair. Startled, she drew in a small breath of air and her hand flew to her mouth. She seemed about to speak a name. Instead, she hesitated and finally asked Helen, "Aren't you going to introduce me to this young man?"

It was a pleasant evening, although it seemed to Dick that both Stephen and Sylvia were preoccupied. He observed Sylvia staring frequently at Stephen. Is she captivated like the rest, he wondered, or only sizing Stephen up?

Stephen, on the other hand, was surreptitiously watching Helen divide and eat a single piece of chicken and a few dumplings.

Dick's thoughts vanished as Billy leaned toward Alan, pointed to the dumplings, and, with an evil grin, whispered, "Grubs."

"Ugh!" Alan's pale freckled face turned one shade lighter.

"William, that was rude and disgusting," Dick said, reprimanding him.

"The very essence of rude," Carol agreed, spearing a dumpling to emphasize that her cousin's remark had not affected her at all. The expression on her face said otherwise.

"I'm sorry." Billy tried to look sorry. "It just slipped out." He emphasized the word *slipped* ever so slightly, and Carol giggled.

"It seemed premeditated to me," Dick replied. "Not another word, understand?"

"Were you that naughty when you were a boy?" Helen asked Stephen.

"Much, much worse," he admitted with a small smile, recalling indiscretions that would destroy the appetites of the adults as well as the children. "However, it was some time ago." Sylvia hooted at his reply.

After the children were sent upstairs to bed, the conversation moved on to European history and customs and finally touched on superstitions. Dick rarely discussed his work with his family, but tonight something compelled him. He began by telling of the dead deer. "Something killed it," he concluded, "by draining all of its blood."

"Oh!" Sylvia furrowed her brows and turned to Stephen. "Some animal, do you think?"

Stephen looked thoughtful. Eventually, he asked Dick, "I am not familiar with your legal system but are your police usually your..." He searched for a word. "...game wardens?"

"No, but we believe what happened to this deer might be related to the death of a young woman four weeks ago."

"Angela D'Amato?" Helen asked. Dick hesitated, then nodded. "But I thought... that is, the papers are saying she was attacked by some maniac with a knife. Uncle, what does this have to do with a dead deer?"

"The reporters have not been given all the facts. The girl did not die from stab wounds. She died like the deer died: from loss of blood."

Sylvia muttered something in Hungarian, then crossed herself. Dick had expected her to be shocked, but he was surprised to see the effect of this news on Stephen. For one moment—so brief that had Dick blinked, he was sure he would have missed seeing it—his young neighbor appeared deeply shaken. Following Dick's edited account of the details of the murder, he commented, "I have heard rumors of deaths such as this, but verifying them was always impossible. Usually they are country tales, you see, not investigated by authorities."

"That's not true in this case," Dick replied. "We have labs in America to analyze evidence and separate superstition from fact."

"I suppose you do." Stephen's voice was so soft, he might have been speaking to himself. "I hadn't considered that." He looked at Dick, his expression troubled, and ran one finger across his cheek. . . .

. . . And the walls dissolved, and Dick had the illusion that he was watching himself. He had become extraordinarily small, as if standing far away. It was impossible to determine where he was; there was only night for the walls and floor and Stephen's solemn questioning eyes. Dick could not hear what Stephen asked, nor what his other self answered. The feeling lasted only a moment. Dick was momentarily nauseated, then blinked, shook his head, and stared in confusion at the empty chair in which Stephen had been sitting. Too much wine, he thought, glancing at Helen, Sylvia, and especially Stephen, who now stood behind Helen, one hand resting on the back of her chair as he replied to some remark of Sylvia's.

Misinterpreting Dick's expression for one of weariness, Sylvia reached over and patted him on the arm. "All this talk of blood has, I fear, made me long for the comfort of my own soft bed. I think I would like to go now, please."

Dick, who planned to be at work early, agreed. As he went to get Sylvia's sweater, she turned to Stephen and spoke in rapid Hungarian. "I extend to you an invitation to my house, Stephen Austra, for tomorrow night. I do this in the old way, you understand? There is much I must tell you then." Without so much as a good-bye to anyone, she walked stiff-legged out the door. It was only her iron will that kept her from trembling.

"Please stay," Helen said to Stephen after the others had left. "You've been so busy at St. John's that I rarely see you anymore. Come out on the porch with me and tell me how the work is going."

She transferred herself from her chair to the porch swing with practiced ease, hoping Stephen would sit beside her. Instead, as always, he put some distance between them, pulling up a metal lawn chair, balancing it on its back rungs so he could rest his feet on the porch rail. Even at that distance he noticed her perfume . . . a subtle blend of roses and white lilacs that mingled beautifully with her own scent.

"You impressed my grandmother, though I am not certain in what way." Helen gave a short laugh. "What was it she told you as she left, something about her house?"

"She asked me to visit. It was a most formal invitation, and I probably shall." He maintained a conversational tone, effectively hiding the turmoil he experienced as he considered Sylvia's words.

"Good. She is lonely and would like the company, especially from someone who speaks her language." Helen's hands fluttered, brushing back a few wisps of hair, then fingering the folds of her skirt. "I've enjoyed your company also." Unsure how to continue, she looked anxiously out at the empty street.

"I am pleased to have your friendship as well," he said, noticing how silver-white her hair had become from the light of the distant street lamps.

He had expected this conversation. Although Helen seemed curiously immune to the magnetism he could only somewhat control, she was still attracted to his vitality. She desired the impossible. He could not give of himself; he could only take.

Helen astonished herself as she continued. "I would like more than your friendship, Stephen, that is, if... No, I should not have said that, I'm—"

"Stop! When a lady as beautiful as you makes the first advance and is refused, it is not she but rather the man who should say he is sorry." He knew the effort her candor had required, and the risk she believed she was taking. It grieved him to repay her with such trite lies. "So I will say it instead: I am sorry. Let me say what I feel, as you have with me. I will be here only a short time and I don't believe love should be so hasty. Please forgive me, and allow me to remain your friend. Our time together means a great deal to me."

So nothing would change, but at least there was friendship. "Of course I wish us to remain friends." She spoke with a warmth she did not feel, knowing that somehow he had lied and that it would be better were he less kind.

The next morning, so early that the recipient of his phone call knew the seriousness of the matter the moment he began to speak, Stephen called New York. Then, while waiting for a reply to his necessary requests, he worked on the rectory windows.

Inside his familiar fortress of glass, he watched the intricate patterns grow under his hands. The fact that he was able to work, and work well, surprised him greatly.

## II

Immediately following shift change the next morning, Dick began reviewing his files on recent homicide cases. It was

quietest at this hour . . . the crimes of the night over, those of
the day waiting to explode in the heat of the afternoon. He set
the week's priorities, pausing, then listing the D'Amato killing in the number-three slot on his list.

One by one he made notes on the cases and, when necessary, arranged appointments with detectives assigned to them.
Eventually only one remained sitting on his desk . . . his own,
D'Amato. He looked down at the manila file, cursing his luck
that, of all the hundreds of murders that occurred each month,
his city had to be the one to get this. He'd received a report
from the FBI, and all the hours he'd spent pouring through his
own extensive files had confirmed their conclusion: Nowhere
in America was there any record of a crime resembling it.

"Country tales," Stephen had called them. Well, if Europe
was the place to begin, so be it. By the end of the day, perti-
nent details of his case would be sent to authorities in Austria,
Hungary, Germany, Romania, and—where in the hell was
AustraGlass headquartered?—Portugal. He doubted any
worthwhile information would come from this, though doubt-
ful leads were sometimes surprisingly productive.

Now that he had taken some small action, Dick found himself feeling extremely protective toward the precious hard evidence the chief had called their "sole link to reality" in this
puzzling case. He phoned Corey and asked the pathologist to
meet him for coffee in the cop shop.

Corey was having more than coffee. There were two
doughnuts and two glasses of orange juice on his tray. "One's
for you," he commented, seeing his old partner's disapproving
look.

"No thanks," Dick said. "I got to watch the weight. It's
been piling on since I gave up smoking."

"So you take it off later." Corey uncovered one of the
juices.

"Later has a way of holding its distance. I prefer to keep it
off now."

"You might be right." Corey patted his bulging waistline.
"On the other hand, I'm not trying to hide approaching middle
age."

"If you were still on the force, you'd have to hide it a little
better than that." Dick mitigated the criticism with a friendly
chuckle.

Corey merely shrugged and reached for his juice. "That plus the dough were the main advantages I found in getting an education. Just try to raise four daughters on a cop's salary." He paused to take a sip before continuing. "Speaking of my job, Sheila Robinson did herself in so you can scratch her off your list. Who'd you want to see me about this morning, as if I didn't know?"

"D'Amato. Did you get a reply from Columbus?"

"They promised me a report by the end of this week. If I don't hear from them by Friday, I'll call."

"The evidence you collected, where did you file it?" Dick was outwardly calm but he sensed an odd tension within himself.

Corey noticed it too. "Do you think someone might try to steal it?"

"It's only a feeling. But yes."

"Hard to do, but I'll move it just in case. Now I have D'Amato's in her file. I wasn't sure how to name the evidence we collected in the valley." He chuckled. "I thought of Vampire, then Bloodsucker, and finally decided on Deerhunter just for convenience. That way I only have to open one drawer to pull out both boxes. You learn to be efficient in college. Tell you what, partner, I'll move them both into one box and mark it 'Sheila Robinson.' Then only you and I will know where it is."

This suggestion seemed so helpful that Dick wondered why he felt such stirrings of hopelessness. "I think that's fine," he said with deceptive relief.

# Chapter Six

## I

SYLVIA LAY IN bed, propped atop a multitude of pillows of colorful and clashing prints. Her gray hair had been brushed back and left to fall against her bare shoulders, and the lacy straps of a black nightgown were just visible above the hand-made patchwork quilt covering her.

Her even breathing told her guest she was asleep, and he knocked once on the door frame. "Oh!" she exclaimed, opening her eyes wide.

"Did I frighten you?" he asked in Hungarian.

"No . . . yes. I was waiting for you but . . ." She shrugged. "Even so, it's always so unexpected."

"Always?"

"And it's been so many years." She reached for the bottle on her night table, but he intercepted and poured the wine for her. "There's a glass for you." She motioned to it.

"No thank you, I never drink wine." The refusal was accompanied by the usual hint of a smile.

"It's good Egri." He shook his head. "Your brother drank, or maybe it was your cousin, your father, even your son. Who could tell? Anyway, *he* drank. He said he loved good Egri."

To the eternal detriment of his stomach, he was sure. "Old woman," Stephen said, using the address as a form of respect. "If you wished to see me, why did you not let me in?"

She chuckled and took a small sip of wine. "If I had let you in, I never would have known, would I? But now I am sure. Oh, I knew you would come, I did."

"And expose what I am?"

"To me! Who would believe an old woman. Half the family thinks I'm a little crazy, you know." She stated this without malice, and it was precisely Stephen's conclusion. "I could just hear them, Dick and the rest, all sounding just like my Lydia! 'Grandma, you had a dream, only a dream.'"

Half her glass disappeared in one gulp. "I usually don't drink like this . . . well, sometimes I do, but only when I'm alone and only good Hungarian." She meant the words to sound gay but failed. "It chases away the ghosts, you see; the memories."

After a moment's pause, Sylvia continued. "I've waited many years to tell this story to someone who would understand. My daughter, she called me a crazy old DP and laughed when I told her how it was."

Stephen pulled up a chair. This was going to be a long, hopefully informative, night.

"I grew up in the hill country near Szged. My family, I suppose you could say they were well off. We owned our land and raised sheep and cattle. An uncle owned the nearest vineyard. There was myself, my brother, and two other sisters. I was the middle daughter. My parents cared for me but I was the least favorite. My brother was the heir. My older sister look care of the younger children and so was useful, and later she married well. The youngest was loved by everyone, for she was as fair as the yellow summer wildflowers that bloom in those mountains. I was not plain myself"—she tossed her well-coiffed head—"but I was willful and exceedingly stubborn. One or two—or maybe it was more—of the local boys would come around to see me but I really didn't care for any of them. When my parents lost patience with me, they sent me to the convent; a sort of offering. But you know how it was. What choice did they have?

"The convent was some distance from our town, built of stones pulled from the mountainside. It was huge and dark and cold, but the gardens were beautiful in the summer and we had many elegant things: needlework we made ourselves—tapestries, quilts, linens, you know. Everyone said my work was excellent; so many compliments I had never gotten before! It was a contemplative order but I liked it . . . the discipline, the silence, the learning. Then *he* came. But understand, I am not sorry; no, not sorry at all.

"He was leading a dark horse with a lucky star on its forehead. I suppose he would have gone past—of what danger is a mountain storm to one of your kind—but there was the horse and it was lame, so he stopped and the prioress gave him shelter for the night.

"I had not taken my vows; indeed, I had been putting off any final commitment, and so I did not wear a habit. I had only seen our visitor from a distance, but he looked young, perhaps handsome. How was I to know he was as old as the Dacean plains? I had never seen one of the mountain lords, though I had heard the legends, yes I had." She laughed, a muffled, bitter sound in the tiny room.

"So I put on my prettiest skirt, blouse, and embroidered bodice and stole into the great hall where he was warming himself by the fire.

"Tell me, are your women as fair, as sweet, as bewitching? Do they turn mortal men's heads with the same sort of elegant words? If they are . . . Oh, why did he ever rest his eyes on me!

"I had meant to flirt, perhaps exchange an innocent kiss, have a brief taste of freedom before I made the decision to put on the habit for life. But one look at him and that life ended forever.

"I blushed and mumbled something about forgetting my prayer book. He asked if I was in the novitiate and, if so, was it wrong for me to stay for just a little while, he was so lonely. And indeed, his eyes did look lonely . . . and dark and beautiful . . . and I had no choice. I stayed.

"He poured me a glass of wine, his wine. It was as dusky and thick as a starless night and tasted like no wine I'd ever drunk before. He said it was Egri and that his family made it themselves from an old recipe. I often drink Egri now; perhaps I've forgotten, but it doesn't taste the same, not the same at all."

She took another sip and propped herself up higher in the bed. In the soft light, Stephen, who had watched so many humans age, could picture with little difficulty the beauty she must have been.

"Not a soul disturbed us through that long night, and we

loved. Oh, how we loved! I should have known then what he was—I was so unlike myself, so bold and passionate in his arms—but I only discovered the truth later.

"This was the man I had been waiting to find! Ever since, he has haunted my dreams. No one equaled him before or after. I won't give you details," she said with a chuckle, "but I know you understand.

"He must have lived far away for no one knew him, but what is distance to one of your kind? We began meeting at night. He would come and I would know and tiptoe down the back stairs and out the kitchen door. He called me his salvation, his one star! Oh, I was so silly, so in love!

"And now we come to the heart of the story, and to why I invited you so formally into my house." She leaned forward and shook her index finger at him as if giving a small boy a lecture. "But first you must make me a promise. What I tell you is of the utmost importance, and I wish something in return. For you it will be a little thing, do you understand?"

"If it is, as you say, a little thing and it places me in no danger, I will try."

"Ho! That's a guarded answer, but it's only what I expected to hear. Now pour me just a bit more wine if you would, then bring me the silver box on the bureau."

He did as she requested. The box was thick and heavy, the carving on it an excellent sample of sixteenth-century art. Sylvia caressed it as she continued.

"We met for nearly six months. I knew a name, Kavil, and there was a last name, too, but it probably wasn't his real one. If I tried for any details of where he lived, what he did, the important things to a silly girl in love, he would become angry. So I stopped asking and trusted.

"I had never made love before but I knew what to expect. He did not disappoint me but he did other things, too, and the last few times we were together, he requested I do them as well. When he asked this, I understood precisely what he was, but by then it made no difference. I would have agreed to whatever he asked. We exchanged blood; do you understand?"

"What!" Stephen exclaimed. "But that is—" He halted. He had been about to say "an abomination."

"And then, the last time I saw him, he gave me this." She opened the box and handed him a thin golden chain containing a glass teardrop similar to the one he wore but of a deep indigo. "He said he had to leave for a little while but that he would return, and when he did, he would take me away with him. How was I to know I would never seen him again?

"We parted. I still feel like a schoolgirl when I think of our last kiss. The next day I was summoned before the Mother Superior.

"Somehow we had been discovered. She asked me to renounce my lover and take the vows, but I refused. I was so in love and happy. She sent me home in disgrace and informed my father of what had occurred.

"I told him my lover would come for me. I told him we were to be married. I told him a lot of silly things, and for that he beat me.

"He said he would give my Kavil two months. Those passed and he did not come, and so my father arranged a marriage for me. The boy was a friend from my youth, loving and kind. He had asked for my hand before but I had refused. Now, feeling abandoned and angry, I accepted. We were married immediately. Two months later we left for America.

"On the boat, I discovered I was pregnant. Matthew, my husband, was so pleased, but I was ecstatic! I had not wanted children so soon, and certainly not to be with child on a long and possibly difficult voyage to a new country. So after I wed Matthew, I had taken precautions and I was sure they had not failed. That meant my child would be his, my Kavil's! I would have a part of him yet to hold.

"I almost died giving birth, but I never regretted the pain. She was so beautiful, with hair like sunbeams and eyes of dark, cloudy blue. No one had eyes like that in my family but I told Matthew otherwise, and how was he to know? Oh, how I loved her and guarded her carefully! She was the only child I ever had; my Lydia; the only one I ever wanted.

"When she was eighteen, I told her the details of her birth. My husband had died a year earlier and I thought that here was the time to explain all to her. She laughed. She said, 'Mother, it was all a dream,' and I remember how hard I slapped her.

"I don't think I ever hit Lydia before, but to laugh at me when I was telling the most important facts about her life? That's when she, as angry as I, called me a crazy DP and worse! Such language from my only child, yet my replies were as terrible. Later we apologized to each other but we were many words too late.

"I had meant to give her the necklace and the box and take her back with me to the Old Country. We had money, we could have lived well, and, had we found my Kavil, she would have been a queen!

"But she never let me speak of it again. Instead she went and married an American. He was a good man, like my Matthew, but oh, the disappointment! I swallowed my hurt as best I could and tried to be a good mother and mother-in-law. *Yoi!* It was hard, but let's not talk about that. They were married for twenty-one years when they both died in that terrible automobile crash.

"But Lydia left something as precious as herself . . . my granddaughter. That is why I brought you here. I want you to understand.

"Lydia's pregnancy lasted over ten months. The American doctors were sure their calculations had been wrong, for Helen looked, if anything, a bit premature. The labor was difficult and Lydia hemorrhaged badly at the end, requiring a great deal of blood. Afterward we were told something was wrong with Helen's heart, for it beat too slowly. They said we should hope for the best. Lydia prayed and I offered encouraging falsehoods . . . this was not uncommon in the family; as an infant she'd had the same problems and more, but I never dared tell her the truth. Like the first time, she would not have believed me, but I rejoiced. My Kavil again!"

As he'd listened, Stephen's expression had grown steadily more incredulous. "Are you telling me that Helen . . . ?"

"Is of your blood? No. But if what I understand is true, she could become . . . and her children, *all* her children. But why am I telling you all this?" She ended with an impatient toss of her hand. "You *know.*"

"Yes . . . yes, I do." No wonder he'd been unable to avoid her; he had no one and she was family. "What I do not understand is why you tell me this."

Her expression saddened. "*Nem*, you are old but you are not yet wise, or perhaps you choose not to see. Before Helen lost her parents, she had been working to overcome the effects of her illness. She is, as you now understand, a strong girl.

And she used to be so independent, so like her mother. Then there was the accident and the shock. Now the shock should be over and it is not. She has seen death and now she will deny life as well.

"And you. My Kavil played at being lonely, I think, and I am sure I was not the only silly girl he snared with that act. But you, you are truly lonely, I think, and I see how you try not to care for Helen, and I know that you do.

"What will life be like for her in a few years? She's beautiful, of course. Someone will overlook her handicap and, if she is willing to settle for that, she will have some happiness. But it is more likely her life will end soon.

"You look surprised. I suppose you should be. Of what interest is infirmity to one of your kind? But understand that when Helen was ill, so terribly ill, the only thing that kept her alive was that wonderful, tenacious part of her that was my Kavil. But her lungs were damaged, and now, with her in a wheelchair, they have no chance to grow stronger. Pneumonia, respiratory flu, either could kill her even with the care of these modern American doctors. . . ." She waved her hand as if pushing the thought away.

"And last, after loving as I have loved, why wouldn't I be generous enough to wish such love for Helen? If the blessing of her family means anything to you, you have mine with pleasure. Take her. Love her. Heal her. Lydia would not listen to me but Helen will heed you, for I know she loves you."

"Yes, Sylvia, she does. But it is one thing to love me; to become one of my family another matter entirely. She has been raised human in a peaceful era. Will she be able to understand the price of that change?"

"Ask her. Then you will know. I think you will not be disappointed." Sylvia reached over to her night table, picked up an envelope, and handed it to him. "Helen's doctors," she explained in answer to his puzzled look. "It pays to have knowledge, does it not?"

As she watched him scan the list, her expression became an amalgam of anticipation and fear.

In response, he said, "You have courage for inviting me here after what we learned last night."

"You were shocked after what you heard last night." She punctuated her reply with a short, dry laugh. "No, I doubt it was you who killed that girl. But even so, I would have asked you to come. I'm old enough and there would be little risk. But no matter." She smoothed her quilt and, for the first time that evening, her hands trembled. She steadied them and held out her glass. "And now, my young-looking man, please . . ."

Some comment, some thanks would be polite, but Stephen found he had nothing to say. As he poured her wine, he reflected on how cruelly she had been used and found it remarkable she was not more bitter. To give such love, then be abandoned without the mercy of forgetfulness was a travesty. Or did her lover really intend to return to her? He probably would never know. "You are a strong woman, Sylvia," he said. "Tell me, how did you recognize what I was so quickly?"

"Once you understand, you hear and you see." She settled comfortably down on the pillows. "But you were easier yet. My Kavil looked almost exactly like you."

Charles? Could it have been Charles? Stephen wondered.

"And now for the promise you made me . . ." She watched him with anticipation.

"I will keep it," he replied, his voice already low and musical and filled with the unique power she would expect. He knew her request.

"Love me," she said in a voice soft and husky. "Love me as he did. I need to feel that passion once more."

Stephen turned off the light. Seeing the spirited girl she once was, that in so many ways she still was, he gave her that pleasure. She cried out once, a name he expected to hear. He held her until she slept.

## II

Dr. David Flatley had just left his office for lunch when he was approached in the hallway by an intense young man who, in the politest of terms, demanded to speak with him. "It concerns Helen Wells. You have the time, yes?"

"Wells?" Flatley considered. "Of course I can spare a few minutes."

An hour later they were still talking. Flatley had unprofessionally let the visitor read Helen's file. But he hadn't any choice, actually, and wasn't this Helen's nearest blood relation?

Stephen scanned each of the earlier entries, absorbing the information so that later, if asked the proper questions, he would be able to recall the data. The most recent entries, he examined carefully. "I must know only one thing, Doctor. Can she walk?"

"Her body may be capable, but it has been a long time since she tried, I assume, and so her rehabilitation will require a great deal of effort on her part. And, of course, much of her paralysis stems from emotional rather than physical causes. I don't possess the knowledge to heal her mind. When her uncle tried to bring her here a few weeks after her parents' death, she became hysterical. If that occurs again, it will be impossible to work with her."

Stephen considered the indecisive prognosis and decided that, while vague, it was preferable to other words he might have heard. He could bring her here, of course, but the effort once they arrived must be entirely her own. "Then I must make an appointment with you for somewhere else. I will bring her to your home tonight at nine."

This man assumed too much! "I gave you my lunch hour and more," the doctor began assertively. "I showed you a file you had no right to see, but I cannot allow you to impose on me any longer. Do you understand?"

Apparently Stephen didn't, for he replied, "Eight is better, yes?"

The doctor tried to say no but found himself nodding foolishly. "Yes." He sighed, resigned.

"Good," Stephen concluded, noticing the doctor's puzzled resentment, then added, "Your time, it is valuable. Put a good price on it."

## III

That afternoon a trash picker who had murdered one of his fellows in a dispute over territory showed up at the station to turn himself in. Dick did the paperwork on him and was preparing to leave early when Corey opened the door.

He laid a large brown envelope on Wells's desk. "Here it is, and you're going to love it!"

Dick noted the return address. "So what did they write?"

"I wish you were standing so I could say sit down. The Blood Disease Research Center tells me there are two of 'em!"

Two? Dick mouthed the word.

"Yep. According to this report, the blood samples were inherently the same but with enough significant differences in composition for the center to determine we have two different . . . ah, types here."

Dick stared down at the envelope. "Don't you want to read it?" Corey asked.

"Nope. I'll take a look at it tomorrow." He unlocked his file drawer and placed it in the D'Amato folder. "Were you leaving soon?"

"As soon as you were."

"Good. Let's get the hell out of here and go take aim at some pool balls like we used to."

Some time later, a more mellow Dick Wells turned to a similarly calmer Bob Corey. "I've been thinking. We have one crime and two critters. Do you suppose the second one might be an ally?"

"I don't suppose anything, but keep up the optimism, partner. I think you might need it."

# Chapter Seven

## 1

"Oooh! Billy, Alan, come here and see what Stephen's got!" Carol yelled from the front porch. In a moment two more young heads popped over the railing to stare down at Stephen, sitting behind the wheel of a new Bel Air convertible.

"Stephen, will you take us for a ride?" Carol called.

"Tomorrow. Now I must go to work." To get out of this heat! He inadvertently glanced at the noonday sun and felt the stabbing pain. *Only mad dogs and Englishmen*, he thought, chuckling at the logical conclusion and thankful that, at least in this decade, men's hats were in fashion. "Carol, I do need your help. Will you meet me out here in an hour?"

"Of course," she purred, and Billy snickered.

As soon as Stephen disappeared into his house, Billy began a teasing singsong. "Carol's in love, in love, in lo-ove—" then lost the entire middle section when she tackled him. "But she's too young for him!" he concluded, laughing at her ineffective punches.

An hour later a more ladylike Carol met a less stylish Stephen as he left his apartment. "Carol, you're getting quite grown-up . . ." he began.

These were exactly the words she'd wanted to hear. She smiled her most charming smile and listened eagerly for the rest.

". . . and I want to request a favor. I will be taking Helen somewhere tonight, and I would like you to watch your brother while we are away. Will you do that?"

Her smile evaporated. "We can't go?"

"No, not tonight."

Carol could not see his eyes behind his dark glasses, but his voice seemed sympathetic. "I suppose I will if you want me to," she agreed as she walked him to his car. "Where are you going?"

"It's a surprise," he said in a soft, conspiratorial tone. "Would you give Helen this for me?" He handed her an envelope and opened the car door.

## II

Early that evening, Helen smoothed her skirt, made one final and unnecessary adjustment to her hair, and wheeled herself onto the lower porch to wait for Stephen. Upstairs, the children were riveted to a terrible television program, odd behavior considering how excited they'd been all afternoon at the sight . . . and potential personal benefits . . . of Stephen's black convertible. Pleased by these few moments of solitude, she closed her eyes and concentrated on the quiet brush of the evening breezes against her face.

"Good evening," Stephen said, startling her, then making the easy jump from his porch rail to hers.

Helen glanced down at her dress. "Is this all right? The note Carol delivered didn't give a destination, so I wasn't sure what to wear."

"You look beautiful, and yes, it will be fine."

Though the compliment was not unusual, the tone in which he gave it seemed to be. "Will you tell me where we are going, or must I wait?"

"I will tell you, and many other things as well, but we must speak in a more private place. Would you have any objection to finally seeing my windows?" His dark glasses reflected the golden tones of the early-evening sun. "It is a perfect time and we can talk afterward."

"It will be a bit awkward . . . with the stairs, I mean."

He laughed, then replied, "I don't think it will be awkward at all. You can't possible weigh very much."

"Oh, I didn't think. That is . . ." With startling candor she concluded, "I thought you were afraid to touch me."

"I was," he confessed, scooping her up, "but not anymore."

He did not put her down immediately but instead carried her from room to room to study the windows . . . first into the empty kitchen where the blues and greens of the waterfall danced across the light walls and floor . . . into the den to view the temple, its ivory tones now pink in the sun's oblique rays . . . then into the bedroom to see the magnificent crimson swirl. "I feel a warmth flowing from this," she said, brushing the glass with her fingertips, "but it is impossible to describe."

"I expected you might. You will notice the effect even more strongly at dawn."

She looked wistfully over his shoulder as they left the room. He took her through the dining room, empty except for one long wooden table that contained, nearly complete, the last of the rectory windows, and into the living room where the seasons glowed. There he placed her on a low, soft sofa.

At first she saw nothing but the glass, but then she noticed the rest of her surroundings. The other rooms in the apartment appeared almost empty—a desk in one, a bed in another—but this room was opulent. The gem-toned glass harmonized with the vibrant colors of the Oriental rug on the floor and the woven cover on the sofa and was reflected in the deep patina of a long, low table that appeared to be formed from a single massive piece of mahogany. Upon that table sat the statue of an animal formed in clear crystal—feline but like no cat she had ever seen—and in the corner rested a huge pear-shaped wood sculpture, beautifully carved. "You have excellent taste," she might have said, but the words seemed inadequate and so she said nothing.

When she perceived she was alone, her eyes returned to the crystal sculpture. She studied the lines of its sinewy body, noted the long incisor teeth. It was stretching, exposing each vertebra in its powerful back. The tail, like that of some hairless hound, whipped between long rear legs, and its expression was intelligent.

"My brother made it. He calls it 'the beast within us.'" Stephen walked through the doorway carrying two cut-crystal glasses and handed her one. "Drink this. You will find the taste unusual but remarkably refreshing."

She took a small first sip, then another, larger sample. "It's like drinking the sea. What is it?"

"Something blended for my family. We find it sustaining."

"You live on this, you mean?" She wondered if he'd used the correct word.

"Yes. As a matter of convenience, or when we can't . . ." He fumbled for the way to continue.

As if it could bestow strength, his hand closed around the ruby teardrop hanging from his neck, and he sat on the floor near her feet. "Helen, you will have to accept much of what I tell you on faith. First, I have been guilty of a great deal of prejudice toward you."

She shook her head but her eyes grew moist.

"I was afraid to touch you, but if I had I would have known in an instant what I held in my arms. Instead I looked at your greatest strengths and saw only weakness. I considered leaving here the day after we met, so troubled was I to be near you. Fortunately I have learned throughout my long life always to trust my instincts, and so I stayed to meet Sylvia, who explained to me that we are only like responding to like."

The last few words seemed sensible but the earlier ones puzzled her. "You make yourself sound so ancient, and both of us so rare."

"I am much . . . much older than I appear. As for us, we are unusual." After allowing her a moment of contemplation, he continued. "The night we met, you said your mother should have lived forever. What did you mean by that?"

His voice was kind but insistent. Helen stared down at the pattern of the carpet, collecting her thoughts before she replied. "Ever since I was a small child, I believed her ageless. I understand all children feel that way about their parents, but this was different, more certain somehow. Although I loved my father as much, his death seemed natural."

"Tell me how you felt at the moment your mother died."

He asked the question as if he knew the answer! She began

to speak, then faltered and started over in a voice that surprised her with its strength. "My parents died while I was at the hospital. They were coming to see me walk for the first time since my illness. Perhaps they were excited and drove too fast, I don't know. I . . ." She covered her face with her hands, and when she looked up, she saw him watching her, his eyes drawing the words from her. "I felt the flames touch her; I felt her pain; I felt her die, and my response was not grief but impotent rage, as if a terrible injustice had been done and it was too late to set it right.

"If I had been alone, I might have screamed from anger and grief, but it seemed dangerous to react. Later, when someone came and told me of their deaths and I had to face that it was real, I screamed her name. I don't believe I stopped screaming it for days. I only remember I missed the funeral, and for that I was thankful."

"Your denial was natural. Though you had no way of knowing until tonight, you and she both knew the truth at the moment of her death. Your mother could have lived forever; so can you." He felt her growing anger and quickly added, "I am being serious. Trust your instincts and you will know I do not lie."

He had always been kind and sensible, yet now he seemed so serious as he spoke of the impossible. *I'll listen*, she thought, and that thought was sufficient.

"I've watched you starve yourself, eating barely enough to stay alive and refusing to do what is necessary to become whole and strong. I cared for you and I had no desire to hasten your death with my needs. Now I understand this apathy. But you must name for yourself what it is you fear."

These harsh words were spoken with such compassion, she was compelled to reply. She looked at the sculpture, the windows, her pictures on his wall. It was selfish to wish to create, to love, to question mortality, yet it seemed so perfectly right. Her hands clenched into demanding fists and she closed her eyes, considering and discarding answer after painful answer until only one, the sum of the rest, remained. When at last she spoke, her eyes were filled with tears but the words came strong and even, as they always seemed to do in the presence of this man. "Time! It will never be enough. Death had no right to my mother, and as for me, what is the difference between five years and fifty? There will never be sufficient time for what I long to do."

"And what is that?"

"Live."

"And if I offered you eternity, Helen, would you accept it?" His words were sincere but possessed a deceptive calm. He feared she would laugh or, worse, refuse.

She bowed her head and wiped away the tears with her fingertips. When she raised her eyes to his, their smoky depths revealed the puzzling hunger she had too long endured.

He had told her to trust her instincts and she obeyed. "I would accept it, Stephen. There are times I believe I would sacrifice everything to possess it."

Her desire was all he had hoped it would be, and so much more, and he knew a moment of uncertainty . . . that she did not care for him but only for that which instinct had already told her he could bestow. Yet she was here, now, with him, and in this portion of eternity her presence was all that mattered.

Helen watched him, her eyes troubled. Eventually she asked, "What are you that you can offer me this? Are you . . . no, no, that's impossible." She concluded with a swift, anxious smile and stared down at her clasped hands.

"Not impossible but not completely correct." For the first time he looked away from her and, in a voice cold with hidden emotion, continued, "I am one of those on whom your legends are based. But I am . . . not human, nor have I ever been. I am a different species; an alien species, perhaps, but one that looks deceptively like mankind."

He sat motionless but his tension crackled in the air like the lightning of a summer storm. "Is it so difficult to look at me when you speak of this?" she asked.

He turned toward her and, in a voice barely a whisper, he replied, "I have learned I must never confess what I am unless I am prepared to see, in the eyes of a friend or a lover, the painful deception that hides the loathing."

"And do you see that in mine?"

"No," he replied, his voice still soft but now triumphant. "I see the eyes of the woman I love."

Helen looked thoughtfully at the windows, becoming more deeply hued in the dying light, and wondered what she must

sacrifice to gain so much. In response, Stephen explained her
lineage, then his nature, its limitations, and its needs while
Helen listened, stunned by the prospect of eternity.

"You must understand," Stephen concluded. "This is not a
gift and there are great prices you must pay. You will have
time to reach a decision. I would not expect you to make one
now."

Looking down at her legs, Helen considered living with
their uselessness for centuries and shared his fear. "I understand how I must begin. And I believe I know what my decision will be."

She held out her hands and he took them, then sat beside
her, his lips tracing a light line beginning at her temple and
moving down the side of her face and neck. She shuddered at
these first touches as she recalled everything he had told her.
Then, as that small barrier of reluctance crumbled, he kissed
her with an intensity that admitted the weeks of frustration
they had both endured.

She had no reason to believe the impossible except that she
had come to trust him; no reason to want to give herself so
shamelessly except that she loved him; no reason to expect
what no person could have except that her entire being demanded it. And so, when he placed his hands on her shoulders
and slowly pushed her away from him, she agreed to everything when he began, "This is what you must do. . . ."

What he demanded first was work . . . frustrating work that
kept her away from her sketch pad and easel; painful work
that kept her awake at night as muscles she had forgotten
convulsed in protest. But whenever she was tempted by self-
pity, she was ashamed.

There was the doctor, who at the beginning had been reluctant to see her, now charting her progress with growing
admiration; and her grandmother, who had no patience with
children, assuming so many of Helen's obligations; and her
uncle, who for the first time in six years had taken a vacation
with the children to visit an aunt in Maine . . . and Stephen,
always Stephen, setting an impossible pace of afternoons at
work, nights at work and, in between, waiting patiently, first
at the doctor's house, then later (when she had the courage to
go there) at the hospital . . . waiting for the moment when it
would become clear she was ready.

Three days after her uncle left with the children, they received the optimistic prognosis: "She will walk. It is only a matter of time and strength."

"How well?" Helen asked, but Stephen, who expected to see her run, made a pretense of flipping through her file and only half heard the guarded reply.

—Now!—his mind screamed —it begins now!—

Thinking Stephen had spoken, Helen turned to him with a puzzled expression. It gave him pleasure to see her so receptive to him, and she read the answer in his eyes.

# III

She waited for him in a house filled with roses and white lilacs, delivered without a card earlier in the day. Breathing in their fragrance of love and renewal, she ventured one last hopeful look out the window. No, he had not returned. Leaving the door unlocked, she went to prepare for bed.

Her hair fell in a pale flood over her shoulders and, as she brushed it out, she studied her reflection in the mirror. Did the strands shine brighter? Were her eyes more blue? Was she beautiful? She had always believed it, yet now she longed for perfection. But the flaws . . . well, she must wait for the flaws to mend.

She undressed, then reached for her nightgown, but it seemed too youthful and she left it in the drawer and slipped naked between the sheets to revel in the unaccustomed feel of her arms against her body, her skin against the cool, crisp cloth. Anticipation filled her and she ran her hands down her stomach to rest on her thighs. *My hands, soon his hands. All those nights I've longed for him and now, please now . . . let tonight be the beginning of my life!*

Her eyes had not grown accustomed to the darkness when she sensed his presence. "Stephen?" she whispered, then saw in the shadows near the door the single teardrop that had gathered to itself the few faint rays of light from the window and intensified them into a deep glow.

—Yes.— He slipped from the darkness and gathered her into his arms.

"You were so late." She spoke without reproach. "I didn't think you would come."

"Didn't you?" The laughter in his voice implied otherwise, and pulling her head against his chest, he stroked the side of her face, then kissed her. "Helen, will you join with me now? We will feel the dawn together."

"Yes, but . . ." Her voice trailed off and she was astonished at her embarrassment. Too many people had been, of necessity, intimate with her body for her to feel modest any longer.

He removed the robe of indigo silk he wore over a loose dark peasant's shirt and wrapped it around her. It had been warmed by him and each touch of the fabric gave a reminder of acts to come. He carried her confidently up the lightless back stairs, then through her uncle's empty apartment. For one moment she stiffened as he jumped from porch to porch with easy grace.

He smiled at her alarm, thinking there would come a day, and soon, when five times this distance would be inches to her and she would feel no fear . . . only knowledge of how much was possible. For the first time, perhaps the only time, life would be his gift. The wonder of her filled him.

In the darkness of his room, one small candle burned low in a cut-glass prism, texturing the walls with light. As he placed her on his low bed and reached down to untie the belt of the robe, he saw her eyes, huge in the darkness, glance in the direction of the flame.

"You are beautiful, but if you wish . . ." He had lit it for her. He had no need of light.

"Leave it." She opened the robe and lay back, her skin golden against the blue silk. "I want to see you."

The emotions waking in Helen startled her. She understood that what they would do tonight went beyond sex, beyond even love, and that soon she would lose with her innocence a part of her humanity. Her body mourned that loss even as it waited for his touch. But her soul, sensing a release from its half-human limbo, filled her with a passion frightening in its intensity.

As he undressed, she watched him, seeking the differences and finding them only in the length of his arms and legs and a body that was as flawless as his face . . . a perfection far from subtle. Her stare was so steady that only when he lay beside her did he realize how much of her boldness was an act.

For one frantic moment she trembled and tried to push him away, but he caught her wrists and pinned them against the wine-colored pillow above her head. Rolling his body to rest on top of hers, he leaned back on his elbows and stared down at her . . . watching her struggle not to look at him, feeling her holding her mind closed to him. As he questioned this sudden panic, he kissed her forehead, her shoulders, the tops of her breasts. —Tell me.—he whispered mind to mind with each light brush. —Tell me . . . tell me . . . do you fear me?—

Since the night he had revealed what she could become, he had used every opportunity to touch her—fingering her hair, kissing her cheek or her hand, resting an arm over her shoulders—and every gentle contact said trust me; love me as you are loved.

"No," she replied, "I fear this desire."

He thought briefly of her future and felt concern, but there was only one way he would allow this night to end. "I know," he whispered as his eyes sought hers, "but desire is life. Take more from me." Holding all other power back, he shared only longing and waited. When she yielded, they met as equals.

He kissed her then, rejoicing in her response, moved his hands and his lips slowly down her body. With each caress she responded with a low sound of need and, the last, the indrawn hiss of pleasure and surprise. "No," she sobbed, and reached down, wrapping her fingers in his hair but only shame protested . . . not her body, not her will, not her soul now fused with his in its own demanding embrace.

—Lie back . . . be still . . . let me give.—As he granted requests she would never have spoken, he found her newborn passion artless and sweet. She floated, lifted higher, then higher until her breath came in ragged pants and she thought she would explode into a thousand crystal shards of colored glass. As he held her at the apex, he whispered in her mind —Do you wish this?—

—Oh, yes.—her soul replied. His warmth covered her and he lifted her hips.

If there was pain, she did not feel it, for she had moved beyond pain, lost to the pleasure of him within her, the movement of him above her. Using the pointed tip of the ruby teardrop, he opened a short, deep cut on his shoulder, then held himself away from her long enough for her to see and understand.

"Now?"

—Yes!—

Her mouth covered the wound, his pressed against her neck, and mind to mind, blood to blood, they merged, they drank, they shared life . . . salty, warm as all life had begun in the womb of the sea. It was a joining silent and motionless, carrying her to an even greater height until she broke and fell with violent spasms into his world. When her legs rose to wrap around his body, he was only momentarily surprised.

Later, resting in his arms, she marveled at all she had felt, and his reluctance to seek his own satisfaction. "But you didn't . . ."

"I dare not; not yet. And there was no need."

"Truly?" Doubt clouded her voice. "Stephen, I want so much to please you."

"Please me?" He laughed with sincere delight at the antiquated term and kissed her palm. "Please me?" The laughter faded as he kissed the curve of her waist. "Oh, my love." His lips covered hers and they began once more.

In the hour before dawn, she slept while he studied her. His eyes rested on the faint bruise on one wrist, the darker one on her thigh, the bright specks of blood on her shoulder and neck. He had intended to be more gentle, but by this time tomorrow, the marks would be gone, or replaced by others. That last licentious thought made him smile.

He fingered a bright strand of her hair and contemplated her nature. In his years he had known only two women like Helen, but they had already changed and he had not been part of those acts. For the first time Stephen, who had known so many lovers, contemplated a unique kind of love . . . a heady blend of passion, admiration, and a strange, parental tenderness.

In that instant a shadow, uninvited and uncomfortably cold, invaded the serenity of Stephen's room. Before he could grasp it, the shadow departed and he moved closer to his lover to gather her protectively in his arms.

\* \* \*

As the first rays of the morning sun struck the ruby window, the room filled with the multicolored display of rainbows dancing off hidden facets, piercing the darkness like a kiss. They swirled across Helen's face, waking her with light caresses.

She stretched. "Stephen." She sighed then, sensing these touches were too gossamer to be real; her eyes opened and widened in amazement. She stared down at her body, at all the places she had been so inexplicably touched, and turned to Stephen, dappled in multitoned flecks. "What is it?" she whispered, her voice reverent.

"It is the dawn. You are feeling the light." To her unspoken question he replied, "No, I do not know why, though, as you see, I have some small control over it." He waved cheerfully at the rainbows, held her close, and in a moment slept. Helen attempted to relax, to do the same, but it was some time before sleep came to her. When it did, she dreamed of the sun.

## Chapter Eight

### june 1955

PLACING ONE INVISIBLE foot carefully in front of the other, Tony trudged down the center of the lightless, empty road; heading east, seeing nothing. He'd tripped on a pothole a mile back and his ankle throbbed, but the fall would have been worse if it had happened on the shoulder and he'd rolled into the ditch. It was sure to be muddy down there, and the jeans and checked shirt he wore were all the clothes he had. Afterward he'd smoked some reefer, hoping it would improve his night vision and steal his pain. It hadn't done either; instead it turned him spooky, on the edge of paranoia, and hungry as well.

He noticed car lights far off to the north, dancing on the tops of small rises, then disappearing into the valleys. Soon the driver would reach the crossroads and might turn this way. Tony considered how his luck had been running and tried not to get too hopeful. When the car did head toward him, Tony hid his knapsack partially down the side of the ditch, prayed it wasn't the cops, stuck out his thumb, and waited.

The car was long, dark, and almost new. As it pulled over, the driver watched Tony grab his bag and transfer a switchblade from it to his jeans pocket. Wise child, he thought, his dark eyes narrowing. This was going to be a delicious evening.

When Tony opened the car door, he saw no overhead light, no dash lights, nothing. He paused for a moment, then thought of his knife. This would be cool; the weed had just clouded his confidence for a minute.

He descended into blackness, closing the door, then turning to the driver, whose silhouette was visible only as a thicker shadow against the night. "Thanks, man. How far ya goin'?"

"Anywhere. I have a need to travel tonight."

There was a restlessness in that voice Tony thought he understood. "I've had plenty of times like that. People can get rough sometimes."

"So I've observed . . . sometimes."

Tony detected the sadness in that oddly pitched voice and laid a sympathetic hand on the man's shoulder. Though he felt a sudden urge to recoil, he ignored it. "My name's Tony. I'm goin' to Akron, or anyplace closer than it."

He could feel the driver trying to look at him. "My name is Charles. I will take you, but you must give me directions. I don't know the way."

Tony's luck was running hot! After thanking the man he watched gray shapes zip by outside the window. "How fast is this bomb movin'?" he finally asked.

It took Charles a moment to decipher the slang before he replied, "I don't know." He might have been saying, "I don't care."

Wild-ass answers were the sort Tony hated most. He sighed and tried to be polite. "I just mean, ya don't have any dash lights, and I think you're goin' too fast. The cops could pull ya over."

"I suppose they could. They never do."

That icy reply reminded Tony of a drug kingpin he'd once met in Detroit . . . good to know, bad to know well. He wished he could see the driver, wished he knew something about him besides the fact that he was young, foreign, and overconfident. The man looked his way again, making him feel like he had in that police lineup: Someone was watching him, someone he couldn't see. The thought was stupid but it made him nervous, and all the times he'd been this nervous were bad times. He beat his stubby fingers against the seat, wishing he was higher and happier.

"You may smoke if you wish."

Tony jumped, now nearly convinced his thoughts were

being read. He was suspicious of the supernatural. The world was goofy enough without ESP and all. "I don't smoke," he replied.

"You were. I can smell it." Charles laughed, the deceptively cheerful sound banishing all of Tony's concern. "I don't *care* what it is, go ahead."

Tony didn't need another invitation. In one practiced motion he pulled a joint out of his sack, lit it, and took a deep pull. "Want some?" he croaked as he held in the smoke.

It had been years since Charles had tried marijuana. The drug hadn't affected him then, but now he had changed in so many ways. Taking the joint from Tony, he raised it to his lips and inhaled deeply. One end glowed bright, then brighter.

In that burst of light Tony got a glimpse of Charles. He was pretty. Some quality in that face made Tony wonder *how* pretty, but this was not the time or place to find out. "Ya got some lungs, man." He made this offhand compliment as he retrieved his weed, letting his fingers rest a moment too long on those of the driver before he pulled his hand away, once more startled. He never gave come-ons to strangers, and besides, he didn't want to risk a rough scene now.

Charles wondered how long he should hold in the smoke and decided that, as this hitchhiker had an aversion for the law, his suspicions would make no difference. Minutes later he exhaled, then took the last third and finished it.

Tony never noticed. Sitting in the silent dark, pleasantly high, had made him feel talkative and he'd been considering how saying too much would be a bad idea. "Got a radio?" he asked.

In response, Charles switched it on. The volume was low, the station classical, and the symphony being played had once been among Charles's favorite pieces. Now it was not what either he or his passenger wished to hear. "Change it," Charles suggested, and Tony eagerly spun the dial. He'd have listened to whatever the driver wanted, of course, but he preferred something with a beat. Eventually he settled on a country station and the drawl of Hank Williams filled the car. He turned the volume up . . . not too high but higher.

In a few miles, the road widened and brightened from a sprinkling of farm lights. Reaching into his suit coat, Charles pulled out a pair of dark glasses and slipped them on, wondering if the drug had altered his vision. "Do you have another of those?" he asked.

"Wow! Ya got one huge appetite!" Tony pulled out a second joint, quite happy for the invitation and no longer concerned about getting too high. If the driver really meant to take him all the way to Akron, he'd be down by the time they arrived. As they smoked, Charles increased the pressure on the gas pedal and the car flew over the rough spots in the road. "Could ya slow down?" Tony asked, no longer worried only about the cops.

If anything, the speed increased. "Is there a reason you're so concerned about the police?"

The way Charles asked his question seemed damned persuasive and Tony had no choice but to reply, "I'm carryin'. Don't want no cops nabbin' me."

"Is it more of what we've been sharing?" The dizzy sensation Charles felt might be the drug or only the smoke, but it had become the greatest importance that he know precisely which had affected him.

"Nope." Tony wouldn't have said anything more but he felt the driver's eyes again. They seemed to be touching him, dragging out the words in spite of his will and, though he should have been wary, he no longer cared. "Got one ounce of white horse . . . ninety-nine and forty-four one-hundreths percent pee-ure." He giggled, proud of his humor and even prouder of the quality of his smack. "Pure," he repeated. "Ya know how hard it is to get *pure*?"

Charles didn't. "How many doses is that?"

"Jolts," Tony corrected. "Maybe three hundred, maybe more. Depends on how it's cut but someone else'll do that later after I sell it. I'm comin' from Chicago. My car lost a wheel and it didn't seem smart to wait for help, so I started walkin'. Glad ya came along instead of someone else." He laughed happily.

Charles didn't listen to the chatter. Instead he made calculations based on centuries of experience. "Suppose you sold it to someone else and got a better price for it. Would you have to take it to Akron?"

"Lots of jumpy junkies in Akron, I guess, but I wouldn't care. Ya want to buy it?"

"I do."

The question had only been asked as a joke and the reply shook Tony. "Why? Ya don't sound like a pusher."

Charles betrayed no emotion when he replied, "I want to kill myself."

Tony convulsed with laughter and beat his hands gleefully on the dash. "Shit, man! For a second I thought you were serious! You are really somethin' else."

"I am." The reply was cold. "And I do."

The laughter subsided, though it took awhile. "Ya been thinkin' about this a long time, ain't ya?"

"Yes." Charles sighed. "A very long time."

"Well, ya won't need that much. Ya won't even need a tenth of what I got."

"I don't know how much it would take," Charles said honestly, "but I'll make you an offer. You help me do this and I will give you all the money I have. . . ." Charles glanced at his passenger, reading the thoughts written so obviously on his face. "I have at least two thousand dollars and there's a title for this car in the glove box. I'll sign it over to you."

"Damn!" Tony exclaimed, then "Damn!" again. The money was way more than enough. And a car besides! He'd never done anything like this before. It would make one hell of a story to tell when he got back home, and he'd have wheels and cash to prove it.

"Well?" Charles asked with sharp impatience.

"Why not? If you're gonna do it, anyway, might as well be me who picks up your leftovers, right?"

"Do you have a needle?" Charles asked hopefully.

"Sure, a new one too. I don't use the stuff much, but if a dealer wants to check out my stash, I sometimes go along. But I always use a new hype and I go first. Ya get sick, ya ain't careful."

In a few miles, Charles turned right and sped down a narrower country road. The weed made Tony drifty, and he tried not to think about what they'd soon be doing. It was growing light and Tony leaned back against the seat and studied the driver. A waste, he thought, too mellow for sadness, and anyway, who was he to interfere? As he watched Charles, he began to fantasize demanding and getting a more personal price for his assistance, but every time he began to think of the right words to say, the fantasy would be forced back into the

murky waters of his subconscious, from which it would
emerge a moment later...a different scene in a different
place. Long before Tony got bored with these daydreams,
someone else did and they drowned. Charles glanced at Tony
then, his expression insolent, and Tony knew he would not—
could never—make it. A waste, he thought, and turned his
head to stare out at the desolate farmland gripped by fingers of
early-morning fog.

The birds had just begun to sing as they pulled off a dirt
road and climbed up a muddy fire lane concealed by scrubby
brush. Charles killed the lights and they drove into the thickening trees until, satisfied they would not be disturbed, he
stopped.

Removing the wallet from his pocket, Charles laid it on the
front seat, then pulled the title from the glove box. He signed
it, leaving the space for Tony's signature blank. He had no
desire to know the boy's real name.

Exiting the car, Charles leaned against its side, pressing his
hands hard against the door so his fingers grew white. As he
tried not to breathe, not to smell the multitude of familiar wild
scents, not to feel the nearly imperceptible dawn breeze, he
knew this place was a mistake. They should have found that
hotel room. He should have made that more intimate payment
then. And after, the four dingy walls, the soiled sheets, and
his disgust would have made this act so much easier. Life
attacked him here and, inside, the beast already responded.
Sliding slowly down, he sat with his back to the car and
placed his hands on his knees, not daring to touch the living
earth beneath him. He knew if he did, he would lose that
rational part of him that wanted so terribly to complete this act
and make it work. Behind him, he heard Tony flipping
through the bills in his wallet, and his mouth twisted into a
travesty of a smile. "Come on! Let's finish this."

Carrying his knapsack, Tony walked around the car and sat
beside Charles. "Got any second thoughts?"

Charles shook his head.

As Tony pulled out his stash another question occurred to
him. "Did you write a note so your people will know what
happened?" It was not a humane suggestion. Tony didn't want
anyone thinking "murder."

Charles hadn't considered a note but he agreed. Finding a

scrap of paper and a pen in his pocket, he scribbled a few lines
in his own language. Let the rest of those magnificent Austras
try to comprehend this! Your people, Tony had said . . . your
people. Defiance melted into sadness. He was the guilty one
and his family deserved better. He added another line, turned
the paper over, and wrote down an address. "Mail this," he
told Tony, never doubting his order would be obeyed. As he
placed the note on the car's front seat, he glanced at his wallet. But no, his family name, his human name . . . the papers
had burned together, the ashes mixing as they fell. No need to
be concerned about names anymore.

Only a few of the brightest stars were left in the sky, and
Charles wondered if the dawn-lethargy would be a help or a
hindrance. "What's lethal?" he asked.

"Two grams will flatten anything that moves."

Charles doubted that. "Make it fourteen. Half that ounce."

Tony exploded. "Shit! I can't fit that in a needle. I can
barely heat it all at once!" The last wasn't true. He had the
white powder divided into two of the dozen lab flasks his old
lady had given him for his birthday. Those flasks made him
feel real scientific and impressed the hell out of his contacts.
No wax paper for this dealer; first-class all the way. He could
heat one of those but he disliked the waste, especially since he
planned on selling what remained when he was done here.
"You're just damned crazy," he concluded.

"I assure you, I am; however, for the moment I know what
I'm doing. Heat it and inject it as often as you must, but do
fourteen."

They had been talking for hours, yet this was the first time
Tony noticed how forceful this man's eyes could be. "Fucking
crazy." Tony upped his obscenity as he lowered his voice.

Charles laid his hands on Tony's shoulders and Tony responded with a rush of emotion that might have been passion
. . . or fear. "I paid for it and I tell you this: Do it all if you
value your life, Tony."

It was only possible to agree. Tony's hands shook as he
removed a flask from its protective paper wrapping, and when
he pulled out the stopper, a small amount of the powder
spilled.

Charles watched it drift down, coating a few blades of
grass like frost, like froth on waves. Memories assaulted him,

keeping his mind sadly occupied while Tony worked until something was thrust into his hand.

"Hold this," Tony ordered, giving Charles a flask one-quarter full of white powder. Pouring water from a canteen he kept in his sack, he filled it almost to the top, took it back from Charles, then used his finger as a stopper and shook it. "Here," he said, smearing the grainy mix adhering to his finger onto the back of Charles's hand. "Taste it. No sugar, no quinine. This is what the *real* stuff tastes like. Very valuable to . . ." He saw Charles's incredulous expression and ended with a nervous snicker. "Fuck it, man. I'm not sure which of us is crazier here." Shaking his head, he flicked on a lighter and began the slow burn, thankful for the gray dawn light and still air.

Charles watched as grain after grain dissolved and was lost to the water. He thought of each as a year of the past: one less . . . then another gone and another . . . until Tony replaced the stopper and, rising to his knees, unbuckled his belt.

For an instant Charles looked up in alarm, wondering who was in control of this encounter. But no, Tony merely pulled it off and said, "Take off your jacket and roll up your sleeve."

"Not my hand," Charles said as Tony reached for it. "Your needle will snap." Tony wasn't sure how Charles knew this but, hell, it was his funeral. He lightly brushed the inside of Charles's wrist but, though it looked promising, Charles shook his head. "Farther up my arm is better."

Tony wanted nothing more than to walk away and let Charles do this on his own. Better yet, he wanted to think of something, anything, to say that would stop this before it began. There were so many things he would prefer to do with this man than kill him and, as Charles in his deadly preoccupation ignored his executioner, the images that returned to Tony's mind were getting disturbingly graphic. Too late, though; he was committed. He wrapped the belt tightly around Charles's upper arm and tried to ignore the feel of his victim's flesh as he prodded and found the best vein.

Tony drew the solution up in his needle and the level in the flask went down a disappointingly short distance. "That's all she holds," Tony said and, looking at it, made a rough calculation. "At least fifteen times, man." He shook his head sadly and stressed the fifteen as if it would somehow hurt.

Though the idea struck Charles as hilarious, he did not laugh. Instead he embellished his earlier warning. "Inject it all, do you understand? When I lose consciousness, keep going. Don't stop if you value your life, Tony." As Tony saw death uncurling behind those huge, lightless eyes, he nodded in complete agreement while some rational part of him searched frantically for the place where his protective fear had hidden. "Do it fast," Charles continued. Tony shook his head and held up the capped flask. "Well, then, as fast as you can and when you are finished, leave this place. Quickly."

As Tony reached for his arm, Charles instinctively wanted to turn his head away but he knew he must watch, must keep himself in control until this act had moved so far that it would be completed and he would know if he would live or die. He felt himself tense but, after a brief struggle, forced his body to relax and accept this unfamiliar invasion.

The needle still might have broken as Charles found metal often did, but it was thin and new and it pierced his skin with only a small amount of difficulty. Tony probed and apologized and, finally rewarded with a vein, pulled a small amount of blood back into the syringe. "Aren't you supposed to push it in?" Charles asked.

"The blood tells you're at the vein. If you don't regis—" Finding himself about to give another drug lecture, Tony stopped and searched for some suitable final words. He could think of none, so he looked questioningly at Charles, who nodded once in reply. Tony shrugged and pushed down while Charles watched with detached interest as the liquid disappeared into his arm. As Tony refilled the syringe, Charles waited to feel something, anything. When he did, the vague euphoria was disappointing.

"Again," he ordered, and his even voice astonished Tony. Afterward, feeling the first real rush, he repeated, "Again."

The man should be dead! Tony decided to turn and run but something held his body in a painful grip. As he found the vein once more, he managed a broken whisper. "What in the hell are you?"

Charles, the drug-induced rapture overcoming him at last, looked up at the brightening sky and smiled. "Something else," he replied, his whisper soft, filled with the antiquity of dreams.

After five injections his pupils grew smaller and sharper as the drug began its merciless assault on his body. Some almost logical part of him began to wonder if time were running backward, if he could keep it running to the beginning and beyond and why, in the growing darkness of this strange dawn, there was no moon, no stars.

"Again," he whispered, and to Tony his voice, because he had a voice, was terrible.

Charles danced with sad dreams that had lost their power to touch him . . . he caressed them, mocked them, and they dissolved into a glowing mist and, in a whisper, vanished. Standing on the endless plain, swept barren by the rush of this internal storm, he saw at last the dawn. The light blinded and he turned away from it, his nocturnal eyes instinctively seeking the darkness . . . hoping to find in its comfort the one he had lost, that perfect memory to show him the way. He called her name but another answered, and he perceived, as only his kind could, the bodiless glory, the bewitching horror of the pure force approaching him. His will was strong, but when the shadow brushed him, he lost all freedom, all choice. He ran.

Something pricked his empty body. "Again," he whispered with soft, fey laughter, and the awe, the ignorant dread of whatever, whoever, had touched him washed over him, restoring reason. His will regained control and he forced his soul back to that empty plain again . . . again . . . again . . .

Each track was marked with a small drop of blood. There were eight before Charles, with his face still to the sky, closed his eyes and let Tony finish on his own.

By now his executioner knew better than to disobey the warning. As Tony reached for Charles the tenth time, he noticed Charles was barely breathing and his face was as rigid as one already dead. But inside, in places he could not see, Charles's body was at work fighting the drug, neutralizing it at a fantastic speed, and that alien part of him was thinking, winning, waiting. . . .

Amazed he could still find a vein to hit, Tony, his body now shaking like a junkie's, plunged the needle again . . . again . . . again.

In response, Charles's features began shifting slowly and inevitably into something more darkly beautiful than his human facade. As he held the last of the drug in his needle,

Tony noticed the change and, having never seen anyone die before, thought this meant Charles was finally gone. Remembering the warning, he finished, wondering if this last jolt would be of any use at all.

He should have listened to Charles, packed his bag and peeled rubber getting out of there. Though he wanted to, he didn't. Instead, Tony removed his belt from Charles's arm and, while threading it slowly through his belt loops, looked down at the creature who was something more than human and made his greatest mistake.

Tony had never seen a man with skin so pale or hair so loosely curled and so perfectly, colorlessly black. The angle at which his head had fallen back accentuated his flawless features, and his lips, slightly parted, held the hint of a smile, as if death were his lover and they shared ecstasy together.

As Tony looked down at this irresistible beauty, all caution vanished. He lowered his hands, leaving his belt unbuckled, and, with no conclusion he dared to name, bent over the motionless, magnificent face of the being he thought he had killed.

His hand brushed the thick curls and he caught one and wrapped it around his finger. His other hand moved down to brush Charles's neck as he searched (he said to himself,) for a pulse. Finding none, he tried again in a different place.

"This is crazy!" he spoke aloud. "He told you. Get out! Get away!" But Tony's body bent still lower, and his fingers hung twitching in the air while he tried to pull them back from their magnetic descent, their independent will, which had them undoing the buttons of Charles's shirt while he watched in terror and helpless fascination.

Had Tony been observant, he would have felt the slight fluttering of his victim's stomach, seen the long, tapered fingers curl and harden. He might have run then, but he was fighting his own internal battle, the desperate, final, struggle of the already defeated.

Tony fell to his knees next to the body, one hand attached to Charles's chest, the other tied to that one lustrous curl. "He's dead. You killed him," he hissed through clenched teeth as he swayed, struggling to hold himself back, to keep from kissing his victim's lips. Sweat beaded on his face and neck as he fought the overpowering compulsion, the bewitching attraction. On the edge of insanity, a final happy thought ended his resistance. "Just saying good-bye," he whispered, relieved the struggle had ended.

It was a lover's kiss, long and deep and utterly revealing. Tony's eyes grew round and shocked, and from his throat came the low grunts of effort as he tried to pull his head away, tried to reach for the knife in his pocket. For one brief, hysterical moment he broke the other's control and managed to accomplish both.

Springing away, he held the knife in front of him; looking down at eyes impossibly, totally dark; at pupils expanded in rapacious interest; at a mouth narrowing, flattening, as it pulled back and back to reveal what Tony's tongue had already discovered . . . those impossibly long feline teeth in a faultless human face.

Tony took a fatal step forward, and one hand reached out to him as if brushing away an annoying insect. Tony's knife hand slashed down, cutting only the air as he doubled forward, shrieking in full-throated agony. He tried to stand, to reform what had been his guts, but that bloody hand was already at his throat.

This was not a merciful gesture, for Charles had moved beyond any thoughts of mercy. But the drug had stolen all hunger, and so he had no need to prolong the life of his prey. Had Tony felt anything, it might have been gratitude.

Charles lay slumped against the body, one hand and his dark hair bathed in the blood until the rays of the morning sun struck him, forcing him into motion. Rolling instinctively beneath the car, he lay in partial dark. Four days later a swarm of flies happily employed in the afternoon sun irritated him into something resembling consciousness, but it was the smell that made him open his eyes.

It wasn't enough, he thought woodenly; but all of it would not have been enough. Turning his head, he lapsed again into a half-sleep, then at dusk rolled out from beneath the car, contemplated the mangled and yellowing body, looked down at his hands, and understood.

His right sleeve was still rolled up, and he saw the individual dry drops of blood on his arm. He recalled nine; now there were sixteen. They brushed away as if they were dirt and, like dirt, no marks showed beneath them. A millennium and the only scars were mental.

He found his car keys in the ignition, then opened the trunk. After removing his blood-encrusted clothing and covering the body with it, he laid aside an ancient crossbow and opened the worn leather valise that had rested beneath it. Taking out a bottle of cloudy water, he washed away all traces of blood and took a long swallow before dressing.

Afterward, he paused and considered this attempt... another deadly lapse into futility. Only one way was open to him now, and pulling a sketch pad from the trunk, he sat cross-legged on the car's roof and composed a letter in a language ancient but translatable. When he finished, he placed it in Tony's shirt pocket. This was a useless gesture: the body wouldn't be found for weeks, and by then the address would no longer matter.

Backing carefully down the narrow road, Charles headed north towards Sandusky. His hunger was impatient. He liked that. He'd make it wait.

# Chapter Nine

## I

WHEN THE THERAPIST strapped on her braces, Helen felt a familiar panic. Before it grew strong enough to threaten her, she dispelled it with a small push of self-control and looked down at her long legs in dismay.

Flatley smiled at his favorite patient. He liked to believe he had something to do with her progress over the past month, though when he examined the facts, he'd done nothing beyond recommending the usual weights and exercises. Her muscles seemed to grow by themselves, almost as if she were willing them into existence. And there were times he believed (irrationally, he knew) Helen's strength had something to do with that pushy young man who used to accompany her to her appointments. He'd asked Helen what had become of Austra, and she'd replied offhandedly, "He abhors illness." Flatley, who cared about all his patients, thought this cold.

Actually, it had been Helen who had suggested Stephen find someplace else to spend the few hours she saw the doctor each week. She had watched him fight these surroundings . . . the sights, the sounds, the scents all throwing him into a quiet panic. And now, if a wheelchair weren't enough of a reminder of how much she belonged here, there were these.

The ugliness of metal and leather meets the vanity of youth. Flatley saw no reason to preach acceptance; she would not wear them long; so instead he suggested gently, "Hide them."

Planning to take his advice, Helen contemplated the discouraging selection of slacks in her closet and called her friend

Connie to arrange a shopping trip for Friday morning. After lunch, Connie could drop her off for her clinic appointment.

Connie agreed, becoming more enthusiastic after she explained she was temporarily banned from use of the family car, and Helen told her they could use Stephen's. "I haven't seen you since we registered, and I can't wait to hear about your friend."

Lover, Helen thought as she hung up the phone, realizing Connie would never hear even half the truth. She sighed, feeling like the phrase her grandmother used to describe Stephen: "old as the Dacean plains." Helen had gone from innocent youth to something far beyond adulthood in a matter of weeks, and part of her mourned the loss.

She began humming as she decided what to wear to town. Catching her reflection in the mirror, she stopped and wondered why she appeared so strange. It must be the light, that deep-toned light from the wine-colored glass that obscured the view from the window above her bed. Her hand closed around the indigo-colored teardrop Sylvia had given her. She could not identify the cause of her concern except that, possessing more than she had ever expected, she had grown greedy. But she could never return to what she no longer was.

Wrapping herself in the blue silk robe, she waited for her lover and was relieved when he arrived early. She needed more kind words, more caresses, more of him as a reassurance that the future would be happier than the present somehow felt.


*II*


Friday morning, far too early for Helen's changing sleep habits, she and Connie began their day in town.

Connie gasped when she saw Helen. "You look so wonderful. Only four weeks and what a difference!" She gasped again when she saw what they were driving. Lowering the convertible's top, she looked at the sky and grinned, "St. Chris, keep me under the speed limit. I can't afford the ticket."

As Connie eyed sensible, and sale-priced, coordinates, Helen pulled out bright tones in loose slacks and sophisticated blouses and developed an irresistible attraction for a magnificently embroidered long red skirt. Gauging its effect in the mirror, she saw Stephen was correct about her changing color needs. It seemed ironic that, as she grew stronger, she also grew more pale. The hot color offset the pallor and restored what had been a naturally rosy complexion.

While Connie was in the changing room, Helen visited the men's department and discovered a rich brown satin robe . . . an ideal replacement for the blue silk. Naturally thrifty, she nearly decided against it when she saw its price, then recalled how this day's shopping was being financed. She pulled out her charge card, wondering if the tuition refund would arrive before the day's bills, then returned to the misses' department to purchase items almost as extravagant for herself.

On their way to lunch, Connie babbled happily about the fall term and, though Helen was tempted to divulge a portion of her new plans, her discretion won. Only Sylvia would ever know them completely; Helen doubted anyone else would believe them. She thought of Chavez, the houses dotting the mountaintop, the creative community below. A new life, a new family.

Connie gave her a playful poke in the arm. "Helen, you can stop daydreaming. We've arrived!"

As they began the time-consuming process that moved her from car to chair to table, Helen felt an unfair impatience to be finished with this methodical transformation . . . to be healthy . . . to run!

Inside the restaurant, the thick Italian smells were oppressive, but as usual, Helen was famished and ordered the heaviest lunch . . . lasagne, antipasto, garlic bread, and, she told the waiter, perhaps dessert.

Connie looked at Helen in amazement and, after she placed her own order, slyly concluded, "Plus a glass of wine for myself and my friend. Burgundy, not chilled." She implied years of experience and the waiter did not question her.

"Connie!" Helen said after the waiter had gone. "We're not . . ." Unexpected laughter bubbled over. It began as a ripple that grew into a torrent of something wild and knowing and almost bitter, but by then Connie had added her own and did not notice. Helen pressed her hands tightly against her forehead, as if she could somehow cap the emotions leaking out before they proved disastrous. "We're not old enough to drink," she concluded, flashing Connie a far from youthful look through spread fingers.

"But we're old enough for other things." Connie winked. "So, do I get to hear all about it, or are you going to play secretive and deny everything?"

"It's a little late for that," Helen admitted, "but you'll have to learn details for yourself." Connie nodded, looking old and wise as the waiter brought the wine.

"Are you all right?" the waiter asked Helen. He placed a hand on her shoulder, and the look he gave her was one of interest rather than concern.

"Quite," she replied, her tone and the hard set of her eyes discouraging him.

As he left, Connie leaned over the table and whispered, "He knows which of us has the experience here." She leaned back and studied her friend, then waved her hand in a dramatic gesture that implied all of Helen. "It explains everything."

"Everything?"

Helen looked so shocked, Connie laughed. "You look radiant, both pale and glowing at the same time. It's obvious you're in love."

"Yes. Yes, I am." Helen beamed at this common explanation for a far more complex misery.

The waiter brought their food, then refilled their glasses. Helen began to protest, but he interrupted. "Compliments of the house for the lovely young ladies." He stared only at Helen, and she needed no psychic sense to understand what he was thinking.

When the man was beyond eavesdropping, she leaned across the table and said softly to Connie, "Let's eat and leave. This place is beginning to make me nervous."

Connie glanced at the waiter standing next to the kitchen doors, then at the bartender, then, with growing concern, at the few male patrons. "You're right." She stabbed her fork into her spaghetti as if already fending off a masher. "Tell me, does this happen to you often?"

They finished their meal in silence, Connie too uncomfortable to talk and Helen absorbed in trying to control that persuasive magnetism which had so abruptly surfaced. Stephen told her she had much to learn; the course load was getting frightening.

## III

Later that afternoon, Dick Wells pulled his car behind the rectory wagon. He saw Stephen hand his house keys to O'Maera and begin unloading the first of three church windows. "I'll give you a hand with those," he called.

Stephen glanced Dick's way and shook his head. "No, Richard, should one fall, I wish the blame to rest entirely with me." He carried the largest of the three up the stairs. Returning for the smaller two, he passed Dick leaning against the wagon. "You would like to speak with me, yes?"

Dick nodded and followed his neighbor upstairs, then waited for O'Maera to disappear into the kitchen to heat water for coffee before handing an airmail envelope to Stephen. "I came by to ask for a translation of one of my replies from Europe." When Stephen looked confused, Dick added, "Old Country tales, not verified."

"Ah, yes." Stephen read through the short letter from the Hungarian Ministry of Police and chuckled. "You must share this with Sylvia. It reads, 'Your murder recalls to us certain rumors that once circulated in the hill country near the Romanian border. Since the revolution, these rumors have ceased. Perhaps our people no longer have a need to create such monsters. We regret we cannot be more helpful.'"

"They don't need to create anything." Dick's tone held little humor. "The monsters are now in charge."

"Was this your only reply?"

"I got one other, a cable in English from Romania. It read: 'Vlad Tepes dies in 1476. Bram Stoker revived him. Suggest you try England.'"

"Succinct . . . and the British are known to be meticulous record keepers. Where else did you mail inquiries?"

"Austria, Germany, and your 'old country,' Portugal."

"I'm Czech," Stephen replied, wondering how carefully police records were maintained in remote parts of his adopted land.

"I hope the officials who have not yet responded are taking this more seriously. Murder, however fantastic, is not a joking matter."

"Perhaps they take their time because they are checking records," Stephen said, and thought, with grim concern, This might be true. He heard O'Maera opening the cupboard. The water had just begun to simmer. It was an ideal time to give Richard a gentle prod. . . .

"Of course, we have other irons in the fire. Corey's persuaded me to try a hypnotist on Linda Freemont. A lot of hocus-pocus, but what the hell, maybe the Rich and D'Amato killings are related. And we've got feelers out in downtown night spots. Somebody must have seen the girl or the killer. Then there are pimps and . . ." Dick was moving in the wrong direction, and Stephen pushed a little harder. "Sunrise Center for Runaways," Dick mumbled. "Bob Moore. August sixteenth."

Dick mechanically accepted the coffee O'Maera handed him. "Thank you," he said, his voice echoing words of gratitude he heard somewhere inside his head.

"Are you through with work for the day?" Stephen asked quickly.

"Yeah. For the weekend too. Thought I'd spend some time with the kids."

"Then perhaps you'd prefer a beer to the coffee, yes?" Stephen had found that these two common drinks were all a single male needed to entertain adequately in middle-class America. A pleasant change from the days when multicourse meals were standard and far more awkward for the host to bypass.

As he went into the kitchen for Dick's POC, Stephen called out, "You weren't expected home until much later. I promised your family a drive-in movie. We could change those plans, or you are welcome, of course, to join us."

"It depends on what you're seeing."

"It was Carol's turn to decide. We're going to *The Day the Earth Stood Still*."

"She actually picked that!" Dick said, astonished. His daughter's tastes usually ran to the more exotic.

His neighbor's eyes flashed mischievously as he handed Dick a glass. "Not precisely. I let her pick three, then I choose whichever I have not seen. Sometimes I lie."

"What else was on her list?"

*"The Creature from the Black Lagoon* and *The Thing,* so as you see..." He laughed, then asked O'Maera, "Are you coming, Patrick?"

"I think not. I always feel a wee awkward at drive-ins." He ran his finger along the inside of his Roman collar. "I must not dress right. Actually, laddie, I'm surprised you like our movies so much. You don't seem the type for such light art."

"The nearest theater to AustraGlass is eighty miles, and the roads are impossible. This is a welcome opportunity. Besides, I enjoy the children and..." The sound of screeching brakes on the hill made them all wince.

Stephen pressed his hands together and bowed his head in mock prayer. "My car awaits, hopefully intact. If you will excuse me, I believe I will go have a few words with the intrepid driver."

## IV

With an optimistic effort, Helen tried to climb the stairs to Stephen's apartment that evening. Her new slacks covered the braces but could do nothing to hide the crutches, nor the deliberate and graceless way she moved. A few steps from the top, she stopped and leaned back against Stephen. "I can't. If I try to go any farther, you'll only have to catch me."

"Then I shall catch you now." His laughter soothed her disappointment as he lifted her. "A month ago did you think you would ever get this far?"

"A month ago reality shifted. Though I admit there were times I thought you insane, and myself as well for believing you."

He sat down, still holding her, and gave her a light, affectionate kiss. "And now, what does the doctor say?"

"He's stopped hinting. He's asked if I've been to Lourdes lately. I told him this was another sort of miracle altogether." She frowned. "This is a miracle, isn't it?"

"That you exist, no. That I found you, definitely." He bent forward, meaning to emphasize this with another sportive kiss, then glimpsed her face, her confusion. "You meant something else, yes?"

"It's nothing, really." She pulled away and shook her head in annoyance. "I've forgotten. It's impossible to lie to you."

Stephen looked at his hand, resting on hers; both so pale, both with that deceptive fragility. She had become more than a lover, still less than family, and he feared any obstacle, every doubt. "Tell me," he said, resigned. And she did . . . first of her uneasiness at the restaurant, then of the taxi ride home from the clinic.

. . . The driver had made it impossible for Helen to ignore him. From the moment he'd helped her enter his cab, he'd entertained her, beginning with light anecdotes about his more unusual customers and ending with a disturbingly detailed but hilarious story concerning the sexual escapades of three inebriated fares he'd picked up in Berea.

His eyes were a startling shade of blue against his olive-toned complexion and she found herself staring back at them too often as he watched her through his mirror. When she moved out of his line of vision, he adjusted the mirror's angle to keep her in view, and with every glance his interest grew. She had hoped to become accustomed to people watching her; could learn, like Stephen, to ignore it, but never before had she been so enticed by the advances of a lewd stranger. His desire filled her; his needs aroused her. She pictured them together . . . him moving above her; not the manner he preferred, but her legs were not strong enough to straddle him, not yet . . . and at the end when his back arched and she held him one motion from completion, she would pull him down and he would scream her name as his blood pulsed through her—No! Impossible dreams! Impossible nightmares!—she was not that strong, not yet. . . .

*Oh, no! Dear Jesus, have mercy on me!* Her past destroyed the vision and she swallowed hard, tasting terror and disgust.

The intensity of Helen's expression betrayed her, and the driver reached back and rubbed her knee. "Where to?" he asked.

With an erratic attempt at control, she pushed his hand away. "Do I have to repeat my destination?" Something in her tone made him mutter an apology, place both hands on the wheel, and drive. Behind him, Helen beat her fingers on her knee until she realized she was tapping them in time to the man's pulse. . . .

"For the rest of the ride I kept wondering what I would do if he dared to pull the taxi down into some park, move into the back with me. I doubt I would have screamed, and I certainly could not have run. No matter how I consider it, no matter how I tell myself I experienced a vivid fantasy, nothing more, I wanted him as much as he wanted me and, in some indefinable way, more than I have ever wanted you." Her voice became small, a child's pleading. "Stephen, will I come to despise myself for how I must live?"

"I do not know; I have had no other existence." He wished he could give her more consolation, more hope. "Please try to understand. You know that I take my life . . . that I feed on you even as I love you. When you change, I can support you for a little while, but you must learn to live independently . . ." He put his hand under her chin and raised her face, then waited until she looked at him before concluding. ". . . to feed yourself."

"So many years, so many lovers." She studied him thoughtfully, as if seeing him clearly for the first time. "How many?" she demanded.

There was no pause, no attempt to consider a number. "Thousands."

She'd expected the answer but not the tone, the look that spoke of year upon year of loneliness. "How many have you loved?" she asked more gently.

"A handful. Most of my blood and most are gone now." Death was not inevitable, and so the sorrow and memories were always more cruel.

"How many have you killed?"

He winced, then slowly moved his hand to rest against her cheek. "I am as you know me. What I once was should not stand between us." For a moment they shared another vision of the afternoon.

. . . the driver falling onto her, dying in her, living on through her, his body resting heavily against her as she drank . . .

She whispered, "So vivid! And such a temptation."

The gentleness of his tone could not salve the hurt of his words. "It is our nature to kill, and humanity, in spite of all our similarities, is an animal like any other. Yet we have learned control. We take life, yes, but we need not give death, as you well know, child."

"But I'm not a child!" Her cheeks flushed with anger, a human response. "You've been hiding consequences from me!"

He made no reply. She spoke the truth and there was nothing to add.

"Which legends describe us the best, Stephen? Vampires and werewolves? They don't seem right, for, though I was tempted, I was no animal caught up in a lust to kill. But the lamia, the incubus, the succubus? I look at you and I feel what is growing in me, and I see my future as one empty conquest followed by another. If that is what survival demands, I don't want it. Nothing is worth such constant degradation."

"It isn't like that. It is a power, a kind of intimacy you don't understand."

"I believe I do. How did you survive here before you met me?"

Thinking of O'Maera, who had been nearly correct in his concern, Stephen replied, "Until a month ago, quite ascetically. At home, surrounded by those who know me, there is no need to hide and no conquests to make. And here, if I had traveled a more anonymous route, I would have been less cautious. I would have taken some rooms at one of your hotels and at night sat in the bar or coffee shop and waited. If I were fortunate, I might have found someone unattached and exciting and taken a lover for the months I was here; it is simpler that way and more satisfying. But because I met you, I did not seek a lover, and my most satisfying night came when I hunted in your river valley."

"That was you?"

"Yes. There were women as well. Most looked like you." He did not need to add this, but he would not make her doubts easier to bear.

"Show me what you do."

He had expected her request, but not so soon, nor with such quiet anger. "I nearly did that the first night we met. Remember how you felt when I first looked at you?"

"Enthralled." For a moment her voice softened, then grew

demanding once more. "Feeling is not the same as seeing. I want you to show me."

"Very well. Later. Late tonight if you wish." She nodded, her mouth a hard white line. He hoped she would be calm. She had felt the attraction, so perhaps she was ready, though it seemed too soon.

# V

Later that night, after the drive-in, they headed east, flowing on a river of traffic, tight as only Friday night traffic could be, with cars of all persuasions and drivers, mostly young, engaged in the elaborate courtship rites of summer. Helen leaned against the door, cradling Carol under one arm. In the back, Dick sat sharing the last of a candy bar with Alan. The boy was too excited for sleep, but his eyes were huge with hidden fatigue and they glowed, with remembered enjoyment of the movie.

A car screeched out of nowhere, too close for anything but an inevitable collision. In that same instant, Stephen screamed a thought to Helen and floored the Bel Air. Pushed to its limits, the engine roared, died, and was revived while Dick's body was shoved violently forward, then sideways, as the car began its impossible turn away from destruction.

Out of the corner of a horrified eye, Dick thought he saw Alan thrown over the side, only to be pulled back by an unseen savior. Following an imperceptible pause, Stephen gunned the car again, this time into the smallest possible opening in the westbound traffic. Behind him, Dick heard the squeal of tires on pavement, the crash of metal hitting metal. It would be a moment still before he understood these sounds should have been made by them.

Beside him, Alan sat dazed, rubbing his bruised neck. In the front seat, Helen released her white-knuckled grip on the door and dashboard, and the expression she had as she stared at Stephen was one of horror. Dick could see only the back of Stephen's bowed head, his right arm still holding Carol and Helen back against the seat. There was no way, no way he could have made that maneuver one-handed, yet he had! He must be okay, Dick thought, glancing again at Helen's shocked expression. He's driving okay, damned okay! He leaned forward and laid a thankful hand on his friend's shoulder and felt a solidity, as if what should have been flesh was bone. Before he had time to consider this, had he considered it at all, Stephen relaxed and lowered his arm, and Carol, freed of the painful vise that had held her, leaned against her cousin and began to cry.

Dick heard the welcome wail of sirens, but Stephen never glanced back, never said a word. Instead he drove carefully west, finally turning to take a different route home.

Somehow he had managed to stay with the car and it had required no effort. Helen's presence might have kept him there, but he could not explain what made him risk his secrecy and Helen's life to reach back for Alan. Too human, he thought, but now there was no admonition. What he had done had worked, and in these happy times he could allow himself to care. Through Carol's dwindling wails he heard Helen's breathing . . . too fast, her thoughts angry.

—Yes?—

—I wasn't prepared. I nearly exposed you.—

—And?—

—Why didn't you show me . . . tell me?—

—Later . . . later.—And the remainder of the evening became more difficult.

Carol and Alan had gradually lost their fright, and both were sleeping soundly when they arrived home. Dick carried one child and Stephen the other and, careful not to wake them, placed them in their beds. As Stephen left Carol's room, he found Dick waiting for him in the dark hallway.

"It occurred to me that I haven't thanked you. I don't know where you learned to drive like that. I don't suppose you've been running shine?" Dick accompanied the remark with a short, quiet laugh. "Anyway, I'm glad it was you behind the wheel, for everyone's sake."

"I am fond of your family, Richard." Dick could not see Stephen's face but he was sure his expression was as serious as his words. "I would not have wanted to see anything tragic befall them. If you will excuse me, I would like to say goodnight to your niece."

"Take your time."

"Pardon?"

"Nothing, I guess. Say good night for me, too, will you? I'm going to turn in now and try to greet this wild crew with breakfast in the morning."

# VI

Helen had removed her braces and pushed her porch swing violently in an attempt to dissipate her anxiety. When the door swung open, she looked up at Stephen, her eyes brimming with anger and dread. "Now," she said, the word both a question and a demand.

Stephen recalled her own words: "She is not a child, yet how like a child she acts." He caught the swing and leaned his face close to hers. She drew back, startled by his fierce, unfamiliar expression. "Now."

Her tension would be a distraction and he knew it would have been infinitely better had she begun as he had, with someone who understood and would yield willingly. For that he had hoped to wait until they reached New York or Chavez, but the act could not be postponed. She waited with fatalistic anticipation, and in response he grinned. "Well, Helen, must I remain here and take potluck, or shall we go for a drive?"

It worked. She laughed, though uneasily and only for a moment. "Take me somewhere you used to go," she ordered less apprehensively.

"Very well. But you shall make the choice for me."

"Do you think I would be jealous otherwise?"

"No, I want you to be attracted to the one you choose."

She became confused. "It would be a man."

"And this need not be sex." His voice had already moved to a more compelling timbre. In spite of his misgivings, tonight had begun to excite him. "You hunt with me and I shall feed as much on your pleasure, your response, to what occurs as I will on the blood of the one you choose."

She found him buying cigarettes at a gas station; no older than herself, with features still softly feminine. Captured by

Helen's eyes, eyes that were not entirely her own at that moment, he accepted her offer of a ride home, sitting without question between her and the silent driver, unable to be polite as he stared at her body with frank longing. But Helen felt no dread, for some consummate force had taken control of him, holding him helpless. She glimpsed swift snapshots of his life, savored his private dreams, and understood that Stephen could arouse any emotion, but because she was here and feared it most of all, he had chosen desire.

She brushed her fingers across the inside of the young man's wrist, feeling his pulse quicken, innately knowing when to give that unspoken command. —Look at me, think only of me.—

A small sound of shameless joy escaped him when she rested her hands on the sides of his face, and she wondered at his rapture while, behind him, the other—the forgotten one —pressed close.

Stephen felt no struggle, no adversary here. This was the sort of first choice he had expected she would make . . . pretty and safe, young as she was young . . . infinitely refinable and far more satisfying than he had anticipated.

As Stephen stole that small bit of life, it exploded within her and, with it, the power! Her mind emptied of all save its presence, and she marveled at what they had done and how much more they could do.

They drove home in silence and only some time after they entered her apartment did Stephen ask, "Shall I stay?"

"I don't have any choice, do I?" He didn't answer, not daring to speak the truth, not wishing to lie. "Just as Sylvia had no choice but to offer me to you." She used her grandmother's name because, in this moment, she did not consider Sylvia any loving relation. Her voice was sharp with contempt.

She felt the force of his anger before he replied. "Look at these." He pointed to a display of her favorite paintings, done over the last two years. Each had required weeks of meticulous effort. "Now these . . ." He waved his hand at a set of five woodland scenes, each completed in hours while they were on an outing, often with the distracting presence of children. They were infinitely better . . . more detailed, more daring in their use of color, and the last was so superior that it made the first appear shabby. "Now look at yourself!" He flung her contempt back. "You are angry, yes? But when have you felt such anger? Such vitality? Such passion? And tonight? Ignore all the morality you've been taught; a different morality applies here. Did you not feel pleasure? Did you not give it and, if so, who has been harmed?"

What she had done should have aroused only disgust in Helen and yet . . . As she began to yield, to raise her arms and ask him to come to her, depleted humanity rallied for one final attack. "Get out!" Helen screamed the words, while upstairs Carol opened her eyes before rolling over in a more ordered sleep. "Get out. I need time." Helen repeated her order in a dwindling voice and, when he still would not move, added, "Please."

He shook his head.

"You would rape me?"

"No, you need only take from me what you wish. I will not force you, Helen, but I will not leave you now."

Again that barely perceptible alteration in tone. He's so sure of himself and so correct. Tonight he had played with another's passion, and though she had been his instrument, she had received nothing in exchange. "Very well, you have had your needs met. Now you shall meet mine."

"I promise I shall." And she was assaulted by that curious inflection, the accompanying soft-focus vision of visions, the touching without touching, which was his form of mental foreplay. But, as it began, she looked at him and, with a simple twist, amplified his thoughts.

He took an involuntary step toward her, then another. Reaching for him, she pulled him down to her and, taking the initiative, gave back everything she had learned, and things she had only imagined, leaving him breathless, empty. He felt her reluctant pause, as if humanity might still win this round, and he kissed her too hard, cutting her lip. She tasted the blood, that reminder of always . . .

With a moan that might have been pain, she took the satisfaction her body demanded. Tomorrow night she would ask to hunt again, and the next night and the next, until she accepted. She would learn, she knew she would have to learn, for what choices were there but life or death?

Later, as he stroked her breasts and stomach and thighs in what might have been the final touches of the night's love-

making, or merely a relaxing pause, he felt her shudder.
—Yes?—

—What are you that you can offer me this?— She rolled so
her body was resting on his, and bent her head down to kiss
him, her long hair falling across his shoulders, her tongue
exploring his mouth, feeling all that was different there, her
tears falling softly, forming bright beads in his dark hair.

# VII

Ed, the bartender at Charley's, was leaning against the rail,
talking to one of his favorite customers when the woman walked
in. Losing his concentration in mid-sentence, he stared at her,
and his look might have been rude, and his comment, "Look at
that bee-oo-ti-fool piece," would certainly have been had both
held less reverence. Dr. Frank Flaherty followed Ed's stare, let
out a silent whistle, and waited to get a glimpse of the fortunate
guy who was with her. It took some time for him to understand
she was alone and, even after her dark eyes glanced his way with
an inviting expression, that she was interested in him.

*"Cochon!"* she swore to herself, lowering her head and
again looking sideways at him from under her winged black
brows. She chided herself for her impatience; it was childish
and she was far from young. Although she did not, as a rule,
enjoy the company of doctors (having found most of them far
too inquisitive concerning certain anatomical differences), she
thought Flaherty passably good-looking, and certainly she
should not judge him, at least not until she knew him somewhat better. No, the swine was whichever of her imbecile
relations was responsible for her sitting in a place as dingy as
Charley's to begin with.

"Lucky dude!" Ed whispered to Flaherty. "This is your hot
night. Ain't ya gonna buy the lady a drink?"

Flaherty walked over to her then, but he'd never felt this
clumsy.

Soon her elegant laughter tinkled through the quiet bar,
making Flaherty feel perfectly at ease, totally in control. She

was French, and every delightfully accented word stroked his desire. He hungered to be alone with her, to unzip that black sheath she was filling so magnificently, but he was happily married and, like a fool, could think of no place to go.

As if reading his thoughts, she rested one beautiful hand over his, cocked her head, and graced him with a sensuous smile. "Your work, they are done now, *oui*?"

Of course they were. It was perfect.

As they walked out, he winked at Ed, who gave him a sly look in return. "Where to?" Ed whispered.

"The office," Flaherty replied with a huge, happy leer.

Ed pictured them in an obscene embrace, his mind considering all the erotic positions they could attempt on those narrow, adjustable tables over at the Blood Disease Research Center. As he cleared off the place where they'd been sitting, he noticed the woman hadn't touched her wine at all.

Two hours later, Elizabeth's Porsche was speeding back to New York, her dark hair flying in the wind. This had been a surprisingly pleasant task with that dear doctor . . . so concerned, so cautious, and, ultimately, so much fun. She was pleased that his conscience would not trouble him; indeed, he wouldn't remember what little they'd done, and she'd made certain it would be a while before he set foot in Charley's. The bartender was far too nosy.

As she drove, she tried to determine who in the family would have been rash enough to have caused this dangerous situation. Unlike Stephen, she was not certain that the murder of the D'Amato girl had been an unnecessary killing. She'd met plenty of women in her day who deserved a premature end, and *poules* were far from exempt.

She tried to imagine a motive. From the details her cousin had provided, this deed had not been done in self-defense nor, apparently, out of need. This left only vengeance and, again, the nagging question as to who had done the killing.

Well, of one thing she was certain . . . she had been successful tonight. Two separate blood types, Stephen had said, and she had followed that order. She patted the box on the seat beside her, hoping someone would appreciate the joke she had gone to such elaborate lengths to prepare.

She edged her cabriolet's speed past ninety and within a

few minutes heard the siren behind her. With a small "*tsk*" of annoyance, she pulled over.

"*Bon soir*," she said to the policeman, her voice bright as moonlight rippling on dark waters. For all the times she had been stopped, she had never received a ticket.

# Chapter Ten

## I

JANET TOOK ANOTHER sip of her pink lady and belched. She found it less depressing to be alone if she was drunk, and she had most certainly reached that necessary state. She'd lost track of how many refills she'd ordered, and of course, there were those bought by the hangers-on, the men who knew where Johnny had gone and why, and who flocked like young buzzards waiting for a chance to rip off a piece of the discarded wife.

*Well, Janet, old girl,* she decided, *it's high time you weave yourself home, and in the morning you'll be too sick to think about anything but yourself.*

"S'cuse me," she mumbled to anyone who might be listening. "I need the can." When she reached the hall separating the bar from the poolroom, instead of turning in to the bathroom, she exited the tavern door. A far easier departure than giving excuses to guys who'd make it hard to say goodbye.

She hadn't walked more than half a block when the fresh air intensified the alcohol's effect and she had to lean hastily against a lamppost for support. Where in this waterfront section of Sandusky could she buy a cup of coffee or something to eat? The prospects seemed as dim as the misty lake at this late hour.

Gulping a few deep breaths of air, she pushed herself into an upright position and continued down the street. Her progress pleased her—she was walking, wasn't she, and in the right direction—when she tripped on a crack and, with legs too wobbly to hold her, fell down hard on one elbow. As she sat back on her knees, rubbing her arm and moaning to herself, someone reached down and offered her a hand.

Janet muttered some thanks and, once she stood, took a close look at her benefactor and thought her knees might buckle again for an entirely different reason. Holy shit! He was handsome. That angular face. Those dark Gypsy eyes.

"Are you all right?" He spoke as if her welfare meant everything to him.

Janet stood a little straighter, trying to acquire some pretense of dignity, possibly even charm. "Nothing two or three cups of coffee wouldn't cure."

He glanced up and down the street, then shrugged. "I would certainly buy you some but . . ."

But? Oh, no buts about it, he wasn't getting away that easy, not if she had any chance of making it otherwise. Let Patty bitch about this in the morning—her friend would have every right—tonight belonged to her. "I'll tell you what, ah . . . ?"

"Charles."

"Oh, that's too formal. Not Chuck or Charlie or something?"

"Anything you like," he purred, and Janet caught the hint of an irresistible accent.

*Hey, Patty, look what followed me home! Is it okay if I keep it?* She giggled, and Charlie, who was paying close attention, pretended not to hear.

The downstairs door slammed shut as Patty was putting the baby's bottle on the stove to heat. Maybe Janet would do the night feeding, an idea that seemed only natural. After all, Timothy was Janet's little boy, not hers, and it wasn't fair of Janet to leave her with most of his care. Actually, all of it would be a more apt description. Since Johnny had walked out on his wife and baby two weeks earlier, Janet had done little more than barhop and, when she came home, nurse colossal hangovers.

Patty appreciated Janet's misery, but she had considered the matter from every side and decided that tomorrow she would go home and let her friend learn to survive this loss on her own.

As Patty walked toward the front door, she heard people ascending the stairs, a smooth masculine voice, and Janet's answering laugh. Sighing, she went into the kitchen and closed the swinging door. Yes, tomorrow she would definitely leave.

Timothy was patiently sucking his blanket when Patty came into the little nursery Janet had arranged in the small room off the kitchen. It seemed the nicest room in the flat with its coat of new white paint, ruffled blue curtains, throw rug, and matching blue quilt to cover the baby. Teddy bears and other small stuffed animals were propped on the sides of the cradle, and above it a musical Raggedy Ann mobile Janet had found in a secondhand store. Her friend had poured a great deal of love onto her child and, once Patty left, caring for Timmy would sustain her.

Patty had picked Timmy out of his crib and was going to retrieve the bottle when she heard a soft cry followed by a louder thud. Could that be Janet? Returning the baby to the crib, she went to investigate.

Patty had always believed in the direct approach, and if this were only the sounds of normal petting, or something more, she would simply apologize and leave. But she guessed Janet was drunk and had fallen, and whatever friend she'd dragged home with her would welcome the assistance. So, anxious to help, she pushed open the kitchen door.

This would have been the moment . . . a chance to scream or to run . . . but all she could do was whisper a small, frightened "Oh."

The man had one arm wrapped around Janet's waist, holding her tightly against him. A hand was tangled in her long hair and his lips—could those be *fangs*?—were pressed against her neck. Janet fought a silent frantic battle but her hands and feet might have been pushing against a rock, so unperturbed was her attacker by her struggles. Two slow trickles of blood flowed down Janet's neck to disappear under the collar of her blouse, and her skin had become ashen pale. This will be a fastidious murder, Patty thought absurdly. No messy slashing here.

Then his eyes caught her . . . dark, beautiful, hungry, and

somehow vulnerable, as if daring—no, hoping—that somewhere in this room was a weapon, any weapon, she could use
to save herself. But she was caught like she had once captured
a roach under one of those clear magnifying paperweights,
each of her efforts—to run, to scream, to fight—exaggerated
yet limited.

Patty was trapped for an eternity of minutes and, when he
let Janet's body fall, he let Patty go also. And she ran straight
into the nursery where she made her final, hopeless stand in
front of the cradle in which Timmy screamed, then fell
abruptly silent.

He hadn't counted on more than one. One was sufficient
but here was another. He should have known about this one
before he entered the flat. Even this tiny slip of his power
gave him comfort, and he licked his lips and smiled, and that
expression of such strange, alien beauty terrified even more
cruelly the woman standing so bravely in front of him. He
could feel her fear, smell it permeating the room like some
rich incense, hear that wonderful young heart pounding. His
gaze was frankly sexual, full of dark promises, and even in
this hour of her death, she was drawn to him.

So quickly that she did not see his hand move, he tore her
modest cotton nightgown from neckline to hem. She stumbled, then stood frozen, painfully aware of her body as his
mind moved through hers, revealing what he saw and felt as
he studied her. When he pulled her against him and covered
her mouth with his, she made no resistance though she trembled as she tasted Janet's blood. Her tongue disobeyed her and
explored his mouth, brushing with reluctant curiosity on the
extra set of pointed eyeteeth. He dropped his arms and she
took one step backward, her eyes pleading for her life, for the
child. He shook his head in sad understanding and pushed her
down to the carpet where she did anything, everything, he
demanded and, in that hopeless finality, found a desperate
fulfillment.

When it was over, her killer, her lover, ran his hand down
her still, smooth torso, kissed her on the shoulder, and covered her with a blanket. He had forgotten the baby, even the
woman who had brought him here and who he'd killed so
clumsily, but as he walked into the kitchen, the calcific odor
of burned milk overpowered him and he retched, vomiting a

dark stream of blood onto the shiny white linoleum. Somewhere in the room behind him, a baby cried in more innocent hunger. He dipped one finger in the creeping red puddle and considered. . . .

## II

Judy Preuss rested a comforting arm over the shaking shoulders of the hapless landlady who had discovered the bodies. Mrs. Poole, in housecoat, rolled-down hose, and slippers, sobbed as she related once more what she had babbled on the phone when she called Judy's office earlier that morning.

". . . and I thought I had seen the worst and that if I could just get through the kitchen past that horrible red puddle and into the bedroom and comfort the poor crying babe it would be all right and I'd go call the police. Then I saw Patty looking almost like she was sleeping and I thought I'd faint. But when I reached down to pick up Timmy and saw— *Oh!* I can't say it! I don't ever want to think about it again. . . ."

She blew her nose into an elegant lace-trimmed hankie. Judy pulled away and said something reassuring, which had no visible effect. "None of us are safe! That's why I called you first. You have to warn people there's a madman loose!"

Judy hugged the older woman, thanked her again—and sincerely—for the phone call and suggested she lie down. Afterward Judy walked to the place where Dick was parking his car. As he opened the door she extended her hand. "Dick Wells, I presume. How do you do. I'm Judy Preuss."

Had they ever met? he wondered as she gave his hand a confident shake. He was certain he'd remember if they had. Her face was attractive but ordinary; however, everything else stood out as distinctive, colorful and flowing, from her blunt, shoulder-length hair to the loose slacks and shirt she wore. The style was masculine but in no shades a man would ever consider—purple and strawberry with a brilliant peacock-feather-colored scarf. Almost as tall as he and taller than many of the police she had been standing near, she was the first person he'd noticed as he drove up and, he suspected, she would be the last.

Opening a notebook, she asked, "I'd like your opinion on this case, particularly if you feel it may be related to the D'Amato murder in Cleveland."

"I'm not in a position to give out information on cases, miss," he replied brusquely. "I'm sure you'll read all about this in your local paper in the morning."

"I'm sure I'll *write* all about it. It was stupid of me not to explain. I'm the crime reporter for the *Sandusky Daily News*."

"Oh, a reporter." That explains everything, the sudden stiffness in his voice implied. "Then you will excuse me." Dick stalked over to two uniformed officers holding by- standers away. There ensued a brief misunderstanding as they motioned Dick away as well, and he was showing them his badge when Bill Daltry, a detective with the Sandusky Police, walked out of the lower flat.

"Dick, I was hoping you'd make it before I had to leave."

The relief in Bill's voice had an ominous sound, and the sudden understanding of what must have occurred upstairs did nothing to brighten Dick's disposition."Who in the hell let on to a reporter that I was coming? I distinctly remember ask- ing—"

"Nobody 'let on' anything. She just knew. She always knows." From his tone Dick realized he'd just picked open a raw wound. "And besides that, she was here first."

"So?"

"So we work with her or else."

"Or else what!"

Daltry sighed. "Let me take you upstairs. Things will be a lot clearer then."

Judy Preuss anticipated their destination and came bound- ing over, notebook and pencil in hand. "You don't mind if I go up, too, do you?" she asked cheerfully.

Dick began to protest but Daltry waved one hand and said, "Why not? You've been there already. I'd think once would be enough."

"I want to record Detective Wells's first words for poster- ity," she said, leading the way and—Dick thought it somehow fitting—lighting a cigar she had pulled out of her shirt pocket.

"Want one?" she asked Dick on the landing.

"I don't smoke." He congratulated himself for his reply.

Dick would always remember his initial impressions of the apartment as a series of pictures like individual pages from the animated flip books his kids owned. An overturned easy chair . . . a curiously pale corpse, not smiling this time, not at all . . . a puddle of viscous blood in the kitchen that must be hours old but looked as wet and shiny as if it had just been poured a few minutes earlier . . . a ripped cotton gown . . . a second corpse, as pale as the first but, like Angela D'Amato, seemingly lost in an eternal erotic dream . . . the cradle, untouched except for a few drops of blood on the pillow . . . and the last, the most obscene picture of all: resting on the fluffy blue quilt, a baby bottle filled with blood.

Permeating the scene was the expected metallic smell, but it mingled with a more oppressive, acrid scent, a scent that made Dick want to run from the apartment, from that case, from that job he had always perversely loved. His first words, when he finally spoke them, were unprintable.

A light breeze from the window wafted the smoke from Judy's cigar in his direction, and he understood with respect why she had lit it. She stood with one hand rocking the cradle, as if the baby were still in it, and spoke matter-of-factly. "After Mrs. Poole saw all of this, she called me. When I arrived, everything was exactly as you see it, except for the baby. He was here in the cradle, sucking on that bottle, his mouth smeared red with the blood. I phoned the police, and later someone took him away.

"I also noticed a great many other things, things I am willing to postpone describing to my readers. I am sure you will both appreciate my discretion and give me some information I can use later."

Damn her! She's pinned us and she knows it. "That depends on what you want to know, Miss Preuss," Dick replied in a barely civil tone.

"Many things, Detective Wells. Such as why the blood in the kitchen doesn't dry, why these bodies haven't darkened where they rest against the floor, what these bites on the vic-

tims' necks signify. I'd also like to know how this relates to
the D'Amato murder. Was she bitten too?

"I want a total story out of this, not tiny pieces of information doled out over weeks. I want to be informed or, better
yet, be there as this story develops, and I will only write the
complete facts when the case is closed. If you do not agree to
this, tomorrow's headlines in the *Daily News* will bring every
kook in Northern Ohio right through your doors." She puffed
on her cigar and, holding it between thumb and forefinger,
tapped the ash out the window. "Deal?"

Dick looked at Daltry, who nodded. "Deal," he replied.

Over the next hour, Dick's grudging regard for Judy Preuss
flourished into full-bloomed admiration. The lady had technique. She made no assumptions and she had a knack for
drawing information out of neighbors, not that any of the gos-
sip looked particularly useful in this case. She also had the gift
of knowing what was out of place in that small apartment and
provided the police with their first real clue.

It was a small piece of decorative glass (flashed glass, Judy
informed them) in distinctive shades of ruby and gold. It had
been cut in the shape of a crescent moon and contained an
etching of a flying insect. The parents of both victims declared
that they had never seen it before.

"This is an antique, if I'm not mistaken," Judy explained.

An idea occurred to Dick. Turning to Daltry, he asked,
"Bill, do you mind if I keep this glass for a day or two? I think
I know someone who might be able to give us information on
it."

"After it runs through the lab you can be my guest. I'd only
have to take it to Cleveland for an opinion, anyway, so you
can save me the trip." He took one last look around, then
headed for the door. "We're done here. There'll be copies of
statements for you at headquarters. Stop by in a few hours and
pick them up."

Dick glanced at Judy as he carefully wrapped and pocketed
blood samples for the Cleveland lab. "If you know of a good
spot to have some lunch, I'll tell you about the D'Amato
murder."

# III

Over endless cups of cloudy coffee, he detailed everything, including the unusual blood specimens, the dead deer in the park, and his own premonitions about how this case would end. Judy took few notes (which relieved him) but she listened intently. When he'd finished, she reached into her briefcase and pulled out a book of matches and, Dick was relieved to see, a pack of cigarettes. Judy appeared troubled, as if she knew what to say but was afraid to begin. Finally she asked, "Have you given any thought to the existence of vampires?"

He looked offended, as if she had just muttered an obscenity.

"Consider the evidence. It may not be *the* answer, Dick, but you had best list it as a possible one. Of course, I'm not referring to the sexless undead"—for the first time she appeared uneasy over what she'd seen—"but possibly some mutation or a totally different species coexisting with ours."

"I've thought of it, all right, particularly your second theory. I've also hunted hit men, psychos, homicidal rapists—you name it, any kind of human beast—and seen what they can do. Now I'm forced to believe I'm dealing with an animal I never knew existed. Sure it's a possible answer, just don't expect me to smile and say how much I like it."

"I find the implications fascinating. Think of it, Dick; we may not be the only intelligent life on earth. This is a story to top any I've ever written or read, and I can't wait to finish its final draft. Which reminds me; I do have to get back to work and pound out tomorrow's headlines, edited though they may be."

He reached for the check and she shook her head. "No, Dick, when I'm working, we go Dutch. It's only after five that I turn into a lady."

Dick knew an invitation when he heard one. "Then, Reporter Preuss, may I buy the lady in you dinner tonight?"

120

Her laugh was thoroughly feminine. "I was hoping you'd ask."


# IV


The restaurant was candlelit, quiet, and elegant, and Dick had just sat down when she arrived. Like this afternoon, Judy was noticed but for an entirely different reason . . . she was one beautiful woman.

Gone were the clashing colors and mannish style, to be replaced by a dress of dusty gold that perfectly complemented her slender body and the flaxen highlights in her hair. Gone, too, was the practical pageboy and, in its place, a hairdo that swept back to accent her heart-shaped face and oval brown eyes. And he had thought her ordinary? This is your lucky day, Dick Wells, because she's here to be with you!

As Dick stood to greet her, he was thankful he still felt satisfaction staring at that fine Black Irish face in the mirror each morning. Even so, at thirty-seven, he felt so much older than she. He might even have gotten tongue-tied, but she had a reporter's gift for drawing out facts, and he found himself telling her everything from family particulars to deeply buried feelings he'd forgotten existed. Only as they sipped their second after-dinner drink did he realize he knew nothing about Judy . . . the woman or the reporter.

"Tell me," he said, "where you learned that trick with the cigars."

"Oh, that!" She laughed and detailed the series of odd jobs that had put her through college in Chicago, finally peaking with a two-year stint as a private investigator for one of that area's smaller detective agencies.

"I learned about cigars the first time I had to take notes at an autopsy. A police sergeant noticed I was turning green, stuffed one in my mouth, and, in a gravelly voice, said 'Breathe!' Now I always carry a few of the smelliest ones I can buy. I confess I'm so used to them, I sometimes light one up just to help me think while I'm writing."

"You're a natural at police work. How come you didn't go into it?"

Her eyes grew angry as she shook her head. "Don't sound so naive, Dick. They'd have me doing paperwork at the station, if anything. I'll get to where I want to go; only I'll have to work a little harder, that's all. And, by the way, this story is one of those opportunities I can't afford to pass up."

She brought them to the very subject they had so pointedly not been discussing. "So who's your glass expert?" she asked.

Only after she agreed to secrecy did he reply, "It's my neighbor, Stephen Austra."

"Austra!" She managed to keep her voice soft, but the tone had the same penetrating quality as the screeches of teenagers trailing after Frank Sinatra. Dick had already seen the effect Stephen had on women as young as his daughter to as old as Sylvia, and this was the first time it had done anything but amuse him.

"You know him?" he asked, trying to sound nonchalant.

"No, I don't, but I know quite a bit about him. Dick, he's from one of the richest families in Europe and you're telling me he's your neighbor. What's he doing there?"

Dick explained the work under way at St. John's, and the artist's reasonable demand for privacy.

"I'd heard something about the renovations," Judy replied, "but no one mentioned Stephen Austra himself would be working there. I suppose he's a lot less likely to be noticed in an apartment on the West Side of Cleveland than in a suite at the Sheraton." She broke into a sly smile. "So he's your neighbor?"

"And practically a member of the family. He spends quite a bit of time with my niece."

Judy nodded sagely. "That sounds like the Stephen Austra I heard about. Robbing the cradle, is he?"

"The cradle! Judy, if he's a day over thirty, I'm an old, old man. Maybe we're not talking about the same person at all."

Judy glanced at her watch. "Order us another drink while I go and make a quick phone call. When I get back I'll tell you everything I know about him."

Judy was gone long enough for Dick to begin feeling edgy. When she returned, she took a sip of her drink and began.

"When I was a child, my parents often visited relatives

near Boston during the summer. Their oldest son was studying
to be an architect and their summer home attracted quite a few
of his fellow students from college. Among them was Paul
Stoddard. He was nine years older than I and quite good looking. I had a crush on him and I suppose I was a pest but I was
also a good listener. He taught me a great deal about artistic
glass. The craft fascinated me. Over the years, I learned as
much as I could on my own. That's how I recognized the age
of the crescent you found this afternoon."

"And Stephen? Why are you interested in him?"

"Well, you see, Paul really didn't want to be an architect.
Instead he dreamed of working for Tiffany, of creating windows or working in interior design.

"But Tiffany had recently died and other firms which had
imitated his methods had closed. Paul told me that if he
couldn't work in America, he would go to Portugal and learn
from the Austras, surpass them and return to create a new
American excellence.

"He wrote letters to AustraGlass. He had others write letters. His persistence paid off. In 1938, he left for Portugal. At
first, he sent letters to his friends, lively descriptions of the
country, his work and what he called 'those mercuric Austras'
. . . their looks, their reclusive habits, their powerful drive. I
read every one I could find. He wrote that he was studying
under Stephen Austra, who was only a year or two older than
himself. Eventually, I forgot about him. After the war, he
came home to head the Austra architectural firm in New York
City. Two years later, he began building the La Pas sky-
scraper. The design made him famous. Stephen Austra came
to New York for its opening.

"I had just begun working as a stringer for a Boston paper.
I thought a private interview with the two of them would be
good for my career. I called Paul. He remembered me and
when I asked if I could interview them, he agreed. When I
went to our appointment, Paul was alone. He said Stephen had
been called away on business. Though I tried for a follow-up
meeting, tried until I was almost rude, I never met him.

"Curious, I read every description of the building and its
opening I could get my hands on. There were no photos of
Stephen Austra. No quotes from him. It was as if he'd never
been at the opening at all."

Judy paused for emphasis. "Remember Paul writing that Austra was in his twenties? Dick, that was seventeen years ago."

"Two different people. It has to be."

Judy beamed with triumph as she shook her head. "The phone call I made was to Paul. I told him I had learned Stephen Austra was working at St. John's and said I'd like to do a story on him. Dick, he was as evasive as ever but it was obvious from the way he talked that Stephen is his old teacher, the head of AustraGlass."

Dick shrugged, more interested in watching how Judy's face glowed as she told her story. Judy set down her drink, her hand almost shaking with excitement. "When do I get to meet him?"

# V

Stephen had just showered and was contemplating the now-familiar signs of exhaustion when he heard the phone ring in Richard's flat. He could not hear the voice on the line, but from Helen's reply he knew it was Richard and that he would not be home tonight. That pleased him, as did the fact that tomorrow was Sunday and he had no daytime obligations. In his fatigue, his body had been reminding him more urgently that he was a nocturnal animal. The sun blinded him even through his glasses and the harsh burns on his face would soon be as visible as they were painful. Nonetheless, he smiled grimly as he studied his reflection in the bathroom mirror. O'Maera's comment earlier today had been correct; by the priest's standards, Stephen appeared much healthier. As he slipped on a pair of clean slacks his own phone rang. It was Paul, telling him of Judy's call.

When Stephen's reply to his news seemed unnaturally subdued, Paul became concerned. "Stephen, was everything in hand before I called?"

"One of my blood has killed a young woman and, now I have reason to suspect, someone else. The detective heading the investigation is my next-door neighbor. Somehow, Paul, a newspaper reporter interested in me seems like an inevitable addition." He concluded with a short, sad laugh that did nothing to dispel Paul's gloom. Sensing his friend forming another question, Stephen hastily added, "There's no danger here, nor do I anticipate any. And what of your work?"

"Going well," Paul continued, pleased to be able to relate some good news, then returned to the murders. "Regarding the matters we recently discussed, we are having difficulty in Europe. Jean Massier is off on his usual inaccessible two months with Laurence and Alec. As a result, we won't be able to determine if anyone in America is drawing on Austra accounts for another few weeks. By then you may already know."

"Perhaps, though I have not been considering this problem as much as I should. There have been other matters that are more important. I suppose I am acting as if the answer will be handed to me. I am optimistic, yes?"

"Too optimistic!" A good portion of Paul's exasperation was directed at himself. "You'll be meeting Judy soon, I fear, and that may be dangerous."

"You fear? Is she really so formidable?"

As Paul considered his answer he glanced out the window of his building, and his pale eyes focused on nothing but the past, then this, his finest commission. "I met her before, when she was much younger, and she was a person to be reckoned with even then, my friend." Paul had spoken with complete sincerity and so was dismayed by Stephen's laughter.

"Then I shall try to be as disgustingly ingratiating as possible, and she can blame all attraction on my charm."

"Stephen, I can arrange my schedule and be in Cleveland tomorrow, if you want."

Stephen considered the offer and declined. "Not yet, but be prepared for that possibility soon, and ask Elizabeth to remain accessible as well. When this is over—however it ends—we may need to move very fast. The Austra name and the firms have been good to us and I cannot consider how, in this modern world, we would be able to start over. Also see that all my obligations in America are canceled. When St. John's is finished, I will be going home."

"Home? Isn't that risky?"

"It will only be for a year or two, and it *is* necessary . . . a family matter. Then I think New York would be a lovely place to die."

As he placed the receiver in its cradle, Stephen glanced at his watch. It was too late to buy a newspaper, but perhaps the news on television would cover the story he believed had broken. He went next door and let himself in.

Helen lay asleep on the sofa in her living room. Sitting next to her feet was a pile of weights, the heaviest pair still wrapped around her ankles. As he unfastened these Stephen ran his hand down one lean calf and felt the growing strength. His was not the only exhaustion. Such glorious persistence! He switched on the TV and adjusted the volume to a barely audible level, then leaned back against the sofa and waited.

Yes, there had been two murders in Sandusky, with a possible connection to an earlier crime in Cleveland. This was all he could expect; details could be acquired from Richard later.

Absorbed in his own thoughts, Stephen did not hear the national news until the announcer broke for an on-the-scene taping of a group of schoolchildren watching a nuclear bomb test under way at a nearby Nevada site. In one sickening instant he returned to Hiroshima, to the only commission he had ever refused to allow AustraGlass to complete because he found, after a few days' stay, that his hunger had grown voracious and the life around him would not satisfy. He'd returned to Chavez panicked, refusing to subject others of his blood, or his short-lived friends, to that tortured, deadly land.

He'd been there nearly two years after the bombing, and now here were children playing while death rained softly around them. The reflection of the rising cloud smoldered in his dark eyes, and as he turned to look at his lover sleeping so peacefully behind him, he contemplated that while it was possible for her to live in his world, there was no longer any way for those of his blood to live comfortably in hers.

## Chapter Eleven

### I

ONE OF JUDY'S heels was creating a staccato rhythm against the floor of Dick's car, the same sort of tension a cat reveals when it flicks its tail while stalking a mouse. All of her reporter's instincts were keyed up. Austra! At last she would meet him!

After he'd parked in front of his home, Dick reached over and stopped Judy's leg from moving, letting his hand rest on her knee a moment longer while he looked happily at her. She tried to return the expression. She had taken a risk in being so forward, but the result had been a satisfying night for both of them—and, she hoped, far from their last.

"There's no reason to be so jumpy," Dick said.

"You're right. Let's get it over with."

The sun slanted off the dirty windows of the vacant lower apartment, and paint was peeling on their frames. It seemed such an unlikely place to find the uncrowned monarch of AustraGlass that Judy had an uncertain moment in which she believed Dick was correct and they had been speaking of two different persons.

"Come up," a feminine voice called in response to the bell.

"Helen's here," Dick said as if he'd expected her presence. He opened the lower door, then stood aside to let her pass.

Bathed in the light of the living-room windows, Helen sat cross-legged on the thick carpet, an intricately embroidered skirt flaring out around her, peeling and eating an orange. On the table in front of her was a disturbing but magnificent sculpture, a bottle of wine, and two cut-crystal glasses . . . one half full, the other nearly empty. The opulence of that room, the beauty of the windows, the presence of Helen herself—all made Judy's doubts vanish. Here was all she'd expected!

Stephen, barefoot and wearing stained slacks and a shirt, walked out of the hallway behind them. He glanced at Judy, then greeted Dick, who, as he made polite introductions, watched Judy's reaction with veiled concern.

So this was Austra! She noticed Stephen watching her with tolerant amusement, making it clear her thoughts were obvious. To break what was rapidly becoming an uneasy silence, Judy looked toward the worktables and asked, "How are the windows progressing?"

"Good. I have been painting. I understand from Paul Stoddard that you know something about glass restoration. If so, you may find what I am doing interesting. In any event, I must finish this section."

He switched on an overhead work light, sat in front of one of the smaller of the St. John's windows, and, as he worked, explained the procedure. "After I clean the glass, I look for the pieces that have to be retouched. It is, of course, necessary to know what type of pigments were used in the original staining, and then I must alter the colors to accommodate for age and, when necessary, for the color changes that will occur when the glass is heated. Once this is done, I can begin." He dipped his brush in a brown ocher pigment and began redoing a large section following some indecipherable pattern.

"But how do you know where to paint? There are no visible lines."

Using the handle of the brush, he pointed out the nearly imperceptible shadings. "It is like writing. Once you know the hand, you can duplicate it. But if the style is unfamiliar, or if you don't know the compounds used when the windows were created, restoration work becomes extremely difficult. When there is doubt, it is best to consult the original artists, yes?"

"But isn't that impossible? They must be long dead."

He handed her a thick, yellowed book. Inside were pages filled with patterns and a numbered code. "That's all I need. The books are time-consuming to compile but treasured helpers later." He switched to a different brush, a second color, and continued. "Few craftsmen know how to restore old

pieces of painted glass properly, and if glassmaking continues
with its advances, soon all painting on glass will become ar-
chaic. In a moment, I will show you."

Dick handed Judy a glass of wine and she sipped it as she
watched Stephen continue. When the section had been finished, he set it in the corner to dry, then turned the huge table
sideways so it rested directly beneath the clear north windows.
Unwrapping one of the new rectory windows, one that he
could admit to having designed himself, he exposed it to the
evening light. The glass itself seemed to create its depth and
design, and Judy saw no indication of any highlighting.

"I created the pattern first, then precisely the colors and
intensities of glass that were required. The color ranges give
the depth of the folds of cloth here, and here." He began
pointing to details as he spoke, and concluded, "The most
difficult pieces were, of course, the wings. The amount of
waste in their execution was no more than usual, but the creation of the colors and pattern took many small pourings over
two years before I decided they were correct."

Judy studied the features, soft yet perfectly formed. "Is
there no additional shading done on this piece?"

"None."

Judy stared at the eyes. "You say the wings were the hardest. I think it must have been these." She ran her fingers over
the small circles of glass and, as she did, Stephen looked
down at his hands, remembering those few hours of pain. As
usual, he ignored it; working close to the necessary fire, the
molten glass, captured by the glory of creation. When he had
almost finished, he'd looked up to see Rachel standing in the
doorway, her face red from the light of his burner.

"Your blood will not add to your design," she'd admonished gently, and he'd looked down and saw that soon the
blood would flow. Barely pausing in his work, he slipped on
gloves to protect the piece. Afterward Rachel kissed his hands
and walked beside him up the hill to his home, never saying a
word, knowing this had been no more than an act of will.
Within a day the burns were gone, and those who would view
the windows for the years they would endure would always
wonder how the eyes had been made.

"May I see the rest?" The excitement in Judy's voice betrayed a compliment she had not intended to give.

He nodded and removed the window, then set the remaining two sections in front of the light. Together they covered the north windows, and Judy pictured how magnificent they would look in full daylight.

The design was exultant, not so much Christian as godly. The left window was a dark angel with arresting black eyes. On the right window, now leaning against the wall, was its counterpart, a pale angel in a color reminiscent of the da Forli frescoes Judy had seen while visiting the Vatican. But this angel was more fair, and both had an exotic, androgynous beauty far from human. The features were in soft focus except for those disturbing eyes. The wings, silver on the dark, gold on the light, were made of beautifully flashed pieces which, through Stephen's art, had acquired the gossamer look of feathers in motion.

Surrounding their heads were deep smoky clouds but in the center where the wings swirled together was a brilliant display of color, which gave the sensation of paradise; of God speaking through his creatures; of her, the viewer, suspended between heaven and earth. Paul, always cautious, had told Stephen the design was dangerous. Judy, viewing the finished work, was awed. Eventually she became compelled to acknowledge their creator and, as she looked at Stephen, she saw glowing in those dark eyes his reply to the words of praise she was unwilling to utter, and a passionate pride in his own magnificent skill.

When she had entered, she had been reluctant to approach him. Now she felt a strong compulsion to touch him, to know he was mortal and not one with his creations. His eyes made her dizzy but, in the moment she thought she might fall, his attention was caught by some remark of Helen's and he turned away from her. "Would you bring me some water, please?" she heard Helen ask her uncle.

Judy gulped the remainder of her wine. "I'll get it," she said, relieved at the distraction. "I would like some myself."

Dick fingered the cloth-wrapped crescent in his pocket, pleased Judy had lost her apprehension but impatient to present the piece to Stephen. He'd seen his neighbor at work often enough that it held little interest for him, and after watching them both for a short while, he went to sit on the sofa behind Helen. She looked up at him with an expression so bright, it appeared mischievous. "Would you like some wine?" She motioned at the bottle, then at a small carved chest against the wall. "There are more glasses inside."

Dick thought of giving her a lecture. Legally she was too young to drink, though he could consider her a child no longer. Her fingers, wrapped around the stem of her glass, were long and delicate, the nails well kept. It's the care she had begun to take with herself, Dick decided; her health is making her beautiful. Walking over to the case, he pulled out two heavy goblets, studied them, and saw the Austra label— the combined alpha and omega—stamped on the bottom. Their weight brought back memories of his mother, of her Waterford crystal, which as a child, he had never been allowed to touch. He felt suddenly clumsy and held each glass with exaggerated care as he poured the sparkling Loire wine. He gave one to Judy, then sat on the floor beside Helen, his eyes moving alternately from her to the crystal sculpture. Both seemed to demand something of him. Though the beast aroused emotions strangely primitive, it seemed the safer place for his gaze to rest.

"We were celebrating," Helen said cheerfully, and detailed what she had been able to accomplish at the clinic that afternoon.

"The most miraculous thing to me has been how hard you've worked," Dick replied candidly. "I was beginning to doubt you'd ever decide to get up and walk, and now..." He put his hand behind her neck, meaning to give her a congratulatory kiss on the forehead, and felt a stab of lust so unexpected that he had to fight to keep from shaking. Looking past Helen to Judy, Dick took reassurance from her presence, then kissed Helen mechanically on the top of her head and moved, as casually as he could, away from her.

As Helen looked at him, bewildered by the sudden change in his attitude, Dick doubted he'd ever seen her eyes so smoky, so dark, so alluring. Had he not known her since she was a child, come to look upon her as a daughter, he would have run his fingers through her long, beautiful hair. A wave of sad understanding passed between them and, after an uncertain pause, Helen held out her glass. "Uncle, I don't care for any more wine. Would you bring me some water, please; the cold from the refrigerator?"

As she spoke, Stephen turned toward Helen and flashed her a reassuring look, a quick nod.

As Dick scrambled to his feet, Judy drained her wine and walked over to him. "I'll get it," she said. "I would like some myself."

Helen grinned. "Then may I suggest Cleveland tap? Tarda water is an acquired taste."

After sampling it, Judy admitted Helen was right. Tarda seemed bitter, too salty, with a metallic undertone much stronger than that of well water. She studied the label, but it gave no indication of the country of origin, reading only "Tarda—Taszgánza." Curious as to what language accented a *g* in that fashion, she pulled a pad and pen from her pocket and noted the name. As she opened the refrigerator to return the bottle, she studied the disappointing contents . . . some cheese, a bag of fruit, a few bottles of POC and Coca Cola, and three gallons of Tarda. Only the last seemed unique enough to belong. The rest of it looked like "entertaining food," food one had on hand in case guests dropped by unexpectedly. On the counter, she saw a jar of peanut butter, a loaf of bread, and some crackers probably intended to go with the cheese.

The compulsion was too great. Without thinking what she would say if she were discovered, she quietly opened each of the cupboards. With the exception of pots and pans and dishes, all of which appeared to have come with the apartment, they were empty.

"What are you doing?" a young voice asked. Judy whirled, nearly dropping the glass in her hand, and faced a pair of wide brown eyes that stared at her suspiciously. "What *are* you doing?" Alan repeated, his voice louder for emphasis.

Judy covered her lips with an index finger and Alan shrugged. Grown-ups hardly ever responded to questions they would demand a child to answer. "I'm hungry. Would you make me a peanut butter sandwich?" He sat at the kitchen table and pointed to a drawer. "The knives are in there." The look on his face implied Judy must have already known.

"Do you eat here often?" Judy asked as she filled his order.

"Sure. Helen's over a lot, and then we have lunch here. Can I have a Coke too?"

Judy opened the refrigerator and asked, "Who drinks the POC?"

"My dad. Sometimes Father O'Maera."

"Really?"

"Only sometimes. Mostly he drinks coffee."

Judy smiled and handed him the Coke bottle. "And what does Stephen drink?" She wanted to giggle. This reminded her of those word games . . . the Englishman lived in the red house, the Irishman drinks tea.

Alan wrinkled his nose. "That stuff in the big jugs. Peugie!"

"Nothing else?"

"Nope." He took a big bite of the sandwich.

"You're Alan, right?" The boy, his mouth cemented with peanut butter, nodded. "Well, I'm Judy. I'm a friend of your father's and I'm pleased to meet you."

Alan gave her what might have been a smile, then headed for the back door.

"Your father's here. Don't you want to see him?"

"Are Carol and Billy with him?"

"No."

"Then I better not. I'm not supposed to be here. My dad wants us to spend the night at Billy's house, but he and Carol went someplace without me." His voice sounded sad. "Don't tell Pa I walked over, okay?"

He looked up at her with solemn, long-lashed eyes of a deep rich brown. His father's eyes, Judy thought as she rested her hands on his shoulders and whispered in a conspiratorial tone, "I promise not to tell on you if you won't on me. Deal?"

He beamed. "Sure! And . . . thanks."

Judy listened to his light footsteps on the back stairs. Feeling much better, she picked up the glasses and was about to join the others when Stephen entered carrying his own glass. "A beautiful vintage, but I've had enough," he said as he poured the wine down the drain, then reached in the refrigerator for the Tarda. Alan, Judy, decided, did not notice everything.

\* \* \*

After handing Helen her water, Judy turned back to the new windows. Calmer, more detached, she viewed them critically and, though she was not religious, she saw something in the design that disturbed her. "Looking at these, I feel as if God is not their creator, but rather that they are somehow creating God."

She had spoken quietly to Stephen, and he responded in an even softer tone only she would hear. "Mankind has always created its own gods to mirror what it chooses to believe."

"Then I suppose we are fortunate that today we worship Jesus Christ rather than Baal or Shiva." Judy had meant this to be flippant, though the thought was sincere. "And what deities do these represent?"

Stephen hesitated, then answered honestly. "The supreme deities; the two sides of intelligence . . . the dark and the light."

"Neither looks evil," she commented.

"Neither is. And where they touch one another, there is the glory of the dawn."

"Have you given it a title?"

"No. If I did, I would have to place them elsewhere. Yet St. John's is where they belong." The last rays of the sun were dying as he wrapped the windows and put them away.

Dick turned from the open porch door in which he'd been standing and pulled the glass crescent from his pocket. He'd become anxious to leave this place and find some quiet spot where he could be alone with Judy. He felt compelled to hold someone tonight and he wanted that person to be her.

Dick's voice always grew officious when he worked, and in that rigid tone, he began, "I have something to show you, Stephen. It concerns murders that took place two nights ago in Sandusky. We believe these were committed by the same person who killed Angela D'Amato eight weeks ago."

Hearing this, Helen looked up at her uncle, her eyes too wide, too shocked. Stephen, on the other hand, listened calmly.

"We found one odd piece of evidence there, and I think you may be the one to tell me something about it." He unwrapped the red-and-gold crescent and handed it to Stephen. "We think the killer may have left it at the scene of the murder. Judy told me it is very old."

Stephen scarcely heard a word Dick said, so preoccupied was he with hiding the emotions, the vivid memories this glass brought back to him. The coincidences were multiplying, approaching some unponderable sum. He managed to keep his voice steady as he replied, "Yes, this is . . . very old."

He turned around, switching on the overhead spot and resting the piece on the table, making a pretense of studying it as he looked again with oppressive sadness at the beautifully detailed design. "A new talent in the family," Charles had said, laughing with paternal pride as he handed Stephen this etching. "If I allowed her, she would spend all her hours in the glass house beside me. I see our youth when I look at her . . . and her mother's face. . . ."

Experts were everywhere, Stephen knew, and there seemed no reason to lie. He turned and handed the piece back to Dick. "I know this glass. Judy is correct concerning its age. It was made approximately two hundred years ago at one of our own glass houses near Moulins in France. It has grown brittle. Someone has taken great care to preserve it. Whoever left it would not have done so by accident. I believe you were meant to find it." And a conclusion, bitter and unavoidable, that fate would bring it to him.

"Was there much of this glass made?" Judy asked.

"Enough that I would recognize it. It is scattered throughout the world, primarily in church windows."

"It doesn't look like a religious symbol," Dick said as he placed it in Helen's outstretched hand.

"It's a mayfly," Helen said. "It's beautiful."

"The person who etched it possessed a great deal of skill," Stephen commented. Noting Dick's puzzled glance, he added, "That is evident even now in this piece."

"Would there be any way to trace the owner?" Dick asked.

Stephen shook his head. "You might try, but I don't believe so. Perhaps it is more important to consider why the killer left it for you. Did he leave something in the first murder as well, something you might have overlooked?"

Dick hesitated before answering. "It's a start. I'll consider it." Helen returned the piece to her uncle, who rewrapped it. "Thank you for your help."

"I wish I could give you more," and he knew, sadly, the duty he must perform. "Miss Preuss, I understand from Paul that you would like to write an article concerning St. John's, yes?"

She was astounded he'd mention it. "Yes, but I didn't think—"

"Well, I have changed my mind. The work I need to do on the outside is nearly finished, and it should be a simple procedure to keep unwelcome visitors out of the church. If you will allow me four more days before you print your story, I will be pleased to give you an interview."

"They will want to run it in the Cleveland papers as well."

He'd assumed as much, but it would not be wise to appear too eager, so he paused and considered her warning. "Thank you for telling me this, but as I said, I believe I will be able to finish in private."

"Thank you!" Now that the opportunity was given, she became anxious to start. "I have my briefcase in the car," she said, hinting.

The offer was tempting. With her gone, even for a few moments, he could learn from Richard a part of what he wished to know. But it would be best to take some time to collect his thoughts and quiet his rushing emotions. "Good. We'll meet tomorrow. Shall we set an appointment for St. John's at two?"

"Certainly." Judy turned to Dick. "Well, it looks like I'm in town a while longer. Can you suggest someplace we could go?"

He could—but not in front of his niece and his neighbor. "Let's go have a drink to celebrate my slim lead and your next story."

## II

As the door closed behind them, Stephen leaned against his worktable, his shoulders rolled forward, his head bowed. There were countless questions Helen wished to ask, but she remained silent, watching him, certain he was expending an enormous effort to dissipate the sorrow that small beautiful piece of glass had aroused.

When at last he looked at her, the anguish had vanished, replaced by feral restlessness. He slammed both hands back against the edge of the table, and the massive wooden structure crashed into the wall.

"It is frustrating for me to have to fight for time." He had meant this to be humorous, but the laugh that accompanied it was heavy and sad. "I wish to hunt, but your river valley is no longer safe for me. I need to rest and I want more than anything to stay with you."

"I can wait for you."

"I know, but I want you with me tonight. I see your concern for me masking your own troubling thoughts. Helen, you need release as well as I." An idea came to him. They had become so closely bonded, he could take her anyplace he wished and the freedom would be enough for both of them.

He had done this before, when he was truly caged... Murano, Rome, Lyons. Once, in the ruins of an ancient dungeon, when the inner darkness had threatened permanence, he had taken Paul with him. The visions of freedom had cleansed them, and they had survived.

He picked up the pear-shaped sculpture in the corner. Sitting beside Helen, he unscrewed its top, revealing twenty tuning keys. Reaching below them, he unfastened two concealed locks, and the sculpture fell into two parts, each similar to a wide mandolin. These he turned to face in opposite directions, then locked the halves together to create a twenty-stringed double-necked instrument. Helen ran her fingers over the strings, wondering how it would be played. "If both your hands are on the necks, how do you strum?"

"With the same hands. It is meant to be played extremely fast, and so gives the player the illusion of running. You can also use each half individually for slower songs, but those could become maudlin tonight, so we will hear the fast, yes?"

He sat in the center of the mahogany table and crossed his legs in a lotus position. Placing the instrument on his knees, he stretched out his arms in a movement controlled and ritualistic, designed to tense rather than relax. His fingers glided once across the strings, recalling their natures; and he began.

The music had no perceivable melody. Had it been slower, it would have sounded discordant, but at the intoxicating speed at which the instrument was played, the notes coalesced into a haunting contrapuntal harmony. At first she tried to watch the playing, but soon it became impossible to see Stephen's hands move. Dizzy from the attempt, she looked at his face and saw that his features had sharpened rather than dulled in the room's dimming light. He looked taut, primitive, and as he reassured her with a sensitive's touch, he began to sing.

Helen had expected Stephen could sing well, but not like this, not with a range so extensive that there were times she seemed to lose the notes, both low and high. The language was alien, simultaneously guttural and lilting, each word curiously inflected. His skill fascinated her, and as she watched in admiration, he glanced up and she understood. Closing her eyes, she lay back and let his voice, his mind, his music take her—strong and unfettered—where he would.

. . . She runs so lightly, she barely feels the ground; sees the grasses pass her so quickly, they blur into shadows. The plains around her stretch for eternity, empty and beautiful, and though this is the blackest of nights, the landscape is clear as day.

Caught in the lust of the hunt, the kill, she is a sentient part of an intelligent pack, gliding, pursuing unseen prey—not by sight but through the vibrations of the earth—with the glory of the chase more important than the identity of the creatures she follows. This is more than a vision, more than a dream; an infinitely detailed reality beyond human, beyond imagining . . . culled as much from her racial memories as from his secret life. As she flows with him, the same wild and primitive desire that fills her during their nights together rises to revel in this remorseless chase.

Within the room only her body inhabited, Stephen's feet began to hit the bottom of the sounding boards at a pace fast and savage. Her heart beats in time with it, her breathing quickens, and, in a resplendent burst of speed, she outdistances her kin. The pursued becomes a shadow before her, powerful and swift, and through strange, keen eyes she sees the magnificent flanks of the smoke-colored stallion heaving in a thunderous, hopeless gallop. Nothing could touch it but the predator she is, and with sinuous grace, she closes the distance.

Leaping onto its back, she grips the mane with one hand and raises her free arm to the star-dazzled sky. The wind

whips her hair as she merges with the beast, sharing its frenzy,
its desperate, impossible escape. As it tires, she reaches forward, forcing fingers between foam-laced teeth, and wrapping
an arm around its straining neck, she brings it down where
together they began the slow, beautiful agony of death. The
beat of distant music grows slow, slower, slower as the thick
blood fills her, warms her. Then, standing triumphant beside
her cherished prey, she hears rising in the velvet dark the
cacophony of unearthly howls, the sounds of her kind.
Throwing back her head, she answers them. . . .

The terrain misted, then vanished. She lay with eyes
closed, hoping through some miracle that she was still on that
starry plain. When she accepted the end, the first thing she
perceived in the room's darkness were Stephen's eyes . . .
nocturnal, beautiful, and almost satisfied. For him this had
been the wrong song, but a more appropriate one would have
terrified her. Soon he would take that risk.

"Was it real?" She prayed it had been, that someday . . .

He nodded. "An old memory. There is more to my life than
time." He placed the instrument aside and held her.

# III

As Stephen was beginning his vision-song, Dick and Judy
settled at a table in a quiet cocktail lounge. Dick sipped his
drink while Judy tried to describe how she'd felt when she met
Stephen. "He's not my type," she began. "He's too good-
looking, too . . ." Her voice trailed off as she sought words to
explain why she found him so captivating, yet so frightening
that she longed to ask Dick to accompany her to tomorrow's
interview or move it to a public, crowded place.

Misinterpreting her pause, Dick chuckled. "Young. You
were going to say young."

"Okay, young. That is, he looks young, but his manner is
not young, his skill is incredible and he obviously knows Paul
Stoddard. If he was the man I once tried to interview, he's
well over forty."

Dick shrugged. Stephen was an Austra. Of course he knew Stoddard. And he could also be the namesake of the Stephen Austra Judy had once almost met. He repeated his earlier question. "So what did you think of him?"

Judy considered lying and dismissed the idea. "When I first looked at him, I felt my knees go weak and my stomach flutter like a love-struck schoolgirl's. And then . . . well, none of it was pleasant."

Dick laughed to hide his possessiveness. "And I suppose you'll tell me next that he made advances to you when my back was turned?"

"No . . . not at all. He was very polite." Judy's tone was thoughtful as she contemplated how she would have responded if he had. "Dick, forgive me if I'm prying, but is he having an affair with Helen?"

Yesterday, Dick would have laughed at the question, but after his brief exchange with Helen, he was no longer certain. The reasonable part of him might have said, "So what, Stephen is damned good for her"; the parental side would, at the very least, demanded he give her a halfhearted lecture. Yet the man, that most primal part of him, overrode the rest and answered what it hoped was correct. "I thought he eventually would and decided I wouldn't object if he did, so long as they were discreet. But with the exception of helping her with her work, he's been very proper . . . like you said, polite." He shook his head stubbornly. "They're just good friends."

Judy persevered. "If so, what's his intense concern with Helen's health?"

"He told me it is the same sort of interest he has in the windows of St. John's: an obsession to see that beauty endures." This also disturbed Dick, so he added, "She is, as I told you, very talented."

"I'd like to see some of her work."

"You did. She painted the watercolors hanging on Stephen's living-room wall." At Judy's blank look, he added, "I suppose you were too busy noticing the . . . ah, windows to see them." The laughter that followed smothered a great many unpleasant emotions.

"I'll see something else of hers if you don't mind. I would prefer not to enter that room again."

She'd given the answer he'd wanted to hear. "Would you

like another drink?" he asked, willing her to say no. She
shook her head and smiled, encouraging his next suggestion.

As Dick unlocked his front door, Judy heard the faint
music drifting out of Stephen's flat. "What is it?" she asked.

"Some more classical stuff. He has a lot of strange
records." Dick opened the door for Judy, but she remained
where she stood.

"What sort of instruments are playing, do you suppose?"
she asked.

He humored her and listened. "Guitars and those wider-
stringed things . . . ah . . ."

"Mandolins."

"I guess. Sounds like three or four people playing." He
shrugged, and they went inside.

Sleep came hard to Dick, and he rolled over and looked
down at Judy, the one good thing to come from these strange
and bloody crimes. Still, he wished they had met under different, better circumstances, for as he pictured her standing outside that Sandusky duplex, he immediately recalled the
victims . . . their smiles, their strange ends. The killer had no
name, no face, no form, yet their minds had fused. They
circled one another, spiraling ever closer, and Dick feared the
fate of anyone caught with them in the center when they
clashed.

Outside of Judy's apartment, this premonition had grown
so strong he'd wanted to say goodnight, turn and leave and
file her away in a mental compartment labeled 'later.' She had
made this impossible and, no matter which direction their re-
lationship took, he would be forever grateful to her for revealing his loneliness. For the first time in six years someone lay
beside him and his world seemed whole and right. Laying a
hand on the rise of her hip, he closed his eyes.

Later, snuggled front to back like a pair of unmatched
spoons, each struggled to escape the same hideous dream as
yesterday's memories were recalled and drained. Forcing herself awake, Judy detected a shadow barely visible in the darkness. But as she reached out to it, it vanished.

Next door, Helen was awakened by the slow sorrowful
sound of Stephen's playing. She could not sense his vision,

for his mind was closed, but names of family came to her . . . Claudia, Ann Marie, Simon, and a last, oppressive with dread . . . Charles.

She tried to sleep but it eluded her, so she waited in darkness until the music, played at the pace of a funeral dirge, was over. When Stephen entered the room, he saw first her eyes, sad and frightened, and knew this was how his must appear to her.

He moved slowly to her, the long brown robe brushing the floor, making him look like some sad St. Francis. As if that part of him could protect her from the approaching confrontation, he took from her and gave to her again, again, until, exhausted, her heart struggling with the thick alien fluid, she slept.

# Chapter Twelve

## I

"DAMN! DAMN! DAMN!" Judy pounded the top of her typewriter in frustration, trying to determine how to best fill the immense holes in her story on Stephen Austra. As if trying to flee her wrath, the ashtray bounced off the side of her desk and she ended up on her hands and knees searching for the hot ash from her cigar. After beating it out, she ripped her sixth lead paragraph out of the machine, threw it in the wastebasket, and, inserting a clean sheet, began with the inevitable slant this story must take. "There are forty-nine gems in the Church of St. John's, each a man-made glimpse of paradise. . . . One hundred ten years ago, the St. John's Parish commissioned two young European artists . . ." As she typed, she found the new words flowed easily. When the article was complete, she read it over, made two minor changes, and decided it was ready to submit.

Judy had wanted to compose the story with the focus primarily on Stephen Austra, but from the beginning he had made that impossible.

When Dick dropped her off at St. John's that morning, she'd reached for the door handle, her mouth set in a grim, hard line. Noting her expression, Dick chuckled. "I'm sure you've interviewed more horrible subjects. I'm going downtown for an hour or so. Should I stop here and claim your remains afterward?"

Judy laughed and nodded, the humor fading as she watched

143

Dick's car disappear around the corner. Squaring her shoulders, she walked up the wide stone steps of the Gothic masterpiece towering above her, her back as stiff as a plaster saint's, her stomach as queasy as the morning of her first professional interview.

Inside, she was greeted not by Stephen but by an enthusiastic Father O'Maera, clutching an old box from which gray patches of dust drifted down to dot his dark cassock. He explained Stephen would be late but had called and requested he show Judy the almost restored windows and tell her something about their initial creation. O'Maera had dug into the church storeroom and found these old records of the original commission in 1844, to Matthew and Edward Austra.

As they walked through the quiet church, he commented, "For the donors who made the building of St. John's possible, there could be no other choice than AustraGlass. The finest religious artists in the world then, and still the best!" As if they would serve as proof he was not biased, O'Maera added, "Did Stephen show you the new rectory windows?" Judy nodded. She'd already begun that portion of her article, with justifiable pride as the overriding theme.

Over the next hour, O'Maera went through the files with her, then detailed the symbolism of every window at St. John's, ending, rather than beginning, with the thirty-five-foot rose. "I saved this for the last so we could spend more time discussing it. It is undoubtedly the finest example of medieval art in the United States."

"Medieval?"

"The colors and patterns, even the composition of the glass, are similar to the North rose of Notre Dame, though, of course, the event portrayed is different. That is the Virgin and Child; this the Resurrection. I visited Notre Dame some years ago. I like our rose better, though I suppose I'm biased." While he laughed, Judy took the opportunity to steal a glance at her watch, a gesture not missed by O'Maera. "I wonder what's keeping the lad?" he commented.

"Lad?" Judy asked, deciding more time with the pastor might be valuable, after all.

"Stephen. He's usually so punctual."

"Has it been unpleasant to have this work done on the church?"

His answer matched what she'd already surmised. "It has been a pleasure, Miss Preuss. Stephen is so considerate when he works, you hardly know he's there. When he is not working, we've had many fine hours together."

Judy sensed correctly that she had stumbled onto another of O'Maera's favored topics. She let him ramble on, only interjecting a question when he seemed about to leave the path she wished him to follow, and so she learned a great deal about Stephen's reclusive temperament and some of the topics they discussed in their afternoons together. "He is a savant on the history of Europe, the Church and its cathedrals. One afternoon he related for me parts of a diary kept by a man who had attended the coronation of Napoleon. He spoke so vividly, I could almost see the Emperor raise the crown above his own head." He continued with a brief mention of Stephen's work hours and concluded, "So we have an ideal arrangement. He said he prefers to work in the evenings, and then he goes at it like a demon. So many times I have had to lecture him . . ." O'Maera turned when he heard the click of hard leather heels on the marble floor.

"Demons in your church, Patrick. They wouldn't dare!"

"One lurks here and, sad to say, he is afflicted with monomania. Laddie, where have you been?"

"Wisely letting you discuss these windows. I'm sure you've done an admirable job."

"He has," Judy said sincerely. O'Maera's enthusiasm had been contagious.

"Helen is in the rectory, Patrick. We're driving out to the country after I'm finished here. An afternoon of work away from work, I suppose you'd call it."

O'Maera winked at Judy, "Monomania," he repeated, then said to Stephen, "Very well, I'll entertain the lass while you continue with *your* interview. Miss Preuss, would you like some coffee when you are done here?"

"Yes, thank you. I told Dick I would wait for him, if you don't mind."

"Of course not. I'll see you both in a bit."

After O'Maera left, Judy fell completely silent and it was Stephen who spoke first. "So Patrick has told you about *his* beloved windows. Is there anything I need add?"

Judy smiled with him. "No, but I would like to know

something about you." Even though she was working, her question seemed an intrusion, and his reply intensified that feeling.

"I agreed to grant a story on St. John's, not on myself. It is, after all, the art that is important." While conversational, his tone had hardened.

Remembering the pride she'd seen him reveal last night, Judy knew the humility to be pretense. "You value your privacy a great deal."

"More than you will ever understand."

"This is not where I would expect to find you," she persisted, hoping these oblique questions would be more rewarding than direct ones, but his look told her he was unwilling to continue. She closed her notebook and laid it and her pen on the pew. "This will be off the record, but please reply. Have some pity for how thoroughly confused I have become."

He decided that if he did not tell her some of what she wished to know, she would only search until she found it elsewhere, and perhaps more besides. "Very well. Off the record, I will answer the questions you ask." He spoke as if they would be irrelevant.

"Are you the chairman of AustraGlass?"

"We are more a family than a firm. As such, we have no chairman, nor any board, but at the moment I am the director."

"And you know Paul Stoddard?"

"Of course. He spent eight years with the firm in Portugal. Once I met him I could not help but be his friend."

"Why are you here?"

His brief hesitation seemed longer than it was. "I have a need to sustain and create beauty, and there is little beautiful or creative about corporate administration. I suppose you could call this a working vacation, and my staying in an apartment in West Cleveland a way of maintaining anonymity, of seeing the real America."

"And you have enjoyed that?" Her question seemed too incredulous, implying that he should not. An American trait he'd often noted . . . disparaging and humble, as if Old World antiquity, merely by endurance, should somehow be more interesting.

"I have enjoyed it immensely. I will be sorry to leave."

"So what may I say about you?"

"My name and the fact that I am a representative of Austra Glass. The house's work did not require an individual's signature for these." He motioned at the windows around them. "Though I suppose the rectory windows will be a different matter, yes?"

"Of course, but you are not so anonymous in America even now. You have other pieces here, do you not?"

"The Merrith House in New York, commissioned in 1945. St. George's outside of Boston, completed in 1949. The three modern pieces in the Baltimore Museum, which were purchased from our private collection twelve years ago. None of those were crafted here; however, all were shipped from Portugal. So you see, this American vacation is long overdue."

"And there were no difficulties with your leaving?"

"Few. The firm is so old, it often seems to run itself. The directorship is no honor, Miss Preuss. We are, indeed, required to spend some years in the position if we have the aptitude. I have a thoroughly competent assistant, quite capable of handling all my affairs for the time I am gone."

"Three months is not so long, I suppose."

"No, it is not, but I had accepted more commissions following this one. Now those shall have to be postponed."

"You are going home, then?"

"I must." He succeeded in sounding unhappy, as if his position were a necessary but unpleasant duty.

Judy asked, "Have you been director long?"

"Since I reached legal age in 1934." His features appeared even younger in the subdued light, and Judy shook her head in disbelief. He responded with a beguiling boyish smile. "No, I would not like you to print that, either. You see, it would probably interfere with my being so affectionately titled 'Laddie.'"

In the next moment they had moved back to a discussion of the windows . . . how much work was needed, how it had progressed, a more detailed account of restoration techniques. "We take the maintenance of our creations so seriously, we promise our major clients that we will assist them in repairs to their windows for as long as our firm shall exist. This is a persuasive selling tool when you consider that our first legal charter dates back to the fifteenth century, though the Austra family has been a glass house far longer than that.

"We keep books such as I showed you last night on every commission and, when the time for restoration arrives, we know precisely what must be done, so it is only natural that our original clients come back to us, yes?" He wondered what her reaction would be if he told her the original artists usually did their own restoration and, if they no longer lived, how difficult it was for another of the family to touch their creations. He suspected she would believe him with barely a question. Paul was correct; she was as formidably open-minded as that.

"We charge a surprisingly reasonable fee for this work, Miss Preuss, though for the rectory windows the donors have paid dearly. They are worth it, yes?"

She agreed, again wondering at his pride. "Yes . . . yes, they are." He waited for her to continue, yet her questions seemed complete except for one. "May I send a photographer here to take pictures?"

"Of the windows, of course. Of me, definitely not."

They walked the length of the nave toward the altar, the loud echoes of their footsteps reminding her they were alone. As they neared the sacristy door, he motioned her to stop and requested she turn around. When she did, he hit the switch and turned off the light.

She sucked in her breath, hissing in surprise and fear as the unexpected darkness surrounded her, then, as her eyes grew accustomed to the dim light, she saw the deep, lustrous colorations from the windows pierce the darkness, as hope banishes despair from a troubled soul. "This is how you felt last night, yes?" he asked so softly, he might not have been speaking at all.

"Yes. Fixed between heaven and earth." She stared at the magnificence surrounding her, her eyes finally captured by the huge delicate rose.

"In the space between being and becoming . . . innocence and wisdom . . . knowledge and grace." He paused as she stared in awe and, at the proper moment, continued. "All art should inspire, but only this is innately inspirational because it is never viewed dispassionately as art for art's sake but rather as art serving a purpose higher than itself."

"Is this why you choose to create such beauty?" she asked, her eyes never moving from the resurrection scene.

"To serve God? No. To create in man a mystical sensuality, yes. Look at these as they are now, bathing the darkness with their ordered glory. Have you seen pictures of the small stone structure this masterpiece replaced?" Judy nodded slowly. O'Maera's file contained a sketch. "I am told the weather on the day of the dedication was similar to today's ... overcast rather than sunny, so the windows shed the same intense tones you see here. No lights were used, save those from the windows and the candles. As the incense rose during the procession you would have seen the individual streaks of color like sunbeams streaming through clouds at day's end.

"Reflect on the splendor, the glory, the pageantry, and the ceremony whose roots extend over a millennium ..."

As she listened, a tenuous vision filled the empty space ... the congregation kneeling in devotion, the choir chanting the responses in ancient harmony, the incense, the sounds of the church organ, and above all, the fervor of the congregation. She scarcely perceived his soft, slow voice, and noticing her rapture, he touched her with the briefest of intrusions and was amazed at her creative power.

"... each individual kneeling here would respond to this beauty with a variation on the same reverent ecstasy, creating an emotional harmony to fill this dark and beautiful place. 'Truly,' all would say afterward, 'this is a house of God.'"

As her vision faded, she detected the hint of mockery in his words and remembered their conversation the evening before. Was he an unbeliever in the service of religion ... or the service of something else? The question rushed rapidly through her mind as he continued.

"Even alone your feelings here are more real, infinitely more intense than any intellectual stroll through an art gallery could ever become, no matter which old masters you viewed. But to assign a creator to this work—to say Stephen Austra did this, Edward Austra that—to become critical and comparative is to detract from the impact of these works. So build your story around the feelings, not the creators, and you will do me and your readers a generous service."

She had wanted to apologize to him then; instead, inexplicably, she had thanked him. Now, looking down at her completed story, she understood. Though these were not the words she had wanted, the totality had become more than she had ever thought it could be . . . and in part it was his gift.

She had misjudged him. There were moments today when she almost liked him. Still . . .

Lost in thought, she absently relit her cigar and watched the thick smoke rise to the ceiling. During the long ride home, not one word to Dick, not one smug smile, not one mature variant of 'I told you so!' And now so many questions she had not asked, so many more she never would have dared to ask. A mystery, but not nearly as mysterious as her own strange inertia.

Resisting some subtle compulsion, she pulled the address book from her desk drawer and looked up the most recent listing for James Prescott, an old colleague and free-lance correspondent in Madrid. The bill for her cable would be outrageous, but she did not anticipate that the cost, or Prescott's expenses, would come out of her pocket. She rarely acted on impulse, and her editor could persuade the paper to pick up Prescott's fees. But even if she had to bankrupt her own small savings account, she would do it—and gladly—to obtain more information on Stephen Austra.

# II

Sifting rapidly through the Monday stack of mail, Dick was rewarded with a heavy manila envelope airmailed from Stuttgart, Germany. Someone had taken him seriously after all, and was intelligent enough to know he might require the information quickly. Inside were copies of medical reports and a three-page letter written in English by the Stuttgart Chief of Police. Dick called Corey's office, but at this early hour no one was in. Glancing only briefly at the medical reports, which were in German and thus doubly indecipherable, he picked up the letter and began to read.

*To my colleague, Richard Wells:*

Copies of your letter to the German Ministry of Police were forwarded to all the major cities in the Republic. I have been Chief of Police here since 1947. I also held the Assistant Chief position before the war until I was "drafted," as I believe you call it, into the German army.

I know of no cases recorded since the war that resemble yours. However, in my second year as assistant, we were confounded by a number of murders that were similar, although the victims were all males.

On August 4, 1933, the body of a young Schutzstaffel corpsman was discovered behind a tavern. He was fully clothed and possessed all his belongings, and there was no sign of a struggle other than that his shirt had been torn open. He died from loss of blood and, as there were in your murder, we found two deep puncture wounds in his neck which had pierced an artery. Upon his chest was carved a swastika and above it the intials SA. The carving had been done before the corpsman's death.

Despite the odd way the corpsman died, we assumed this to be the work of anti-Nazi terrorists, perhaps a large group that had held the corpsman quiet and helpless while one of their members marked the victim. Two nights later a second corpsman was found dead in precisely the same manner. A week later two more were murdered—one on the twelfth, the next on the fourteenth of August—again in the same manner.

We had by now determined there was no group of strangers in town and ruled out local Nazi resistance. Instead we became suspicious of the Schutzstaffel itself. All these young men had been first in the Sturmabteilung (a plausible explanation for the swastika and initials), and we were convinced the bloody rivalry of these two groups had led to the murders. Apparently some of the previous SA members began to assume this as well, for they banded together, forming a group of nine and were never seen alone in public. At night they shared a farmhouse on the outskirts of the city; assuming, no doubt, that no large group could approach them without being seen.

However, on the evening of September 2, the same band

*of assassins apparently walked through their door (we found no sign of forced entry) and killed them all. Except for one, these were more normal killings. In the house, furniture was overturned and broken, plaster in the walls had been smashed by bullets and the force of objects thrown against it. All the lights in the downstairs rooms had been shattered, so part or all of the fight had been in darkness. The carnage was everywhere, and the struggle between these two groups must have been incredible.*

*We found two bodies on the stairs leading down to the central foyer. Both had broken necks. In the main room were six more: one with a broken neck, three with their throats cut open as if by some powerful beast (is this what occurred with your victim? Your letter was not specific on this point), one had his ribs crushed and the pieces of bone had pierced his heart and lungs, and one had been disemboweled. All had the same carving on their chest, though in these the slashing was done after death. Two of the corpsmen had also been shot, apparently by their fellow victims during the struggle, but the wounds were not a factor in their deaths.*

*The ninth corpsman, the one who had been leader of the SA band, was propped against the wall just inside the front door. His spine had been snapped, but low so that had he lived, he undoubtedly would have been paralyzed from the waist down. Whoever killed him first unbuttoned his shirt, leaving a trail of blood down the front of it, then made the carving before killing him by draining his blood. From the young man's horrified expression, it would appear he had been conscious throughout part of the slow process that led to his death, though his agony must have been unbearable. Indeed, he may have been one of the first attacked because we found traces of paint from the floor of the porch beneath his nails and long scratches on the paint just outside the front door, as if he had tried to escape and had been dragged back into the farmhouse . . . not once but three times!*

*After these killings, the persons responsible apparently went upstairs and bathed, for there was a puddle of bloody water on the bathroom floor and stains in both the sink and bathtub. I found such blatant confidence thoroughly unbelievable.*

*These murders, particularly the last, were among the most ruthless crimes I ever encountered in my years as a police officer. There were no witnesses and few clues, and we never solved them.*

*As I read this old file concerning these murders, I notice how undetailed our investigation appears. Please understand that in the time after Hitler rose to power, the Schutzstaffel and Sturmabteilung operated above the reach of the law. At first great pressures were placed on us to solve this case, but as we conducted our investigation it became clear that the Schutzstaffel was withholding much useful information. They, and the SA as well, had engaged in many murderous acts, and the relations and friends of their victims who were courageous enough to come forward and demand justice were themselves destroyed. I suspect these murders were done by paid assassins in retaliation for some crime to which even the corps dared not admit. I also believe the corps knew from the beginning who was responsible for them.*

*Should your case ever be solved, Detective Wells, please write and tell me how it ended. To have murders so ferocious and unusual remain a mystery is, I am certain you will understand, troubling to me even after these twenty-two years. If I may be of any further assistance to you, do not hesitate to write.*

*With my sincere regard and sympathy,*

*Helmut Schlaker, Chief of Police*

Dick reread the letter, then slid everything back into the envelope, intending to walk it over to Corey's lab and study it further while he waited for his friend to arrive for the day. On the way, however, he stopped in the cop shop and saw Corey already sitting in the corner, sadly stirring a cup of black coffee. "No doughnuts?" Dick asked as he pulled up a chair.

Corey patted the roll of fat above his belt. "Day three of the Dr. Corey bread-and-water diet. On it you might live to be a hundred, but you're guaranteed to wish you'd died young."

He didn't follow this with his usual boisterous laugh; instead he added, "When you got critical you started me thinking. I saw a doctor Friday afternoon. He says forty pounds has got to go. Once that's off, the cigarettes have to follow. The blood pressure goes down, or this coroner will have a coronary." He sipped the coffee and grimaced at the taste. "I sure as hell don't want the ghouls on my staff doing my autopsy *before* I retire. I suppose I should thank you, partner, but I don't have the heart." He managed a weak, regretful grin and, anxious to discuss something else, pointed to the envelope's foreign stamps. "Another reply?"

"Yeah." Dick slipped it across the table. "Watch the blood pressure when you read this."

Corey glowered as he pulled out the reports. "Don't rub in your good health, okay?" Dick nodded, understanding a few words too late how much of his problem Corey was keeping to himself.

"What's a Schutzstaffel?" Corey asked when he first encountered the word.

"SS, remember? Those friendly guys we met during the war."

"Sure. Welcomed 'em with loaded arms. Small loss, I'd say. One less for our side to shoot."

Dick waited for the inevitable explosion. It didn't come. Instead Corey sat up straighter, occasionally whispering a key word: ". . . broken necks . . . disemboweled . . . three times . . . bathed. Christ, this is a confident beastie!" This last was said with more amazement than distaste.

When he finished the letter, Corey scanned the rest of the files, rapidly isolating the universal medical data from the foreign language. Only then did he react. "Damned Kraut fools! They never typed the blood."

"Schlaker said this would look undetailed."

"Amateurish is more like it! At the very least they should have typed the bathroom. A lot of lead flew in that battle. Someone must have scored a hit. Now the idiots just raise more questions."

"Five of the victims were killed the same way as ours. I'd say that's answering a major one."

Corey read the letter again. "Someone played with that last victim like a cat with a half-dead mouse. I don't give a damn if he was human or not, he must have had one hell of a reason for slaughtering those Nazis."

"He?"

"Okay, it . . . or she, or both of them. Or, assuming there's two, and there's lots more than two, the whole pack descended on that house."

"A whole pack never would have made it through the door. The action would have started outside."

"Well, if we go back down to two to nine, we might as well say one to nine. Lousy odds either way."

"Remember the prints in the valley? Something that can run that fast can probably move like a wild animal in closed spaces too. Besides, one to nine makes more sense. We had one victim die from loss of blood, but when our killer tried for two he didn't have the capacity. With the SS it was one at a time until that last night. Then he saved his preferred mode of execution for the last."

Corey looked respectful. "Listen, partner, you might be on a roll. How about the two of us going back to that dingy cell you call an office and building on what we've got."

They did. One hour and innumerable arguments later they had something only a little better than nothing . . . male, long-limbed, slender, good-looking (they had plenty discussion on this, but Corey won; healthy people were handsome people), incredible reflexes, eyes that see well in darkness, European-born, possibly mid-to-late forties, odd dietary habits, but outside of long rear teeth, his features were unknown.

"Doesn't make it as a description for an APB, does it, partner?"

Dick stared at the ceiling and beat his pencil on his chin. "Let's try a long shot. He hates Nazis, so he was probably a foreigner in Germany also."

"Damned foreign."

"Specifically foreign. Foreign enough to hate Nazis, not so foreign that he wouldn't fit in with the population. Jews and Gypsies," he said thoughtfully, recalling the Nazis' favorite targets. "Let's assume dark hair, dark eyes, and a pale olive complexion."

"If you're wrong . . ."

"It won't be the first time, but it feels right. It *feels* right, Cor, but it won't make any difference. When we lay eyes on that killer it will be because he walks through the door and says 'Here I am,' and that feels more right than anything. Just in case I'm wrong, I'm going to talk to Daltry in Sandusky then mail him a copy of this letter."

But after Corey left, Dick called Judy first. This was a perfect excuse to hear her voice again.

# Chapter Thirteen

## I

—CONTEMPLATE THE SILENCE, and when your thoughts are still, sense my presence, reach out and unite with me. . . .—

So had begun that first experience. Extension, Helen called it, and Stephen, who possessed no word to describe the power, said it would suffice. The first union took days to achieve; the second was easier, and as he promised, the process eventually became spontaneous. Now she practiced it like a game of skill, and the more she trained, the sharper grew her aim.

Here was an ideal day and place for practice. Comfortably crisp and breezy and, under the thick whispering trees, the sunlight made no painful intrusion. Lying motionless, Helen had already determined eight different species of birds within her range (Stephen said he sensed twelve) and had begun the more difficult detection of persons by sex and approximate age when she heard his question and answered, also aloud, "I like it as well. It pleases me to have you dependent on me if only for such a small thing as that."

Alan, absorbed in his fourth unassisted game of chess, did not even glance up from the board.

—Small? Woman, you speak of my life! (laughter) But are you impatient?—

—I am learning patience. I've come a long way. I used to wonder why, after all these centuries, you would even take the time to look at me.—

Alan moved. "Your turn," he said, and Stephen reached for his rook.

—I feel as if I am snapping my fingers. There will never be enough time; not now, not after we go.—

"Tell me more about your home."

"Chavez? A tiny whitewashed town surrounded by vineyards and mountains. The firm is located a few miles from it; self-contained, you could say."—You will like it, I believe, but becoming overly attached to any one place is hazardous. —"The Portuguese government grows unstable and we already have plans to move the glass house to an area I have desired for some time but have postponed considering until travel to the site became easier."—Later I will show it to you, but now I think I should devote more attention to this game. Alan is displaying a remarkable aptitude for strategic thinking in one so young.—

After a thoughtful half hour, Alan began losing interest in the game, and Stephen chose to mate. "You get better every time," he told the boy as they put away the pieces. "Does your father play?"

"A little with Carol."

"Well, now he will be able to play with you also, and soon I think you'll be able to win." Alan's face glowed from the praise as he turned to Helen and announced he was hungry.

Helen reached into the pocket of her pink sundress, handed Alan a dollar, and sent him down the path to the hot-dog stand. Stephen watched him go and said, his voice already nostalgic, "I shall miss them all when we depart."

"Yet you are anxious to go and cannot. Will he come, do you think?" Responding to his puzzled expression, she added, "Since the night you saw the etching, Charles is a part of all your thoughts. If he read Judy's story, would he come?"

"I believe so. He is only doing what I expect by taking his time. I've added two months to my lease. I hope I do not have to stay that long. I wish to leave with you in September."

Helen did not comment; she'd already decided she simply would not go without him. "Why do you think he killed those women?"

"I don't know. Perhaps he is insane and destroys unintentionally. He has always been a creature of strong emotions . . . his own as well as what he chose to take. When we were young, he would search out the gentlest, most innocent persons and reveal to me their private hells. It was a form of juvenile sadism, but he never completely outgrew the habit. In good times he will abandon it, and in the bad he practices a poisonous gluttony born from despair. But understand, he is no monster. At his best, he is as potently irresistible to our own as to humanity.

"But now I believe he has become what he has taken. We are all naturally cautious, but he is acting in such a rash manner, it seems as if he is daring the world to . . ." Stephen could not continue. He had reached the impassable wall.

Helen, already sensitive to that barrier, let his thought remain unfinished. "And he was my grandmother's lover; my grandfather."

These were not questions. "How did you know?" he asked.

His astonishment surprised her. "You just told me." If Stephen had not been completely certain of Helen's lineage before, he was now. "Will I meet him, do you think?" She spoke as if anticipating a visit from an eccentric, troublesome relation rather than a possibly deranged killer. She could no longer conceive that Charles could do her any harm, nor view his terrible deeds with anything but detached curiosity.

"When he comes, you will meet. It appears inevitable." The rest of that thought, that cold and formless horror he sensed from that meeting's outcome, he did not contemplate as much for his own sanity as for hers. Indeed, he did not wish to discuss his brother at all, and so he moved the conversation in a different direction. "Charles would find it amusing that I have exhausted myself to finish St. John's and now have nothing to do but await his arrival."

"St. John's is finished!"

"Three or four more nights. The rectory windows can be installed at any time. If it were not for this waiting, we could leave." He stretched out beside her on the blanket, resting his head on his arms, and stared at the treetops and patches of deep blue that leaked through them as they swayed. The breeze rippled his indigo peasant shirt, and the subtle beading that was part of the collar embroidery pressed coolly against his neck. The whole shirt was handmade, a ten-years present from Rachel. She'd mailed it to him in Tunisia and by some miracle it had reached him. "I couldn't wait," she told him when he finally returned home, and for that familial reminder he had been pathetically grateful. Those had been bad years, though no time away from family was pleasant. Now, another reprieve and an unanticipated delight for a future.

"Have you said anything to Richard yet?" he asked.

"Hints. I told him I would not be starting school this fall and that I have been considering travel but nothing more. I thought I would wait to be definite until I received a more formal invitation from the Austras."

"Formal?" His voice grew droll. "I am the director and mine will not suffice?"

"Try explaining your intentions to my uncle," Helen said, teasing.

In better circumstances he might have tried, but potential honesty was another of the things Charles had inadvertently destroyed. "I don't have to explain," he began then reconsidered. Richard, after all, was family in an indirect sense. "Very well. Wait for Rachel's letter. That is what you mean by formal, yes?"

"Or what you meant by discretion not so very long ago." She began to sit up.

"No, no. Lie back and tell me of the people around you." At that moment Helen spied Alan walking up behind Stephen, balancing three drippy double-dip cones in his two dirty hands. She suppressed a laugh, then gave Alan a thankful smile as he handed a cone first to her then to a surprised Stephen.

"I wanted to share because you brought me with you," Alan said with youthful solemnity to his neighbor, who sat speechless, staring at the chocolate and strawberry custard dripping slowly off his fingers.

Helen diplomatically sent the boy back for napkins and laughed. "Tell me of the people around you," she repeated in a playful imitation of Stephen's tone and accent. "You looked so startled. Did he really sneak up on you?"

"I expected him but not this gift. I hope you're very hungry." He passed the dripping cone to Helen, then walked down the path to rinse his hands at a convenient water fountain. Staring into the dense woods, he sniffed inquisitively. So much about this place called to him.

"Is Richard coming later?" he asked when he returned.

"He promised he would." Dick and Corey had started their

Saturday with a dawn fishing trip and were planning on stopping in Sandusky to see Daltry and, Helen was certain, Judy Preuss. Carol was spending the weekend with a friend, and she and Stephen had taken pity on Alan, who was trying not to complain about the dismal prospect of an entire day alone with Billy. "You want to send Alan home with him, don't you?"

"Of course. Do you believe I could spend a day on the edge of such a magnificently lively forest and not wish to remain after nightfall?"

"More education?"

"Of a sort. We're far from any town. We will hunt tonight."

She looked incredulous. "I can't run."

"But you can walk." How well they had kept that secret! And that was a kind of discretion too. Her efforts and his blood had given her unnatural strength until, when she found herself deceiving even her doctor, she dropped therapy altogether. Flatley appeared relieved to see her go.

"We'll leave for a time, then return when the area is deserted. There is a fire trail on the way that winds up the ridge. We'll take that."

"And then?"

"You and I will take a walk and you will help me find my prey. But tonight you must choose the most difficult. I wish us to run." And he grinned, his expression sharp and feral and humorous. So similar to the night of her first choice and, like on that night, this unlikely blend of the mundane and the fantastic bewitched her.

## II

By the time they reached the Huron park, Corey and Judy were on their way to becoming good friends. She enjoyed his lively humor and bad puns and the way he treated her with the same unqualified respect she received from Dick. That a good portion of this respect stemmed from Dick's high regard for her intelligence and Corey's own regard for his ex-partner did not diminish Corey one bit in her eyes.

As for Corey, he had been prepared to dislike her. Women as forward as Dick hinted she had been the night they first met were usually cheap. Instead he found someone secure enough not to stand on a lot of stupid gender-based formalities. Dick deserved her; he'd been lonely long enough.

Following their introductory conversation, Dick had asked, "Are you still free to get corrupted in the big city tonight?"

"If we make it through the door without a phone call, you're on!" She went for her overnight case, while Corey grinned at his friend in good-natured envy.

As they walked to the car, Dick explained he had to stop near Norwalk to claim his son. "Stephen and Helen have watched him all day, and I promised to free them from his intrusion. I hope you don't mind."

"I'm getting used to him," Judy replied. "Besides, I haven't asked him what he thought of my story on St. John's."

Curious, Corey asked what traits in Stephen made Judy uncomfortable.

"Have you ever met him?" Judy asked, as if it would explain everything.

"No, but I've heard plenty. A candidate for sainthood who performs miracles with his car, or so the rumor goes." Corey looked slyly at Dick. He'd heard that story at least six times —which was five times too many.

"And I heard you're a candidate for the Sherlock Holmes Observation Award, so please use your elementary skills and tell me later what you think of him. I'd like to know."

Corey bowed with mock dignity. "Fair lady, I shall treat him as if he were suspected of everything."

Though Corey had meant the words to be humorous, from the moment Stephen had stood and they had shaken hands and looked appraisingly at each other, he had done just that. It was difficult but he persisted, and it had taken only minutes before his curiosity was thoroughly aroused.

Stephen noticed Corey's interest but interpreted it as no more than the sort of glances he usually received. He was fully aware of how the investigation was proceeding—the German reply was interesting but useless, the description of the suspect a surprise but vague—and he felt secure. In another time, he'd been naturally distrustful but he had outgrown constant suspicion, as the world had outgrown personal barbarism. On this beautiful Saturday, surrounded by friends, his instincts slept. Ignoring Corey, he began to discuss the St. John's article with Judy.

Though he had already read it and so could quote it back word for word, Stephen made a pretense of scanning the copy Judy gave him. "The descriptive passages flow beautifully," he told her, and because he knew these were not his words but the outcome of her own vision on that dreary afternoon, he added, "Have you ever considered creative writing?"

Her puzzled glance implied she was not certain if the comment was intended to be a compliment or an insult. "You write elegant prose," he explained. "It would lend itself beautifully to fiction."

"I've been told that before," she replied, her voice warming to what she now perceived as praise, "but I'm too busy writing facts." Her eyes were filled with stubborn idealism and Stephen saw her goals were already set.

As they talked, Corey surveyed Stephen with quick, precise glances at his clothes, his hands, his feet, and the way he sat and spoke and smiled and laughed.

They stayed only an hour, then Dick gave his son a piggyback ride to the car. Following a few yards behind, Judy asked Corey, "Well?"

She'd enjoyed the visit, feeling no uneasiness at all, and so expected Corey to make some joking remark about Stephen's looks. Instead he concealed his observations behind an enigmatic expression and the soft evasive question, "Do you know anything more about him than what's in your article?"

Did "off-the-record" include Corey? Though Judy didn't believe so, she nonetheless replied, "Only a little, but I have a friend uncovering information in Europe. The paper is paying —grudgingly, believe me—though I'll admit to you the investigation is more to satisfy my own curiosity. My friend is fast when he's asked to be. It's been over three weeks, I should get a reply soon."

"When you do, call me. I'd like to read it myself." Anticipating her questions, he rapidly added, "I'm just curious, that's all." Corey lied. He had no basis for what he was thinking, so he had to be cautious.

# III

The woods were hushed in the velvet darkness. The scents heavier, more stimulating; the ground rich and pliant with year upon year of life ended and begun. He held one arm around her waist, supporting her as they walked in wordless communion beneath the arched and waiting trees. As it had been the evening she had shared his vision, the world had grown vivid and distinct as she perceived their surroundings with purer, keener eyes and ears . . . senses that were now her own.

He released her and she stood alone, her hands and arms held away from her body, her clothes a distraction as she carefully brought into focus the life surrounding her.

—Extend.—She obeyed and with his help went further than ever before, penetrating the life around her. He slowly unwound his power from hers and she held the vast space alone, exultant.

—No intelligence . . . only you and I . . . small things there . . . there . . . below.—She might have been pointing and he following her gesture or she might have been following his, for in this broader reality uniqueness dulled. Quickly she discarded all but the healthy, the swift, the tireless.—That one . . . the doe . . . the grace . . . beautiful . . . beautiful eyes . . . her!

—Merge with it and come with me.—

She sank slowly to her knees in the small clearing, her mind here and there, and watched her lover, alien no longer, dazzle her with the predatory change. His eyes held her in a sidelong gaze of brief, fierce intimacy, then, with a quick shake of his head, he was gone. Closing her eyes, she ran with him and from him, fluid as the night.

He extended the chase, directing his prey, touching it and letting it run, circling it, surprising it. She felt the building terror, the splendor, the careless grace, always the grace as they moved naturally, confidently, through the enveloping dark . . . and longed to be a participant in body as well as soul. They ran higher on the ridge and there was effort, at last, in that climb and the pleasure of challenge until the moment when he stumbled, then jumped, then paused in surprise only long enough for him to see, and her scream to rend the silence. For one terrible instant, she awoke as from a nightmare and, surrounded by loneliness, returned to her lover.

He directed the pursuit toward her and moved in for the ecstasy of the kill, ending not so near that she would be forced to see the conclusion but close enough that she could join him if she chose. When she heard the soft rustle in the leaves, she returned to herself. Forcing her body to stand, shaking more from emotion than weakness, she grabbed a tree for balance, then walked unsupported that short distance to where he knelt. His back was to her, his head bowed as if he mourned the dying prey. His face was pressed against its neck, one arm extended the length of the body to hold it firmly helpless. She stood in a silence broken only by the sounds of her quick breathing and, twice, the hopeless thrash of the animal.

When it quieted yet still lived, he lifted it and, standing, turned toward her, holding it in outstretched arms, his forehead resting against its back so she could see only the doe . . . and his hair darker than the night . . . his hands pale as the absent moon. She felt herself a goddess as she walked forward through the familiar musky incense to accept this offering.

When the life had ended, he led her back to the leaf-carpeted clearing and she remembered the hideous sight that had marred the chase. "What did we see on the ridge? Was it . . . ?"

"Something died. It does not concern our kind." His voice was compelling, yet she would have protested. But he stole the words before they formed.—This is our concern.—He slipped the sundress straps from her shoulders, then ran his hands down her arms, her back, her thighs, feeling her . . . lean and sinewy as a young animal just entering a long, long prime. . . .

Sometime during the lengthy drive home, as Helen lay against Stephen, picking bits of leaves out of her clothes and hair, she had a sudden, lighthearted insight. Resting her hand on his knee, she gave it a strong affectionate squeeze. "I'm not sure where we fit into the legends but I know what animals we are. We're chameleons, can't you tell?"

He laughed, but only out of courtesy. Masks, silver bullets, and now small lizards, he thought. Such is the Austra coat of arms. He might have found some humor there but he didn't see it, for they were returning to the waiting and Charles already lurked insidiously on the edge of his thoughts.

## Chapter Fourteen

### I

THE MORNING MAIL brought negative but polite replies
from Austria and (Stephen would be relieved to learn that
night) from Portugal. Disappointed by this, Dick studied the
police reports from other Ohio cities but found nothing out of
the ordinary.

Pulling out his files, he began updating them from weekend investigative reports. It was placid, mindless work and he
glanced often at the clock, looking forward more than usual to
a half-hour break with Corey.

Punctually at nine-thirty, he walked down the stairs and in
the back door of the cop shop. Corey sat in their usual spot at
a table that appeared forlorn and uninviting with only the two
cups of black coffee on it. "Anything new?" Corey inquired as
Dick sat down.

Dick told him about his negative replies, the disappointing
—if you looked at it in a certain way—statewide reports.
"Nothing. It may be a boring week."

Corey thought of Stephen, then of Judy's anticipated information. He thought of Bob Moore's Wednesday appointment
with the Freemont girl. Hardly boring. "Yes," he agreed,
"midsummer doldrums are setting in." He sipped his coffee.
Without cream it tasted bitter, as if it were a prescribed, rather
than a chosen, stimulant. Corey grimaced in dramatic disgust,
which caused Dick to laugh.

Wrapping a finger around the waist of his pants, Corey
pulled it up and down. "Three weeks and things are already

getting loose. You know, I feel so frisky, I may learn to enjoy starvation. The missus sure is." He turned the conversation briefly to their stop to pick up Alan, then commented, "Speaking of loose clothing, does your neighbor always dress so comfortably?"

Dick recalled the slacks and peasant shirt Stephen had been wearing Saturday. "He does. Even his suits are cut full. He says he prefers comfort to style."

"That shirt was stylish. Not *American*"—Corey stressed the word patriotically—"but elegant. That's interesting too. Most foreigners try to look as American as they can."

Dick chuckled. "I don't think Stephen gives a damn, and if only a part of what Judy believes is true, he can afford the insolence."

"I wouldn't think going barefoot in that park would be comfortable. Too many stones around, and the parking lot was gravel."

"Stephen told me once that he spent the first half of his life in sandals or nothing at all, weather permitting."

"Sounds painful. What nationality is he, anyway? I can't place those looks."

"Czech." Dick looked quizzically at his friend, then laughed. "First Judy and now you. Where's this obsession going to end?"

Corey shrugged. "Judy asked me to observe, so I observed. Besides, anyone in good shape interests me these days. Even you interest me, partner. So tell me, how did you manage to give up smoking?"

## II

The sun dodged dark thickening clouds when Carol came out into the yard to sit on the swing next to Alan. As usual, his humming irritated her. She'd had a bad dream the previous night and was feeling particularly unsettled. "Could you shut up!" she demanded. "I'd like to listen to the birds." Alan obeyed, and as he stared at his neighbor's windows he thought of what he'd seen that morning. Carol didn't act very friendly but he asked, anyway. "Is it all right for Helen to have someone over at night . . . without asking Pa's permission, I mean?"

"Sure," Carol replied absently. "She has Connie over sometimes, doesn't she?" With reluctant curiosity, Carol inquired, "How come you want to know?"

His sister's sharp expression told Alan he never should have said a word, but now it was impossible to avoid answering. "Because she had a friend stay over last night and I wanted to know if she would get in trouble if Pa found out. I saw . . . the friend when I woke up early. I had a bad dream and—"

Carol cut him off abruptly. "It was Stephen, wasn't it?" Her voice had become so gloomy, Alan knew she was swallowing tears. Not understanding her reaction at all, he nodded.

Carol sniffed. "That was wrong," she said without looking at her brother. "I'm going to have to tell Pa."

"No!" Alan jumped off his swing, stood in front of his sister, and continued in ignorant righteousness. "No, you can't do that! You can't get her in trouble. Helen never tattles on us!"

Filled with all the dangerous emotions that accompany jealousy, Carol stood, too, and faced her brother. She was half a head taller and bristling with anger. "They both did something very wrong," she said in a voice colder than ice.

Stephen too? His cousin and his friend? "You can't," Alan insisted, and as Carol tried to walk past him, he grabbed her arm. "You musn't "

She unleashed her anger on her brother. One fist shot out, catching him just below the eye. The second followed and he doubled up and fell to his knees to look up at his sister in dull surprise as he waited defenselessly for another painful blow.

"You damned moron!" Carol said fiercely. "You're too little to understand anything. What they did was wrong. It was sinful. I have to tell!" She kicked at the dust in front of Alan, barely missing his fingers, and ran into the house where, in the privacy of her room, she allowed herself to cry.

Alan crawled to the swing and sat without moving until he could breathe without pain. Though he hadn't wanted to hurt anyone, he had, and he felt so guilty. It was late morning.

Helen would be up soon . . . or Stephen . . . and he couldn't
face either one. His head was bowed and his shoulders rolled
forward in a dejected slump as he walked through the yard to
the back alley. Feeling the first raindrops, the beginning of the
storm, he looked up at the black clouds and knew he'd soon
be soaked. He didn't care. The weather matched his mood
perfectly.

Stephen and Helen, what had they done? And worse, what
had *he* done? These two questions occupied most of Alan's
attention as he rounded the side of the garage and stopped
abruptly, finding himself face-to-face with a stranger who
looked as if he'd been waiting for him. The man spoke silently to him with solemn, penetrating eyes . . . eyes that
seemed to sympathize with how he'd just been hurt and that
hinted they knew all the answers to all his questions.

Alan wasn't supposed to go near strangers but this one
didn't allow him any choice, and the man looked so much like
Stephen that the boy felt secure. Taking his hand, the man led
him into the dark narrow passage between the two end ga-
rages. Though the roof overhangs kept out most of the rain, an
annoying drip kept hitting Alan on his head and interfering
with his concentration as he told this understanding man
everything Carol had done to him.

—Why?—the stranger probed.—Why?—

Alan told him the rest; as much as he understood.

The stranger's eyes now commanded him to continue. Alan
gulped and tried to look away. He shouldn't do this. It was
wrong to tattle on family and friends.

—Answer me!—

The order could not be disobeyed. As Alan spoke, he wondered if the places where this man's fingers now gripped his
shoulders would bruise.

When Alan finished, the man stared at him the way Billy
stared at the candy in Mr. Becker's store. "I could eat you
up," Alan's great-aunt used to tell him as she bounced him on
her knee when he was little. Alan recalled how terrified he'd
been when he'd first heard these words. While they stood
silently, the water found a path down Alan's back and he shivered.

Following a roll of thunder, the man looked up and seemed
to notice the storm for the first time. Without loosening his

painful grip on Alan's shoulders, he moved the boy sideways so Alan's back pressed against one garage, the man's against the other. In the few inches separating their bodies, the rain fell.

—Your sister.—The man's eyes burned through the boy's defenses, exposing his soul. The thoughts promised justice, revenge, relief.

Alan had wished for all these things constantly but knew the desires were wrong, and so he shook his head quickly, sorry he had allowed himself to yield and listen even for a moment to these beautiful temptations.

The dark eyes ignored this reply and the wonderful promises continued in terms a seven-year-old could understand— . . . never hit you . . . never tease you . . . never . . .—As the stranger recited, he magnified the injustice, the hurt. Alan's tiny conscience never had a chance.

He was right! Carol had done awful things! "Yes, yes! She deserves it!"

The stranger released his grip on Alan and spoke for the first time in a voice sweet and smooth as milk chocolate. "My name is Charles and I will be your friend. I will come to you, and when I do, I will make your sister answer to me for all the hurt she has given you. May I do this?"

Alan nodded. "Yes," he replied in a guilt-filled whisper. "Yes, you can come."

—By name!—

"Yes, Charles, you may come."

—Good.—Charles cupped one hand under Alan's chin and raised the boy's face. The heavy raindrops beat against Alan's cheeks and eyes like someone else's tears, then were stopped by the back of the man's head as he bent and kissed Alan on the forehead. As if this touch had broken the powerful bonds that held him, Alan sucked in his breath and ran, determined to never, never say a word to anyone about what had happened. But when he thought about it later, he realized he could not tell, because he did not understand.

On the other hand, Carol understood too much. She could not let her misery show when she told her father what Helen had done. If she did, she would have to face the embarrassment and, even worse, her father's knowledge that her revelation was inspired not by a desire to correct a wrong but out of revenge. Throughout the night's dinner, she considered the problem until Dick, wondering at her unaccustomed silence, took a close look at her, saw her red-rimmed eyes, and asked what was wrong. Alan paled, glanced at his father in shock, and, without asking to be excused, left the room at a pace just shy of a complete bolt.

"Something is wrong," Dick said to Carol, "and I want you to explain it to me."

Faking reluctance, Carol did. Not about hitting Alan, of course. That was a matter between the two of them, but about what Alan had seen, had told her. "That is not your business," Dick reprimanded her when she'd finished.

Carol wanted to ask if her father was going to yell at Helen and Stephen, but she knew that question was even less her business, and besides, her father appeared so furious, she dared not continue. She finished her suddenly tasteless meal in silence and asked to be excused.

Once Carol had gone, Dick cleared off the table, then rinsed and stacked the dishes for his children to wash in the morning. The mindless routine restored some sense of perspective and he tried to consider this situation with the calm it deserved. "If they were discreet," he had said to Judy. Well, they had been discreet. It was an accident, really, that they'd ever been found out. What gnawed at him more than the affair itself was that he had learned about it from his children and, unless the two were spending the night in Helen's living room, they were making love under his own daughter's bedroom. *You are irrational, unreasonable, and stupid*, he told himself far more than once. Absently, he pulled a bottle of POC out of the refrigerator, sat at the kitchen table and drank it while he debated whether to say anything to them at all.

Stephen's lights were off and his car missing when, long after his children had gone to bed, Dick decided to take a walk. He stopped briefly downstairs and told Helen he was leaving for a little while. Sensing his turmoil, she looked at him inquisitively. "A rough day," he lied and left.

He walked past the playground where he used to bring Carol when she was Alan's age and Mary was occupied with the new baby. He sat on a swing and thought of Carol's sixth birthday, the last he and Mary had planned together, and how

that night he'd carried her small exhausted body up to bed.
"She's growing up," he'd said to Mary that night. And now?

Growing up. They were both growing up and there was no
way to protect them from that misery.

He continued on, stopping finally at a neighborhood tavern
where he knew the bartender like an old friend. When he left,
he wasn't drunk but, as a policeman might testify to a jury, his
judgment was impaired. Would he speak to them? He'd let the
fates decide.

## III

Stephen's car was parked in its usual place though his
apartment was dark, but as Dick walked up the stairs to the
lower porch, he noticed Helen's front door was cracked. She
no longer waited; they were together. The fates had decided.

He did not wish to catch them at the obvious, so he didn't
conceal his entrance. Instead, he knocked before walking in
and sat in the darkened living room. "Helen, Stephen, I want
to speak to both of you," he called in a stern, parental tone,
it's impropriety heightened by the hint of a slur. He had taken
only two deep breaths when he heard the brush of fabric on
fabric and the light flipped on. The accused had been in the
same room with him all along, sitting side by side on the sofa
while he, the judge, sat in a chair across from them.

Stephen's look merely inquired. Helen's, on the other
hand, stung him with its fury. "How dare you!" she began,
then stopped as Stephen reached out a hand and covered one
of hers in a subtle reminder.

Stephen's expression was so subdued as to imply boredom,
and Dick remembered something Judy had said. He'd been
through scenes like this before. Robbing the cradle . . . with
Helen, with his children, and though he reminded himself how
unintentional that last had been, he concentrated what he now
believed to be just wrath at his neighbor.

"I've trusted you," he began in an unsteady voice. "I've
treated you less like a friend than like family, and this is how
you use that trust."

"Take your time," Richard had said a month ago, although the invitation had been a bit belated. Something of that irony leaked into Stephen's words as he replied, "Your friendship was repaid in kind. I did not think I owed you sacrifice as well."

He's so cocksure of himself, Dick thought, looking at Helen. Her skin appeared pale in contrast to the deep blue robe she wore. It was a loosely wrapped covering, he was certain, nothing but her body beneath, and in the shadow between her breasts a cobalt-blue teardrop flashed as her chest rose and fell. He looked at the stone for some time and struggled not to consider the body it rested against, then broke his eyes away from her and met those of his neighbor. "I expected some restraint. You're staying only a few months. Or is that what made an affair so damned inviting? I'd like to know your intentions if you—"

"His intentions are not *your* concern!"

Helen was magnificent in her anger, Dick thought, magnificent. "And when he leaves, Helen, what then?" The reminder was intended to be cruel. Dick wanted to hurt her as much as she now hurt him.

Helen turned to Stephen, and Dick got the insane idea they were speaking without words though their expressions did not change. In a moment she turned back to him and said, "I leave too." Helen thought the revelation better suited to a calmer moment but—Stephen was correct—there would be no calm opportunity in which to discuss her plans again.

"Leave too? To stay with him?" Helen nodded, unable to conceal her happiness. "You cannot. I forbid it!" The parental tone had vanished, replaced with an unthinkable jealousy, and he rose from the chair and walked across the room until his legs were only a few inches from her knees. "I forbid it," he repeated, and his voice broke.

"Sylvia is my official guardian. There is nothing you can do to stop me. So why don't you go upstairs to bed, Uncle." She watched him with uncomfortable intensity for a moment, then added, "Your own."

Dick reacted by slapping her as hard as he could. Her head did not move, nor did she cry out, but beside her, Stephen sucked his lips between his teeth and, where his fingers gripped the sofa arm, the thick fabric ripped. Dick glared at

him with an expression full of surprise and disgust. He wished
Stephen would hit him so he could savor the pleasure of slug-
ging him back.

Instead it was Helen who stood with careful balance and
faced her uncle, the place where he'd slapped her showing the
red print of his palm. Almost too quickly for Dick's eyes to
follow, her hand was raised, but as it came down to strike
him, Stephen's flew between them, catching Helen's wrist and
stopping her blow. Helen lost her balance and grabbed Stephen for support. As she did, Dick sensed another wordless
exchange. "Very well," Helen said, her anger redirected at
Stephen, who so calmly controlled her. "But I will not be
treated this way. I am no child, am I, Uncle? Look at me and
tell me, am I a child?"

Dick expected her to untie the belt of her robe, so provocative was her tone. Instead she stood motionless, her body only
a few inches from his. He looked at her but he could not
touch, and though he wished to (damn, how he wished to!),
he did not *want* to. Rather, he wanted more than anything to
run from that room. He must have had more to drink than he'd
thought, though, because he felt so numb. No, not numb.
Frozen. And something was playing strange tricks with his
mind because he felt . . .

—No!—

The order was directed to Helen but it was Dick who
obeyed it, walking with shaky relief back to his chair while
Helen stood her ground. The battle was over. Dick knew he
had lost, and though he was not sure which of the other two in
this room had won, shame deadened his curiosity.

Stephen rose and enfolded Helen in his arms. "You are
ready," he whispered with compassion, "but not with him, not
with these emotions. For us anger is a dangerous luxury. Or
were you seeking something more by way of retribution for
his desire?"

He knew! Her legs grew weak and she sank, still holding
him, down onto the sofa where she stared at the floor as if it
had suddenly become the more precious thing in this room.
Her hair fell forward, hiding her self-disgust.

—This is what I meant by a different sort of morality. The
only degradation is what you choose to take to yourself.—

Her uncle! Helen shuddered. Could any power have erased

that night if Stephen had not been there to stand between them? She did not need to look at her lover to know his concern as he ran his hand lightly over her bruised cheek. She was amazed Dick would leave this room unharmed.

—Alive.—Stephen corrected.—When we attack, we kill. —After I return, we have much to discuss. He motioned to Dick, and the two of them walked into the darkness and kept on going, traveling over a mile down the quiet streets before either said a word. As they walked, Stephen carefully cracked the shell containing Dick's emotions until his loneliness and frustration and his fears for the future of his children spilled out.

The compassion he received from Stephen, who was no stranger to loneliness and whose race paid a horrible price for the privilege of their few cherished children, restored much of their friendship. When the time came for explanations, Stephen lied so beautifully about Helen's future that after they'd returned to the house, Dick could say good night with no animosity. Later, as he lovingly checked on Carol and Alan, he did not even wonder—or wonder why he did not wonder —where Stephen would be that night.

When Stephen returned, Helen still sat in the same place, in the same position as when he and her uncle had left her two hours earlier, frozen in meditation on all the complex emotions that had attached themselves like leeches to her soul. She could not turn back time (nor did she wish to), but she needed desperately to understand why she had contemplated such a terrible deed. Though she had waited impatiently for him, when Stephen finally walked through the door she looked as if she feared he would strike her and, he saw clearly, she believed the blow would be deserved.

He offered comfort but she would not be consoled. Instead she spoke in a halting voice. "You and Sylvia both tell me I have much to learn. Was tonight an example?"

"Yes. People react to you—to all of us—strongly. You've known Richard is attracted to you, and tonight, in your anger, you let his desire build. It was understandable."

"Understandable?" She covered her mouth with her hands to suppress whatever hysterical sound might escape.

"Strong emotions are great temptations when you do not comprehend the power and limits of your nature." As he moved toward her, she pushed out with her palm, motioning him away. He ignored her and sat, but at enough distance for his body to be no threat. "You are ashamed. There is no reason to be. Tonight you sought fulfillment, a kind of fulfillment you will never receive from me."

"Never?" She looked so sorrowful, he was certain she'd misunderstood. As he searched for words to explain, Helen found the courage to continue. "And must I leave you, then?"

He shook his head and the relief on her face was an unexpected gift. "No, though tonight I thought you might wish me to go." He could conceal only a portion of the sorrow he had borne when, speaking of loneliness with Richard, he had contemplated a future without her.

She reached for his hands and pulled him closer to her. "To send you away from me? When you have given me life?" His expression was so incredulous, she smiled through her misery. "A month ago, I may have thought differently, but now, even with my confusion, I am grateful you interfered with my future. As I waited for you to return, I thought of how I would feel if I had never known you and I could find only hollow places . . . places now filled with joy. You were so right to refuse me that night I wished you to leave. When would I have known such passion, such love?"

And she would have been happy, but there was still the shame and the self-conscious fear that stemmed from knowing that forces were awakening inside her which she could barely understand, let alone control.

"I can explain but I cannot teach you all you must know," Stephen said, feeling unreasonably possessive as he considered how she would learn. Her misery was as real to him as if it were his own, and he realized she could not remain here filled with constant apprehension that she might have to face her uncle, or someone else, alone and provoked. Duty had pulled him in two directions but now his course grew clear. "I will give Charles one week. If he does not come, we shall leave. Can you be ready?"

She'd never expected to welcome the good-byes. "As soon as you wish," she said, her voice filled with thanks.

# Chapter Fifteen

## I

JUDY'S FIRST REACTION to the thin envelope on her desk Tuesday morning was disappointment. She had anticipated something bigger, heavier, possibly even a small box. Opening it, the first thing she saw was James's invoice. "There had better be something in here to justify this amount, or you can keep on starving for all I care," she mumbled and, placing the bill to one side, began his letter.

> *Dear Judy,*
> *A most fascinating assignment! I am sure you will appreciate my speedy reply as I, of course, will appreciate your speedy draft to me of fees and expenses (receipts attached).*

Attached obviously, James, obviously. . .

> *I drove first to Lisbon where I checked AustraGlass records. All are in order. They moved their glass house (quaint term, isn't it?) from Austria to Portugal in 1910, a most beneficial relocation when you consider the mess about to erupt in most of Europe. While in Lisbon, I was able to determine the following facts about their directors.*
> *From 1911 to 1933, the president and director (of the glass house and all of AustraGlass respectively) was Denys Austra. He was born in France in 1886, died in 1934 in a climbing accident in the Alps. The body was not recovered.*

*Though he was a mere twenty-four when he took those top corporate positions, he was ancient by comparison to his successor.*

*His successor was Stephen Austra (your Stephen Austra?), born in 1916 in Czechoslovakia. He ascended to that lofty joint title in June 1934 at the age of eighteen!*

*While I was in Lisbon, I checked with various exporting houses hoping to locate some ex-employees of Austra-Glass. Nada. When I returned to Madrid, I called on antique dealers and local firms who manufacture decorative glass. Mas nada. As a last-ditch effort, I went to the University of Madrid Art Department. Bingo! An instructor referred me to Herr Josef Doehring, a retired history professor.*

*Herr Doehring is in his mid-sixties, though he looks somewhat older. At first he seemed reluctant to speak to me and sent me away. The next morning he phoned me and said he had reconsidered but would write you a letter instead of discussing the firm with me. Then he requested I come and take the letter and post it for him. He had sealed it, but I confess I read it. Had it been filled with senile ramblings, I would have searched further for an insider's view of the Austra operations.*

*I won't comment on the letter's contents except to say that after I had finished reading it, I was curious enough to travel south to Barcelona and tour Omega Ltd., the Austra subsidiary there. It manufactures Oriental-design rugs—a most modern operation—yet the patterns and colors are so exact, I have been assured by experts that no one but an expert can tell them from the real McCoys. You'll appreciate the fact that I was given the tour by Theresa Austra (the female VP of operations, and in Spain!). She was a beautiful creature even when she talked shop, which she did, alas, continuously.*

*Since Austras interest you so, I shall enthusiastically describe said lovely VP: five feet eight, unruly black curls, delightfully dark eyes, and a knockout figure! I offered lunch. I offered dinner. I nearly offered a night of passion, but decorum won. No luck; I was spurned!*

*She also introduced me to the president of the firm, James Austra. I noticed a remarkable resemblance between them, though Señorita Austra (there is hope!) told*

*me they are only cousins. I also spotted two, perhaps
three, other people who must be family as well.*

Here James had penciled a small letter A and circled it.
Judy turned to the last sheet, blank except for the letter and
scribbled comment, "If Stephen Austra bears this family resemblance, I can see why you're so interested in him. But,
Judy old friend, how . . . how . . . *how* did you get that paper to
spring for my fee???" Judy reddened, then smiled. How like
James, she thought as she remembered their brief, uncomplicated affair. She shredded, then threw away, the note and returned to her letter.

*I contacted a genealogist, Emma Bright, who does a
flourishing business tracing Old Country roots for bored,
rich Americans. It seems your Stephen is one of twins,
born in 1916. Stephen and his brother, Charles, had their
births registered by their father in 1918. In that year the
Czech began keeping records and, if children were not
baptized, the word of the parents was accepted. The father
is listed as Francis, the mother as deceased.*

*Mrs. Bright also traced birth records for some of the
following Austras born after 1900. Other information was
a matter of public record. If you wish me to continue past
this rather sketchy listing, please let me know. I did not
wish to knock you over with huge phone and travel bills
before receiving further instructions.*

*A colleague of mine spent an afternoon delving into
Austra corporate records in Vienna. Directors there, as far
back as the records go, were:*

*Steven Austra (Czech, 1870–1910). Served as Director
1892–1910. Drowned, body not recovered. One of triplets; also Claudia and Edward.*

*Michael Austra (Czech, 1853–1892). Served as Director
1878–1892. Retired (at age thirty-seven?).*

*Matthew Austra (Hungarian, 1830–1877). Served as Di-
rector 1850–1877. Died on hunting expedition in Africa.
Buried there.*

*I then collected, via phone, what I could of the Spanish, French, German, and Irish records and discovered the following.*

*Presidents, etc., Omega Ltd., Spain (firm est. 1838):*

*James Austra (Czech, 1918– ). Father, Michael; mother, deceased. Also has twin sister, Rachel, according to Mrs. Bright's investigation.*

*Theresa Austra (Hungarian, 1932– ). No additional information.*

*Presidents, etc., Alpha-Ireland (firm est. 1920):*

*Daniel Austra (French, 1932– ). Assumed presidency 1951. Father, Denys; mother, Danielle Austra. Mrs. Bright expressed some confusion over this. Apparently Austra was the mother's maiden name. Perhaps the couple were cousins?*

*Robert Austra (Austrian, 1904–1943) Father, David; mother, deceased. President of Alpha 1935–1942, when he resigned. Died in plane crash during World War II. One of triplets; also Elizabeth and Sebastian.*

*Janos Austra (Hungarian, 1884–1932). President 1920–1932. Cause of death not listed. Father, Charles; mother, deceased. Also had twin sister, Mary.*

*Ann Austra (American! 1914– ). VP of Operations for Alpha. Father, Charles; mother, Claudia Austra. (Cousins again?) Also twin brother, Laurence.*

*Austras in France:*

*David Austra (British 1926– ). Director of Austra Studios, Paris, from 1946 to present. Firm was established in 1946.*

*Daniel Austra (no data available). Manager of Moulins Glass House (est. 1644) from 1920 to 1935. Operations suspended 1935 to 1946. Manager after war to present, Alexandre Massier.*

*Austras in Germany:*

*Matthew Austra (Czech, data unknown). Manager Austra-Glass–Stuttgart, 1933–1934. Operations suspended 1934–1946. Current manager is Jean Savatier.*

    The Austras certainly start young and die young, don't they? On the other hand, they save a bundle on funeral plots. And all those poor motherless twins and triplets! Only Danielle and Claudia seem to have possessed the stamina to live to tell of the awesome travails of bearing the family litters.

    You didn't ask about this, but my "informed source" for the European banking community estimates Austra assets well in excess of one billion dollars. There are direct holdings in Portugal, Spain, France, Ireland, Germany, Canada, and New York, plus innumerable investments elsewhere. Monies are primarily held in old, revered Swiss banks, some in numbered accounts.

    I rang up AustraGlass in Chavez, asked to speak with Stephen Austra, and was informed he is visiting America. I would assume the Stephen Austra at St. John's is the firm's director. But if renovating church windows is his idea of a vacation, I wonder how he goes at it when he works.

    Can't wait for you to mail me a copy of your story, though from this beginning I'd say you could easily dig around and accumulate enough for a complete book . . . possibly pulp fiction. Want to collaborate? Let me know. . . .

Always,
James

    P.S. Tarda water is bottled by a small state-owned firm near Cluf, Romania, and exported solely to AustraGlass. The firm also bottles mineral water under a variety of labels for more general consumption, primarily in the Balkan states.

Judy put James's letter aside and picked up Josef Doehring's. When she finished it, she understood why Corey hadn't given her a flippant answer on Saturday. He had had some intuition and had been waiting for her evidence... circumstantial but damning. After phoning him, she began the long drive from Sandusky to Cleveland. On the way, she reflected on how thoroughly unpleasant Dick's life was about to become, and was astonished to find she felt more concern for Stephen.

## II

Corey and Dick were finishing their second cups of coffee when Judy arrived. While they had waited for her, they'd been reviewing their slim evidence in the D'Amato and Sandusky murders. Judy held Prescott's envelope in her hand, anxious to pass the letters around. But after they'd said their good mornings, Corey asked her to sit down, then concluded, "... he left us that piece of antique Austra glass and has a relation, of sorts, in the neighborhood, correct?"

"Correct," Dick said.

"Then may I present to you, suspected solely of hunting deer—and possibly Germans—without a permit... your neighbor, Stephen Austra."

Corey waited for Dick to burst into laughter, and yesterday Dick probably would have. Today, however, his face went white and his eyes moved from Corey's to Judy's with the same shock a convicted murderer shows when given the death sentence... this was inevitable, this was unspeakable, this was expected.

Corey and Judy exchanged a concerned look while Dick held out his hand for Judy's letters. "Don't forget Bobby Rich," he muttered as he separated the two, handing Prescott's to Corey and keeping Doehring's for himself. His hands shook so badly, he laid the papers on Corey's desk, then hunched over them to hide the misery on his face as he read.

*My Dear Fräulein Preuss:*

I am an old man and the doctors tell me I do not have long to live. I am telling you this not to obtain your pity but so you will understand why I am writing to you at all. Upon my dismissal from AustraGlass, I was required to sign an agreement not to reveal information on the private workings of the Austra firms. I suppose this applies primarily to the skilled glassmakers and other craftsmen, but should word that I have written this letter get back to the firm, I might lose my very generous monthly pension. I will risk it now, but I trust to your discretion in not revealing your source of information. I would, you understand, rather finish my remaining year or two with accustomed comforts.

I began working for AustraGlass in 1913, a few months after I received my doctorate in history from the University of Berlin. I had been interested in historical research, and someone on the university staff (I never determined the name of my benefactor) referred me to AustraGlass. When they contacted me, they offered me a position and a salary, both of which I was loath to refuse.

My duties were most unusual, and I have never heard of any other corporation possessing a department such as the one in which I worked. All corporations, of course, are chartered in perpetuum but I know of no other that takes its longevity so seriously.

I was the Assistant Director of the Department for Historical Projection, a department that apparently goes back almost as far as AustraGlass . . . well into the seventeenth century, I believe.

Our staff was headed by an economist, then myself and a banker as co-assistants. It also included a psychologist, a retired agent for the British Secret Service (with outstanding contacts, the anonymity of which he guarded well), a sociologist, a philosopher, and, under us, a staff of fifteen. Just before I was forced to resign, we added two scientific advisers to the staff as well (an inevitable addition considering this modern world).

Our duty was to analyze world trends—economic, political, social, and so on—and to determine the most advantageous locations for Austra subsidiaries and the most

*stable countries for Austra investments. It was this depart-
ment that had suggested Portugal as the ideal European
country for AustraGlass headquarters during World War I,
and it did this in the year 1894. While I was on the staff we
successfully predicted the year of the Russian Revolution
and its inevitable conclusion; the alliances, duration, and
outcome of World War I; postwar inflation in Germany; the
rise of Hitler; the year of the beginning of the Spanish Civil
War. . . . I could continue, but let me add only that our ac-
curacy was unquestionably superb.*

*I cannot tell you much about daily operations elsewhere
in AustraGlass because I had little contact with the creative work of the firm. We reported directly to Denys Austra, and he was the only member of that family with whom
I had more than a nodding acquaintance. Even then, I did
not see him very often. The Austras are extremely clannish
and they have rather palatial estates far up in the mountains, while those of us who worked for them generally
owned homes or rented rooms in the nearby towns. I did,
however, see a great many members of the Austra family at
our yearly meetings.*

*It is difficult even after twenty-one years to discuss these
meetings. At them were the heads of all the Austra subsidiaries and key persons within these organizations. In at-
tendance would be thirty to forty people, all but ten or so
family. These meetings would run for days, often twelve
hours or more daily. Exhausting but not impossible. What
was more demanding was simply being in the same room
with so many Austras . . . all so handsome, all so young, all
so similar, and all with eyes so incisive and solemn. Until
my first meeting, eight months after I started, I thought I
was wonderfully overpaid. After it, I was not sure they
could ever pay me enough to make me go back.*

*It would begin with our director updating our previous
reports on individual countries. You would assume that no
change would mean success, but then someone would ask
how we could justify our conclusion in light of this event.
That event . . . and so on. On the other hand, if there was a
change, why had we made it now? What facts had we
overlooked when we made our report the year before? Five
years before? And the last question, always the same: How*

*did each of us feel about our conclusions? As if we could
all be entirely apolitical, totally devoted to a firm we did
not own. They placed great importance on our answers to
this last question, and before my first meeting, the British
agent was gauche enough to warn me not to lie. I never
liked him after that, though I suppose he was attempting to
be helpful.*

*He was the only one of us, by the way, who did not
become perturbed by these meetings, but I suppose his
training had taught him to withstand such intense grillings.*

*After discussing individual countries—all countries in
which AustraGlass had general investments—we would
begin more specific reports on countries in which AustraGlass had subsidiaries, and from there we would discuss more general world trends. The Austras barely
glanced at their carefully detailed reports and they took no
notes, though they could quote back to you verbatim something you had said four or five days previously. And the
way they asked questions was likewise disturbing. There
was no order I could determine, yet questions would be
asked as quickly as they were answered, no two persons
ever speaking at the same time.*

*After a time, a palpable tension would begin to grow in
that meeting room—a subdued, incomprehensible paranoia—but whether it came from us or from them, I was
never able to determine. As an example of how disturbing
this tension could become, in my third yearly meeting the
psychologist (who had been with the department for twelve
years) began to sob uncontrollably. He was under no
greater pressure than the rest of us, but he was a slow,
thoughtful man and the length and rapidity of what could
only be termed an interrogation had pushed him to the
breaking point. When this happened, we were given a re-
cess of thirty minutes while one of the family (Robert, I
believe) led the psychologist away. When we continued, the
psychologist had returned, surprisingly composed, and
they seemed gentler with him afterward. (As a matter of
fact, he became director of the department in 1934. I was
surprised when I heard of that choice, for I had anticipated
they would select someone more emotionally stable.)*

*I might have stayed with AustraGlass until my retire-*

*ment, but in 1933, Denys Austra went climbing in the Swiss Alps and never returned. Two months later, Stephen Austra was elected to the position of director at the age of eighteen. I am told the family reached the decision quickly and unanimously.*

*I managed to be present in the corporate offices the afternoon he arrived. Stephen Austra was greeted by the staff as less an inevitable nuisance (for what could a mere child know of vast corporate matters?) than of a king returning unscathed and victorious from a long crusade. The director's secretary (thirty-two years with the firm), businesslike and loyal as corporate secretaries who grow old at their desks frequently are, began to cry. "I knew him as a child," she confided to me. Afterward there was a staff meeting and, anticipating their request, I left before it was made.*

*One of Stephen Austra's first official acts was to demand the resignation of the director of my department. A day later I was summoned to his office.*

*The director's office faces south and west, and the windows extend from ceiling to floor. The view would be spectacular but it is completely obstructed by ornate glass designs, the colors of which made the room seem less businesslike than intimate. As I walked into that office, I noticed the conference table had been replaced with one half its size and that a heavy wooden worktable had been added, upon which an intricate pattern was already in place. Denys Austra was no artist, but this director, I thought, planned to take his glass-house duties more seriously.*

*He greeted me in excellent, but dated German, and I pictured his language teacher as an ancient classics scholar. He was impeccably dressed and did not appear uneasy in his role. Indeed, I had to frequently remind myself this was a boy of eighteen, for I had the disconcerting feeling I was speaking to someone far older. He asked if I had enjoyed my work with AustraGlass. I replied affirmatively, mentally preening, as I assumed this conversation meant I was being considered for the directorship of my department. Not so. Rather, when I was comfortable and secure, he looked at me and, with an unreadable expres-*

sion, asked how we could have misjudged the rise of Hitler to the chancellorship of Germany in 1933. We had predicted 1934, I responded, so we were off by less than a year, and as our reports had noted for some time, Germany was very unstable and would likely soon be the cause of a second major European war.

He questioned how this mistake could have been avoided. I told him his predecessor had considered our predictions too precisely, that a year's anticipation—or, better yet, two—would always be in order on such major events. He said he was inclined to agree with my advice, then asked what, as a German, I thought of Adolf Hitler.

I am not bitter, Fräulein. Indeed, I now feel only sorrow for the way our meeting went. Later, after the defeat of Germany and the reports of Nazi atrocities, I remembered our conversation and was shamed that I, who had worked in such painstaking research, should not have believed my own carefully compiled facts on what would soon occur in my country. Unquestioning patriotism, Fräulein, is much more a defect than a virtue.

I replied honestly that I was a loyal German, that the settlement following World War I was a travesty, and that the Weimar Republic had, from the beginning, been a tool of the British and French. German nationalism, while extreme, would eventually diminish as Hitler pursued a more moderate path, and the predicted world war would be avoided. The turmoil in Europe would be tremendous, I added, and suggested that, as a precaution, the firm close all Austra subsidiaries in Central Europe. To be brief, Fräulein Preuss, I said everything I felt, and none of what I should have known, and I made myself into a total fool in front of that precocious child.

He then informed me that six months previously, the Sturmabteilung had entered the small Austra subsidiary near Stuttgart, separated the few known foreigners and Jews, and executed them, later denying the incident had ever occurred. The SA did not, however, harm the Austra family, and the facility was closed and abandoned within the week, as were other subsidiaries in that region.

I replied it was fortunate the family had been spared. I thought this a properly respectful answer, but it would *have been better had I said nothing at all. Stephen Austra looked at me, his black eyes hard as stones, and replied that the SA correctly sensed that they were persons best left untouched. I did not respond to this, though I was somewhat surprised the SA had let them live. They would not have killed the Austras outright (that would have been too public for the SA at that time), but to have them simply disappear, to be disposed of later, would have been a different, easier matter.*

*He told me any loss of life was unacceptable, then quickly added he did not hold Historical Projection responsible. "We had the ultimate responsibility," he said, "but, as you so succinctly noted, did not use your predictions properly." He appeared sincerely grieved by this error, and I expressed my sympathy.*

*"I was there when they were killed," he said so evenly that I felt a sudden sorrow as I contemplated how much of that horror he was now attempting to hide.*

*I said rather inanely that I had lost a brother during World War I, and while I had mourned, I eventually learned to accept the loss. Perhaps when he was older, I suggested, he would grow more understanding of the inevitability of death.*

*Commenting coldly that he doubted that, he slid a sheaf of papers over to me. It was my resignation. "You have done an admirable job," he said, "but we require more neutral minds."*

*He never intended to keep me, and I became angry. But as I was about to speak, he looked at me quite dispassionately and I knew nothing I could say would make any difference. I signed and within a week was gone, having obtained information from the firm on the teaching position at the University of Madrid. There were some turbulent years, but I was superbly prepared to face the worst from the work I had done for the Austras.*

*I harbor no ill will toward Stephen Austra. I even believe he was right. I was not unbiased, and it would have affected my work. The reason I am writing is more complex than revenge.*

*When your representative, James Prescott, contacted me and asked if I would give him information, I immedi-*

*ately said no and that night questioned why I had replied
so negatively and so quickly. It was not because of my
agreement with them, but rather because of some compulsion toward silence that has been with me since that day in
1934.*

*When you do not entirely control your will, you do not
control your destiny, either, and my destiny weighs heavily
on me now, Fräulein. I am, therefore, not easing my conscience or writing to create difficulty for AustraGlass (as if
this letter could somehow do that!) but rather to regain
that total freedom which will allow me to face my end in
peace.*

*With most cordial respect,*

*Professor Josef Doehring*

When Wells had finished Prescott's letter, he looked up, his
expression so subdued and sorrowful, it appeared he had just
learned of the unexpected death of a close relation. In one
sense, he had. "You knew, didn't you, Cor? You knew Saturday."

Corey nodded, his expression one of sympathy.

Dick recalled the previous night with uncomfortable clarity. "How? What did you see that I missed all along?"

Kicking himself, Corey thought. It was natural. He picked
up a small pad from his desk, keeping his eyes on the terse list
rather than on Dick's face as he spoke. "First of all, if Judy
hadn't asked me to observe, I never would have noticed a
thing. But she did and I remembered Linda and so . . ."

Dick's knuckles were rapping loudly on the arm of his
chair, and Corey glanced at him. Just get on with it, Dick's
look said, and squaring his shoulders, Corey slapped the pad
down on the desk and continued. "Well, it was subtle. A lot of
it too subtle to mention without something more concrete to
back it up. It seemed we'd waited this long, so a few more
days wouldn't matter.

"The first thing I noticed was how he moved; deliberately
slow, as if he were in the middle of some controlled dance.

"And there are those shy, boyish mannerisms. Say something funny to him—and I said a lot—and he looks down
when he smiles or laughs. Someone with as much conceit as

you say he has ought to throw back his head and bellow to all the world. With that in mind I took a good look at his face. His cheekbones are high, but they're further accentuated by a powerful jaw and rear overbite."

Dick stared down at Prescott's letter . . . all those mother-less twins and triplets started young and died young. Though he was already convinced, he noticed Corey's pause and asked him to continue.

"Okay. There's two interesting things about his voice. The first is the low, even pitch, as if he's hiding its full range. I also caught an odd lilt. I assumed it's the remains of an inflec-tion from his native language. Czech or Bohemian accents don't sound like that, so, regarding his nationality, he most likely lied to you."

"It says here he's Czech," Dick replied, patting Prescott's letter.

"It also says he's thirty-nine. Shall we assume that's a lie too?"

"Why were you so interested in his clothes?" Dick asked.

"I didn't care about the slacks, really. He's got long legs, but so do a lot of men. I was more concerned about the shirts with the wide sleeves. You see, while I watched him, he never held his arms straight down at his sides. The sleeves hide a bend. However, when he was lying on the blanket, the wind flattened his sleeve against his arm and I would say it was a good four or five inches longer than it should have been."

"Which brings us to his feet, right?"

"Among other things. He had no shoes in sight and, like I told you, that park is no place for bare feet. I got a good look at their soles; thick-skinned but no calluses and, for someone who said he grew up barefoot, that's most likely impossible. I also looked at as much of his body as I could and, with the exception of a scratch on his neck, there's not a mark on him. For someone who works with glass, there should be cuts on his hands, or scars from clumsier days. I'll bet big money on the fact that what I didn't see is just as flawless.

"But I suppose the fact that made me decide I had to be right was the same one that made me wait until now to tell you this. You said it yourself over and over. How did he make that car turn?"

Dick recalled that night and the hand he was now certain he

had seen pull his son back into the Bel Air. "So I should arrest him for exposing himself to save my children's lives?"

"Arrest him? I haven't suggested that."

Dick snapped his reply, furious at Corey, at Judy, most of all at himself. "Sure I can! I can haul him in on suspicion of murder, and after we have the blood tests . . ." Judy's shocked exclamation silenced him. "What in the hell am I saying?" He smiled despondently. "Besides, my family would never forgive me. I'd even have trouble forgiving myself."

Judy walked behind him and wrapped her arms around his neck as he continued. "Children, family . . . this really hits hard. Every time I've looked in the back hall and seen the open places on the stairs that until a month ago held a wheelchair lift, I would feel so grateful to Stephen for forcing Helen to work. Now she tells me she's leaving with him and, unless he doesn't go, I can't see any way to stop her. You see, I think they're two of a kind. Cor, that expression of yours is dead right: I should have been a priest. Easier a Father than a father." He clenched his fists and pounded them once on the desk in impotent anger. "I thought he was a friend, and now I discover I don't know a damn thing about him at all!"

"It would be to his advantage to be ingratiating," Corey suggested.

"It would be more to his advantage to be a recluse!" Judy retorted, then spoke to Dick. "You saw his reaction when you handed him that glass. Then he did an about-face and gave me an interview. I'd say he's putting himself at risk to find whoever committed these crimes. You have no proof he's harmed anyone. I just can't believe that someone who could create such beauty could also be a murderer."

"Killer," Dick corrected. "Only people murder people. You're right, though; I may be jumping to the worst conclusion. We don't know anything, but we're sure as hell going to find out." Now that a decision had been thrust upon him, Dick was impatient to act. He arranged an immediate appointment with Bob Moore, then walked Judy to her car. "I'll call you tonight and let you know what happens," he promised.

"This afternoon, please." She kissed him good-bye with impetuous passion.

On their way to Sunrise House, Dick reviewed the cases from this new angle. He still believed Stephen could not be responsible for the D'Amato murder, even if it were possible for him to be in two places at once. As for Rich, any part Stephen played in that was most likely self-defense. Regarding the Sandusky murders, Stephen's alibi was irrefutable. He'd been with the Wells tribe at the drive-in.

Dick's hopes for the outcome of this appointment were charged but ambivalent. Was Stephen his friend? If so, would friendship be a strong enough reason for him to assist in this case, or should Dick have something more substantial with which to bargain?

He considered the worst possibility . . . that his conclusions were totally wrong and Stephen had killed Angela D'Amato. He pictured himself at the trial, sitting with the prosecutor, his entire family and parish priest as character witnesses for the defendant who, he was certain, would have the best attorney old money could buy. And he saw Helen on the stand, the star defense witness until the prosecution blew her reputation apart. There was a hopeless humor here . . . the kind that provoked strained laughter and, he thought grimly, the resignation of a veteran cop who loved his job.

When they'd nearly reached their destination, Dick said, "I feel like a born fool. Do you know I've never seen Stephen eat or drink anything except water?"

Corey used an old comeback. "Confucius say that which is as close as nose on face is easily overlooked."

This time Dick didn't even crack a smile.

## III

Moore's office was basic beige with just the right blend of bland magazines to make it appear authentically medical. The only touch missing was the proper smell . . . no alcohol or disinfectant here, just old smoke and air freshener. If the lack of color was intended to soothe, it did nothing for Linda. The girl paced the room a number of times before settling into a chair and pretending to read a *Good Housekeeping* while her eyes darted from floor to wall to door.

Moore's receptionist had the week off and the psychologist, looking healthful and tanned (from his ten-week "workshop," Dick thought cynically) and far too fair-haired and boyish to be an expert at anything, motioned Dick into his office. There Dick explained, in as much detail as would be plausible, what they hoped to learn from this session. He left out only the things Moore had no business knowing, like the fact that the girl's rescuer most likely wasn't human.

When Dick concluded, Moore explained, "I don't have the facilities here for you to observe her from the beginning, but I'll tape the session. If I am able to induce a trance, I'll push open the door and you can stand behind her and observe, but please, not a word until I'm finished."

Moore led Linda into his office and left the door cracked. For a while all that could be heard in the hall was the murmur of Moore's voice explaining the procedure while he put the girl at ease. Then he began. "Now, Linda, I want you to uncross your legs and let your body relax in the chair. Pick any object in front of you and study it carefully.... Good, very good.... It's a pretty picture, isn't it? Now relax and breathe deeply and listen to my voice...."

Moore turned on a metronome. "Count with me, Linda. One...two...three...four...one...two...three...four..." Linda's voice followed, first anxiously, then with increasing calm, as the metronome wound down. "Close your eyes and relax and listen to me. The only thing that matters is the sound of my voice. Now I am going to ask you some questions about..." As he spoke, Moore moved slowly to the door and pulled it open, motioning Corey and Wells to step inside.

And everything was going fine—the event had happened exactly as Dick had believed until Moore asked who had ordered the dog to "stay" and the girl began to scream.

Moore tried to quiet her. "It's all right, Linda, you don't have to think about this. Just relax and listen to my voice. That's better...."

Linda repeated how Rich had counted, how she had run, how the dog had sat in front of her, and, beside it, Rich pointing his gun.

"Did he point the gun at you?"

"No... no, at someone else," she said, faltering.

"Did the person Rich pointed the gun at have a weapon?"

"No."

There was little cause to rejoice, but Dick wanted to applaud, anyway. For the moment his job appeared saved.

"Who was the gun pointing at, Linda?"

Without any warning the girl screamed once more.

When Linda was ready, Moore tried a new approach. "Did you hear anyone speak?"

"Yes, I heard Bobby say 'Kill.'"

"He ordered the dog?"

"Yes."

"What happened after Bobby said 'Kill'?"

"The man asked, 'Is that the command?' and Bobby said 'Yes,' then repeated 'Kill' again." She paused, moving nervously in the chair. "Then the dog! I saw the dog leap on Bobby. He never even raised his arm to shoot! His face! It was . . ." She began to cry, then abruptly fell silent.

"What happened then, Linda?"

"I . . . I fell?"

She fainted, Corey mouthed to Dick, and Moore, catching the exchange, nodded curtly.

Moore then approached the main event from the other direction. "You remember eating at the diner, don't you, Linda?"

"Yes." She smiled. "The hamburgers were good."

"Do you remember driving to the diner?"

"No."

"Do you remember walking to the car?"

"I couldn't. My feet were cut."

"How did you get to the car?"

"I was carried."

More hesitated to request a name. Instead he asked, "Did the driver carry you?"

Linda squirmed in her chair. "That's all right. You don't have to answer," Moore said quickly. "Did the person who carried you talk to you while you were going to the car?"

Linda looked at him blankly.

"Did you go directly to the diner?"

Linda stared without replying.

"Do you remember anything at all before seeing the diner?"

"He kissed me?" Her tone was uncertain, as if she were recalling a vague dream.

"The driver kissed you?"

Linda did not answer, and Moore had the impression that as long as she didn't try to speak, she wouldn't scream. He decided to ignore these silences. "Was there anything else? Anything you remember about that kiss?"

"There was blood. I tasted blood."

Moore glanced up at Dick in frank bewilderment. Whose blood? Dick mouthed, and Moore, holding his breath in an unhappy expectation of another scream, repeated the words.

"My own," Linda answered calmly.

Moore exhaled audibly at the surprising reprieve. "Why did he kiss you, Linda?"

"So I would forget."

"Where did the blood come from?"

"Somewhere." She smiled and turned her head so that Dick saw her profile and recalled with a shudder the faces on which he'd seen that kind of smile before.

"The person who kissed you, can you describe him?"

Again Linda remained silent, but her hands began gripping and releasing the chair arms. "Relax, breathe slowly," Moore ordered and, when she was more composed, asked, "Why did he kiss you?"

She shook her head. "He said I was brave and he kissed me."

"Did you like being kissed?"

"Yes. It made me . . . not afraid."

"He kissed you and you felt brave?"

"Yes."

Moore finally felt it was time. "You are feeling more relaxed than ever before. . . . Your breathing is very slow. . . . You are nearly asleep. Now I am going to ask you a question and you will answer it without any emotion, do you understand?"

"Yes," Linda whispered.

"Was the person who kissed you Stephen Austra?"

"No!" And whether she meant *no it wasn't*, or *no, she wouldn't say* became irrelevant because she started to scream again, more hysterically than before, and Moore, his hands covering his ears to screen out the searing sound of her voice, was a long time in quieting her. Then he finished as he had begun, repeating, "One, two three, four . . ." until she opened her eyes.

Afterward Moore could tell Wells no more than the obvious. "You're welcome to make whatever you wish of the strange things she said. I do understand that she believes she must protect the person who saved her life. Hysterical amnesia is often a willed disorder. As long as she doesn't want to remember, there is nothing I or any other therapist can do."

"I saw how you reacted in there. I heard you were better than this," Dick said bluntly.

Moore didn't deny it. "I felt like an amateur, but I doubt anything I could have done would matter. Her mental barrier is too strong."

"Could we try again?"

Moore's head began to pound as he considered the question. He massaged his temples. "No! That is, she's too emotional. You'll have to wait weeks, and even then I don't believe you'll get the information you want."

As they were leaving, Dick remembered the tape Moore had made. "I'd like to take it with us."

"No. If you need it, you'll have to write up a formal release and have the girl sign it. Until then, it stays in my files."

After the three had gone, Moore took the phone off the hook, leaned back in the same chair in which Linda had been sitting, and imagined himself walking slowly down a long flight of stairs. His head was still pounding. He had three patients to see later that afternoon and needed the next hour to acquire the necessary composure. He considered rising to take some aspirin; however, a suggestion intruded and without leaving his self-induced trance, he reached for his phone and dialed a number.

"Yes?"

"This is Bob Moore. You requested I call you."

"The officers with your patient, what did they wish to know?"

Moore told him.

"Did you tape the session as directed?"

"Yes."

"Would you play the tape for me?"

"Of course." While it played, Moore sank back in the chair, totally content. A short time later he returned to the world feeling far better than when he had left it, puzzled only by the empty reel spinning on a machine he was certain had been switched off.

# IV

Stephen hung up the phone and soberly contemplated all the likely consequences, not of the few facts Linda had been instructed to reveal (and which, if needed, would serve as his defense) but of what Richard now understood to be true. Stephen did not know if he was viewed as a prime suspect in any of these murders or merely as a potential informed source, but no matter: The time had come to act.

He first had the operator dial Paul's private number. Paul, in conference with representatives for a new client, answered on the third ring, and even though he spoke to Stephen, he sounded annoyed.

Stephen was relieved Paul had guests. They would prevent him from worrying too much over the requests he was about to hear. "I will only be a moment, so you need not ask your clients to leave. First of all, have Elizabeth call her acquaintance in Columbus late tomorrow morning. Second, as soon as possible, speak with our legal advisers in New York and have them place the best criminal defense lawyer in Cleveland on an immediate retainer."

"Defense?" Paul's voice was so doleful that in spite of this situation, Stephen responded with a laugh meant to reassure.

"I've been in worse predicaments, my friend. Far worse. But there are many, shall we say, awkward components to this one. Should the unlikely possibility arise, I will wish immediate counsel."

"Of course." Following this automatic reply, Paul recalled the constant pacing from one corner to another to another and how soft, endless footsteps in complete dark had nearly driven him mad until . . . "Of course! I'll do it immediately and call you back."

"There's no need. Let the lawyer here contact me while you return to work."

"Work?" The three visitors in his office, now staring quizzically at his back, had been almost forgotten.

"Paranoia is a once-a-year luxury, remember? I am merely prudent. *Insgavani*."

"We have a bad connection. Was that an order, a question, or merely a suggestion?"

Stephen heard Paul's smile. "Call it a suggestion. By the way, is your guest room available?"

"Yes, and if it weren't, it would be."

"Good. Denys and you will not be needed here. I will be coming to New York instead. Expect to see me on the twenty-second. Plan for two, by the way; myself and a friend."

"One room . . . and a friend." This seemed too trivial a matter to alter Stephen's plans now, and some of Paul's disapproval leaked into his tone.

Stephen chuckled. "Paul, you sound like a very British gentleman's gentleman I once employed. He didn't last. However, this is not what you think. Helen is one of the family, one you haven't met. I will do what is necessary, and when I leave here, our secret will be secure." Stephen paused, and when Paul did not reply, he added, "And now you have something far more intriguing to consider than the mob with the torches and wooden stakes, which is not congregating outside my door. I'll call you at home tomorrow. *Insgavani*."

Prudence, he had told Paul. Prudence and instinct: the most powerful combination. Fortunately he had heeded both and laid precise plans. There was a danger in what he would do now, but more in waiting any longer. Picking up the phone, he dialed Richard's work number and prayed to whichever old gods still watched over his kind that his neighbor was alone in his office. When Wells answered, Stephen spoke three words to him in a language he would hear from no one else, then broke the connection and began the waiting. If the deed were not done, he would know soon enough.

# Chapter Sixteen

## I

THE CHURCH OF St. John's stood dark and empty, save for the single spotlight near the altar under which Stephen worked, completing the repairs to the last window. Midnight approached, and he felt, rather than heard, the whisper-light footsteps, sensed the shadow moving toward him. —Hello, Charles.— He paused to finish cementing the corner before looking up.

"Stephen, have you no warmer welcome for your brother?" the voice, so like his own voice, purred back in Latin.

As Charles walked forward, Stephen studied him, noticing the subtle, yet in his immutable kind, hideous alterations . . . the skin merely a shade too ashen, the irises of his eyes flat black, like unheated coals, while behind them glowed an angry, rapacious light. Charles could go to Chavez now, sit in that chair, rightfully his for the next two decades, and, outside of surprise at his unexpected return, none but family would detect the change and know how unfit he had become for that station. Yet in his brother's presence, Stephen could not avoid taking a step backward to place more distance between them. Charles winced from this instinctive recoil, and Stephen detected his brief stab of expected pain.

Charles's shirt and slacks were new, and on his back was strapped his crossbow and a sheaf of short, thick arrows. Stephen's eyes rested on that bow as he spoke. "I've been reading too much about you, Charles. I've been picking up pieces of yourself you have left behind. Far worse, you used the family name! Why, Charles, why would you place us all in such mortal danger?"

"Mortal danger? A bad choice of phrasing, little brother? You're treading on unstable ground, ground pocked with quicksand. Walk carefully or you'll fall, like me, into limbo to become nosferatu." His words were bitterly sarcastic, delivered in a tone of terrible lifelessness. "Nosferatu . . . we are nosferatu." The words echoed back in a monochromatic chant: tu . . . tu . . . tu . . .

"No, no, no," Charles said, as if admonishing the echoes. "I am wrong. Stephen is an Austra, the prince of the blood . . . the heir apparent, though apparently the monarch will never die."

Not a thought leaked from Stephen's barricaded mind, but his expression was easily read. Charles responded with a brief, humorless chuckle. "Look at you! I say one simple little word and you are so profoundly shocked. If the monarch *ever* dies . . . *if* he dies . . . if he *dies*. He waits for it, you know. When the world ends, he won't come to you." Charles shrugged and dropped the thought. "How long has it been, Stephen?"

"Forty-five years." Nearly half a century of waiting for his brother's touch, and now he could not raise his arms for an embrace. "We searched for you but you left no trace. What have you done with all this time?"

"I submerged myself in life; I tried to drown in it. Oh, I have been busy, Stephen, and I've learned many things. Did you know I can pass, Stephen?" His voice softened as he spoke that sentence and, at the end, broke. "It seemed so clever when I first said it . . . pass." He leaned against the front pew and lowered his head. When at last he raised his eyes, Stephen shuddered from their chill. "I have come from burying my dead."

"You were responsible for all of them?"

"Yes. And more, brother . . . the deaths of those I cared for, those I despised, and those I never considered at all.

"Don't look alarmed. It's only recently I grew careless, but not long ago I was reminded of my people by a most unlikely source. I promise you, no more inexplicable remains; except, of course, for the final inconvenient corpse."

He walked away from the thought, slowly strolling the

length of the communion rail as he continued. "You know I was with Father for a while; driving him mad, he said, so he sent me away. Yet at the beginning he had the parental kindness to tell me what I must do, and I tried and failed, even at so simple a thing as that."

This was no longer his brother. This creature who spoke of the inconceivable, who hinted of acts that could not be consummated, was a being inexorably altered by grief and rage and loss into something alien even to his own. Stephen found he had nothing to say except to repeat warnings given centuries ago, and then they had been said too late. Instead he leaned warily against his worktable and listened.

Charles circled the church, waving a hand at each darkened window. "What is it they say of the Austras? The only glass artists whose works equal those of the High Middle Ages. How do you think they would react, Stephen, if they knew who built those cathedrals or, better, if they knew our names . . . the ones we've used when we haven't been restricted by religion or glass? Do you suppose when faced with such magnificence they might accept what we are?" At the rear of the church he turned and applauded. "Beautiful, Stephen, though far from the best family work. Or so the more knowledgeable critics say."

Flowing silently back to the pool of light, Charles ran his fingers over the textured surfaces. "I envy you this even creativity, this constant drive. Alchemy, Stephen, remember when we tried it? Total failure but here"—his nails clicked on the glass—"here is success. You have taken your native earth and turned it into something more beautiful, more enriching than gold.

"I remember how Father warned us at the beginning, saying recognition would place us in constant peril. You were right; in the end the family followed you, after all. Perhaps I should have remained behind, one loyal son at the side of the patriarch. Those thick stone walls would have been the perfect container for my addiction."

He patted the crossbow. "Remember how we would hunt when we were young, betting which was faster, the man or the bow. You always won, but I preferred the weapon. To you the challenge was everything and the terror merely a mild seasoning. But for me, terror was always the main course . . . a potent, dangerous course, yet so thoroughly satisfying as all we remarkable Austras know.

"I loved to stand at that distance, to wait until my choice thought it was beyond danger, and then to feel the despair, the agony so much more than physical when that arrow, that first jolt, hit. Now, well—" He broke off with a harsh burst of laughter, then pulled four arrows from his sheaf and thrust them into his brother's hands. "I made these for you."

—To use or to receive?— Stephen wondered.

Charles ignored the nebulous question and continued. "Notice the tips. I made them of glass, our glass, so there will be no chance they will deflect. And the shafts, over an inch across . . . a wooden stake is a fitting end for one of us, don't you think? Look at them, little brother . . . invasive, deadly as no small bullet could ever be."

Stephen barely heard the words as he stared down at the arrows, twirling them in his fingers, admiring in dull bemusement the simple elegance of their design; nor did he see the crossbow until Charles held it out to him. "To give," Charles said.

Stephen had begun to reach for the bow but, on hearing this obscenity, whirled and slammed the arrows on the table. His mind extended in instinctive self-protection, and he knew he dare not touch that weapon . . . he dare not feel pity or sorrow or love for this creature with whom he had once shared the womb.

Charles laid the bow next to the arrows, then rested his hands on Stephen's shoulders. Feeling the tension, he moved back a few steps and spoke their language, the swift inflections filling the church with arrhythmic music. "I thought my life would end as I lived it; in debauchery, in blood . . . that I would be hunted and found. Humanity has the advantage of numbers, after all, and a certain plodding intelligence. If they did, I would fight. I would have no choice, would I? Yet I had believed they would be victorious.

"But then you told me you were here, my brother, my other half, and I appeal to you for what love we have shared with each other and the love you have for your people . . . save them from the rogue who is one of them no longer. For them you will do it." He returned to Latin and concluded in a voice solemn and determined, "I want you to kill me, Stephen. I wish to die."

Stephen turned. "Say it!" he ordered, and Charles repeated the sentence. "No! Say it in our own language." When he received no reply, he added contemptuously, "We possess no words for the impossible, Charles."

Without warning Charles sprang, his hands open and dangerous. But before he reached his brother, he dropped them instinctively to his sides, backed off, and breathed swiftly, attempting to consume his own rage. "What did you think I would request of you? Solace and comfort? Would you like to try to heal me, Stephen? I give you permission, though it will drive you mad and I don't wish to be healed. Life only causes me . . . pain . . . you see." His words grew clipped as he concluded and saw his brother's eyes condemning him to an eternal sentence.

"I did not come here to make this request lightly, Stephen. I have attempted suicide many times. I have put a gun to my head and found my hand would jump when I pulled the trigger. Once I almost succeeded and woke in a small country hospital where a nurse with troubled, inquisitive eyes told me how lucky I was to be alive. I had lost much blood, and they were curious how to replace it, the fools! I took the nurse and left them with a new riddle . . . how a man who should be dead could kill then disappear.

"I tried drowning, only to wake on shore not remembering how I returned there. I tried starvation . . . now that *was* insane, but then you know how long we can starve. . . ."

Charles's voice had become so soft, only another of his kind would be able to hear the words. They move closer to each other, finally standing motionless only inches apart, their eyes locked, and the air around them hummed with words . . . half spoken, half thought, quick visions of the past.

". . . and at last I tried love, human love. I would have held her, my Sylvia, for as long as one can take solace in mortal woman, and then, through her I would have found my death."

Not death! Not them! Stephen held back thoughts of Sylvia and of Helen, but the wall he'd erected could be sensed and Charles watched him more closely while he continued. "Eventually she fled. So much for salvation through mortal love.

"And now it comes to this: to what I need and what you

say you cannot give me." Charles walked the few feet to the altar. "Pity it isn't Lent. They still erect those huge wooden crosses, don't they? 'What greater gift doth any man possess' and all that other righteous vindication for constant self-immolations." He shoved the thought away with a downward thrust of his hand and stared intently at the huge crucifix suspended above the altar. "This one is occupied but I believe there's room for two." He extended his long arms and asked cheerfully, "Will I fit?"

An icy stare was the only reply, and Charles gave a low, sardonic chuckle. "I caught that, brother. You nearly said 'sacrilege.' You eternal caretaker! You beautiful Quasimodo! You've been in churches far too long. And what do you gain, Stephen? What is your reward for this effort?"

Stephen's brows flicked together in annoyance. "You know the answer. The creativity, the beauty, the fervor . . . it sustains me, Charles, as it once did you."

"Once did?" Charles rested tight fists on his hips and stared up at the dark rose. "Yes, I was once that foolish. But no more. Ah, brother, it isn't me who should be contemplating that cross, it should be you, for only a martyr would create such beauty for the satisfaction of his enemies."

"I don't consider them such."

"Don't you? Then why don't they *know* you, Stephen? Why is it that in a millennium you haven't had more than a score of true human friends? And from whom do you protect your own except from your enemies? No, don't try to lie to me, be content with self-deceit." He pointed to the crossbow. "Pick it up, ready it, and let's get this finished. Better you than one of them. If they do the deed, they'll ask questions I'm sure you would rather not answer."

When Stephen did not move, Charles frowned. "Perhaps you're concerned about afterward, is that it?" He tilted his head and smiled as if from a sudden delightful insight, then moved to the priest's position in front of the altar and ran his hands over the white linen covering the marble stone. "When you're through, lay me here and consume me . . . devour my body and blood like the animal you are.

"Animals," he whispered, and pounded his fist once on the marble altar stone. It responded with a deep pagan boom. "Animals!" he screamed in his own language, and the guttural reverberations screamed back softer, ever softer, until the word hung, another whispering wraith in the air.

"What have we defied, Stephen, besides some petty morality that never could begin to apply to us? What have we done to deserve the persecution? Where is the justice that we, who were meant to be worshiped, are hiding? I wish I could feel terror. It would be a relief compared to this frigid detachment, this rage, this surety that whatever powers created us would not have had the perversity to spawn them too."

Between the real sorrow and exaggerated hate lay the truth, Stephen knew, and the truth was that Charles had chosen this despair, though fate and family had hastened it. His brother had been the strongest, the one most able to absorb pain, to tolerate grief and loss. They had leaned on him and he had broken. For his own unwitting part, Stephen believed himself guiltiest of all.

"I am drawn to darkness, Stephen, as you are drawn to beauty. I do not seek it, for it surrounds me. In the streets I brush against humanity, and their souls confess. You would look at a young girl and see her eyes, her silken skin, and I would feel her fear of time and decrepitude. You could take me into a forest so pristine, humanity has left no footprints there, and I would tell you its end is near. And this church, this glorious church you have labored to restore . . . its beauty will be worthless when the storm they all await shatters, then melts this glass back into the earth from which it was wrested.

"In the years that have separated us, I have laughed at you, little brother. You have the most powerful mind ever seen in the family, yet you bury your powers and move among these flaccid masses, a god in hiding. But you can have the last laugh, though you are far too kind to do so, for you are wonderously happy. And I? I am assaulted by my memories and by the future of humanity, running so aimlessly, racing toward death. I have longed for serenity, Stephen, and for too short a time I found it. Even now I search for it, but always I find only fear."

"You find only fear because you seek only fear! Death is not so simple, Charles. Go home, as we all must go home when the world moves too close. Brush against your own and let their power blur the sharp edges of your past, and their presence restore your distance. Life will not release you. Accept that and live."

While Stephen had spoken, Charles paced behind the altar, setting definite limits to his range, as a panther paces within only a section of a cage. Upon hearing his brother's counsel, he halted, the entire power of his mind directed at his reply. —No!—

The force of this response ended all of Stephen's ill-conceived hopes. "Charles, what is it? What have you done?" He was prepared to accept the most horrible reply.

Charles walked to where Stephen stood and gripped his shoulders. "Do not press me for an answer, little brother, but I beg you . . . look at me as you have not done since my arrival; touch me and understand!"

This was a plea rather than a command, and Stephen complied. But whatever love, whatever compassion he had wished to impart was swept away by a wave of emotions so desolate, so desperate, and so foul that his hands shot up and circled his head as if to block the input. He fell slowly forward until he rested against Charles, weakened by an agony that would have been infinitely easier to tolerate had it been physical.

Charles released his brother's shoulders and wrapped his arms around him. "Little brother, if I sensed these emotions in you, Austra or no, I would feast on you. Do you see now? No power can heal me, and because I am no less than any of you, I cannot take this sickness home. My disease is contagious and there is no longer any solace for me on earth—especially with what was once my own kind."

Stephen was unsure in which language he spoke, or if his reply was vocal or mental. He only knew it as an assent that meant "Yes, I understand" and "Yes, I am helpless."

"Then you will do this for me." The inflection was insistent; no question, only a demand for immediacy.

Stephen pushed back to arm's length from Charles. Their eyes met briefly, then Stephen severed the contact and shook his head. "I am unable . . . I cannot . . . do this to my own."

Charles thrust him away and Stephen lost his footing, clutching at the edge of his worktable for support, inexplicably afraid to turn his back even for an instant.

"You cannot!" Charles screamed the words in Latin, his body taut with rage. "Are you some animal caught in primitive instinct? Is it honor that you force me to live when I only wish to die? Understand, you fool, the only choices left to me are death or madness, and I have too little time to decide!"

"Madness." Stephen considered the implication. "If there were another way, any way at all, I would try, but this"—he motioned to the bow on the table—"or this"—he held out his hands—"are both useless." He spoke fiercely.

"But it's so easy, Stephen." At these words Charles leapt with deadly speed, his hands a white blur as he reached for his brother's throat. But Stephen moved, grabbing Charles from behind, forcing him to the ground, pinned and helpless.

Later, the chilling implication of these few moments would grow to occupy much of Stephen's thoughts but now he was merely weary of this impossible dialogue. "When you tried debauchery, brother, you should have considered the consequences. This might have worked had you been fast enough." He released Charles and reached out his hand, but instead of taking it, Charles rolled out from beneath him and onto his feet in one fluid motion.

"I know them all," he growled, then cursed in a language well suited for cursing, and his voice grew louder until the church rang with the words. "I will make you regret this refusal. I will take from you one after another all those whom you value, all those whom you love. I will hound you, Stephen, for as long as I am able, until you grant me this request."

Charles walked stiffly past Stephen and retrieved his bow. His eyes rested briefly, hopefully, on his brother. Then he disappeared into the shadows and was gone.

Stephen leaned over the glass table, seeing nothing but the four arrows . . . those indecent reminders of Charles's obsession. He took a deep breath, and another, and turned to stare into the dark sacristy, his tone resigned. "Well, Patrick, I can see by your expression that you've been standing there a while. I suppose you would like an explanation, yes?"

With no hesitation, Patrick O'Maera walked into the light and embraced his friend. "Only what you choose to give me, laddie." And the love in his touch and tone banished all trace of evil from St. John's.

When O'Maera released him, Stephen said with profound sadness, "Stay with me, Patrick; it will be only for a while. I would rather not follow the format or ask for absolution, but would you give the seal of confession to what I tell you tonight?"

"Of course."

"Good. Then I will work as we talk . . . and don't lecture me. I need to keep my entire self occupied."

In less than an hour, Stephen interrupted their conversation to declare "It is finished. Have someone . . . No, I'll put this last window in place tomorrow. I wish to see the work complete and I should speak with you further but not now; the night has grown too dangerous." His mind scanned the darkness beyond the church's walls. They were alone.

"I will walk you to the rectory, Patrick, and I want you to bolt your door and not open it for anything until morning. If you hear noises here, let God take care of the demon in his house. Promise me!"

They walked into the cool, dewy night . . . the kind of evening Stephen would savor were it not for the danger waiting in every shadow . . . a danger directed not at him but at those for whom he cared. And each of them was so pathetically vulnerable.

As he drove home, he considered his debts and decided there were none. He contemplated his responsibilities and concluded he had none. Nothing held him here but his own inclinations. And they formed powerful bonds.

## 11

Hours later, still absorbed in indecision, he heard slow, careful footsteps on his stairs and looked up to greet Helen with whatever cheerfulness he could muster. Yet as she leaned against the archway, a vision in deep blue and gold, he saw her expression was as somber as his thoughts.

"I did not wish to disturb you," he replied to her gentle, unspoken reproach. The words were almost true. His terrible dilemma was not a problem he wished to share.

"You know I don't sleep at night anymore. I hardly sleep at

all." Her look questioned, and in response he held out his arms.

Would what she had become be enough protection? Would Charles touch before he killed? What if he never came close enough to know? For an instant he saw her dying, a short, thick arrow in her chest.

As he held her he weakened; his only obligation lay here in his arms. "How soon can you be ready to leave?"

"All I need are a few clothes. The rest can be sent for." As she replied, she considered the urgency of his request and thought of how carefully Dick had avoided her that evening. "My uncle knows the truth about both of us, doesn't he?"

"He does." And in a few short hours, Richard's knowledge had become no more than a minor inconvenience. "Don't be concerned about your uncle. I must leave for a different reason. We'll go this afternoon." Before she could inquire further, he continued, "And now I think I would like to forget the hasty farewells." He locked his door and helped her rise.

"I thought . . ."

"Is there any need for discretion now?" He sensed they would be safer here than in the house next door, though he wondered whether the rest for whom he cared would be spared or placed in greater peril when their only possible protector had left. "I know them all," Charles had said. But did he? The uncertainty was a blessing.

# III

As he left for St. John's later that morning, Stephen met Alan sitting on his front steps clutching his treasured chess set in both small tanned hands. "Would you play with me?" he asked, holding out the box. His expression implied he expected Stephen to refuse.

"If I weren't going to work." At these words Alan looked so relieved, Stephen sat beside him on the sandy stairs and, taking off his dark glasses, studied his young neighbor. "Did you think I was angry with you?"

"Carol said you were. She said you were mad at both of us." Alan stopped, bit his lower lip, then added, "I'm sorry, you know."

"I know, and Carol is wrong."

Reassured, Alan broke into a happy grin. "Can we play when you get back?"

Stephen began to refuse, then changed his mind. "One game," he promised . . . one last game. And if Richard wasn't there, some hard farewells. If he was home, there might be no farewells at all, only a furtive leaving. He rested a hand on Alan's shoulder and bent forward, meaning to give the boy a kiss on the forehead, when Alan looked up at those dark eyes and hair and his expression distorted into mute terror.

A thought flashed as painfully as noon sun through Stephen's mind and, as quickly as it came, he discarded it. If Richard had said anything at all to his children, Alan would not have dared approach him. "What is it? Answer me." At this unpleasantly familiar command, Alan clutched him and began to cry.

Stephen rested his cheek against the boy's soft hair and sifted through what resembled guilt trying to find a tangible cause for this sudden misery. Young children were difficult to touch, their facts and fantasies both so real, and Stephen obtained only hints. Once Alan's sobs subsided, he managed to blurt out a few words that told Stephen the danger would remain here whether or not he stayed. There would be no farewells today, no final game of chess . . . if he left, he might as well kill them quickly first. It would be a gesture of mercy compared to the terror they would later face.

Though he had no power over his brother, no course of action that could be conceived let alone pursued, he could not leave this place, these people, so helpless.

As he quieted the boy, Stephen looked up and saw Helen standing in his doorway, her expression severe. —You met him and so we were to leave?—

He lowered his eyes and turned his head away. An assent.

—Do you remember what you told me?—

Stephen unwrapped Alan's arms. "It will be all right," he whispered to the boy, then turned to face Helen with the same caution with which he had met his brother. "You are leaving without me." No question, no order . . . merely a fact.

"Do you remember what you told me?"

"Yes, but it no longer matters."

"I will not leave." This also was a fact.

"Is yours the blind confidence of an ignorant child or the too noble bravery of a woman in love? No matter, your presence will be a maddening distraction as I do what I must."

She refused to be baited by the mockery in his voice and stood unsupported, hoping that independence would lend power to her words. "Is it possible for me to be brave when I feel no fear; to be blindly confident when I know with absolute certainty that if I leave, I will never see you again? You said it was inevitable that Charles and I meet. Aren't your instincts and mine a powerful enough combination to override your paternal inclinations, Austra?" She used his name as an accusation, a reminder.

He gripped her shoulders, his eyes flinty. —Heed me! He means to kill you all!—

"And especially me, is that it?" Her expression did not change as Stephen nodded. "He will not harm me."

Her serenity calmed him. "Is this a comforting belief or something more?"

"I know what will occur if I leave, but if I stay. . ." Using the rail for support, she sat heavily as what strength she had vanished. After a lengthy, bewildered pause, she concluded, "I don't know. It is too difficult to view my possible . . . death with the necessary detachment."

So close and probably so right! He sat beside her on the staircase. "You say you are not brave, yet you shame me. Very well, I yield."

"Then we will wait for him?"

"No!" His reply was so fierce, she flinched. Knowing she did not understand, he continued more calmly. "Charles has asked me to destroy him. To raise my hands against my brother would be an act so unspeakable, it would lead to my own annihilation."

"Your death?"

"No, something easier to contemplate and probably far more terrible: the destruction of what I am. If you choose to stay, you must let me deal with him in my own manner."

"Do what you must." She leaned against him, her fingers brushing against the cut on his neck, the mark of last night's passion, and for a moment she thought only of the happiness of touching, of loving.

"You will be a pleasant distraction," he said with grave tenderness, "and a welcome comfort."

The phone rang. "It's Richard," he said.

"Are you going to answer it?"

"Eventually." His voice was sly.

# IV

Dick had gotten no work done that morning. He hadn't expected he would function; that he came to work at all was a miracle. *What in the hell is he? A friend of the family? My niece's lover and . . . what is he?* These thoughts revolved in his mind like a scratched and skipping record. He ought to do something; he didn't want to do anything. He avoided morning coffee rather than admit to Corey that he had made no decision, and simply sat and thought.

A finger tapped the turntable. The needle moved into the next groove. Whatever Stephen might be, he must be questioned. Dick began to call the DA, then thought better of it; potential allies deserved some respect. He decided to try the police approach and phoned Stephen instead. As he counted the numerous rings, he tried not to wonder whether his neighbor was asleep or merely occupied. When Stephen did answer, he began with a brusque, "Yes, Richard?"

Following a quick, stunned silence, Dick replied, "I want to see you downtown this morning. You are not a suspect but we want to ask you some questions concerning a number of crimes committed in this area."

Stephen's response was immediate and firm. "I will not come, Richard. You cannot place me in one of those windowless cells you call an interrogation room and expect to obtain any lucid, let alone worthwhile, answers from me. You need my help, yes? I will give it on my terms. You will meet me alone, Richard, in one hour at St. John's."

"And if I refuse?"

Stephen's laughter was not pleasant. "Eleven, Richard, in the rectory at St. John's. Just you and me and Patrick." The click on the line said "end of conversation."

# Part
# Two

Stephen-Austra

*august 1955*

## Chapter Seventeen

### I

WHEN WELLS ARRIVED at the rectory, he found O'Maera expecting him. In the roomy kitchen, the curtains were drawn and a pot of freshly brewed coffee filled the air with an inviting aroma. Dick accepted a cup from the priest and they sat in strained silence at the table. To hide his uneasiness, Dick reached into his shirt pocket and pulled out a toothpick . . . one new habit to replace the old one. This was the stage and time, only the star was absent. "Where's Stephen?" he asked, attempting to sound calm.

"He'll be along. Did you come alone?"

"I didn't get any choice, did I?" Dick's reply held sharp edges. He would have been infinitely more comfortable questioning Stephen downtown but was thankful they were meeting in the rectory rather than the church. This, at least . . .

"Is neutral ground," Stephen concluded, walking into the kitchen from O'Maera's office, stopping just inside the connecting doorway. Though he was dressed entirely in black, his clothes were far from somber and more elegant than usual. The pants fit snugly, flared at the cuff to accommodate a pair of high European boots, and Dick saw that in one conclusion Cor had been wrong: it was possible to disguise the length of one's legs. As usual Stephen's shirt was of loosely woven cotton, cut low in the front, and the facing, collar, and cuffs of the long, wide sleeves were lavishly embroidered in an intricate leaf pattern in gold and wine. Around his neck hung the ruby teardrop, and what Dick had thought no more than an artistic eccentricity now appeared as alien as its bearer.

Dick stared, reluctantly fascinated, trying to see everything Corey had seen. Stephen returned his look. Then, with a courteous bow, he stretched his arms up and out, finally crossing them midway between the top of the door and the nine-foot ceiling. As he did, he spoke a few words in an elaborately inflected language. Listening as much to the melody as to the syllables, Dick detected the thought—the time has come for us to hide from one another no longer—but whether this was his thought or Stephen's, he did not know.

Stephen lowered his arms and walked with quick feline grace to sit in the chair across from Dick. When he spoke it was in a tone so casual, he might have been discussing the possibility of rain. "I was planning on spending some time talking with Patrick this morning, and when you called it seemed an ideal opportunity to speak with you as well. Thank you for the telephone call. The formality of a squad car would have been so much more awkward to refuse." He pressed his fingers together beneath his chin and stared down at the table. "I would have refused, anyway, of course." Smiling as if at some private joke, he looked up at Dick with an infuriatingly indifferent stare. *I am waiting*, it seemed to say. *Ask what you will*.

But the questions would not flow. Instead Dick thought of Doehring's letter, Prescott's research, Cor's observations, and the nine-to-one odds.

"Ah!" Stephen exclaimed merrily when he'd absorbed these.

On cue, Dick exploded.

His tirade was similar to that of two nights earlier, but now, fear, not jealousy, prompted the outburst.

Long before his temper was exhausted, O'Maera snapped, "Dick shut up! Mother of God, show some mercy if you can't find any tolerance in your heart."

Dick directed his wrath at his pastor. "You know how powerful he is, yet you defend him?"

"That is a power he will not use here—"

"No, Patrick," Stephen interrupted. "It is a power I would rather not use here. So you see, I have no need for your defense or of Richard's mercy or of anyone's tolerance. Continue your tirade if you must, Richard, but when you are finished, I will settle for no less than your respect."

That soft voice only added to the feeling Dick received as he looked into Stephen's eyes . . . as if he had just been centered in the cross hairs of a rifle sight and the weapon was held by someone capable of pulling the trigger with no hesitation. "It was you who massacred those Germans, wasn't it?"

Stephen responded first with a cold laugh, then replied in that same quiet tone, "I will not hide what I am, Richard. They deserved that fate, and I admit I yielded to the reasonable temptation of enjoying the evening's destruction immensely. I have rarely killed with such a delightful lack of regret." He looked inquisitively at Dick, then added, "Thirteen less for your side to shoot, yes?"

Again that private smile. Dick inwardly shuddered and recalled the huge orange tom he'd had as a childhood pet. He'd smuggle that cat into bed with him, hiding it under the covers, enjoying the pleasure of its soft purr and the feel of its fur against his bare chest. That casual intimacy stopped the first time he watched it gleefully destroy a rat nearly as big as itself. He viewed his pet differently after that—with less affection but greater regard.

"Regard," Stephen echoed. "Yes, the time has come for us to talk. . . ."

"Stop that!" Dick ordered.

Stephen arched one eyebrow. "It will be necessary later, but for now, as you wish."

O'Maera's noisy breathing had quickened during this exchange. "I don't understand what you are discussing," he ventured cautiously. "You killed some people, Stephen?" In the chair to O'Maera's right, Dick lowered his face into his hands and chuckled humorlessly.

Stephen looked sadly at O'Maera then more intently at Dick. "Does what I say here regarding Stuttgart remain confidential?"

O'Maera nodded. Dick ran his fingers down his face as he slowly looked up. "Yeah. From what Schlaker said, those guys probably deserved what they got."

"They did." Stephen turned to O'Maera and began. "In AustraGlass we have a department whose sole function is to alert us to sudden political upheavals, as well as more gradual social changes. Though they rarely make mistakes, they misjudged the rise of Hitler to the Chancellorship of Germany by nine months. Hitler seized control in March 1933, two months before we were to move our small operation from Stuttgart to the safety of Portugal. After his coup, we found it impossible to obtain transport for our equipment or to unfreeze our assets in the local banks. It might have been wiser merely to leave, but the SA and SS did not trouble our operations and it seemed that, as long as we provided a livelihood for one hundred and fourteen German citizens, we were in a more desirable position to bargain with authorities.

"In July, eighteen SA corpsmen invaded our factory and seized the eleven foreign workers and the four of my family who comprised the executive staff. They took us into a storage room, separated us from our workers, and, while three of the SA held their useless rifles on us, the rest executed the workers . . . not quickly, but one by one. After shooting the first five, seeing their numerical advantage, the more vicious pulled out their clubs. They had come well equipped to teach a lesson to the Austra Gypsies who would drain the Fatherland of its unearned wealth."

Stephen stared at an empty space, his eyes reliving the horror of that afternoon. "It was not so terrible watching, listening as the blows—such deceptively soft sounds for the damage they did—fell. What was more disturbing was looking into the eyes of the two victims who knew the truth and who watched us, the Austras, in the vain hope that we could do something to save them, and almost understanding why we could not. While I held my niece and shared her agony as she felt her lover die, I promised her those murderers would themselves die knowing precisely why they were being executed."

"You couldn't stop them?" Dick asked.

"There were eighteen SA thugs and only four of us. It would have been an easy matter to stop them, but what then? How would we explain the corpses to all those good German citizens milling outside that room? If you mean stop the act, that was impossible. Of the family present, only my mind had the power to command, but I was already occupied keeping my niece in control. The death of those we love gives indescribable pain to us. Ann was only nineteen. This was the first loss that truly touched her, and the circumstances were hideous.

"Afterward, I brought the police, including Helmut Schlaker, to our factory to view the carnage. I went through the formality of taking him aside and asking if we could obtain any justice in Germany. He said he could arrest the SA members who had done this, but they would never be brought to trial. He implied that if we insisted he act, we would all most likely be attacked. We heeded his honest warning, closed the factory, and everyone except myself left Germany.

"So you killed them, alone and unarmed?" Wells asked.

"Unarmed, Richard?" Stephen looked amused. "Yes, I suppose I was unarmed. You understand, of course, that I did not kill them all. Eighteen SA members invaded our factory, but five of them were hardly more than boys along for a thrill. If they survived the war, they're probably fine German citizens today: good members of the Republic who have tried, perhaps even successfully, to forget the murderous follies of their youth. No matter, they disappeared from the ranks of the SA soon after that July day, and I let them live. The other thirteen were a different matter." He described the hunt, the fear he instilled in them and how he made it appear that the "blood purge" of the SS, begun throughout Germany a few months earlier, continued on in Stuttgart.

"The killing of the first four forced the remainder together, out in the country where they could be on guard and, they believed, remain safe from their own allies. I had hoped to continue taking them one by one. But I heard they were leaving for an assignment near Munich soon, and so, one evening, I paid them a visit.

"I walked barefoot up to their house, wearing dark clothing and smelling of brandy. The corps leader met me at the door with a gun and a sadistic smile. I told him, with a heavy slur, that I had come to execute them all for the murder of my employees. He thought me drunk or mad, of course, and I knew precisely what he planned to do with me once I was inside. Nine armed men to one crazy Gypsy seemed excellent odds to him . . . amusing odds, you might say, on such a boring evening in so secluded a place. My bare feet were much on his mind, and indeed they were the first things he felt after I walked through that door.

"Helmut Schlaker was correct. The corps leader was the first to fall and the last to die—and so persistent in his attempts to escape. We were over a mile from the nearest house, three miles from town. Where would he have gone?

"I suppose I could have let him crawl and retrieved him later, but I wanted him to hear the cries of his comrades, as I had heard the cries of mine, and to know that when the sounds stopped, he would be next. I admit that when his turn came, I took my time."

Though Dick had listened impassively to this account, inside he cheered. "And afterward you took a bath?" he asked incredulously.

"No. I had to remove three bullets. I had some distance to run that night and it would have been painful to leave them in. By the time the bodies were discovered, I had crossed the border near Strasbourg."

When Stephen had finished, Dick sat silently for a moment, then asked a question that had nagged him since he'd first read Schlaker's letter. "Weren't you afraid those men might have killed you instead?"

"No. Had the act not been possible, I would not have gone. . . . That is instinct."

O'Maera walked over to the stove and picked up the coffeepot. As he poured more for himself and Dick, his hand shook. "You promised me a history, Stephen. Will it all be like this?"

"No, Patrick. But clearing up that mystery seemed the best place to begin. Now Richard doesn't have annoying questions to try his patience while I relate the tale I promised you." Stephen stood, pulled a bottle of water from the refrigerator and poured a glass, then turned and leaned against the counter. "Are you expected anywhere later, Richard?"

"I don't know, but it doesn't make any difference. Nobody knows where I am."

"You would admit this to me?"

"Why not? Hell, you probably know it, anyway."

"I do, but thank you for that trust." As Stephen lifted his hand, meaning to clap Wells on the shoulder, Dick flinched, and his pulse—impossible to control—quickened. With barely a flutter in its motion, Stephen's arm crossed above Dick's head and he picked up the glass from the counter.

When they were seated, Stephen turned to O'Maera. "This is still in confidence, yes?"

"Of course, laddie."

Insanity, Dick thought, a priest and a... Stephen's dark eyes moved to his, and the look in them was smug, as if he were about to finish another unspoken sentence. Instead he asked, "And you, Richard. What use will you make of the information I provide?"

"I'm trying to catch a killer."

"Our purposes are similar, then, but if you wish my aid, you will have to agree to hold what I say now in absolute secrecy. General knowledge you may use, but facts concerning my family remain confidential. Is that understood?"

Dick had grown wise. His assent was silent and significant. Stephen watched him a moment, and there was a disturbing depth to his gaze. Then his eyes became mischievous, and the accompanying broad grin hid nothing. Dick tried not to stare.

# II

"I will begin by saying that in eras when the earth was thought flat, we possessed names for the moons of Jupiter and for the satellites of stars scarcely visible in your night sky. My father, the father of our race on earth, has no early memories, but now, in an era in which humanity reaches for the stars, it does not seem fantastic to assume we are a race whose origins are alien.

"As for myself, I suppose it is only in these times that I must begin the story of my life by telling you I am alive, not dead; I possess an abhorrence of coffins, particularly my own; and I was born, not created.

"The year was 718, the place northwestern Romania in the high reaches of the rugged, barren, and delightfully private Carpathians. At that time, my people had recently migrated from the central grasslands into those mountains in order to live untouched by what to us were the constant and annoying invasions of peoples from the east... the Huns, the Slavs, the Magyars, and those who fled before them.

"My mother died in childbirth, the usual occurrence for women of my race who choose children. At the end, I have been told, my father offered her his blood in an effort to save her. Sometimes this works. This time it did not. I am said to much resemble her.

"Legends tell that our newborns rip their mothers apart in their birthing, but this is not true. Our infants possess neither tooth nor claw; they live on milk, not blood, and for the first few years are barely distinguishable from your own small babes.

"Their mothers die, we believe, because their life forces are depleted by their developing children. For all our strengths, we are creatures more reliant on balance than yourselves. There is our blood, so thick that developing fetal heart's could not pump it, and so the mother's blood thins. There is our remarkable ability to heal, an ability that would undoubtedly lead to miscarriage and so is diminished. Along with this, somehow the will to live is also diminished. My mother, for example, refused my father's offering, as others have refused before her. Those few women who do survive childbirth rarely regain full strength afterward and I know of no instance where a woman of our kind has given birth more than once.

"Although our women control their fertility, nearly all choose to bear children and, because multiple births are as common among my people as individual ones, our numbers stay nearly the same . . . there are a few more of us during times of peace, a few less during your own unstable eras.

"Don't look so surprised, Richard. Some of us have died; our young are particularly vulnerable. But unlike yourselves, who delight in finding more unusual and efficient means to dispose of one another, our strongest—indeed, our only—prohibition, is not to kill our own, except to save the life of an infant in childbirth. The prohibition against murder is so strong, we possess no word for that act in our language. There has never been a need to create one."

"Never?" Dick was incredulous.

"Never. We are not physically able to kill blood kin. You might as well expect us to turn into bats."

"Truly civilized," O'Maera commented.

"On the contrary, were we more civilized, this prohibition

would not need to be so strong. We are predators, Patrick, and without this structure we would undoubtedly have consumed each other long ago. Only as small children do we fight among ourselves with any kind of controlled violence. By the time we reach adulthood, our tempers are difficult.

"I matured in changing times. Then we were the dominant ones, the lords and protectors of those few of your people who shared the safety of those mountains with us. Yet sovereigns must be ever wary of those they rule. I was raised a prince, venerated and powerful, and taught both the superiority of my nature and the need to hide my special gifts from your super-stitious masses. Even then, we had accepted the inevitable: our time was nearly over. Already we were becoming your myths, your legends, the bogeymen with whom you terrify your disobedient children. Today, with our protection complete, you refuse to believe your own senses, even when you have been given all the proof you need to know we exist.

"At this time we existed on the same external cultural level as humankind. Our society was loosely feudal, though we demanded little from our serfs except their respect and our privacy. Our scientific knowledge was as primitive as your own, except in the area of astronomy, in which, as I have noted, we were far advanced. Medical knowledge, with the desperate exception of midwifery, was unnecessary. But in art we excelled.

"Our paintings, our needlework and tapestries, our pottery, our weavings all had a colorful, detailed realism. Most of my family members possess a great deal of innate ability and, as an added advantage, our senses are so much keener than your own. Of course, we also have the tremendous advantage of time . . . time to consider our designs, to prepare our materials, and, above all, to perfect our skills. For example, the building of just one set of church windows took an average of ten years, roughly half the adult life span of a medieval man. One set of windows might be all the creative work he would ever do; for me it seemed a few moments, nothing more.

"As I have said, the mountains were not our homeland, and we missed the plains we had abandoned. Even I who was born after the move, felt the longing. This was not nostalgia but, rather, a reaction similar to withdrawal from a mildly addic-tive drug . . . undefinable, elusive, and unpleasantly real. Instead of passing in time, however, the feeling became more troublesome.

"Those plains attracted us for reasons still inexplicable. Evolution suggests we would be more comfortable in a colder climate, where the prey is larger and more challenging, the sun less fierce. Even those mountains were more suited to us, but to the grasslands we were drawn. Eventually, a handful of my people returned to those plains. They found them settled and civilized, yet they stayed for a while, merging with the inhabitants; foreigners among foreigners in the larger enclaves.

"There was one among us, old and wise, who believed the strength of our people might lie in some quality of the plains earth itself. We owe him much, for when those wanderers returned, he brought with him quantities of that earth and requested we use it to line the walls and floors of our keeps. This we did, and we thrived.

"They also brought two priests who were spreading the word of your god throughout those mountains. The two came willingly, anxious in their ignorance to make new converts. From them we learned to read and write Latin and to understand the basics of a number of the then modern European languages, so we would be better prepared should we ever need or desire to move.

"The teaching of these educated men created new aspirations among many of my kin. The encroaching human settlements in our mountains made it only a matter of time before our unique natures were revealed. We feared becoming trapped in an eternal diaspora, the size of our group making us all the more noticeable as we traveled.

"Those who had returned from the plains reported how easily they had lived among humanity and how their artistic works had been much in demand. It would not be difficult to thrive, they suggested, and offered as proof the fact that they returned to us far wealthier than when they had departed.

"Others, more conservative, disagreed and questioned whether communal creatures such as ourselves could endure living in near isolation. Discussions on this subject occurred frequently. Changes were approaching.

"The priests who were so influencing our lives were as alike as fire and water, bound together only by their love of

Christ. The first, Peter, was jovial and possessed a sharp intelligence and curiously innocent faith far more contagious than any rational religious teaching could ever have been. He had been well named, for like St. Peter, he was an uncomplicated, steadfast man. The other, Cyril, fervently preached the approaching death of all things and the hell that awaited unbelievers. Our frank amusement at both these notions only fueled his zeal.

"The unlikely pair had apparently seen a great many unusual peoples in their travels, for if our nocturnal and mysterious dietary habits disturbed them, they made no comment. We in turn adopted a similar laissez-faire attitude toward them, and what they ate was a much a mystery to us as what we ate must have been to them.

"This reasonable arrangement might have gone on more than a few months had not Cyril been either suspicious or insomniac one night and stumbled into the midst of one of our small hunting groups. I'm sure he decided he'd been living amid a pack of demons, for his reason cracked in that instant. We brought him down as he ran screaming for the keep.

"Of that group, I alone possessed the ability of mental control. I tried to reach some steady, logical portion of his mind, failed, tried again, but there was nothing. As I released him and turned away, he attacked me. I was his fatal mistake."

"You killed him?" O'Maera asked, again shocked.

"No, Patrick, someone else reached him first." Stephen waited patiently for this to be accepted, then continued. "His death, or rather the revelation I received as a result of it, changed my life and the lives of my people forever.

"We brought the dead priest's body back so his friend could perform whatever burial custom he wished. Peter accepted our half-accurate account that beasts had attacked and killed his companion. He invited those of us who wished to stay and share final prayers for the repose of Cyril's soul.

"I was among the few who did. As I have told you, he was not well loved. I stayed out of curiosity and because I knew Peter did not wish to be alone with his grief. Most of all, I stayed because I believed myself responsible for Cyril's death. When I failed to control the priest's hysteria, I became angry and released him too abruptly. Had I calmed him first, he would not have attacked.

"And so I participated for the first time in the inexplicable last rites of the church and thought them an elaborate ritual to perform over a piece of already decaying meat. As I listened to the words, I wondered at their meaning. I had never doubted the existence of souls . . . but their immortality? And if human souls were immortal, what of the life forces of lower animals? Of ourselves? Was this belief a mere optimistic myth born of human fear of death, or could it be real?

"Hours passed. It grew light, and I and the priest were the only ones left . . . he alone in his prayers and I absorbed in my own soliloquy on the nature of souls and death. I had moved away from the window into the protective shadows, and as the sun rose, a ray of light reflected off a small ruby-toned bottle of Holy Chrism and onto my bare arm. Instead of the usual burning, I felt warmth . . . a languor like the sensual touch of a beloved. I knelt motionless and concentrated on that small patch of light. The longer it rested on me, the more intense the feeling of well-being. It had the same beneficial effect I experienced when I had first held our native soil, and so much more!

"I immediately assumed the Holy Chrism itself imparted this warmth. If so, I was prepared to accept and preach this religion, for it must mean salvation for those of my blood. Peter, mistaking my presence as affection for Cyril and my interest in the bottle that had belonged to him as a desire to possess some memento of the man, offered it to me. Emptied of its blessed contents, it still had the same wonderous effect. We knew something of glassmaking, but I had never encountered glass with this property. I inquired where it had been crafted, and Peter told me it had come from a glass house in our homeland.

"Understand the importance of this discovery. Our keeps were dark stone edifices, shuttered by day to keep out the scalding light. This glass, both transparent and soothing, gave us the pleasure of your daytime, the beauty of its light. My existence from that discovery to the present has been directed . . . nearly a millennium in which I have created multicolored jewels more precious than those that decorate the fingers and wrists and necks of the wealthy. Those gems exist. Mine— from the blending and the melting and the pouring to the drafting of the designs and the final execution—were created with a purpose.

"I have enriched humankind, given your believers a glimpse of the ever-present eternity, and I have provided in nearly every country on earth daytime sanctuaries for my people. Above all, I have served myself. Every piece I have made—from the small windows here to the masterpieces at Lyons, at Beauvais, at Chartres—has been my pleasure."

"Chartres?" O'Maera whispered in awe. "You built—"

"The windows, yes. There existed, of course, a long period from the discovery of the properties of my native glass to the building of Chartres, but it seemed only a moment. At first I went, alone or with others, to the nearby glass centers and worked alongside their craftsmen. Later, at home, I perfected and improved on the techniques I had learned.

"Through long hours of experimentation, I expanded the color range and the transparency to levels unheard of in Europe. Then I began designing windows for our own dwellings. They were crude compared to the work I did later, but they were the first *aughkstras* anywhere in the world, and they had far more magnificence than I had ever anticipated achieving. As I expanded my skills, I began to consider more detailed designs that could not be worked in our small structures. I hungered to create. It was then that Peter suggested we go to France.

"Ten years had passed since Peter came to us. He had been middle-aged then, he was old now, though with a curious sort of antiquity that affected only his appearance. He had the same energy, the same robust health as when he first came to us; both the product, no doubt, of living among people who never experience illness.

"By now, of course, Peter knew us for what we were. We did not repeat our earlier mistake; instead, when we perceived he had scores of politely unasked questions concerning our timeless, mercurial culture, I told him the truth. I was chosen to do this, for only I loved him as I would kin.

"This was the first time I ever explained our natures to a human being, and as I did so, I felt an unwelcome surge of fear for him. His life rested on the decision he would make that night. If there were any possibility he would reveal our existence to his world, he would remain a prisoner with us until he died. I told him everything, including the truth about how Cyril had died, then gave him time to make his decision. He had lived among us long enough to understand and, when he gave his promise, he did not lie.

"I was thankful, for it was that man, more than anything else, who made me want to leave our home and mingle with others like him. Eventually, I and my brother Charles and two of our kin decided to take the risk and leave with Peter. The year was 1123, and carting the native minerals necessary to make our special gem-colored glass, we departed. In ten years we reached the first of many milestones . . . the Abbey of St. Denis in France.

"Yes, Patrick, Saint Denis . . . the prototype of Gothic churches. Though Peter had been absent for many years, he came from a powerful family and easily arranged an interview for me with the Abbot Sugar. Sugar saw samples of my glass and my designs and immediately discarded all consideration of Venetian expatriates. I was his glassmaster from our first meeting.

"The abbot had drawn into his plans for the church an ornate, though bulky, oculus that he planned to fill with solid-colored glass. I designed for him an *aughkstra* window . . . airy and delicate as a snowflake, impressive as the evening star in spring.

"Our requests of the abbot were simple . . . a private place in which to work and the freedom to live as we chose without interference. Skilled craftsmen of the time were clannish, secretive, and often eccentric, so there was nothing unusual about either request.

"As the walls rose, our glass was being blended, melted, and poured. Charles supervised this while I worked with the abbot on the designs. He wanted to symbolize the flow of time, the mystery of eternity, the majesty of God-as-always. He wanted every worshiper lifted into paradise. I fed on his aspirations and together we created a masterpiece.

"During the first winter at St. Denis, Peter died. He who had been so timeless for a human of his era returned to France to see in the faces of his friends and read in the familiar names on stones in graveyards his own mortality. These reminders, more than his age, killed him.

"He should have stayed in our mountains, learning from

firsthand observers the history of the world. His time was over, and when death came, it was surprisingly gentle with him. Even so, this was my first loss of a close human friend, and so the hardest, and to this day the most sorrowful.

"But for my kind, life in your world was just beginning. People traveled from all over France to watch the wonderous cathedral rise. Many were common, some were powerful, and the most prestigious of all were treated to the expansive hospitality of the abbot. As his protégé, I attended many of these gatherings, and Sugar and I made a formidable pair in our zeal for our creation. The combination of his religious fervor and my commanding gifts created an epidemic that infected all of of France.

"Stephen Austra built the church at St. Denis, but he would have been far too old to work at Chartres, so that labor went to a cousin, Matthew. A third Austra, Michael, built the Lincoln Tree of Life in 1250, and Santa Chiara in Italy. Others created sections of Notre Dame, beginning in 1260, and Orvieto in 1342, and many more. At some sites, I supervised the building; at others my brother or one of our kin would be in the public eye. After a while our family achieved a reputation that could not be equaled.

"What windows we did not build we designed for others, or provided their craftsmen with rare tones of glass. Builders were willing to pay, and pay handsomely, for what we offered. One third of the wealth of France went into the construction of these churches, and a sizable portion of that wealth flowed to us. When the French Renaissance ended, the Austras had wealth, power, and the immense protection of the Church.

"My people also benefited from the work in a more important way. Your sun, your burning star, we tamed for ourselves. Our suns are those roses. The windows you hold so sacred are sacred to us as well . . . as a symbol of harmony, of unity, of a power—a god, if you wish to call it such—that made our races so similar, we could survive undetected in your world. Buried within your Christian symbolism are our own beliefs. You will not find them; it takes our eyes to see.

"As I walked through Chartres, surrounded by the synthetic rubies, amethysts, emeralds, and other precious tones, I could feel in the darkness the peace, the inspiration, the wisdom all people would discover, and I received a satisfaction from the creation of that beauty, which was so intense that no emotion has ever equaled it. Those *aughkstras* sang to me in a chorus of light and color, and their voices were magnificent!"

Stephen paused a moment, then continued on a sadder note. "As I said, the abbot and I created an epidemic throughout France. Only after a century did I pause to notice the deaths; the short, wasted lives; the wasted lands. 'Enough!' I longed to say. 'Go home to your families, your farms, your manor houses. *Ite missa est.*'

"But already the recessional had sounded. One by one the great projects were abandoned, many before completion. The only religious fervor to equal it before or since was the building of the pyramids. But those were built by slaves to honor the dead. My *aughkstras* were a symphony to delight the living, and however tremendous their cost, to this day they serve their purpose well."

"That's the fourth time you've used that word so like your name," O'Maera commented. "What does it mean?"

"The word had many meanings, depending on inflection. In the most common, the day inflection, it means 'rose' or 'flower'; in the neutral, 'circle'; and in the night, 'star.' It is a typical noun, with the night term the most important. *Aughkstra* also has a philosophical meaning . . . the large or beginning, which is the star; the small, or the end, which is the flower, and between them, the cycle that is eternity." He fingered the ruby teardrop resting against his chest. "The alpha and omega, you might say."

"How about food?" Dick interjected sourly. "What is your word for food?"

A pause, then another disconcerting grin. "We have no general word for food, though we have countless adjectives, many of which you would not comprehend, to modify the neutral term that is 'blood.' In the night inflection, the noun becomes 'prey' and, in the day, 'humankind.'"

"So we're a snack, huh?" Dick retorted.

Stephen laughed. "Precisely. Believe me, Richard, it is quite disturbing to devour creatures which so resemble ourselves and which are able to protest quite eloquently their own destruction. Only in extreme need would we kill a human being, and as for those we know and often love, to give death would be nearly impossible."

Dick did not miss Stephen's point. "When the Germans attacked your workers, what would you have done if they had included one of your own?"

"We would have destroyed everyone. Had it been necessary, we would have leveled that factory. Our lives are not expendable. To what lengths would you go for your own family, Richard?" Without waiting for a reply, he continued, "This is an excellent example in another way. When we kill, it is for vengeance or defense. If we yield to the luxury of feasting on our victims, it is unimportant, for they would die in any event." He felt O'Maera's distress and added, "When you sent requests to Europe for information on killings similar to yours, how many did you receive?"

"Schlaker's. That was all," Dick replied.

Stephen turned to O'Maera. "So you see, Patrick, the world has changed, and we have changed with it. You live in a comfortable era in a remarkably free society, but I have lived in times and places when life and death hung on the whims of a few powerful men."

"And did they find you out?" the priest inquired sadly.

"Some suspected. Some who were my friends, I told. Those who were my enemies and knew, died. I don't apologize; *szekorny,* I survive." He reached out, covering O'Maera's folded hands with one of his own. "I must be honest, Patrick, for many important reasons." Stephen paused, and then went on, answering the unspoken questions.

"Our longevity has usually been simple to conceal. The invasions, the plagues that began in the filthy sewers of your overcrowded cities, the civil wars, the world wars—all have made it possible for one Austra to die and another to take his place.

"We have likewise been careful to have no portraits painted. Of course, now there is a need for photographs and documents for passports and visas. This paperwork makes secrecy far more difficult but not impossible, as necessary documents—genuine ones—can always be obtained for a price.

"It is simpler to live in free countries, and we have usually anticipated the whims of history. AustraGlass has moved six times already, and there will be a seventh in the next twenty years. For protection, we have scattered our monies and holdings world-wide rather than risk our fortunes on the rise or fall of just one nation.

"AustraGlass sustains us, but there are nameless times for each of us. In these we paint, we sculpt; we become more creative and build reputations around aliases. Some of us are writers or excellent historians. For myself, Patrick, the most satisfying vacations were during those years when I could hide nearly all my eccentricities behind the length of my arms and my height and the strong soprano tones that are so easy for me to reach. Sometime, Patrick, I'll sing you the songs as they were meant to be sung."

O'Maera appeared first confused, then expectant. His face lit with a broadening smile, and Dick looked quizzically at both of them. "Do you know anything of the castrati?" Stephen asked, his voice at a clearer, higher pitch than usual.

When Dick finally understood, he looked down at the table in embarrassment, wondering what else Stephen had had to do to survive.

"Whatever was necessary," Stephen replied ambiguously. He remembered that there had been something he had cherished far more than the magnificence of the music: the luxury of being viewed as unique, as a creature forbidden and attractive. Though it had not been his true nature humanity had perceived, it was to that they responded, "I found that era an education, Richard. A glimpse of how acceptance would come if man was civilized."

O'Maera comprehended. Dick did not. "They created monsters," Dick muttered, then stopped and stared at Stephen's face, at its faultless beauty. His uneasiness intensified to the level where, for the first time in twenty years, he wondered if he was blushing.

"Not yet," Stephen responded, humored by the fact that this admission should disturb Richard so much more than his tale of killing an entire squad of soldiers. Each era held its own surprises. He sipped his water before continuing.

"Nothing endures. Our windows were no exception. By the eighteenth century, many were in need of restoration, and those who did the work often destroyed, in their ignorance, as much as they saved. It was then that AustraGlass began the tedious necessary task of saving these treasures . . . a task that became most time-consuming following the world wars in which so many treasures were destroyed.

"Now AustraGlass builds windows. Its subsidiaries throughout the world also design the buildings that contain them; the sterling, china, and glassware that decorate the richest of tables. In southern Spain we manufacture the finest Oriental-design rugs in the world using dyeing techniques acquired before I was born. My people excel in craftsmanship and art, and AustraGlass is guilty of blatant nepotism in its hiring practices.

"We have likewise selected some of the best talents mankind offers . . . people such as Paul Stoddard. He only needed a free hand to create his own architectural masterpieces, so perfectly harmonious with their landscape that they require no adornment to make them beautiful.

"But now we must speak of what is most on your mind. Your killer, Richard, is my brother Charles."

## Chapter Eighteen

### I

DICK HELD HIS breath as Stephen continued. "I will not tell you his history except to say that his talent is immense even among our kind, and it has never been restricted to windows or canvas. Yet like so many of your own great artists, the heights and depths of his excesses have destroyed him. But humanity has played its own major role in his downfall.

"The mayfly you gave me brought back cruel memories. It was etched nearly two hundred years ago by Anna Louise Austra, when she was eleven years old. It is a fitting symbol of her life, for a year later she was dead, a victim of the guillotine. Her crime? She was an Austra and, though untitled, rich and foreign. How foreign her executioners never suspected. She was Charles's daughter and he could have saved her, but he did not know she was in danger until she died. He had gone to Italy but, before he left, he had sent her to safety in Switzerland. She never made the border. Her escorts betrayed her for the fortune they thought she carried, and the French killed her with the same efficient savagery they used on their own countrymen.

"Hers was not my brother's first loss—he was far too old to have avoided loss—but her death was the first to leave him in despair. Together we hunted the escorts, and when we found them and my brother claimed his vengeance, I thought he was at peace. Yet he never trusted anyone in your world the way he had before, and in his hatred he did no work destined for the eyes of humanity for many years.

"In the times that followed his daughter's death, he became increasingly reclusive, until Claudia Austra became his salvation. We do not marry, but she stayed with him for half a century, her beauty, her joy, and her love bringing him back from the dark places into which his mind had wandered. He told me he wished to work, and we had just accepted a handful of commissions in your country. I suggested it . . . so civilized, so peaceful, so safe.

"While they were here, Claudia became pregnant. By now medical advances had made childbirth safer for our women, and only a small subterfuge was required . . . papers from European doctors explaining her anticipated difficulties, a substitution of the blood sample the hospital needed for typing . . . and her delivery was a success! Two boys and a girl. And Claudia survived!

"But living and thriving are far from the same, and in her weakness, she longed for her people. 'Take me home,' she told Charles. 'The children need family and there I may grow stronger.' So, being able to refuse her nothing, he agreed. Forty miles south of England, a German U-boat bombed their Spanish freighter. The Germans apologized for the mistake, diplomatically and perhaps even sincerely. The ship, after all, had not even been bound for Britain.

"The freighter did not sink immediately, and so there was ample time to radio for help and give coordinates. Then, as in the cliché, it was women and children first into the one intact lifeboat. Claudia and her children, scarcely three years old, were among them.

"'Help will come soon,' Claudia told Charles. 'There are blankets. The children have jackets and bonnets. We will survive.' And so the boat pulled away in choppy water, bearing four precious lives.

"In less than a day a rescue ship found Charles and a few others clinging to a bit of the hull. But help came to the lifeboats only after four days, too late to avert the tragedy. I heard the story weeks later from a courageous British woman named Ann Reeve, who had been with the family in that lifeboat. . . .

"Claudia wrapped her children in the blankets and listened with growing fear as, after a day, the whispers started. 'Why don't they eat? Why do they drink only water?'

"'The children still nurse,' Claudia said. 'Here are the bottles, and as for me, I cannot keep anything down. Save the food for yourselves.' For a moment only, her companions were thankful.

"The second day brought new mutterings. 'Why are the children, who are so well covered, so red from the sun? And the woman, the woman looks like she is burning up.' The British were sympathetic, but some of the European women, along with the crew manning the lifeboat, crossed themselves, and muttered the word *vampyr*.

"The bottles were empty by the end of the third day. The children were losing control, and Claudia, protected by the night, nursed them the only way she could. Then, weakened, she collapsed against her only friend on that boat, Mrs. Reeve. The widow wrapped her arms around Claudia to comfort her through the moonless night.

"For the frightened and superstitious in the small boat, the dawn brought new terror. Two of the wounded had died, and here was the British woman, who had slept beside the hellish one, with the marks on her neck.

"'I tried to explain that I was well and that Claudia hadn't moved from my side all night,' Mrs. Reeve later told me, her tears flowing with the memory. 'But they would not listen.'

"'Keep them covered,' Claudia had whispered to her. 'You are their only hope.' Then, as two crewmen lunged for her, she jumped overboard."

"But why?" O'Maera asked. "Would they have killed her?"

"They might have tried, and had they harmed her, she would have had no choice but to fight, and there would have been no question what she was. And there were so many. She might have lost the struggle or tipped the boat. Then what of her children? Weak though she was, she made the correct decision. By leaving everyone in doubt, she gave her children and herself a chance to live. But that chance was too slim for Claudia. We never recovered her body.

"Mrs. Reeve now had allies. Horrified at what they had witnessed, three other women joined her in guarding the children and defying anyone to touch them. But that night, weak and exhausted, the one on watch let her eyes close. In the morning, the boy, Simon Austra, was gone.

"'He fell overboard,' the crew insisted. But there was blood on one old sailor's shirt, and some passengers ex-

changed guilty looks. That afternoon the lifeboat was spotted
by a Portuguese tanker.

"When you've learned to expect so little, it is astonishing
to find someone who would give so much. On the tanker, Ann
Reeve demanded a cabin for her young charges, then, with the
utmost in British common sense, did everything necessary to
care for them.

"She knew their family name, and a discreetly worded in-
quiry soon brought a reply. Three weeks later I arrived in
London to claim two healthy, beautiful children who, with the
innocent callousness of youth, already called their puzzled
caretaker 'mother.'

"I wish Charles had gone for them instead. Had he sat and
heard the entire account from the human being who risked her
life for his family, I might not be here repeating this sad story.
At the time Charles was frantically searching the coast, hoping
somehow that Claudia had survived. He stopped seeking long
after he knew she had died. This time he did not take solace in
revenge nor, as he wrote me, could he bear to be near his
children, both of whom so resembled their mother. So the
children went to Portugal and Charles disappeared. Only here,
recently, did I learn how he has fared in these last forty years.

"He has felt too many losses, too much grief, and now
there is no beauty in his life, only anger, despair, and an
oppressive hidden guilt. He no longer lives; he exists.

"Existence is possible for a little while—ten years, twenty,
a human lifetime—but for us it is not enough. Life is too
strong to be our adversary, yet Charles has been wrestling with
it for years."

"And killing the living," Dick said, interrupting. The story
irritated him. He preferred his murderers human, and their
troubles anonymous.

"Yes. But he is not killing for its own sake. He wants to
die."

"If that is truly what he wishes, laddie, why does he not
kill himself?"

"As I said, Patrick, we are incapable of murder—including
murder of self. He cannot physically perform the act; even its
contemplation is a Herculean task, and so he searches for
death obliquely. He killed at first because he thought the tales
he heard as a child might be true: that his soul might walk into

the arms of death with the soul of his victim. He must have come close in that first murder, for he was tragically careless."

"Damn! What in the hell am I doing here!" Dick said. "Forgive me, Father, but I was willing to suspend all reality and sit for an hour and listen to this incredible story, but his talk of souls is too much. I have seen death, and it is far from complicated. And you!" He stood and pointed an accusing finger at Stephen. "Just what sort of game do you think you're playing?"

"Sit down, Richard." Stephen's command was angry. "I suppose I was optimistic when I assumed you would deduce you were dealing with something alien when you examined your own evidence; that you would believe the word of a priest who has known you since you were a child; and . . ."

"I'm not questioning what you are." Dick tried to interrupt.

". . . believe your faith that, since before you could read, told you that you indeed possessed a soul. I was mistaken, but unlike Christ with his doubting Thomas, it is dangerous to show you what I am. However, if you are willing, we will indeed play a game . . . one that I hope will prove more convincing than any evidence you've collected so far. Agreed?"

Dick, who seemed to have no alternative, agreed.

Stephen pushed back his chair and stretched. "Patrick, if you do not mind, would you take your phone off the hook for a little while? I would rather not be disturbed."

O'Maera rushed to do what was requested, and when they were settled, Stephen began.

## II

"Have you ever hunted, Richard; taken a gun or bow and stalked some wild game? That is a small satisfaction compared to what the hunt means to us. Closer, perhaps, is how you must feel as you pursue a killer . . . studying his movements, sensing his emotions, becoming so intimate with him that you seem to think as one. Apprehending him gives you gratification, yes. But there is more gratification—though you may not admit it even to yourself—in killing him."

"There's some truth to that. But I don't apologize."

"Even if your victim was innocent?"

"Innocent! I have never—"

"Never? Weren't you in combat during the war?" Stephen thought of his own actions during war, other wars, countless wars. "And weren't there times when that killing felt more satisfying than any other experience you'd ever had?"

"But that was war, and war is . . . different."

"It is killing, the same act, but it has been sweetened with valor, with chauvinism, even with religion, until you feel free to express your love of giving death. But for the most part, the combatants you face are as innocent as yourself."

Dick began to protest, but O'Maera cut him off. "He's right. I was a chaplain, and I heard the confessions."

"And in the name of religion and politics, human beings can engage in acts so atrocious that they sicken me. I, who thought myself immune to the sufferings of humanity, visited one of those death camps hours ahead of U.S. forces, and it was . . . no, words cannot describe that horror and despair."

For a moment the memory solidified . . . the scent of death, the sounds of the dying, all permeated with that acrid stench, which in the final, furious annihilation, had slaughtered so many. Later he took little comfort from the lives he and the others had saved, or the glory he felt in that killing. He thought only of the glass in the Stuttgart cathedral. Was this the majesty of man? The end? Though he had witnessed crimes more terrible than this, the reason had never been so personally unbearable. . . .

"But you say they were innocent," Dick challenged, breaking that short, sad pause.

Stephen glanced up and for an instant looked surprised. "The boys *your* boys killed were. No, the death-camp guards were guilty of hideous crimes, but I find it amazing that the leaders of your country could be so self-righteous at Nuremberg after ordering the bombings of Hiroshima and Nagasaki. To the victor goes the vindication."

Stephen paused, gauging Richard's reaction. "No, I do not preach pacifism, but I cannot depersonalize death as you do. For all my kind, death is an intimate act. With a gun there is distance. With a knife there is still that metal barrier. Even with your hands, you do not feel death. I do. Look at me,

Richard. If you wish to enter the mind of your killer, I will show it to you."

Stephen's eyes were slivers, as hard and black as onyx, and as Dick stared into them, the first small stirrings of fear began.

"Consider, Richard, you and me," Stephen continued in a slower pace. "I have captured you. The physical battle is over. You cannot resist me now, though you wish to struggle, to break away. My hold is already too intimate for escape."

—Try!—

Dick obeyed but found he could not move, could not force his eyes from the lightless hollows drawing him dizzily forward in an endless fall.

"Your pulse is faster, Richard. Do you fear me? You should, for I can reach out and take you like this."

Stephen's hand moved quicker than thought to Dick's neck. The fingers stroked with a delicate, arousing touch that made Dick want to pull away. The contact lasted for what seemed an eternity, until Stephen found the strongest pulse point and Dick felt the nails press into his skin.

"It is here that I would feed on you, Richard. You would scarcely feel my teeth. Like the cut of a razor, the wound would only hurt later, though you need not worry about the pain at all . . . there is only the now, you and me."

Dick thought of the corpsman waiting for death, knowing he was helpless and his end unavoidable . . . counting the minutes. . . .

—Hours, Richard, as there are hours for you and me—
"All the time I need, all the time to take anything, Richard, anything I desire from the best to the worst you have to offer. For love, there is that wonderful devotion you have to your children. For sorrow, there is that loss from years ago, which could be recalled as if it occurred yesterday . . . and for a deliriously refinable horror, I could amplify at whim the uneasiness you felt from the brush of my fingers against your skin."

Stephen's face was inches from Dick's, and as he spoke, he lowered his head, his hair grazing Dick's cheek, the side of his neck. When Dick inhaled, he detected a scent wild and beautiful. —Desire, Richard.—

Judy, Helen, Mary . . . the early conquests and the recent ones and those he had only imagined all merged into one

intoxicating longing that did not equal the attraction he felt for
the creature that held him now. He ached. "Please," he whispered, pleading, "sweet Jesus, no."

—Silence, Richard.— "When I will you to feel a thing,
you will feel it. When I order you to do a thing, you will do it.
You are mine, Richard . . . for a moment, for days, for as long
as I wish to hold you. Be thankful we are friends. I made you
a promise, yes? Now I will keep it. Now I will show you your
death."

"A game," Dick muttered, and the reminder might have
comforted, but as he said the words the knowledge vanished.
This was real! First him, then Patrick . . . Cor, Judy. Security,
what better security than the death of those who know; and he
would be the first! He trembled, he tried to shout some cry of
defiance, but it had become impossible.

"Listen to your heart! The deer in your so lovely valley did
the same. Of all the emotions, fear gives the most distinctive
flavor to the blood, and yours is perfectly seasoned now."

Dick blinked, and when he opened his eyes, Stephen stood
behind him, his fingers still pressed against the same spot on
his neck, his other hand resting on Dick's shoulder, that gentle
pressure holding him more helplessly than any tight grip could
have done. Stephen's voice had deepened, and Dick felt the
warm breath on his neck and was thankful he could not see the
mouth that spoke.

"Death has a fearful embrace, does it not, but not for long.
I take you now, and your heart, which is beating so strong and
fast, gradually slows. As the pressure of your blood dimin-
ishes, you feel flushed, as if lying in the warm sun or in bed,
after sex, wrapped in the arms of your lover. . . . Your heart
beats slower. . . . Slower. . . . Now my strong slow pulse unites
with yours, our hearts following the same waning cadence as
we move in this inevitable . . . this intimate . . . waltz. . . .
You'll dance beyond fear . . . beyond feeling . . . as we spin
slower . . . quieter. . . . Your will surrenders . . . but your body
. . . fights on . . . seeking life. . . . I marvel . . . at the strength
. . . of that . . . final defiance. . . ."

Dick felt nothing now except the two small pinpricks on
his neck. All his being, his future, his reality, was sucked
through those holes into a hot and rushing whirlpool where
only a voice was his companion. Wait! Stephen moved with

him, supporting him, and something else as well...
ponderous, enduring, and, in some primitive fashion, terrified. As he fought for breath, his surroundings roared and his
being faded.

"Death is reaching out... its stagnant hand... every cell
... in your body... vibrates one... final shudder... of
protest... of denial... and still I am there... with you...
until your soul... reaches back.... And now... I leave you
... as I must leave you... lest I follow too far... and lose my
self... in you... following you down... into nothingness
... to become... nothing...."

The words softened, slowed, and were gone. Dick wanted
to raise a hand, feel, but his hands were gone; to look to
O'Maera for reassurance, but his eyes were empty. —No! Not
here... not now!— And he felt the laughter, mocking yet
comforting, and through it he heard the words that gave him
freedom.

"No, this is not your time... only a valuable game... a
glimpse of the reality of myself... of your killer. All life is
the same.... Animal or human, it makes no difference... to
me or to death... I kill to live.... Your killer acts for a reason
I am barely able to comprehend... he kills to die but always,
at the end... his soul gropes its lonely way back."

Stephen had gradually quickened his speech and, along
with it, Dick felt his heart return faster than a normal pace. He
shook as Stephen removed the fingers from his neck and his
own shot up to the place, rubbing, then pulling away. He
looked down at them, amazed to see no blood. "I might have
been drowning," Dick whispered.

"So we were, but this is, as I said, a game we are playing.
And now, how do you feel?"

Dick answered honestly. "Relieved. Was that my soul that
felt so afraid?"

"Your soul had the understanding; your body knew only
terror."

"Is it always the same?" he asked slowly.

"Death? Yes, there is always that satisfaction."

"Satisfaction! You want me to believe I should be concerned about someone else's victims when you speak of death
as satisfaction?"

"I told you before. Life is life and all the same. I take no human prey."

"Then you've been hunting?"

"Your wild valley, no. You made that somewhat dangerous. But understand, I need not kill. There are many emotions nearly as potent as terror and, I assure you, just as gratifying. You don't attribute any of your victims to me, do you?"

Dick thought of Rich, then dismissed the notion. "No," he replied.

"And do you honestly believe that I need take anyone unwillingly?" There was no pride in Stephen's voice.

Embarrassed at the implications of that question, Dick looked elsewhere, his eyes finally coming to rest on the kitchen clock. "Two hours," he said in amazement.

"You make a challenging adversary," Stephen commented.

Dick walked unsteadily into the rectory office and replaced the phone's receiver, then picked it up and called downtown. "Just checking in with Cor," he said in response to O'Maera's puzzled glance from the kitchen. After a few words to a secretary, he left the rectory number and returned to the table. If it was souls Stephen wished to discuss, Dick was ready now to listen.

But Stephen no longer seemed interested in the subject. "You understand what Charles tried to do with that girl, yes?"

"I think so."

"Well, it did not work, so he decided on a dangerous alternative. He killed in the bloody manner he did so you would search for him. He believes you will find him and destroy him. Then, through my interview with Miss Preuss, he learned I was here. I wanted to know why he was killing; I had never expected he would be insane enough to demand death from me. I, who have fathered no children because I could not bear to bring destruction to one I love, am the last Austra able to grant his request, yet, because of our intimacy, the only one capable of comprehending it."

A call came in for Dick, and while he took it, O'Maera decided to ask a question that had been troubling him all afternoon. "Stephen, do you believe in God?"

"Which one, Patrick? Jehovah? God the Father, Son, and Holy Ghost? Allah? Osiris? Baal?" He added other names, some long forgotten in the history of mankind. "All of them,

good or evil, are manifestations of the same force. I respect
that force, but I do not find it the whimsical being man now
adores and glorifies. The force I respect does not reward or
condemn for isolated acts and, if in the end we are judged
(and of this I am not certain), it will not be on the basis of
belief but on the value of what we chose to become. I hope
that, at the end of your world . . ." His sentence was left unfinished.

# III

It was Corey on the phone, and he was furious. "What in
the hell is going on with you!" he shouted. "First I get a call
from the blood center and some *ass*-istant director named Flaherty starts chewing me out. 'Bat's blood,' he says, 'you sent
us bat's blood.' Then he says that if I'm going to play expensive tricks on them, they weren't going to do us any more
favors! I told him they were lunatics, and when I went to get
another sample to send, I found that all the evidence on our
killer and his hunting relation is gone."

"Gone! Do you know who took it?"

"Don't you play me for a fool, partner. You signed those
boxes out yesterday. The sergeant watched you do it. Right
now I am in your office staring at spotless vials and slides,
cracked pieces of plaster and ashes in your wastebasket, which
are probably all that remain of my evidence. One question,
Dick: Why did you do it? Was it the chief's idea or did a bribe
seem more important than your job?"

Dick didn't attempt an answer. Instead he hung up the
phone with exaggerated softness and turned toward the
kitchen door. He remembered with sinking clarity the odd
vertigo he'd experienced the first night he'd discussed the
D'Amato murder with Stephen. He'd done this, that damned
inhuman beast! Any understanding Dick might have felt, any
grim, philosophical humor he might have taken in the obvious
elaborate practical joke was overpowered as the fear he'd felt
earlier twisted into a lethal rage. He reached inside his coat for

his gun, unsure of what he planned to do with it, and discovered that the shoulder holster was empty.

His eyes searched for a weapon, any weapon, and decided on a hammer resting on the sill. Dick picked it up and found its weight reassuring. His mind questioned the prudence of this act, even as he sprang silently at Stephen's back.

The weapon landed on air, the chair already empty. Dick whirled to see Stephen behind him, and with a blur of motion, one hand gripped his upper arm while the other put a stranglehold on his neck.

Dick's rage evaporated into astonishment as he saw blazing in Stephen's now huge, dark eyes an innocent and deadly fury belonging to something ancient and primitive, something that could kill. As the edges of Dick's vision began to vibrate, he heard O'Maera's voice calling, muffled by the pounding in his ears, "Stephen, put him down!" But the anger was already draining from Stephen. His grip on Dick's neck slackened, and with casual disdain he dropped Dick back into the chair.

As Dick slumped forward, forcing air down his constricted throat, Stephen spoke in a voice cold with contempt. "There is a force within us that can scarcely be controlled. I understand the anger that prompted your attack. I have been waiting for its release, and it was that which saved your life . . . that plus the fact that you are a friend, and this"—he lifted the hammer from Dick's hand—"hardly a weapon."

His speech had an odd, sibilant sound and Dick was sure that Stephen's face must be altered in some way as well. But Dick was fascinated by Stephen's hand resting on the table. Tensed, every muscle and tendon accentuated, not only on the back of the hand but on the tops of the fingers as well. No wonder Stephen had an unbreakable grip.

Stephen paused, sucked his lips between his teeth, and began to breathe deeply and slowly. As he did, Dick saw the muscles in that strange curled hand relax and re-form into a softer human shape. When Stephen spoke again, it was in his usual voice, the tone sincere and sympathetic. "The game is ended now. I am sorry if you were hurt, but I wished to give you some small indication of our mental power and our physical strength and an understanding of how carefully we must control our emotions."

"Control!" Dick snapped. "You must be a real killer in a barroom brawl."

"On the contrary. I've often had a reputation for being an arrant coward."

"My God!" Dick exclaimed as he remembered.

"Do you think we exist by luck? We are deadly, Richard, deadly. Act with care should you ever have to face my brother alone. Do not threaten him, not even with words, or your life will be worth no more than . . ." He picked up the hammer, holding it loosely in one hand and snapped the handle with a flick of his thumb. ". . . than this." He tossed the broken tool on the table, then reached into a kitchen drawer, pulled out the revolver, and slid it across the table.

Dick looked down at his weapon, uncertain how his body would react were he to reach for it. "Do you know where your brother is?" he asked without raising his head.

Stephen paused, then laid a hand on Dick's shoulder. Though he felt the resulting revulsion like a familiar obscenity, he ignored it as, caught up in his own struggle, he forced the words to continue. "No, Richard, I do not. . . . I want you to find him and kill him."

Dick wrenched himself out of Stephen's grasp. "Your brother! How can you think of this?" he said with loathing.

"Because I must, and you must trust me," Stephen replied simply.

Dick grew livid. "My evidence has been washed away and burned by my own hands, and now you ask me to kill your brother and expect me to trust you. You are a monster, damn it, and I'm a cop, not an executioner!"

Dick had not been aware he was standing until Stephen shoved him back into his chair. —Don't play the hypocrite with me!— "You've understood from the beginning how this must end. If my honesty offends you, you had best remind yourself that you will have no opportunity for defense should Charles choose to attack."

"Me? Why would he—"

"Before you begin your questions, let me conclude. I am here only because Charles has left me no choice, as you have no choice except to be thankful I did not merely wipe the slate clean and depart as I had planned. Last night we became allies in this struggle. My brother visited me here." He described what had occurred between them, then what Alan had told him, and concluded, "Your family is no longer safe."

A terrible fear clawed at Dick, its touch more painful than Stephen's. "So we are sitting here when, right now, Carol and Alan . . ." He refused to list the possibilities.

"And Helen," Stephen added with such infinite tenderness that O'Maera knew this would be the loss, if any, that would peel away his friend's civilized veneer, perhaps irrevocably.

Stephen looked at the windows, the drawn curtains diffusing the scorching summer sun. "Don't be concerned. It's a clear day." His voice grew soft and sad. "My brother never tolerated the sun as well as I, and he is weaker now, a creature of darkness. So if you must face him, face him by day and, even then, not alone. When you find him, do not try to . . . arrest him." Stephen's voice faded, and he spoke with difficulty. Whispering something in his own language, he continued, his voice still strained but coherent. "If you must shoot . . . aim for his head . . . not where he is . . . but where he will . . ." He clutched the edge of the table and bowed his head, unable to finish.

Dick wanted to shake Stephen. His family was in danger and he wanted no less than omnipotence from this ally. Yet he saw in Stephen's struggle the incredible effort it had taken for him to ask for this help. He waited, feeling mercy for the first time.

O'Maera spoke softly. "Stephen, you said there were more of your people in good times, less in bad. Tell me of those who are no longer here. What happened to them?"

Stephen did not look up, though he attempted to separate the question from its implication. O'Maera repeated his words, and when Stephen answered, he began easily. "Simon drowned. Claudia . . . no, I will not speak of that again. Robert was in an airplane shot down over France. There was a fire and it was daytime. Mark and David were caught in the bombing of London."

He stood and turned away, resting his hands on the molding above the door, his head sideways against his shoulder. "I see it; I feel it, Patrick," and both sensed the profound unending sorrow. "We are . . . ."

"That close, laddie. I thought you might be."

"Can you help us at all, Stephen?" Dick asked.

"I am not sure," Stephen admitted. "I know your children should stay close to Helen and me. I cannot harm Charles, but I can prevent him from harming others while you do the work you do best."

"Shouldn't I send the kids away? They have an aunt back East."

"What if Charles meets you alone one night and takes their location from your mind? What if he waits until they return? How many weeks or months of anxiety are you willing to endure?"

Dick rubbed his neck and found the bruises comforting. His ally was powerful. "What do you want in return for helping me?"

"That this case remain unsolved and my family's secret be undisturbed."

"How?" Dick braced himself for an answer he knew would be unpleasant.

"We face him alone."

"And then what?"

"While I hold him, you will do what Charles and I cannot do: You will pull the trigger. Afterward there will be no questions, no . . . autopsies. That is the price for my aid. Agreed?"

Stephen held out his hand, and after a brief hesitation, Dick clasped it. Though this seemed a simple act, that voluntary touching required tremendous effort, and Dick was aware that Stephen understood. With a bravery that stemmed from accepting the inevitable, Dick met his neighbor's eyes. "Agreed."

Stephen cautioned, "This will be a dangerous battle; one we may both lose."

"You?" Dick asked, amazed.

"In either event."

Dick believed he understood. "You said you could protect my family, but what happens if Charles attacks you?"

"He cannot."

O'Maera, who had listened sadly as this agreement was made, frowned and said nothing.

Dick left an hour later, mulling over how to explain this to Corey, how to get him to promise secrecy, and how to avoid speaking to Judy at all. Stephen remained behind, to give

O'Maera details Dick was not prepared to hear.

"Did you have to be so hard on him, laddie?"

"He is a stubborn man and far too brave. I only hope I was hard enough."

"You lied to him." O'Maera's voice held no reproach. "Can you fight back?"

"Self-defense is the strongest instinct. Hand to hand, I will win. If he should use a weapon, I don't know. I've never had to learn."

"If he was able to attack you, can he goad you into attempting the impossible?"

"I fear he can and, worse, that I will succeed. But I must not be the one to kill him, Patrick. To sin against our own makes us separate from our own. If I do as Charles demands, I will become as he is. And Patrick, I do not have the strength to be forever alone!"

"What was his wrong?"

"He will not tell me." Stephen drained his glass and went to the refrigerator to refill it.

"How long can you live on that?" O'Macra pointed to the cloudy contents of the glass.

"It is hardly more than mineral water. A few days; longer if I must."

"I cannot condone what you and Dick are planning, but if I can help you in other matters, please ask."

Stephen tried to be solemn. "Thank you, Patrick, but I think I'll manage." He cocked his head and studied his friend. "You're curious, aren't you?"

O'Maera fingered the crucifix of his long wooden rosary. "It isn't always what you did with Dick, is it?"

Patrick's reluctance was natural. "No, hardly ever. I am not a sadist, and you would not be compromised."

O'Maera considered carefully before replying. "Then yes, laddie; I am curious . . . more than curious."

Stephen would never have asked, and could not, for the same reason, refuse an acceptance so rare and beautiful. His hand enveloped O'Maera's, which still clutched the crucifix and a few beads. "Then trust me, Patrick," he said, not wishing to begin without his friend's complete assent.

O'Maera nodded. "I do."

The experience Stephen imparted was powerful, mystical

... an amalgam of the beauty of his countless years. These were visions, an emotional ecstasy O'Maera would savor for the remainder of his life.

As Stephen raised the priest's wrist to his lips, he felt a gratitude rich and intense. While he took life, he ran his perfect fingers over the ends of the crucifix, the rough wooden beads, and O'Maera slowly lowered his head to rest on Stephen's shoulder, his free arm circling his friend in a reverent embrace.

# Chapter Nineteen

## I

UPON RETURNING TO work, Dick phoned Corey. "I figured you'd be back sometime," Corey snapped, then appeared in record time carrying a cigarette and his own ashtray. Without a word he planted himself in his favorite old chair and stared coldly at his friend as he smoked and waited for an explanation.

Dick found the tobacco smell intoxicating. "Did you mention the missing evidence to anyone?"

"Of course not! What in the hell has gotten into you?"

Dick sighed in relief. "I've had one incredible day and I'll give you details, but only if I have your word nothing I say is passed from you to anyone. I need your help, and a whole lot more than my job depends on it now."

"I was right about Austra, wasn't I?"

Dick didn't even nod. Instead he sat in a chair across from Corey, crossed his legs, and played with the ribbing on his sock.

"All right!" Corey growled. "I'll keep your damn secret."

And Dick told him almost everything, savoring the changing expression on his friend's face until he explained the threat to his family and saw Cor's sympathy. "You got problems, partner."

"At least I have help."

"After Austra tossed you into this mess, the least he could do was hang around to drag you out of it. Your reputation's going to take a big beating, but if it all works out the way the

253

two of you planned it, nobody will ever know the evidence is gone. Don't worry, I'll cover your ass just like you've done to mine a whole lot more than once." He studied Dick. All day sitting in the rectory drinking coffee and he looked like he'd run an obstacle course through Death Valley. "I wish I'd been there."

Dick was thankful he hadn't been. "Cor, can you imagine creatures that can actually feel the death of someone in their family, then remember the event, even from centuries before, so strongly that you want to cry with them? Think what it would be like if people were like that. What do you think . . . ?"

Doses of reality, Corey thought; administered fast. "The way we croak, we'd all go insane in no time. Mass depression. People sobbing on street corners. And consider the on-the-job discomfort for a coroner. Every stiff on the table would make me bawl. No thank you, I prefer humanity just as heartless as it's always been. Let's leave long-term sorrow for the immortal few."

"That's the saddest part. They're not immortal. They just think they are."

Corey patted his diminishing belly. "I'm working hard to make sixty-five. Anything over one hundred is immortal in my book."

"Well, I hope Stephen has plenty of time left, because if he cashes in his chips now, he's most likely taking part of the Wells clan with him." Dick hesitated, then asked, "There's one other favor I want to ask. If anything happens to me, blame Charles if you can, and try to keep the Austra family name out of it."

"You trust him that much?"

"He didn't ask it, but one thing's clear: he's not sure what he's doing, and I have a niece to consider. If it ends bad for me, I'd at least hope her long future will be a pleasant one."

"Point made. I hope I won't have to do what I can. Did Austra explain anything about her?"

Dick slipped on his suit coat as he replied, "A little. He said I should get the whole story from her or Sylvia. I prefer to talk to Helen, and now's as good a time as any. I suppose I'll start by asking her if she'll settle for a nice healthy life to, say eighty-five, or if she's going the full route to Armaged-

don. If she tells me Armageddon will have no effect on her,
I'll know for certain what she's become."

As he drove home, Dick considered the difficulty of facing
Helen after what had occurred two nights before. Well, there
were fantasies he'd have to learn to ignore; so would she.
They began with mutual apologies, then Dick listened to
Helen relate Sylvia's tale, understanding perfectly by the end
Stephen's interest in his niece.

"Don't you have any regrets for what you're leaving?" he
asked when she'd finished. She answered with a sweet smile
to soften her "No," and because she had become so beautiful,
so healthy, so much a woman instead of a child, he accepted
her decision and tried to consider all the benefits and none of
the disturbing consequences.

Afterward Dick sat in Helen's kitchen, finishing the last of
a sandwich and coffee, anxious to return to work but not
wanting to leave until Stephen arrived. Sensing this, Helen
said, "He's next door now." She looked past him—or maybe,
he thought, through him—and added, "You can see him if
you wish."

Dick shivered. "Yes, I do. I'll be back late tonight." In the
living room, Billy and Carol were beginning their usual evening argument. Alan was stretched out in front of the TV,
already sleeping. After Dick carried the boy off to bed, he
kissed Carol, then asked Billy to leave.

"Aw, do I have ta?" Billy whined.

Dick nodded and Carol said, "Good! He's been a brat all
night!"

"Well, I have a quarter for a chocolate sundae, and I ain't
waiting to share, so there!" And with that courteous good-bye,
Billy ran past his uncle and up the hill to Becker's Grocery.

Helen followed Billy outside, leaned against the porch rail,
and watched him go, wondering if Dick should have driven
him home and had a talk with his parents. No use worrying
them, she decided. That pint-sized glutton was probably the
safest Wells of them all. The breeze touched her, the scents in
the air enticed. Here was a beautiful evening no one would
enjoy.

When Dick walked into his neighbor's apartment, he found
Stephen stretched out on his back on the sofa. He appeared

asleep until he commented, "So you're planning on working nights for a while?"

"Yeah. I want to talk to my night-shift people first. Our suspect is more visible then, right?" He could not bring himself to say a name . . . not in this place, not to Stephen. Following a long pause, Stephen rolled languidly up to lean on an elbow.

"Wise. But be careful, Richard."

Dick spoke confidently. "You're not the only one with instincts, you know. In my line of work you learn to trust them fast. Mine say I'm more useful to your brother if I'm alive. Look, I've got to go. Shouldn't you . . ." Stephen gestured for silence and closed his eyes. When he opened them, Dick continued, ". . . be next door?"

"The children were too distracting for what I am doing."

"Which is?"

"Observing the space. Helen calls it extending."

"Extending?"

"It is something we do when we hunt, but it is useful for other things as well." He paused again, his eyes dreamy. "A squad car has just parked in front of your house. The policemen are Parker and O'Reilly. They both think their assignment insane. They're being quite graphic about it."

Dick walked onto Stephen's porch, relieved to depart that lush and uncomfortable room. The car and officers were there, as Stephen had described. "Do you mind having them outside?" he asked when he'd gone back in.

Stephen shook his head. He did mind, but he understood.

"How far can you, ah . . . see?"

"For as many hours as I will do this tonight, not far. Picture a circle, the radius almost to the corner store."

"And you're doing this now while we talk?"

"No, Helen is."

Dick beat his fists once against his thighs. Nothing would ever be the same again. "And will our—"

"Charles," Stephen said, his voice sharp. "You do yourself and me a disservice by trying to be kind. And, yes, if Charles comes too near, he will sense we are watching." Dick flinched at his tone, and Stephen continued more softly. "Would you like a sketch of Charles?"

"Of course, but your secrecy . . ."

"I am as anxious as you to end this, Richard. If you run it in the papers, all I ask is that you not use any name with it. Charles is not using 'Austra,' anyway. I will work with Helen on the picture tomorrow."

"Can't you draw the picture yourself?"

"Under the circumstances I wouldn't expect my hands to function well." He stood and seemed to gain some of his usual energy. "Would you introduce me to the two in the squad car before you leave? I don't want them to confuse me with their suspect when I go to Helen's after the older distraction is also asleep." At Dick's puzzled look he added, "No, I could remain here, but in this matter I am not logical, Richard. I know I am being overprotective; I don't care."

Dick was suddenly glad he'd stopped. It had just become far easier to leave.

# II

At Becker's Grocery, Billy immersed himself in the sensual pleasure of hot fudge on chocolate ice cream. Although he didn't have enough money for nuts, Becker had supplied a few, anyway. Billy was, after all, the store's most steady customer, and he could afford to be generous.

It was sunset and the sky had taken on a deep orange hue. The street was deserted, the store—except for Billy and himself—empty. Becker decided to place the CLOSED sign out a few minutes early when he noticed the stranger standing on the stoop outside the shop door. Laying the sign next to the cash register, Becker waited to see if the man would enter.

Charles stood in the evening light a few minutes longer, watching first the Wells house, then only Helen as she sat on her porch rail, the teardrop pendant now glowing a rich green in the evening light. A few moments after she went inside, he sensed the newborn power of her mind. Forty years became yesterday as he recalled Sylvia. Instinct! Was it Helen rather than Stephen who had held him here for so long? If so, the meeting with his brother had been a tragic mistake.

He entered the store, sat on the stool next to Billy, and politely requested a glass of water. It tasted of chlorine and Lake Erie. He sipped it, watching Billy until the boy briefly stared back with wide-eyed insolence. "You seem to be enjoying that sundae," Charles commented, a touch of humor in his voice.

"Um-hum." Billy didn't bother to look up again as he replied.

"Are the chocolates in this store as good as the sundaes?"

Here was a subject to spark Billy's interest! "You bet!" He grinned for emphasis. In the dull, reddening light, the chocolate stuck to his teeth reminded Charles of more nourishing things.

Becker moved down the counter to stand in front of Charles. "Is there something else you would like?" he asked, his meaning unmistakable.

Charles replied first with an ingratiating smile, then said, "I would like to buy a pound of chocolates as a surprise for a relation of mine, one I have not yet met. Her name is Helen Wells. Perhaps you know her?"

"I do," Becker replied.

"Sure!" Billy piped up. "She's my cousin." He peered at the man, thinking he looked less like one of the Wells family than like Stephen.

"I'm related to Sylvia," Charles said, then waited with concealed expectation for a reply.

"To her grandma, huh? Well, she lives around here, too, you know?"

"Well . . . ah?"

"Billy."

"Well, Billy, if you're related to Helen, perhaps you know what kind of chocolates she prefers."

"Chocolate-covered cherries, chocolate creams, maple . . ." Billy began naming his own favorites.

"Dark-chocolate butter creams," Becker interjected, eyeing his young customer so sharply that Billy flushed and went back to devouring his sundae. "Every time Helen comes in here, she buys butter creams. It's good to see her out again and looking so well. Poor thing was so sick for a while. Now she's blooming. Why, just yesterday she walked up. I never expected . . ."

Charles prodded him on and soon knew a great deal about Helen and her parents, as well as a few facts concerning Sylvia, though not her address. He pulled out his wallet and pointed to the case of chocolates. "Would you wrap up a pound of Helen's favorites, please? And do you have a card?"

Becker handed him one, then began wrapping a gift box. When box and card sat together on the counter, Charles requested a second purchase. "Please put four chocolate creams into a bag for my delivery boy." He looked over at Billy. "You will deliver this, won't you?"

"You bet!" Billy finished his sundae quickly, then stood, anxious to earn his reward.

As Becker handed over the change, Charles's eyes were caught by the number on his arm, barely visible at the edge of the short-sleeved shirt. At his intent stare Becker looked down at the mark, then up to his customer, to the unreadable emotion etched so clearly on his face.

"I don't hide this, nor do I display it. I leave it there as a reminder that I have gained salvation because I have been through hell."

Charles stared at the shopkeeper and dropped his hands to his sides, curling his fingers into tight fists, finding it impossible to turn away.

Becker grew confused. "You're the right age. You're foreign but not German? You understand, don't you?" When Charles still stood in silence, Becker filled with compassion. "Wait outside," he said to Billy, handing the boy the bag of chocolates. Though his head did not turn, Charles's eyes followed the boy, his expression one of hopeless expectation.

Reaching across the counter, Becker gripped his customer's shoulders. His accent, barely noticeable earlier, thickened with emotion. "Many of us had great losses then. Was yours a parent? A brother or sister? If so, I regret my unintentional reminder. But the dead are gone, as those days are gone. It is best to forget."

Charles reached out a hand, one finger brushing the numbers on Becker's arm. "But you remember," he began in a voice redolent with sad music as his eyes filled with the horror of those years. Becker felt tears come to his own, but Charles shook his head, denying the sympathy, and continued in German, "It was myself. I lost myself. You never should have touched me, for I am Gvura and I roar with the dark glory of how much your people endured."

The light streaming through the store's window had turned a crimson shade that reflected from the mirror behind the counter into the eyes through which Becker was thrust viciously back to that horrible year. He was tenacious, but his aging body could not tolerate such a vivid resurrection of despair. Powerful bonds squeezed the air from his chest, and he fell forward against his tormentor. Charles dropped him gently to the counter, picked up his packages, placed the CLOSED sign in the corner window, and left, pulling the main door shut behind him.

"Here." He handed the chocolates to Billy, careful not to touch even the boy's fingertips. "Take these to Helen." His voice had become a mockery of merriment, and Billy looked at Charles's face and saw that it was a ghastly shade . . . dead white tinged by the bloody sun. He ran.

When he reached Helen's, he charged through the door and thrust the box into her hands. "These are for you," he blurted, then turned and ran from her as well. He didn't stop running until he reached the safety of home, of mother and father.

Billy's fear told Helen enough that she covered her mouth with one hand as she reached for the card with the other. Before she opened it, however, she saw Stephen standing in the doorway. "Becker's chocolates," she said in a tiny voice.

When he'd detected Billy's flight, Stephen had cursed the police car; now he was thankful it was nearby. "Wait," he said, and went to speak to the officers before returning to sit on the arm of Helen's chair. "Open it."

On one side was written in English: "When we meet, Granddaughter, I will show you eternity." On the other were words in a language Helen had heard only recently, had never seen written. Stephen translated. "Do not take her before me, Brother, for she was destined to be mine from the moment of her mother's birth. She is my salvation."

"Do you understand any of it?" Helen asked.

"A little, but I will not surrender you to the monster he has become."

—Inevitable.— He glared at her and she was thankful so much of his anger was directed elsewhere. Curious, she opened the box and shuddered at its contents.

The sirens sounded . . . a police car followed by an ambulance. Helen's fortitude dissolved into grief, and she lowered her head to the chair arm and began to sob softly; weeping for her ravished humanity, for the little she could still care.

Stephen had no sympathy for the shopkeeper he'd never met but so much for Helen . . . so weak, so young, and trying so hard to understand. His hand swept down to grab the box, to fling it against the wall. Then, cursing once in his own language, he stalked out and up the hill. By the time he reached the top, he remembered who and where he was.

A curious crowd milled around the door of Becker's Grocery, waiting for the officials to emerge. When Dick arrived in his unmarked squad car, they all turned his way. These were his neighbors and they knew his title, wondering why he had come and why his face looked so grim.

Since hearing O'Reilly's request for an ambulance at Becker's Grocery, Dick had searched for the strength that would allow him to identify his nephew's mangled body, to go and see his brother and his brother's wife, to give them the sad news . . . their only child. His eyes found Stephen's; his look accused. Parker whispered something to him, and Dick leaned against the side of the car in a relief that turned to a lesser grief as they carried out the victim.

"What was it?" Dick asked the attendant.

"Looks like a heart attack. He might make it." The accompanying gesture said Becker probably wouldn't.

Someone tapped his shoulder and Dick turned, surprised to see Corey. "I'm listening to my police radio. When anything happens near your home, expect to see me."

"Thanks. They tell me this is a heart attack but . . ." But Stephen had been there. "Let's go see if this concerns us."

When Dick walked into Helen's flat, he nearly stepped on a butter cream. "Charles—my grandfather—sent me chocolates. Billy was the delivery boy, and for that poor Mr. Becker . . ." She turned her head away and held tightly to Stephen's hand. He bent down and whispered something to her. Then, for a moment, his eyes became unfocused.

"Stanley Becker is a survivor," Dick said. "He'll surprise us all." Helen gave no indication she'd heard. Hers was more than grief, and she would not be comforted.

As Dick went to call his brother and check on Billy, Corey sat fascinated by the couple across the room from him. Stephen returned his gaze, and from the pressure of those dark eyes Corey knew his sincerity was being tested. Apparently he passed, because when Dick returned, Stephen handed him Charles's card and translated the words. "The shopkeeper, tell me what you know of him." Stephen did not ask, he interrogated.

"Stanley Becker, damn it!" Dick snapped back. "He's a person. He has a name."

Though only Dick seemed angry, the cold reply stung Corey harder. "This house and these people, Richard. For them I will be responsible. The shopkeeper, the child down the street, the various extensions of your clan, even the two officers who now sit so vulnerably in that car outside your door are not my concern. Caring is a luxury. Do not expect me to be indiscriminate."

"If he's not your concern, why are you interested in Stanley Becker?"

Stephen's voice grew frigid. "Because my brother did not feed on him, and I wish to know what Charles hoped to take."

Corey gulped. The fantastic had suddenly solidified. Dick replied, "He's German. A practicing Lutheran, but a grandmother was Jewish. If you look at his arm—"

"Enough. Charles revived those memories. He probably could not resist once he knew of them and his choice was too old." Stephen's expression was indifferent. He gave only facts.

Dick muttered through clenched teeth, "I'm going to burn that alien bastard—so help me God, I will."

Helen stiffened and Stephen commented dryly, "Isn't it wonderful how we're all working toward the same end?" He spoke to Helen. "Would you call your grandmother and explain what has occurred? Ask her if she would prefer to come here or to arrange to stay with someone else?"

As Helen left the room Corey gaped at her in open amazement. Just a few weeks ago she'd been on crutches! Though she still had the obvious bent-knee gait of polio victims, the change was incredible. He looked at Stephen. "I gave her only strength, Dr. Corey. The rest she did herself. She has determination, yes?" His expression held fierce, possessive pride. No one would come between them now . . . not Charles, who said he would; not Dick, who said nothing at all.

The phone call had been brief, and Helen returned to relay the message. "Sylvia told me, 'What possible change could occur in forty years in one of his kind? I hope he finds me.'"

Stephen shrugged. This was only what he'd expected to hear. Sylvia had been warned. That was sufficient.

While they'd been talking, Corey had been sporadically scooping up chocolates. The whole ones he returned to the box; those too mangled to eat, he placed in an empty glass that he began to carry to the kitchen. "I'll make some coffee," Helen said, following him.

In the kitchen, Helen took over while Corey watched the easy, graceful way she moved. "I've known you since you were a little girl, and I've never seen you look so beautiful."

She acknowledged the compliment with a short nod. "At last I know who I am."

"Are you sure?"

"If I were not, I would still be in a wheelchair painting pretty, meticulous watercolors. I've grown bolder in my life, as well as in my work, and I'll survive even this." She stood in the kitchen door and looked toward the living room at her uncle and Stephen. "But I look at them and sense a dangerous end."

Corey knew enough to ask, "Is that your instincts?"

"Partially; the rest only pessimism." She worked as she continued. "Stephen called New York when he returned from St. John's and told Paul Stoddard we would remain here another week or two. He said nothing new had occurred, that all was well here." She shook her head sadly. "Well . . . When the conversation was over, I asked if there was anyone else in the family who could help us. He said this matter concerned only him and me, and that no one else could be trusted at the end. I don't know what makes him think he'll be any different.

"And my uncle acts as if he barely cares about what has happened to me. I know he's preoccupied with his own children, but his reaction is so subdued, it worries me."

"I understand from Dick that Stephen frightened him, almost literally, to death."

"And I understand why he had to do that. Yet fear may have destroyed what remained of their friendship. If so, what will happen if Stephen becomes vulnerable? Will Dick decide to burn two 'alien bastards' instead of one?"

Damn! She was honest. "He's never even hinted at anything like that."

"But if the chance comes, he'll consider it; we know he will."

Nine armed men and one crazy Gypsy.

"So you see, Bob, that's why I'm concerned about them both."

Helen handed Corey a cup of instant coffee, then turned to the stove to pour another. "There's more, am I right?" he asked.

"Yes. I don't expect you to understand, but what they are planning is wrong, Bob. No matter what they do, it will end the way it must end . . . with Stephen and Charles and I . . . and there is destruction for any one who would come between us."

And the dangerous end, Corey thought. He took the coffee into the living room, and the conversation lightened until the phone rang. Stanley Becker hadn't made it.

# III

There had been no rain for two weeks, and the lawns and parkways had baked brown in the sun, while in barren places the ground cracked. It was a cruel season, one in which Frank Larson was thankful for his unusual downtown assignment . . . traveling from bar to bar, Coke to Coke, circulating the suspect's picture.

Finally one person recognized the suspect, and when he looked at the sketch, he said, growling, "Sure as shit I know him, and I hope I meet him again because if I do . . ."

Larson listened to the story Jim Simons—owner, bartender, and bouncer for the Golden Anchor Pub—told him, then called Dick, who arrived an hour later with his neighbor. At his first sight of Stephen, Simons raised his fists. "Wrong guy," Dick said nervously, moving between them. Simons might have swung, anyway, but the look Stephen gave him made him back off.

"You've met this man?" Dick asked, pointing to the picture.

Simons glanced at it, then longer at Stephen. "Yeah, I guess it ain't your friend, though. Anyway, he came in here last night and sat at one of the back tables and started ordering brandy with bottled water for chasers. Only he wasn't drinking the shots. Seems he asked the waitress what she liked and started passing them to her. After the third round I noticed she was a little woozy, so I asked her what in the hell was going on. She acted kind of confused—drunk, I guess—so I went back and asked this jerk to leave. He stuck a twenty in my pocket, grabbed his coat, and walked out the door arm in arm with the bitch. I would of decked him if the place hadn't been packed."

The corners of Dick's mouth twitched upward once. "So then what?"

"The bitch shows up for work this afternoon like nothing happened. I asked her where she'd been and she said she couldn't remember, damn drunken slut. I took a good look at her. There's no way she could of forgotten. She was a mess."

"I would like to speak to her." Stephen's tone was imperious, and Simons glared at him, then bellowed "Cynthia" in the general direction of the back room.

A moment later a petite brunette appeared. She wore a short, low-cut black uniform over which she had added a long pink gauze scarf and flimsy red overblouse. The effect was becoming (the colors reminding Dick of Judy) but clearly not what Simons expected from his help. Dick held out the picture. "Do you remember this man?"

She shook her head. "Slut," Simons muttered.

"Shut up," Dick ordered.

Simons ignored him. "Come on, Cynthia. Take off the doodads and show them what a night you had."

Cynthia's eyes darted nervously from Stephen to Dick. "Go ahead," Dick said with sympathy. "There's no need for you to be ashamed."

When Cynthia had complied, Dick moved her into the tavern's kitchen where the light was better and looked at the slashes, the bites on her neck and chest.

"And up the inside of one thigh too," Simons added with a sneer.

"And who gave her the black eye and the bruise on her cheek?" Stephen asked.

Simons swore and stomped out of the room.

Still embarrassed by what she could not remember, Cynthia covered her face with her hands. Dick noticed the bruises on her wrists. Before he could question her, Stephen reached out, his long fingers covering the marks from his brother's hands. Looking down, Dick saw similiar bruises on her ankles. Some night, all right, and for that the jerk had slugged her?

"Are you in pain?" Stephen asked, lowering her hands from her face.

"No." He had spoken with such concern, she smiled faintly. When she did, she bore a remarkable resemblance to Claudia, and Stephen inadvertently looked away. What he must do would not be pleasant.

From a corner, an old dishwasher eyed them sullenly. Dick motioned him from the room, then shut the door and leaned against it so no one could enter. If he were asked to leave he would, but Stephen only requested he turn off the lights. Dick did, and the room became dim, the only source of light a dirt-caked window facing a narrow alley. Lifting an already passive Cynthia onto the counter, Stephen moved so their faces were only a few inches apart and began.

As it had in the rectory, his voice deepened and slowed, the cadence growing more pronounced. "Though you don't recall this, last night you were with someone who subjected you to a great deal of pain. It is important that we know where you went with him."—Think of nothing, except for me. . . . The man who took you from this place looked very much like me. Look at me and remember.—

"But . . ." Her eyes, almost dark enough to be Claudia's eyes, begged him to stop.

—No. There will be no pain . . . not with me.— He raised her arms over her head and held her wrists just tightly enough to serve as a reminder. —Don't speak . . . remember.—

Dick watched, waiting for facts and hearing nothing. They stood close to each other, motionless until she began to struggle . . . useless attempts to kick, to escape, quickly fading to a weak quivering. She surrendered, leaning toward him, and in response, he moved closer, dropping her arms and pulling her to him.

This was markedly different from Moore's approach, Dick thought; more exotic and certainly quieter. The technique would earn any practicing psychologist a malpractice suit, but it was effective. Dick had been prepared to wait hours; in five minutes Stephen released the girl. If Simons had been here, he would have tried to slug somebody at the end.

"Did she remember?" Dick asked.

"She doesn't. I do." Stephen glanced appreciatively at the girl. "Thank you."

"You're welcome." She gave an automatic reply and left the kitchen quietly.

On the way to the car, Dick asked, "Why did you thank her?"

"Because we were closer than most lovers will ever hope to be, because she let me touch old wounds, and because, once past the externals, she doesn't resemble Claudia at all." Stephen sighed. "We are going to the East Park Hotel, Room 414. He was there at eleven. Checkout time is four P.M."

Dick radioed their destination, then listened as Stephen detailed the layout of the room and hallway. As they drove, Dick thought of Cynthia's passivity. She should have been hysterical or, at the very least, shown some sign of fear from the night before. It seemed unwise to mention this possible mercy to Stephen now, or even to dwell on it, so Dick turned his thoughts to the near future and steeled himself for this dangerous attempt.

Once he decided he might be able to assist in some way in "ending" his brother—the euphemism *end* being the easiest to contemplate—Stephen had considered and discarded a host of methods. The one he had discussed with Richard appeared the closest he could come to the actual act, but still he'd cautioned, "I cannot be in the same room where the deed is done, or I will kill the attacker."

Dick only blinked at the statement. "Attackers," he'd corrected. "I see no way we can act alone."

Stephen had protested, but on this Dick insisted. "If we face him in some lonely spot, maybe it could be you and me, but in the places where you tell me he will likely spend his days, we'll have rooms to empty, hallways to clear. If we act alone, there will be more witnesses and more questions, not less."

They compromised. Dick would face Charles alone with the same two policemen on each shift assisting, and if there was a need afterward, Stephen would take the facts from them. Groundless rumors, they both well knew, soon died.

The first shift pair, Walker and Larson, were sitting in their squad car near the hotel entrance when they arrived. "He's here. He knows we're here. I want to see him first." Stephen spoke woodenly.

"Can he talk you out of this?" Dick asked.

"Not anymore. I will meet you outside the room, Richard."

## IV

The door to Room 414 stood open. Stephen had been expected. He entered the thickly curtained room and looked down at his brother, stretched out on the bed. Charles's eyes were closed, his mind studying the space around him. "I see you've decided to help me, after all," he said after a moment. The tone seemed flat in spite of the inflection, a premature requiem.

Stephen was thankful Charles had chosen speech, and in their own language. Despite what he would do here today, he had longed to hear his brother's voice one final time. "You left me no choice, did you?"

"I suppose not, though I thought we'd meet next in New York. You would have an ally in Elizabeth when I came for Paul."

"I could not ask anyone in the family to assist me in this act. As it is, I can comprehend it only with extreme effort. No, Charles, it is better here."

"Good. You understand that much." Following a lengthy pause, he added in English, "They're clearing this floor, and the rooms above and below. Your friend is carrying a remarkably lethal weapon, perhaps a Thompson? Walker will never shoot me. I don't know about Larson, and as for Wells, he

does what he must." For the first time Charles looked at his
brother, his stare moving deeper than Stephen's regretful expression. "So you're to hold me, are you? I'm sure you'll
make a noble effort, little brother."

"You asked me to do this, Charles. Have you changed your
mind?" Stephen's speech quickened. He dared to hope.

Charles laughed. "Would your policeman face me if he
knew your staunch resolve, I wonder? No, little brother, I
have made my decision, but not here in this place or in this
fashion."

"What else am I to do?"

Charles gave his brother a patronizing smile and sat up.
"Sophistry does not become you, Stephen. Abandon this ridiculous attempt, face the inevitable, and bring her to me."

"So you may destroy her as you did the other?"

Stephen's eyes bored through the mocking facade, and
Charles's smile faded. "Even were I to explain, you would no
longer help me willingly. I have moved beyond your trust.
Still, I will survive this day, and I will come for her and for
you, and we three will meet death together."

"I am the stronger. If I must, I will stand between you."

"I expect you to try, but you are not stronger than fate,
Stephen. Or have your powers grown even that great?" He
laughed maliciously, mercifully, and Stephen spun and moved
toward the door. "I notice, little brother, that you haven't said
good-bye."

Charles expected and received no reply. He laughed again
and was still laughing when Dick, magnificently armed, entered his room. "How do you do," he purred amiably. "I am
Charles Austra, and if you are wise, Dick Wells, you will put
down that useless weapon and I will let you live."

Stephen emerged to find Dick waiting with Larson beside
him, Walker at his post at the end of the hall. "Go!" he ordered, then leaned against the wall and directed his mind back
to his brother, to spin the bonds and pull them tight.

As Stephen's mind toiled, Dick entered the hotel room,
faced this more than human enemy, and pushed the door shut
behind him. The lonely click of the lock marked the point of
no retreat.

". . . and I will let you live," Charles said. Fantastic, but had he no reason to assume Charles might be speaking the truth, Dick still would have believed him.

As Charles stretched and stood with lazy nonchalance, Dick saw he was taller than his brother, leaner, with a more blatantly androgynous beauty. As they studied each other, Dick thought of short, thick, hairy men wielding huge broadswords and wondered how anything so fragile could have survived such savage times. In response he felt Charles's mind rip into his. A stab of pain coursed through his body, and for an instant he fought the urge to run.

Charles laughed, the sound high and clear, fading in and out of range, the sound of fingers circling a crystal wineglass. "You are wise to fear me, Dick Wells. Now put down your weapon." His will wavering, Dick began to obey.

*What in the hell am I doing?* Dick asked himself as something screamed —No!— in his mind. So Dick leveled his gun, held his ground, and waited for the order to fire. Despite all he knew, looking at that face made him feel like a murderer. When Stephen's mind grasped his brother, Dick saw Charles's eyes widen in fear, as if he were a wild creature that had just been caged. Dick wanted to squeeze the trigger, but he waited for the order, and in that moment Charles made his move.

In the hallway, Larson had stood contemplating thoughts more intense than his own. This was not justice but an execution! You did not shoot a man as if he were some sort of animal. He had to stop this; he must! Using the passkey, he went into the room and pointed his revolver at his superior's back. Dick heard Larson enter and dared one quick glance over his shoulder. "Put that gun down," he ordered, and received no response. "Then just get the hell out of here!"

The gun did not waver, and Dick felt the sigh. —You and me.—

Stephen waged a battle of his own. He held his brother's body, protected Dick's mind. Now he struggled to grasp Larson as well, but there Charles constantly bested him. As they fought, Charles's thoughts to his brother darted between pleas for mercy and screams of defiance, though his outward expression remained confident.

Walker saw Larson disappear. He ran down the hallway

and stopped a few yards short of the door, staring at Stephen with growing horror.

Stephen's head was pressed so tightly against his chest, Walker was sure his spine should snap from the force. His hands were clenched into white-knuckled fists that beat against the wall convulsively, and blood trickled down from the corners of his mouth where his teeth had bitten into his lips.

—You're going to have two deaths on your conscience, little brother . . . no, look at you! It will be three!—

Stephen began to open his hands in what looked to Walker like a hopeful gesture until he saw the blood-covered fingers curl into claws. —Run!— Walker needed no further suggestion.

Inside, Charles, briefly freed, took a few steps toward Dick before he was pulled to a halt, and the struggle for control of Larson intensified. The gun swayed, Larson's body shuddered, and he was about to collapse when Charles moved again and steadied him.

"Stephen can control ten of you helpless creatures, but one of his own is nearly impossible for him. He won't last much longer. Shall I order my pawn to shoot you, Dick Wells, or will you call off this battle?"

"I won't. I'm here to give you only what you want. Death, Charles. I will give you death. Let Larson go and I'll finish what we've started here. I know where to hit, and I'm a crack shot. I'll try to make it painless. Let me." —Hold your brother, damn it! I'll take my chances with Larson.— He received no indication that Stephen had heard.

"I thrive on pain, Dick Wells. I don't order my pawn only because I want to take you myself." Charles's lips pulled back in an expression far from a smile, and as Dick watched in fascination, Larson crumpled and the order was given. —Fire!—

Dick tried but never managed a single shot. His gun was pushed up, then ripped from his hands and turned sideways, the clip grinding brutally into his chest until a stronger force pushed it away. Charles's face was inches from Dick's, the pupils of his eyes expanding beyond the iris . . . to become as huge as great cat's eyes in moonless darkness. Dick saw his face in those eyes and received the sudden, hideous illusion that he was seeing not his enemy but himself.

In that moment Dick was thankful for his helplessness. It would have been a struggle to stand his ground were he free. From years of occupational practice, he tapped the strength to hold an unwavering stare. His look was bold enough to be a challenge, and when he saw that Charles understood, the grim line of his lips turned up in a tight smile.

The bravery became bravado when Charles hissed, "So courageous, Dick Wells. So noble. So almost pure. Consider your position. You are my brother's only soldier in the field. I could kill you now, but it would be fast and extremely sloppy, and I seek something you alone can give. I will wait, and when next we meet, you will know my sparing you this day was no act of mercy."

Charles turned to leave, then looked back. "Stay in this room. The hall may be dangerous." Still holding the gun, Charles left, slamming the door behind him.

"Walker!" Dick rushed out of the room, but Charles and Walker had gone. Only Stephen remained, sitting with his head resting on his bent knees, his clothes and the carpet around him speckled with blood. On the wall were two red streaks marking the path of his hands as he'd slid down. The gun lay at his feet; it would never fire again. Charles had come through a hell of a lot better than this, Dick thought. There was no hope.

—You're wrong. Never once did he attempt to control me.—

Stephen looked up . . . his face! Larson staggered out of the room and Dick moved, shielding Stephen. The rumors alone would be bad enough. "What happened?" Larson asked.

—Neither will remember.—

"There's been a fight. Go find your partner. You can head back to the station, but first tell the manager to send someone to clean up this mess. Afterward the guests can return to the floor."

When they were alone, Stephen stood and went into the empty room where he leaned against the wall for support. His head throbbed, his eyes were stabbed by the pain of the sunlight leaking through the cracks in the drawn curtains. "Well,

Richard," he said, barely moving his lips, "Charles is not in the hotel, but he can't have gotten far. Shall we try again, just we two?"

Dick sank carefully into a chair. Looking at his ally, he asked incredulously, "Where do you get the strength?"

Stephen muttered a musical phrase, then repeated it in English. "I do what I must, that is survival. . . . Now, shall we continue?"

"Let him go."

"I'm glad you know when to quit for the day, Richard."

"Who said anything about the day?"

"I did." He noted that Dick stood up stiffly, breathing shallowly to avoid the pain. "Another few pounds of pressure and your ribs would have cracked. Where do *you* find the strength?" Without waiting for a reply, he pulled out his wallet and handed it to Dick. "We have two hours to check out. Please call room service and have them send up a cold bottle of spring water, no ice, and order whatever you'd like for yourself. While we're waiting, I will take a shower. I need one, yes?"

"You're a mess," Dick agreed. "It's a good thing you wore brown today."

"I expected this," Stephen replied, then went into the bathroom.

Dick stared after his neighbor, thinking that if Stephen's confidence was an act, it was the best one he'd ever seen.

After he ordered, Dick stretched out on the bed and attempted to relax, to ignore those eyes that still seemed to tear so perceptively through his defenses, exposing hidden places in his soul. He heard the water run and thought of the ruthlessness of his ally. There was, he understood, no enmity between these brothers; indeed, they were bonded so tightly, they were closer, even when apart, than he ever would become with anyone in his lifetime. How could Stephen act with such deadly calm, and worse, how much more merciless would he be if his victim were human and anonymous?

These were questions Dick would never ask, but Stephen sensed them, anyway, and ignored the temptation to answer. He turned the shower to scalding but even this did nothing to melt the sharp-edged, icy crystals coursing painfully through his veins. If only they had acted alone; if only he had blocked the entrance, if . . . if . . . if . . . if . . . In spite of their love, of their infinite years together, he cursed his brother as, leaning against the tile, he watched his blood mingle with the water and disappear down the drain.

# Chapter Twenty

## I

IT HAD BEEN eight days since Judy had given Dick her information concerning Austra . . . eight long days in which he had called for only one brief phone conversation following Moore's appointment. "Self-defense," he'd told her, the relief in his voice obvious even with their noisy connection. He promised to phone again when he had more information, but he never did. Neither Judy Preuss, the reporter—nor, more especially, the woman—could tolerate his behavior.

This morning, with her schedule clear and her patience exhausted, Judy decided to do some investigating on her own.

She began by visiting Detective Daltry. With her usual lack of formality, she strolled unannounced into his office and found him genuinely pleased to see her. "I was going to send this over to you. It's a sketch of our suspected killer."

Judy looked at it and her eyes widened. "Austra!" she whispered.

"Did you say something?"

"No, I was only surprised because it's so . . . artistic."

He chuckled, pleased to see her flustered for once. "Are you sure you weren't reacting to how damn handsome he is? Most of the females who see this sketch want a chance at rehabilitating him."

"Does he come with a name?"

He shook his head.

"Don't lie to me. I know it already."

"Then you know more than I do," Daltry retorted. "Wells

said you might think something like this. He said I should tell you to be sure."

Judy ignored her anger. None of this, after all, was Daltry's doing. "Thanks, Bill. We'll run it tomorrow morning."

She'd slipped the picture into its envelope and turned to go when Daltry stopped her, asking with uneasy hesitation, "Judy, I don't want to seem like I'm prying into your private life, but rumor has it you and Wells hit it off pretty good. Do you know what's going on in Cleveland homicide?"

"What do you mean?"

"I never said this, understand?" Judy nodded, and he continued. "The grapevine says Wells is driving his staff like a madman in a effort to find this killer, but that he had this sketch for five days before deciding to publish it. We also hear the men assigned to this case have orders to locate the suspect but not to apprehend, and if they should be threatened by him, whether he's armed or not, they are to shoot and aim for the head. Now what kind of orders are those?"

Judy understood them perfectly, but there was no way she wanted to explain the situation to Daltry, so she answered evasively, "You know how rumor exaggerates, Bill. Why not call Dick and ask what part of them are true."

After dropping off the sketch and submitting a brief story to run with it, Judy checked her notes and phoned a Cleveland number. When someone answered, she broke the connection without a word. Every piece of the puzzle had just fallen neatly into place

*II*

"Come in." Judy heard Stephen's invitation before she pressed the bell and ascended the dim stairs to the darker flat above. When she reached the landing, she saw that only the workroom was dark; the living room filled with light and color. Stephen walked forward to greet her. He reached out to shake her hand but she backed away, afraid to touch him.

Because she knew her behavior was rude, she became ruder still.

"I came to ask you what you are."

There was an instant of silence, then his laughter, musical and intentionally irritating. "If you knew enough to ask that, Miss Preuss, you also know the answer. My question to you is: How do you intend to use that knowledge?"

Although they were nearly the same height, he seemed to tower above her. It was his manner, she decided; confident, patrician. She disliked it. "I shall write about it, of course. It will be an excellent story."

"An excellent story." He mocked her triumphant tone. "At the cost of how many lives?"

"Don't accuse me," she retorted. "You aren't pure, you aren't innocent. . . ."

"Nor are we guilty. We are . . . what we are. But you would destroy me and my kind not even because of that but, rather, to further your own ambitions. Do not speak to me of innocence."

"It's my job and I have the proof."

"Do you?" he asked, and motioned for her to sit down. When she did not, he sat himself, stretching his legs out on the mahogany table. Unwillingly, she again found herself admiring the beauty of that room, and how right he looked in it. "Do you have proof?" he repeated.

"I have statements, reports . . ."

"Circumstantial evidence? A letter from an old man with Old Country ways? We, Miss Preuss, have modern lawyers, the best that can be bought, and they are well equipped to deal with slander. No one will run your story . . . no one legitimate, that is. Would you enjoy working for a tabloid? A sad waste of your talents but often the last refuge for those who know the truth."

"I was promised this story. I will be given access to the evidence."

"Gone." He held out empty palms, tilted his head, and gave her an engaging smile, as if he had just bested her at an inconsequential game of cards.

This was not the way she had planned this meeting to begin, nor the news she had come to hear. She had decided that to remain had become pointless, but Austra said in a cordial voice, "Sit down, Judy, and tell me why you are really here."

She balanced on the edge of the chair and folded her hands in her lap. Her tension gave her a stern appearance, though her words were conciliatory, "You're right. I had no reason to drive all this way for the exchange we just had. I don't know why I said any of it."

"You came about Richard, yes?"

"I did. We were working together and then he . . . stopped taking my help." She was certain Stephen knew what she meant, but still she continued with the awkward deception he was finding both antiquated and charming. "It's been days, and he hasn't called me. I'm concerned about him. This is dangerous, isn't it?"

"You know that. What is it you want from me?"

"I want you to release whatever hold you've put on him."

"Judy, he is not mine to give." He felt the sorrow she tried to hide and added, "Of course he cares for you. Stay away and allow him some small amount of peace."

She'd never suspected Dick might be protecting her. "But I want to be a part of this," she protested.

"So you can write your story?"

"No, damn it! So I can help. You know I'm no fool."

"And you are brave. You came here alone."

Uncertain if he meant this as a compliment or a threat, she overlooked the remark and persisted. "Isn't there anything I can do?"

"Judy," he wanted to say, "take the family next door and put them into your car and drive as far as you are able, and tomorrow and the next day drive some more." Yet he knew that course would be utterly wrong. All of them were needed here, as if they were characters in a play, building through the sum of their parts to a shattering climax. So instead he told her what had occurred and what they were now doing, then offered soothing advice. "Go home and wait. The end is coming soon, and I believe Richard will not be hurt by it."

This was half a lie and Judy believed none of it. She looked at the windows filtering the afternoon sunlight. "Could I see him, do you think, if I did not stay too long and left before nightfall?"

Such a small request. Still, he wanted to refuse but, thinking only of Richard, he agreed. "Go, lighten his burden for a little while, then leave for home early. The air is oppressive. There will be a storm tonight."

She started to stand but he motioned her back down. "Richard is not in his office but he'll call me soon. While you wait, would you care for something to drink? I have coffee, or perhaps you'd prefer another glass of white wine?"

She smiled. "Coffee, please."

While he was in the kitchen, Judy noticed a stack of books on the floor. Curious what sort of writing would interest Stephen, she scanned the titles. All were modern, and the selection, in a variety of languages, eclectic. At the moment Stephen appeared to be halfway through *Lord of the Flies* and, idly paging through it, she saw an inscription in a familiar hand:

> *To Stephen,*
> *The fervent agnostic on the eve of his 27th sabbatical from the willing pupil and friend who owes you more than his life, Paul.*

"Why does Paul Stoddard feel he owes you so much?" she asked Stephen when he returned to the living room.

"He doesn't, but he believes he does."

She frowned at this, and reached for her coffee.

She saw him glance at the huge wall clock above his empty worktable. "Does this waiting make you anxious?" she asked when he was seated.

"Of course."

Judy enjoyed that frank admission, the human weakness. "Is there anything I can do to help?" she asked nervously.

"Yes. Yes, there is and we might as well conclude our earlier discussion. Please stand."

She set her cup on the table and complied, her knees barely holding her. "Now walk onto the porch. Remain close to the door where you can hear me." Judy glanced at him, obviously bewildered, then did as he asked. When she was in place, he continued.

In the beginning, Judy knew, he read only her mind, but soon he began stating what would happen before it occurred, then finally, "That dark-haired girl, the brunette in the blue blouse. Watch her."

The girl Stephen described was walking down the street, talking with a friend. As they passed the house she stood still, then turned and gaped up at the porch. Her friend continued on, speaking only to the air until she noticed she was alone. "Andy! Andy, what are you doing?" she called. But the girl appeared deaf; she was moving deliberately toward Stephen's stairway.

"And I release her." The girl looked away, shook her head in bewilderment, and ran to join her friend, who stood laughing as if she were the target of some incomprehensible joke.

Judy walked inside and sank back into her chair. "How do you live with such power?" she asked.

"It is a part of what I am. I rarely use it."

"I find that impossible to understand."

"That is because you are human and I am not." The off-handed statement of what Judy already knew was unsettling. "My family has adopted many of your emotions, but love of power—the kind of power humanity so delights in wielding—is a vice we dare not claim. We use our talents sparingly and we survive. Perhaps it is best for both our species that we must hide. For this reason the greatest aid you could give me is your promise of secrecy."

His voice grew frigid as he continued. "There have been eras when those of my blood were hunted and destroyed for what we were and, more often, what we were thought to be, but those persecutions were mere inconveniences compared to the plans your modern world would have for us if it knew of our existence. I see myself employed as a weapon, a piece of mental artillery in your eternal conflicts. I speak eighteen languages fluently, I have an eidetic memory, and there are few minds I cannot force. I would be ideal in espionage, yes? The only traits lacking are the proper degree of chauvinism and the ability to self-destruct, but I am sure whichever government recruited me first would search for the means to surmount both."

"But there are laws and protection," she said, protesting.

"I have been informed we may have no rights, if that is convenient," he responded dryly. "Yet if any of my family were threatened or harmed, there would follow a slaughter such as you could barely imagine."

He ran his hand down the back of the crystal sculpture, drawing Judy's attention to it . . . the magnificent and deadly power it implied. "Charles created this, and the force it symbolizes is as much a part of me as those windows behind you. I have always had a fondness for the beautiful things—to create them, to possess them—and this has sustained me. But because of what I am, I could learn to thrive on danger and destruction. I could go through aeons, my jaws tensed, aching for the kill. I don't relish that thought. Do you?"

Judy experienced a surge of excitement when she considered what he would become, then shuddered in revulsion for what she might have done had she revealed his secret. Stephen watched her, his unruly curls highlighted by the multitude of colors filling the room, his beautiful face deliberately blank.

"No," she whispered. Convinced this was her own conclusion, she said it more loudly. She would have reached for her coffee, any motion to hide her disgrace, but her hands were shaking.

He moved to sit close to her on the edge of the dark wood table. When she looked at him, he spoke softly. "Thank you. I would not wish you for an adversary."

The distance separating them had become painfully narrow, and she felt a return of the odd vertigo she had experienced when she'd first viewed the rectory windows. She repeated her offer, and though her voice was far from calm, she thought herself daring. "I would help you if I could."

"I do not need your sacrifice."

"If it were more than that?"

"You wish to be as I am? That was to be the price for your silence? I cannot give you that power or that time. I can give you pleasure and take what I need, that is all." Judy flushed and began to turn her head away, but he held her chin, stopping the motion. As she looked at his dark eyes, she saw beyond their beauty to their sincere compassion. "Were it possible, there would be no need for you to bargain." The clock began to chime the hour. "Now go and answer the phone." As he spoke, it began to ring.

# III

Since staring into those huge, empty eyes Dick had desired nothing more keenly than to conduct the search on his own ... to seek, to corner, to kill alone. As he worked, he grew more certain that all he need do was dismiss his men and walk down any empty hallway and he would find himself once more facing his quarry. The intensity of this compulsion troubled him, and heeding Stephen's frequent warnings, he never traveled unaccompanied. Even in restaurants where he stopped for lunch or coffee, two officers always sat with him. As days passed, he grew to resent their presence, an unpleasant reminder that the hunter was also the hunted.

Home was more confining. He would wake in the dark hours, feeling intangible waves in the air. Though he believed he was politely ignored, he found himself moving at a snail's pace, fearful that should he reach out or walk too quickly, he would brush against the protective bubble surrounding him. One night he was roused from sleep by a rude mental nudge. —Your son— Stephen's thoughts said, and Dick had walked into Alan's room to find the boy trembling, crying in his sleep.

"Thank you," he'd whispered to the empty darkness. As he lay awake holding his child, the sky grew brighter. Once the sun touched the houses, seductive laughter, almost audible, tinkled like distant wind chimes.

How much did the children know? He considered this as he sat in the intimate darkness of the Lakeview Lounge and ordered a drink. Judy was to join him here. They'd arranged that on the phone. Two nights ago he'd arrived home early enough to find them awake. Helen was the one absent and reportedly asleep. Stephen sat cross-legged on the floor, looking less like the beast he'd glimpsed in the rectory than like some adult-sized Peter Pan as, with dramatic emphasis and grand gestures, he related ancient mythical tales. In front of him sat both Dick's children, listening with wide-eyed wonder, too enthralled to question why they were indoors while their friends were outside playing kick the can and catching fireflies in the thick August night.

He should be thankful for the aid, he thought as he sipped his drink, but the brief rebellion in which he now engaged gave him callous satisfaction. He had decided that he would not sit in this cool and private place with his lover while Larson and Walker stood in confusion somewhere nearby, their presence rendering even small intimacies impossible. So he ignored Stephen's advice and sat alone and exposed, searching dimly lit corners, daring a materialization of that deadly gaze and smile. But he sensed no one, and for the first time in days he felt independent and free. When Judy entered, he walked to her with a broad smile, his first genuine one in days, and led her to their table, isolated by velvet curtains on three sides.

He asked about the ominous weather, her job, and other pleasantries until the waitress brought Judy her drink. Then he looked down at his own and played with the ice in his glass as he began hesitantly, "I wanted to call you before, but there was nothing I could say. Everything I promised you is gone, and I made . . . another agreement."

"Stephen told me, and I'm relieved the evidence is gone. Now it will be impossible to submit to that terrible temptation."

The change in her attitude was so abrupt, Dick asked anxiously "What did Stephen do to you?"

She shook her head. "It wasn't like that. He only told me what would happen to him and to his family if their existence was revealed. In spite of their power, or even more because of it, I can't expose them to our world, not the way it is."

Though his promise had been forced, perhaps because of Helen it had become his decision as well. Now relief lightened his voice. "I'm glad we agree, Reporter Preuss. Now, if you will pull out your notebook, I'll tell you what you can relay to your public. . . ."

As Dick began providing Judy with details, a waitress stopped at the table on the other side of their curtain. "What can I get . . ." Her voice trailed off as her customer looked up.

"I'll have brandy, neat, and a glass of bottled water for a chaser." She rushed to fill the order and return, while her customer cocked his head toward the curtain, listening with interest to the words of the couple beside him. Tonight was the last night of his life, but he'd never anticipated as luscious a bon voyage as he'd soon receive.

". . . so he was here?"

"Yesterday. Apparently he wasn't alone. We're checking area bars. We'll find the girl . . ."

Wells certainly reached hasty conclusions. But in this instance he was correct. Actually, it had been one of the hotel's maids, and though she didn't remember, she'd been more than a pleasure. Now he had a passkey, and soon that would become a most convenient tool.

". . . and we have two unmarked squads in the neighborhood plus a plainclothesman in the lobby."

Blatantly obvious and totally futile. Still, he'd taken the precaution of using the service stairs. There was no reason to overextend when common sense would suffice. His waitress brought his drink, then stood, beaming down at him. He handed her a ten-dollar bill, letting his fingers brush deliberately across her palm. "Keep the change. What time do you leave?"

"Eleven."

His smile was suggestive, as was her response. "Watch for me. I may be back." By the time she'd reached the bar, she'd forgotten his face. Later, should he need her, she would remember. Growing impatient, he sent a subtle push to Judy.

She leaned over the table and ran her index finger in figure eights over the back of Dick's hand. "Stephen said I was supposed to 'lighten your burden.' Let's not talk shop."

But neither really had anything else to discuss, so Dick described part of his experience at St. John's. Once they'd finished their drinks, they sat silently and stared at each other until Judy chuckled at their clumsiness. "How many hours have you worked in the last week?" she asked.

"A hundred, maybe more."

"Don't you think you deserve an afternoon off?" Her mouth turned upward with the hint of a smile, her look already intimate. Rarely had she felt so aroused or so bold.

Dick had the money for a room, but the squad and plainclothesman would be awkward. "I'll take care of the room while you order us another round," Judy suggested.

"Pay for it now," he said, slipping her a twenty, "and

there'll be no questions to answer when we leave." Neither
considered how quickly they had reached their decision to
abandon their afternoon plans. They were too preoccupied
with each other.

The drinks arrived a moment before Judy returned. "Mr.
and Mrs. Paul Stoddard have been promised a cool, comfortable night in Room 315. It's past check-in-time. Shall I take
up our glasses and wait for you?"

"Please. I have to make the necessary excuses or my men
will conduct a room-to-room search." As Dick watched her
leave, he was fascinated by her legs moving beneath the
loose-fitting slacks. Provocative. Seductive. For an instant he
frowned, then chuckled with a sound so soft and deep, only he
and his hunter could hear. It's the woman, he thought, it has to
be!

The room lived up to the manager's effusive description
. . . cool, comfortable, and undeniably plush. Entering through
the long, narrow hallway between the bath and closet, Judy
set her oversize purse and the glasses on the long, white,
provincial-style credenza, then reached down and slipped off
her socks and shoes and wiggled her toes in the thick green
carpet. Though she'd been tempted, she had never taken an
afternoon off from work to be with a lover, and the wicked-
ness of it aroused her.

Dick arrived a quarter of an hour later. "I've never had
such fun telling lies," he confessed as he glanced around the
room, then looked longer and more appreciatively at the
woman standing in the middle of it. She kissed him and her
hair smelled fragrant, the skin on her neck cool and smooth
under his fingers.

When she moved away from him, he looked down at himself apologetically, then bowed with excessive politeness.
"Lady Judy, would you excuse me, please? I must shower. It's
seems like it's been days."

She motioned regally in the direction of the bathroom and
laughed. "Then by all means go. Besides, I have to call work
and make up lies of my own, you know."

In a neighboring room, also cool and comfortable and pre-
sumably unreserved, Charles stretched his long legs out on the

bare mattress, leaned against the connecting wall, and waited. While he eavesdropped on Judy's conversation with her office, a wry smile played on his lips as he anticipated the upcoming hours with unrestrained delight. The slaughter would no longer be necessary. Instead he'd have the man... the woman too. He'd have them both together.

After completing her call, Judy hung the do-not-disturb sign on the door and, as an added precaution against inquiring maids, attached the chain. Thoughts of the deeds that had tempted her earlier that afternoon returned, and she found that even the avoidance of them made her feel unusually lascivious. She slipped off her slacks and rummaged in the bottom of her cluttered handbag until she found the small bottle of Shalimar, her one feminine affectation while she was working. She sprayed herself lightly, then turned back the covers and sat on the edge of the bed, playing with a strand of hair and meditating on the near future with single-minded sensuality.

When Dick reappeared, wrapped in a towel, she greeted him with a wolf whistle and a sultry look. Judy liked watching his body as much as she loved being near him. Dick didn't know it yet, but he was trapped... possibly for life. She held out her arms. "Come here, Detective Wells, we're about to commit a misdemeanor. Unless you'd prefer to try for a felony?"

"I'll try whatever you like, so long as you don't report it." He dropped the damp towel over the back of a chair, sat on the bed, and hugged her. "Even with all the work and worry, I missed you. Eight days is seven too long." As he kissed her, he undid the buttons up the back of her blouse and slipped it off. They stretched out under the sheet, too occupied to hear the faint click of the lock and the door opening.

Charles reached one hand inside, gripping the chain, twisting it, pushing slowly inward until it snapped with one small sound. Closing the door, he leaned against the hallway wall and considered possible introductions. He decided quickly, and went to lean against the credenza and wait, silent as a shadow, to be noticed.

Dick saw Charles first. Judy felt him tense as he stared at a point beyond her. She began to turn, to follow his eyes when he whispered, "We're not alone," and his tone told her who shared their privacy. She rolled over with exaggerated care, as if their visitor was a poisonous snake preparing to strike, then gazed at Charles with emotions that traveled with startling velocity from fear to curiosity to fascination.

The clothes he wore were tailored and, though expensive, bought off the rack, the lengths inadequate for his long-limbed body. Like his brother, he had a preference for black, and the cotton shirt contrasted sharply with his pale, youthful face. He appeared to Judy a gangling, innocent boy thrust into an ancient, vile role, miserable at the miscasting. Inexplicably, she longed to comfort him.

"I inspire that, Judy," he responded in a silken voice, "though I've never understood why. Comfort, however, is not what I intend to take."

Dick's eyes rested on the revolver sitting on the chair next to the bathroom. Noticing his interest, Charles pulled it from the holster and held it out. "Would you like it?"

. . . do not threaten him . . .

It occurred to Dick that he'd already made that mistake four days ago as he reluctantly replied, "No . . . no, leave it," then demanded, "What do you want?"

"I wish to feed . . . first on the woman, then, when you are ready, on you."

As Judy shuddered and pressed closer to him, Dick succeeded in ignoring his fear and his anger as he watched Charles with icy calm and guarded thoughts.

Charles bowed his head in a gesture of respect. "You are wise, Dick Wells. True bravery is not suicidal. If you do not attack me, I will let you both live. Then you can remember all I do here."

Judy had never heard a voice like his . . . so soft, so musical, yet not weak or effeminate but consummately male. She had thought Stephen handsome, but Charles, now engaging the complete measure of his seductive powers, intoxicated. Lowering her eyes, Judy vowed not to look at Charles again, but her resolve was useless. Her will had been captured.

Charles smiled, a serpent's smile of anticipation. "You wish for equality, Judy Preuss, yet in your fantasies you submit. You strive for independence, yet you worship power. Very well, tonight you shall worship me."

The words crawled through her body, plucking nerves that responded with deep, sonorous vibrations. "No," she begged, her voice caught between a whisper and a sob, and pressed her legs together as if she were about to be violated.

"Precisely . . . precisely that." Picking up the revolver, Charles tossed it behind Dick. "If you do not attack me, I will let you both live," he repeated, and added, "Your children will keep their father." He slid closer to the bed and, in a gesture seen only as movement, flung off their sheet leaving the gun barrel pressed against Dick's side, a cold insistent reminder of what he was. "Now let her go."

Dick's only response was to hold Judy more protectively. "It's me you want, isn't it?" he asked.

A ravenous gleam enhanced the beauty of Charles's face. "Of course, though not in the usual sense. I shall feed on what you will feel this night . . . and on what I shall make you feel."

The implication was impossible to avoid; nonetheless Dick replied, "Let Judy go and I will not struggle with you."

The answer began with taunting laughter. "I see you do not understand, Dick Wells. I will take you as an adversary, not a martyr. Were I to spare this woman, you would attempt to meet your bargain, and that would be a paltry meal compared to the feast I anticipate consuming during the hours we shall spend together. Besides, I would not wish to deprive you, or ultimately myself, of your possessiveness, your jealousy, and your devasted sense of masculine duty." His eyes flickered over Judy's body. "And I would not wish to deprive myself of this beautiful beginning to what is hopefully my final self-indulgence. Now, Dick Wells, stop trying to be noble and release her." When Dick refused to move, Charles added, "It's true. I never asked you to obey . . . but you will."

He pierced Judy with her own longing. "You bargained with my brother for eternity. He was a fool not to lie." Judy looked up at Dick and nodded before turning her head away in shame. "I wish I could give you that life, Judy Preuss. You would be a magnificent addition to the family . . . strong and beautiful and realistic. You know your desires and when to submit to them. Your lover is only prolonging a useless struggle. Shall we show him? Shall you tell us now what you wish done to you?"

Judy's fantasies and needs became as real as the room, the

bed, the arms holding her. Her eyes rested on Dick's face as if the sight of it could block out the images ravishing her mind. It didn't. Instead her passion rocked her lover like an ocean wave. He thought he'd known her, had satisfied her. Perhaps he had, but not like this. He stared down at her body, glowing with the first flush of excitement, her stomach hard, her legs tensed. He felt desire and despair. He wanted her.

Charles spoke. "I demand only your honesty, Judy. Do you desire me?"

"Yes." The word was torn from her throat, and tears came to her eyes.

His voice embraced her. "And what may I do to you?"

"Anything." This reply came quick and strong. She had surrendered. Squeezing Dick's hand, she pleaded, "Let me go, love, otherwise he'll—" She broke off, suddenly occupied only with resisting the urge to begin clawing at Dick's arms. "Please," she begged both of them.

Feeling her struggle made Dick forget his weapon. Instead he wanted to use both hands to tear Charles into small, insignificant pieces. Had Judy not been the cause of this fury, he might have tried and, he was certain, died in the attempt. But she lay beside him and he believed Charles would keep his promise. With deceptive tenderness, he replied, "I understand. I was there for a little while, remember?"

"Yes, be thankful my little brother prepared you well. Now release her." Dick obeyed, and Judy scrambled to her feet, relieved to stand free, if only for a moment, from both of them.

Charles stared at her, his eyes cold, dark pools, and as Judy fell into them, she shivered. "Sad that you are so cold but please finish undressing. I wish to see all I shall possess. Then I will warm you."

As his lover reached back to unhook her bra, Dick considered there were worse things than death, and he was seeing one now. His hand inched slowly toward his revolver, but when he finally gripped it, he pointed it toward the window. Before he could squeeze the trigger, however, the gun was wrenched from his hand and flung across the room to strike the wall. Dick hoped it would discharge on impact but instead it fell silently to the floor.

"Luck is not with you, Dick Wells. I suppose I should take

offense but I can afford to be magnanimous. I suggest you try
to enjoy yourself." He turned his attention once more to Judy.
"I certainly shall."

As desire flowed between them, Judy longed to run to him.
Ashamed of her response, she moved as far from him as possible to stand with her hands behind her, her palms spread flat
against the wall, her head thrown back as she refused to meet
his eyes.

"An interesting coincidence," Charles commented to Dick.
"She is standing in the same manner as our children when they
give up on a fight. I think, though, she means something else.
But I will not go to her. She must come to me."

He pressed his palm against his teeth and tore at it sav-
agely, then sucked. As he extended his arm to her, the blood
pooled in his cupped hand. "Come to me, Judy." She shuddered but did not obey. —Look at me!— Her eyes sought his
in amazement. "Now come to me." His voice embraced her
and she walked forward and bowed her head over his hand.

—Kneel.— And she knelt.

Words that had been so terrible when Dick first heard them
returned now to comfort him. —When I will you to feel a
thing . . . — Dick looked from Judy to Charles, whose rapacious eyes locked with his, and in their depths were promises
Dick dared not consider.

Charles's hand pressed up on Judy's chin, and when she
rose to her feet, he pulled her against him and kissed her with
an insistent passion that swelled with her response into something more savage. His fingers moved down her back, the
hard nails lightly scratching, not intending to arouse, not yet,
but only to hint of acts to follow.

As he struggled to remain helpless a foolish hope came to
Dick. In response, Charles lifted his arms and undid the buttons of his shirt cuffs. Judy unfastened the rest with a willing-
ness Dick tried to view as merciful.

They sank together to the carpet, and soon Dick heard a
low inviting moan. At that pathetically familiar sound, he
tried belatedly to attack and found his body had deserted him.
All that would obey were his hands and he pressed them
against the mattress frantically, trying to force some other part
to respond.

—Desire, particularly under these circumstances, is a savory first course, but you, Dick Wells, will be the remainder of the feast. During our time together you will find I am an excellent cook.—

Dick watched. When he tried to look away, he *felt*. It was better to watch.

Miles away, Stephen stood on his porch, his clothes and hair whipping in the rising wind. Richard was not due to call until eight-thirty, but by that time the phones would undoubtedly be out. He had already called Richard's office and been informed he'd gone off duty. Leaving a message, Stephen attempted to reach Corey, first at his office and then at home, but no one answered in either place.

He narrowed his eyes as the gale lifted the dust from the streets. Was there a genuine reason for this anxiety, this vague dread that gripped him as he watched the clouds create an early night? It was six-thirty. If the phone lines went down, this was one time he would welcome that ridiculous squad car with its police radio.

Patrolmen Frank Parker and John O'Reilly had returned to the station and were preparing to go to their accustomed seven P.M. assignment when they heard the emergency announcement. There were more pressing needs in the city tonight than watching over a small group of people at the Wells home. On the south side, power lines were down, phone lines were severed everywhere, and some low-lying roads were already flooding. In addition, two more storm systems were building in fury over the lake, awaiting their destructive turns.

"Ned Beaumont's going to have to wait," Parker grumbled. "We're actually working tonight."

During this puzzling assignment they had alternated . . . one reading aloud with the aid of a flashlight while the other watched the house. It had been the perfect arrangement and they would have ended their first book tonight if the weather hadn't intervened.

"We'll radio him later," O'Reilly suggested. "Maybe he can pull us off whatever wet duty we'll be doing."

"Fat chance! They've only been humoring him, anyway. He'll never get a squad tonight. Even Dick Wells's alien monster is no match for a Lake Erie northeaster." Parker burst out

laughing at his mention of what had become the department's
most popular joke.

As Parker dug around in his cluttered locker seeking his
boots, O'Reilly slipped the slim paperback into his pocket and
patted it. "It never hurts to try, and Wells still has plenty of
clout around here."

# IV

Charles dropped her long after she stopped responding,
then paced silently to the window to pull open the heavy
drapes. Outside, the rain pounded wildly against the glass,
obscuring the view of the clouds.

Dick's eyes traveled slowly . . . first to Judy, unconscious
and probably in shock, then to Charles, hard and beautiful as a
classic statue, his skin marble-white in the colorless flashes of
light.

Feeling Dick's gaze on him, Charles turned and drifted, to
stand beside the bed. Reaching over to the night table, he
poured a glass of water from a pitcher that somehow had become filled. The flowing liquid sparkled in the flame of a
single candle, another mysterious addition to the room.

Dick closed his eyes and concentrated and finally remembered the lights going out, the knocking at the door. How
uselessly he had struggled for that slim hope while Judy had
stretched and rolled over, their eyes meeting briefly before
hers moved past him as if he were another piece of the furniture. And then there was nothing until his eyes had opened to
focus despondently on the couple twining in the soft light. As
he had watched, the whisper began in his mind . . . name upon
name. Some were familiar, one he knew well.

—What do you want from me . . . my admiration, my
pity?—

—Am I in danger of receiving either now? No, Dick Wells,
I just want one human being to hear them all . . . to know who
I was, someone who won't care.—

The bed moved, there was warmth beside him. Called back

from his sad contemplation, Dick saw his captor watching him thoughtfully. "Would you like some water?"

—No.— Once he accepted his captivity, Dick had tried to cry for help so often that Charles had taken speech from him.

—Would you like to talk? We can converse in this manner. Actually you've gotten quite good at it.— The corners of his mouth twisted upward. —Quite good.—

—No.— Dick clenched his teeth and tested his invisible bonds, then waited stoically for whatever torment would follow.

—As you wish.— Charles took one last sip of water, then, setting down his glass, he brushed his fingers over Dick's temples. His touch was electric and Dick tried to flinch, to pull away. Though his nerves responded, his muscles were chained.

—Wait!— The hands moved away. —How can you do this?—

—Easily.— The laugh had the sound of cold music. It filled the room, Dick's mind. "You beg for time, Dick Wells, but I will answer you. I do this the way your children pull the wings off butterflies or set fire to cats, the way your adults destroy one another with only feigned regret . . . your existence means nothing to me, and in my years I have grown callous as humanity." His fingers, their touch feather-light, stroked the length of Dick's chin, then moved to his neck. As Stephen had done, Charles sought out and pressed against the strongest pulse points, sharp nails marking the spots before descending.

—You're lying. If you were as cold as you attempt to be, you . . . —

—Perceptive! Particularly now.— "I grow hungry for you but I will tell you the other half of the truth. In those quiet times when the beast inside me is not clawing at my guts, I feel fear. Tonight you will hold that fear from me and I will take not pleasure, though I promise there will be pleasure here, but your shame and your rage and your pain. I shall devour your humanity, and it will give me that special sustenance I need to do what I must do this night. Pray, Dick Wells, that you give me enough."

Charles's hands moved down Dick's arms to rest on his open palms. In response, Dick gripped those hands in a hopeless final effort to stop Charles from touching him. As Charles returned the pressure he lowered his head to Dick's shoulder and Dick swallowed hard, fighting waves of emotion more horrible than any he'd imagined . . . not dread, but desire. —I can't even move.— The thought brought relief.

. . . and when I will you to do a thing, you will do it . . . hours, Richard, hours . . .

A sob caught in Dick's throat. —Stephen! God, I wish you were here now.—

Charles shook with quiet laughter. —I've called on both on occasion. Stephen, I assure you, is the more invasive. Call him the way we are speaking now. Come, I will help you and we will reach him together, but just once . . . —

His hands squeezed to the edge of pain. His lips brushed his captive's neck and for a moment the response brought only disgust, then a sudden, vivid revelation of how far they would descend.

—Stephen!!—

—Stephen . . . ?—

"Just once. Later we will call to him again, later he will share in all that you feel; but now we shall become far too busy to be concerned about whether he heard us or not." His captor's voice had acquired a more definite lilt. As he spoke, he released Dick's hands and moved to lay sideways at the opposite end of the bed. "Let us start with bravery, Dick Wells . . ." And within the merciless silence of visions, Dick's ecstasy, his nightmare began.

# Chapter Twenty-One

## I

STEPHEN EXPECTED THE CRY long before he heard it. Instinct was not needed when logic could apply. He'd already attempted to reach Dick through the nearest police call box and found it as unresponsive as the private phone lines. Out of curiosity he tried starting the BelAir but, as expected, the wires were soaked. Muttering self-directed oaths, he returned to Helen's and resumed guard. Within minutes the scream shook him and he retreated. As his eyes focused, he saw Helen looking at him, her expression mirroring his own.

"You sensed it?"

"When it reached you. Charles and my uncle are together, aren't they?"

"And Judy as well." His stupidity astonished him. "How far is Dr. Corey's house?"

"About five miles; shorter if you cut through the park."

"Good. I'll risk leaving you that little while." She gave him directions while he slipped off his shirt and shoes.

For the brief time Helen remained alone, she sat in the darkness and considered this struggle. That morning she had begged Stephen to let Charles come to her and he'd refused. "I did not stay to watch you and my uncle attempt the impossible," she'd retorted with what she believed was righteous anger. "I stayed because I know Charles and I must meet. Isn't it better we meet here and now, rather than wait for the sorrow to come as we bury those who will die because we have failed to trust?"

His reply had been so calm as to be inconsiderate. "You see only the meeting. I sense its outcome and I will not yield. I am tenacious, Helen. I have fought worse battles and won."

"With your own kind? Consider, Stephen, that you are evenly matched and your hands are tied." She stopped abruptly; she was his main constraint.

Too weary to be angry, he had lain back on the dark cushions and closed his eyes as the rainbows colored his face. "You need not remind me of what I already know."

"Someone will die," she'd wanted to repeat, but stopped the words because he knew that. She did not understand how such a terrible fact could make so little difference. Instead she'd pulled away and prepared to leave. Though he did not speak, he'd opened his eyes to follow the motion of her hands and arms and body as she began to dress. Conscious of his gaze, she turned and saw his expression of passionate intensity . . . hunger devoid of love or desire. He had never appeared so alien to her as in that moment when she held her breath and returned freely to him. Later, when her lips moved to his neck to consummate that final act, he stopped her. "I have nothing to give you . . . nothing," he whispered, and pulled her head down to his chest, stroking her hair in a silent plea for understanding.

Her contemplation ended as she heard Alan cry out in his sleep. She went to him and gently patted his shoulders until he woke. "I saw Pa and Judy . . ."

"It's just a dream," she lied. "Here, I'll lay next to you for a little while." As she rubbed the boy's back and listened to the storm, her mind wandered, seeking Charles, asking him to come. But the night was empty, and, tapping all she had learned, she built a wall around her thoughts.

The weather made a good excuse. Corey's two youngest daughters were terrified of storms, and his wife catered to their fear. When the lights went out, everyone else headed for the basement while Corey, armed with a lantern and a Zane Grey novel, sought the welcome solitude of the garage and the police radio in his car. As he listened through the static for news of Dick, he stretched out and began to read.

The wind, the hard rain, and the branches beating on the

roof kept Corey from hearing the pounding on his garage door until the lock was ruined and the door lifted. Before he had time to react, Stephen stuck his head in the car window, his hair dripping water onto the seat. "You have to find Richard; he's with my brother."

"You're sure?"

"Dr. Corey, I would not be here if I weren't," Stephen snapped. "I don't know where he is, but Judy is with them. Find them and don't go alone."

Corey was about to ask another question but Stephen was gone.

Corey drove his own car the way he used to drive squad cars. Twice he hit puddles that stalled his engine, and he had to pull over and wait for the heat under the hood to dry the wires. Afterward he was more careful, and it took him nearly an hour, often driving half blind, to reach the downtown station. He found it nearly deserted, two lonely dispatchers sitting behind the huge front desk.

He checked the records and noted that Dick's last call had come from the Lakeview. If he'd stayed there with Judy, Austra might be wrong about the danger, though Corey doubted it. But this could be a scandalous situation and he hoped his friends would be able to appreciate his discretion.

He began with a multitude of time-consuming lies, finally getting Parker and O'Reilly released from traffic duty. Afterward it had taken the two officers the better part of another hour to travel back downtown. When he'd heard they'd been reassigned, O'Reilly began to grumble. "It's nearly midnight and we were due to punch out at eleven."

In exasperation, Corey bellowed back a reply. "O'Reilly, if I hadn't gotten you pulled off traffic, you'd still be outside up to your balls in water praying a wire wouldn't fall close enough to fry your progeny. Now say thank you and shut up!"

Corey insisted on taking the wheel and soon found police cars suffered the same ills as private vehicles. He finally slid over and let O'Reilly drive. The car was O'Reilly's baby, and he nursed her along, not quickly but constantly, while Corey explained that Dick might be in serious trouble. He was deliberately vague as to why.

# II

... it must have been the experience, centuries of experience, that made him know just how to touch, to stroke ... when to be soft, to be hard ... perfect, so damned perfect ... no one, no one had ever ...

Tonight, the laughter, the same mocking laughter he'd heard so often, brought him back from the dream. When his vision returned, he saw Charles sitting cross-legged at the foot of the bed, his elbows on his knees, his head resting on his cupped hands. Charles flashed him an exquisite smile—It's close to eleven. You're surviving remarkably well.—

Dick thought of the corpsman, the hours.

"That was vengeance, Austra vengeance ... time-consuming but pure like my brother. He touched only terror, but tonight you will learn the complete manner of stripping a man."

Dick hardly listened as he stared at Charles with dry, half-open eyes. Something about his own body puzzled him, and incredulously, he understood.—You never ... !—

More laughter.—Disappointed? No, of course not.— He raised his arms over his head and arched his back, a cat's stretch Dick's aching shoulders envied.—I've been touching your mind; becoming educated, so to speak, but it is late and I've lost patience. You have a powerful will, Dick Wells, and until you submit, the most important ingredient is missing.—

Too exhausted to be baited any longer, Dick looked out the window at the wild night, wondering what could be left that he hadn't given already. They'd run the gamut—bravery, nobility, sorrow, fear—and as each was taken, the others expanded to fill the void in his soul. Like the day at the rectory, what remained lay benign as planted bombs waiting for a signal to detonate. He sat vacantly staring, and the invisible bonds loosened. Tentatively, he tried to lift his arms, and though they seemed unnaturally heavy, they responded. Dick rested his head on bent knees and let his shoulders roll forward, reveling in even this small relief. Speech was still impossible, he found, when he tried to ask the obvious question.

"I want nothing less than complete surrender. When I take you, there will be no restraint, and so I will taste the purity of self-disgust . . . soon, very soon." He gripped Dick's shoulders, powerful fingers pressing where the muscles met the spine, kneading hard with a soothing circular motion.

A thought, almost humorous, emerged.—Getting me ready for the next round?—

"Precisely."

—You're insane.—

Dick intended these words as something between an expletive and the obvious truth, but Charles responded seriously. Pointing beyond the window, he asked, "How many people have I killed in the last three months? How many could I have killed? No, Dick Wells, I am not insane, though I fear I soon will be. Consider me insane on this violent night . . . an omnipotent, sentient carnivore slipping silently from room to room, turning this hotel into a blood-soaked mausoleum . . . and then tomorrow night . . . and the next? And if I did, who would stop me, Dick Wells. You?

"Stephen understands how dangerous I would become . . . how easily I would betray the precious Austra secret once I move beyond caring. The likely betrayal is the primary reason he dares the impossible with this frigid resolve, but he has been correct all along. We value our own lives too greatly; no mere act of will can tap his deadly power."

—No hope.—Even sorrow had dulled.

"Ah! But there is, and so we return to you and me, Dick Wells, and to what I shall take." Charles moved to crouch beside Judy, his fingers brushing her neck.

—She'll be all right, won't she?—He felt some interest, little concern.

Charles stood with exquisite grace, the flashes of lightning accentuating the angular lines of his face, his ancient, pristine body . . . the voracious beast above its prey. His reply was deliberate, the words brutally arousing. "I promised you that, didn't I?" He spread his arms out in a languid move. "The town is paralyzed. It's a perfect night to pay my respects to your family. I promised Alan something, too, remem—"

The bomb exploded with silent rage as Dick sprang with all

the force of his stolen emotions. But before the fight began, it was over. When his hands were inches from his foe, Dick's arms were caught, pulled up, and wrenched tight in Charles's incredible reach. His feet left the floor, but before he could raise a knee for a satisfying hit, Charles slammed him crosswise on the bed, holding his extended arms over the side and pressing his back tightly against the mattress. Dick waited to feel the tendons snap as his shoulders dislocated, but Charles only held him, letting him push every muscle to its limit, trying to break free. Dick longed to kill, but that was impossible, so he begged instead, tears blinding him as he whispered, "Use me. Kill me. Do whatever you want with me, but leave them, leave them alone!"

"You've achieved it, Dick Wells! Though you've broken our agreement, you've attained perfection. We will begin now."

He felt something important, something precious, wrenched out of him then. As his vision cleared, he saw the face so insistently seductive, hovering above him, tantalizing with its distance. Had his hands been free, Dick was no longer certain how he would have moved them, save that he longed to touch. The only choice left was the freedom to surrender. —My family . . . promise me—he pleaded faintly one final time.

The face moved lower until he saw only eyes, so beautifully vivid in the oddly scented darkness, and there was no sound but the penetrating purity of thought.—You will give and I will take . . . no promises save you and I.—

As Dick prepared for the weight and visions that never came, he was acutely aware of the position of his body . . . how his head was bent, his neck stretched; the rest taut, exposed, waiting. The first soft touch seared more cruelly than the four hard nails that followed, scoring him from thigh to shoulder. His mind roared one final protest and received no reply. There were no words, no thoughts, no terms to this surrender.

He tried to count the lightning flashes, to think of nothing else. He managed five before his body called him back to that bed, to his tormentor, his lover.

. . . And in the apartment below his own, the one who had promised to protect howled with him and for him, knowing that now he stood alone and the battle had barely begun. . . .

With Stephen, there had been only hints, but now, as his will was swept away by desire amplified, refined, and made into something more brazenly pure, he understood.

"—Kiss me . . . yes! . . . here and here, more . . . and now, take me—" The music surrounded him and moved in him as the suggestion grew into a potent, beating demand. "—Take . . . take . . . take . . . —" until he obeyed, moving slowly to fulfillment and, on the edge of release, flung aside, rearranged, and entered.

For one terrible moment, he stood away from his body, watching them both. But he did not struggle against the one pressing behind him, did not push away the hand that cupped him, aroused him, then held him back. Instead, with a cry of passion, he moved his hands back freely to pleasure. With this final surrender, an arm wrapped around his mouth and chin, raising his head to press against his lover's shoulder. His spine was arched at an impossible angle, and in protest at the pain, he bit down, tasting the blood, too rich, flowing thick as cold honey to fill his mouth. As he forced his head higher and spat, moist lips kissed his neck, then teeth pressed down, striking something vital.

—This is how animals couple; without tenderness or mercy.—

—Yes! And this is how I take you. Here is our common bond, the only place we truly meet. Give me how you feel, my love, now that your humanity has been peeled away and there is only the beast . . . give it to me!—And they traveled toward a shared fulfillment, violent as the storm.

He convulsed, quick, silent spasms that brought no release from the arms that held him. "—Again . . . —" the melody persisted. "—Again . . . —" And as they moved, his being drained.

# III

The opulent lobby of the Lakeview Hotel glowed softly in candlelight that quivered and threatened to die as Corey, flanked by Parker and O'Reilly, walked through the door. Motioning to the officers to wait at the entrance, Corey marched up to the desk. "I'm looking for a couple who are checked in here."

Placing aside a magazine he had been attempting to read in the unsteady light, the clerk looked at Corey in irritation. He should have been relieved at eleven, but no help had arrived, and although he had become resigned to spending the night there, he needed no additional annoyance. Wearily, he opened the register and, adjusting his glasses, asked the name.

"They're not using their own. Let me see the book." Corey's tone allowed no protest, and the clerk handed it over.

Corey had hoped to recognized Dick's writing but none of the signatures looked familiar, so it must have been Judy who registered. When he gave Judy's description, the clerk looked at him stupidly and shrugged. "I came on at five. What time did the party check in?"

Dick had called the station at four-fifteen. Corey swore and the clerk eyed him with distaste. "All right, then," Corey growled, "who was the first person to register after you came on?"

The clerk pointed to a name and Corey counted eighteen signatures on the list ahead of it. "What time is check-in?"

"Two. All these people signed in after two."

"Can you tell me which are regular customers?"

The clerk could eliminate only one name. At Corey's next suggestion, he opened the register and pulled out personal checks that had been used to pay for the rooms, canceling five more from the list. "Lots of people pay cash, don't they?" Corey mumbled. Misinterpreting this as a slur on the lofty reputation of the Lakeview, the clerk glared.

Irritation only sharpened Corey's logic. "Do you keep records of out-of-town calls made through your switchboard?" he asked.

The clerk held out his arms, then flopped them down to his sides in a hopeless gesture. "The day operator is gone. Her replacement never came in. I don't know where they keep the log. I was writing notes for long-distance calls until the phones went out."

Corey leaned across the counter, forcing the clerk to take a hasty step backward. "Now listen to me, you asinine incom-

petent! You go and find that log because if you don't, I'm
going to visit the twelve remaining names on that list, and I'm
sure your guests will not appreciate the intrusion. Wait a second . . ." He walked over to O'Reilly, grabbed his flashlight,
and thrust it into the clerk's hand. "No use setting fire to the
place with that damned candle. Now go!"

In a few minutes the clerk returned with a two-page list
containing not only the calls and room numbers but the times
the calls had been made. There were three to Sandusky but
only one in the late afternoon. "Who's in Room 315?"

The clerk ran a finger down the register. "A Mr. and Mrs.
Paul Stoddard."

The name sounded familiar . . . he'd been mentioned in
Judy's article—he had something to do with AustraGlass!
"Give me a key."

Bristling, the clerk refused. "These rooms are private. You
can't just barge in—"

"I can have my associates break down the door. Do you
want to take responsibility for that?"

"No. You'll knock first, won't you?"

When Corey nodded, the clerk sighed with relief and
handed over the key and flashlight. His concern returned,
however, when he heard Corey tell Parker and O'Reilly, "Wait
fifteen minutes. If I'm not back, both of you come to that
room. Be prepared to shoot."

The clerk's face reddened. "Now see here! There were police swarming like vermin all over this hotel today. This is the
most respected hotel in the city, and you are not—"

"I hope we are not, either," Corey snapped as he walked
away.

They moved as one in that slow, warm, comfortable
whirlpool . . . around and around . . . Judy was gone . . . his
soul was gone . . . there was only his body, the body holding
his . . . two hearts crowding one chest, beating united . . . the
cadence slowing . . . descending . . .

A quicker knocking broke their rhythm.—I think we have a
visitor.—Three more knocks, louder.—Love, is this a friend
of yours? . . . Ah, Corey, yes?—

—No.—The thought was nebulous, a negation of too many
things.

—We need him safely away tonight, we need everyone away . . . I have calls, remember?—

—Nonono . . . —

—I promise everyone in this room shall live.—

Three more raps, their usual code, then, "Partner, are you in there?"

The body beside Dick departed and he felt an odd twinge of loneliness. And, where Charles no longer touched, incredibly cold.

"Oh, hell! Can't I take just one night off? This had better be important, Cor."

Corey felt like a total fool. "I'm sorry. Stephen said . . ."

"Damn that alien bastard!"—Technically correct, Dick Wells, but the intent was exceedingly poor.—"Listen, who's here with you?"

"O'Reilly and Parker. They're downstairs. I—" Corey cut off the sentence and, as best he could, the thought, amazed it had taken him so long to comprehend Stephen had been right.

"Let them wait. Just a second. I'll be right there."

The door swung open and, after Corey entered, closed behind him. "How do you do, Dr. Corey? I understand you've been interested in meeting me. I'm Charles Austra."

Corey eyed him with wary interest and brushed past him into the room where his eyes rested on Judy, then, beyond her, on Dick. His attention returned to the body on the carpet. "Is she alive?"

"Of course." Corey moved toward her but Charles stepped between them. "You'll have to trust me. Please take a seat. You're a bit early but perhaps that's just as well. I've missed having an audience since I finished with Judy, and that was hours ago."

The meaning was obvious, and Corey stared at his friend. Dick stared back, and the few feet separating them extended to miles. Corey sat, immediately gripped by transparent bonds.

Charles stepped over Judy and sat beside his second victim, his fingers lightly stroking Dick's shoulder; a lover's touch. His dark clothing, pale hands and face, and the ashen body lying beside him created a stark study in black and white. "Try to relax, Doctor, and to think pleasant thoughts. Your health, after all, might otherwise suffer."

Dick rubbed the cloth of Charles's shirt between his fingers. It was nearly over. His eyes grew sad, and shamed by that sadness.

"Not yet, love," Charles whispered, "though soon,."

Charles lowered his head and Dick turned his sideways in a gesture Corey thought was surrender. Corey could understand surrender, but his heart began to race as he watched his friend raise his arms beneath Charles's loose shirt, touching flesh to flesh as he pulled his lover closer.

Charles pushed and Corey's pulse quickened. He pushed again.—Think of your health.—Damn! Corey couldn't think of anything else.—I'm sorry I have to rush, Doctor, but we both know why I must hurry.—

Corey swore silently.

—And you, Dick Wells, have been a feast. Now pray for yourself, for the woman you love, and for my people that I succeed tonight.—

In the time that remained, they stopped speaking even in thought, and as life flowed from one to the other Dick felt the warmth sweep over him, bringing the ambivalent finality of unconsciousness.

Paralyzed, his body tortured in a different manner, Corey struggled to breathe, fighting to survive, sure he was losing. But, running amid his pulse's frantic rhythm, he detected a lower, stronger beat . . . pressure . . . release . . . pressure . . . release. The feel of a gunshot at the police shooting range or a bass drum in a loud dance band. Pressure . . . release. Corey managed to slump forward, attempting to force his rebellious body to calm, and saw Dick's revolver on the carpet beside his chair. He attempted to move, and his body reacted with quick jerks. Maybe Charles had begun to lose his hold. Maybe it had been too many hours; maybe he didn't know; maybe . . .

"Maybe I don't care."

Corey looked up and saw Charles watching him, clearly amused. "I'm through here, Doctor. Fire that weapon and you'll only bring half the hotel through that door." He accompanied those words with a wave at the bodies on either side of him, and Corey felt his muscles free, his heart slow mercifully. He managed two deep, marvelous breaths of air while his hand swayed above the revolver. Before he reached any decision on its destination, Charles shoved him upright and, grabbing that arm, snapped it.

Corey screamed. "God damn you!"

"I doubt it," Charles replied gravely. "I've served God well and I think he owes me far more than damnation . . . as do you. A broken arm is far less unpleasant than a coffin; though, for my purposes tonight, just as useful. But don't thank me for your life, thank him." He motioned back to Dick. "He's put me in a generous mood and so I keep my promise and let you live. Now I think I had best depart, before your friends arrive. Please inform my little brother that I have calls to make." In a mundane gesture amid the fantastic, he patted his pockets and his keys jingled. Opening the window, he waved roguishly to Corey and, with a quick glance down, jumped.

Ignoring the pains—the sharp one in his arm, the duller, more dangerous one in his chest—Corey knelt beside Judy and searched for a pulse. Finally he found a weak, swift flutter.

He became conscious of motion behind him and turned to see Parker and O'Reilly with their weapons drawn. Parker's eyes searched the dim corners, seeking the attacker, while O'Reilly gaped at Corey and Judy, then last and longest at his superior. "Holy Christ! Who in the hell did this?"

Corey's reply was sharpened by his pain. "Dick Wells's alien monster. Parker, grab that sheet and make me a sling for this arm. And O'Reilly, stop gawking and go radio for an ambulance. Tell them it's an emergency. Tell them . . . there's been an accident and two people are going to be taken to . . ." He paused and considered the safest destination. "To Elmbrook. Have the ambulance come in without sirens and meet us at the service entrance." O'Reilly turned to leave and Corey added, "And tell that moronic clerk everything is fine up here but that I tripped and had an accident. The ambulance is for *me*, understand?"

O'Reilly nodded. He understood perfectly.

Later, while the victims were being carried down the service stairs, Corey used the flashlight to scan the room. There was no blood on the carpet, only a few easily overlooked drops on the bed . . . no sign that anything unusual had occurred there. Number 315 was a hotel room, just like any other, in which the occupants had quietly checked out. Corey even remembered to leave a tip for the maid next to the room key.

# IV

This was a night on which the extraordinary could be overlooked. Only after he made sure that O'Reilly and Parker would spend the remainder of it in front of the Wells home and that Dick and Judy were ensconced on the same floor at Elmbrook did Corey take the time to have his arm set. As he waited patiently for his turn in the crowded emergency room, he decided it was possible, even likely, that what had occurred at the Lakeview would go unnoticed by the ravenous snoops of the local third estate. What Parker and that idiot O'Reilly would say upon returning to the station was another major problem. Though, on the brighter side, if they talked, no one would laugh about Dick Wells's monster again.

After his cast was in place, Corey was informed he should stay overnight at Elmbrook himself. "You've been through an ordeal, Doctor," the ER attendant told him. Ordeal, hell! He'd barely seen the tip of the iceberg.

"If I'm in, I want to be in the same room with Dick Wells." Corey had chosen this hospital because he had connections here. The staff had followed his instructions earlier and they followed them now. As a result, he was sitting by Dick's bed when, hours later, his friend reentered the world.

"Hello, Cor." Dick spoke like an addict coming off a nod. Moving only his eyes, he scanned his surroundings, recognized them as a hospital room. He did not remember why he'd been brought here until, noticing the IV and the blood dripping into his arm, the night returned. He pulled his knees up to his chest and shivered. "Are the kids okay?"

"Yeah. Parker radioed a message."

"And Judy?"

"She'll be fine. She's in the room across the hall."

After the first few words, Dick stopped paying attention. His mind had moved back to that hotel room. He was about to ask another question when the answer came to him. "Some sight, weren't we?"

Dick might have been inviting a smart retort, but Corey couldn't think of any. Instead he grasped his friend's hand, a gesture meant to reassure, and felt the shudder of revulsion as Dick pulled his own away. That instinctive reaction spoke more vividly of the night's torment than the IV, the slashes, the bruised and swollen wrists.

"How did you know to look for me?"

"Stephen told me."

"I see." Dick swallowed hard. "I screamed for him. All those miles and he heard." He tried to push himself up higher in the bed and found that, for all his strength, Charles might as well be holding him. "God, I hurt! There isn't anywhere I don't hurt . . . my arms, my legs, my mind." His eyes returned to the IV, the life flowing back. Maybe tomorrow he'd be thankful he'd survived.

Corey attempted to be cheerful. "In the morning you can see Judy."

"Judy." The word sounded so bitter, Corey wondered if Dick blamed her for their attack. His silent question must have been obvious because Dick continued, saying, "No, Doc, it isn't like that. In a way it's worse." He stared at the ceiling, then went on. "In the ambulance I came to for a few minutes, and I looked over and saw Judy lying on a stretcher next to me . . . so still, pale like he was pale. Her hand was hanging down, brushing the floor, and it looked hard and cold. All those hours, never moving. I was sure Charles had lied and she was dead.

"I reached over and squeezed that hand, praying for a response, and it felt so good when her fingers tightened around mine. Her eyes opened, though I don't think she really saw anything. 'Where is he?' she whispered. 'It's okay, I'm here,' I said. She rolled her head slowly sideways and looked at me . . . so many hours, such calculated savagery . . . and I saw the disappointment, the longing in those beautiful eyes. . . ."

Dick's voice faded, then tapped some reserve of anger. "It's not over, Doc; not until I burn that beast . . . all those beasts. So powerful, so vicious! Nothing deserves power like that, nothing! Damn it, Doc, he . . ." Dick faltered, seeking words to explain. "The times I hated him, the times I wanted to scream, those were the good times because at the end I . . ." He couldn't finish, could never finish. For the second time that night, he began to cry.

A nurse making routine rounds heard him and returned with a sedative. "Set it down," Corey said. "I'll call you when he needs it."

But it appeared a more natural sleep would claim Dick until he noticed the cast on Corey's arm. "He got you, too, huh?"

"Yeah. He had my heart traveling way past speed limit. Then I guess he decided what he was doing was too dangerous. He said he promised you?"

"He made lots of promises, kept every one. Oh, Jesus!" Dick tried to sit up, to swing his feet over the side of the bed. "He said he was making calls tonight. He promised Alan . . ."

Dick's vision began to blur, filled with sparks of light so bright, they hurt. "You have to help me, Doc. We have to . . ."

Corey didn't bother to call the nurse. For Dick the hypo was just another small spot of pain, lost among all the rest.

# Chapter Twenty-Two

## I

THE RAIN FELL softly on the tile roof of St. John's, its quiet murmurings barely audible inside the great stone structure. Charles sat cross-legged and barefoot on the candlelit altar, the water dripping like tears from his clothes and hair. Setting aside the bow that had been resting on his knees, he lowered his head and waited.

O'Maera took the time to dress properly . . . not only in his usual cassock but in full vestments. He chose not purple for mourning but white, the symbol of purification and, as a final touch, added the heavy silver cross he had been given by his family when he was ordained. It allowed him no power over the one in his church, but its pressure around his neck soothed. He faced death tonight, and should death claim him, he wished to end his life with this small comfort.

It had been too many days . . . days in which he had seen a friend tempt his limits, a family exist in fear. He was a priest, and like Dick Wells, like Stephen, he did what he must. When he heard the call—the whisper in his mind that woke him from a troubled sleep—he responded.

O'Maera entered St. John's through the front door and pulled it carefully closed behind him. Once inside, he abandoned his soggy raincoat, wiped the water from his face with a handkerchief, smoothed his vestments, and walked slowly down the center aisle as if he carried a crucifix at the head of a holy-day procession. He coughed twice, his lungs protesting the penetrating damp. As he moved forward, a chanting rose from the altar in a powerful soprano, chilling as ice, piercing as fire, *"Pax huie domui. Et omnibus habitantibus in ea—"* The beginning of the rites for commending a departing soul to God.

When O'Maera neared the altar, the chanting stopped. Looking up, he saw a face cleansed of emotion, magnificently angelic. Ignoring his fear, his just anger at this blatant desecration, he boldly asked, "Are you truly a demon in my church, or do you seek the solace only a priest can give?"

The voice that replied had the hard, beautiful ring of offertory bells. "I seek many things from you, Father. Solace is not one of them. My soul wishes release from this immortal body. I have come for my last rites."

O'Maera's denial was immediate and firm. "You cannot seek them from me, for I know what you are contemplating."

"Would you withhold the rites from a prisoner awaiting execution and prepared to die? You understand my death cannot come from my own hand." His arms moved outward, encompassing night. "Listen to this storm! When even God has aided me, can you deny me your power?"

The face! The voice! Both so much like Stephen's, but what torment O'Maera sensed in this soul. "Have you been baptized in the faith, then?" he asked with growing compassion.

Charles watched the priest with ancient, unblinking eyes as he replied in a solemn, flowing cadence. "I have been many things . . . a poet, a sculptor, a painter, a teacher, a father, a monk . . . a millennium of lives, and in that time I have been baptized in your faith, in many faiths, for sudden conversion is often the wisest course for survival."

"And do you believe in God?"

A long silence broken only by distant thunder. Then, "The coincidences have become too fantastic for me to believe otherwise."

Fear released him. The dark angel no longer hovered above him. "Then I cannot deny you your request. Usually the rites begin with confession."

The being above him inhaled deeply, then exhaled with an uncertain sound, one trapped between a sigh and a hiss. His eyes clouded with sorrow as he began. "I seek absolution for one sin, the only sin I have committed against my kind, and among us it is most grievous. When Claudia—my sister, my wife, my friend for a thousand years—came to me, her eyes filled with fear, and told me her time for children approached, we made a pact that she would live because I would not let her die. But in her pregnancy, she weakened; she demanded the choice our women are allowed. She made me agree . . . yet as she lay dying, I broke my oath and denied her death. I held her while they forced the blood into her veins. I beseeched her. I screamed into her mind, 'Do not leave me. I cannot take another loss . . . not you, not now, not even for the sake of these new lives.' And I brought her back, back to three years in which she existed with me and with her children, filled with unspoken despair at the prospect of years upon countless years of life.

"Though we might have hidden the truth from the family, there was no way Claudia and I could hide from each other, and so, because we could tolerate our loneliness no longer, I arranged for us to go home.

"Enough of our women choose to survive childbirth that our brother believed the letter we wrote him after the children were born was the truth and, afterward, that Claudia's death had been a vain effort to save the children and herself. Had Stephen seen her before her death, he would have known the reason she gave for dying was a lie. Claudia was physically weak but her mind remained as powerful as mine. Do you think she was no match for a few ignorant sailors? They would have jumped had she commanded them. No, she chose her death, and even then, it was days before it claimed her. I searched for her though I knew what she had done, and I felt death when it came and ripped her apart. Absolve me of this, Father, for it is my only sin and I have done my penance, for I have lived for forty years with her final memory, that terrible guilt, and the emptiness of belonging to nothing on this earth."

So close, they were all so close. O'Maera automatically raised his hand to absolve, then stopped. "You came to a human priest to seek absolution for a sin committed against your own, yet you confess to none against humanity?"

"Sometimes, not often, I am surprised by remorse. But never guilt, and without guilt there can be no sin. We exist in the same world, that is all. I feed on you but you are nothing to me. You are not my kind."

"Then seek your absolution from one of your own, for I am not worthy to cleanse you!"

O'Maera spun and began to walk down the aisle but Charles reached out his mind, stopping him. "I require many things from you, Father. We have much to accomplish before this night ends." O'Maera turned his head first; then, more slowly, his body followed and, with a will not completely his own, he moved back to Charles whose eyes—so beautiful, so implacably sad—called to him.

As he approached the altar, the chanting resumed. *"Confiteor Dei omnipotente, beate Marie semper . . ."* The beginning of the general confession. Was this a compromise?

—Call it such if it comforts you.— With no pause, the solemn music continued. *". . . mea culpa, mea culpa, mea maxima culpa . . ."* Acting only on reflex, O'Maera waited to absolve, then entered the sacristy to prepare.

During the next hour O'Maera recited the prayers and followed the ritual anointing, unwilling to question the propriety of his act. As he reached up to touch Charles's eyelids with Holy Chrism, the sleeve of his linen alb fell back and Charles saw the wound on O'Maera's wrist: his brother's mark. His eyes were drawn constantly to it as the priest's hands moved.

When the rites were complete, Charles reached down and, grasping O'Maera's wrist, raised it to his lips. As he did, he released the priest from his control and felt a brief, powerful ecstasy. Charles stood and, picking up the oil, began to repeat the sacred ritual. *". . . et bene dic nostre conversationi: sanctifica nostrae humilitatis ingressum . . ."*

—Why do you do this?—

*". . . qui sanctus et qui pius . . ."* —You also await death this night.— *". . . es et permanes cum Patre et Spiritu Sancto in saecula saeculorum."*

"Amen." —You would kill the priest who just gave you absolution?—

*". . . advertat ab eis omnes contrarias potestates . . ."* —I do what I must, that is all.—

The ancient ritual before death continued.

When the chanting stopped, O'Maera waited quietly, trying to accept whatever end would be chosen for him. He had

always thought himself an earthly man but, had he viewed his
face in a mirror, he would have been astonished at the beatific
transformation. He was ready to die, though he wished to
understand why death must claim him this night. He turned to
Charles, standing beside him wearing an expression of merciless sympathy.

"I take no pleasure in ending your life, Father, but before
you die, you will know, as Stephen must know, that I am
capable of any depravity that will lead to my end. I act quickly
and desperately out of love for those who were once my people."

O'Maera found the truth consoling. "Then why is there
such enmity between you and your brother?"

"Ah, Stephen!" Charles glanced at the west windows, his
brother's works. "He does what he can to help and what he
must to survive. The call to life is too strong to allow us the
luxury of sacrifice, and to destroy me would be, for Stephen,
the ultimate sacrifice. But we shall see if his will can be made
to overcome his instincts; if his love for his people and for
Helen is stronger than his love of self. I wish you to summon
him here. If you do this freely—"

"No!" O'Maera stood resolute, knowing the consequences
of his decision.

"Then you foolishly seek martyrdom for a cause you do not
comprehend. Very well, I will not deny that gift to you, and at
the end you will still do as I command."

"Were I assured it would be only your death I would hasten
this night, I could not willingly help you."

"As you wish."

O'Maera looked with love at his church, his altar, thinking
there could be no more fitting place for his life to end. It was
difficult for Charles to hide his pity as he added, "I will have
my time later to prepare. If I leave you alone for a little while
to say your last prayers, will you swear not to seek help or to
leave this place?"

This was so much more than O'Maera had expected to
receive, yet it seemed wrong to agree, as if by doing so he
would condone his murder. He shook his head. "The Lord will
understand why I have not prayed."

"No matter, you have your time." As Charles moved silently down the aisle and merged with the darkness, he asked

with the finest subtlety, —Where is Sylvia?— and O'Maera, not even aware of the question, replied.

After the huge wooden door slammed closed, O'Maera moved toward the sacristy. A few feet from it, he turned and walked back to the altar. He tried again, with no better luck, then attempted to reach the main aisle and was halted at the communion rail. He could not scream above the wind, and there was too little with which to start a fire. Of all the possibilities, only the one Charles had suggested seemed reasonable. With a moan of frustration and despair, he knelt before the altar and prayed.

## II

The wine bottle was half empty, the deep red Egri in the glass beside it so opaque the firelight did not reflect off its surface. She recalled another night . . . the storm, the fire to warm him. He would come tonight, she knew, if he came at all.

How silly Helen had been, warning her as if Kavil's coming would somehow be a threat to her. No matter how many deaths he had caused, no matter what he had done, they had shared love and he would not harm her. Her only fear had come when she looked in the mirror at a face that, while dignified with age, was beautiful no longer.

Earlier, she had searched in her closet and found the long skirts and the loose shirt she had worn when she and Matthew had gone to the folk dances at church and to picnics with those who had also come from Europe and looked nostalgically back at the old ways. After she had dressed, she looked at herself in the mirror, her features softened by the candlelight, and felt a pang of sorrow for Matthew more real than any she had felt the day he died. When it passed, she went downstairs, poured her wine, and waited, sleep finally claiming her in spite of her expectation, the noise of the storm.

Feeling the light touch on her shoulder, she opened her eyes and looked into his. And the years fell away.

He studied her face in silence, wondering what it would have been like to stay with her . . . watching the lines form, the eyes lose their brilliance, the hair thicken and gray while he remained untouched by time. But no, it would not have been that long. Twenty years, twenty-five at the most, and then there would have been the child and he would have found his release. It was far too late for explanations to matter, but he wanted to know. "I came to ask why you deserted me." There was no reproach, no bitterness in his voice. He was prepared to accept any answer.

"So you did, finally, go back?"

He understood. "Yes. They said only that you had married and gone to America; a very large place, even for my kind. I had no way of finding you or the child." He had never tried; never even considered trying.

"You knew about her, then?"

"Of course, though she was not my reason for leaving." But possibly the reason he had stayed away too long. He looked at the fire, wishing he'd begun their conversation differently. "I should not have spoken of your desertion. I did not return for nearly eight months, and by then you would have been sadly compromised."

"And even two weeks is an eternity for a silly girl in love." She chuckled. "We're getting maudlin, Kavil. We were never that before." For the first time she touched his face, and her fingers were as dry and smooth as parchment. "I might have waited, even with the shame, had I been meeker and less willful. But then you would not have chosen me, I think. You wanted passion, not submission."

It had been less than a year after Claudia. "I needed it desperately. But tell me of our daughter," he concluded in an effort to brighten the conversation.

"Her wedding picture is on the mantel if you wish to see how she looked." He took it down and studied it as she continued. "She was as willful as I; perhaps even more stubborn. When her head barely reached my waist, she would stand firmly with her feet pointed straight ahead and say she would do this or that and no one could alter her course. Yet she was so magnificently kind and generous that I could not help but love her." She told of their argument concerning Lydia's lineage.

"Would you have believed your mother had she told you that?" Charles asked with a trace of humor.

"Probably not, though with Lydia I thought I must try." She described Lydia's marriage, Helen's birth, and their daughter's death, then concluded, "Now there is only Helen."

"And is she as obstinate as her mother?" Charles asked in an off-handed tone.

"In her own way, even more. She never argues as Lydia did, but she is like the wind, which listens to no one. She is your granddaughter and mine. Our heritage is evident." Sylvia chuckled with satisfaction. "And soon she will be one of you."

"I wonder if she will find those countless years a blessing or a damnation."

The wine tricked her senses, Sylvia decided. He could not mean those words to sound so serious. "Ho! Do not think so lightly of centuries to someone my age, Kavil. Would that I could have that life!"

He returned the picture to its place on the mantel, then turned and faced her. "Would that I could trade places with you or, better, that I were human and we had met and grown old together. Then were I to die first, you could place flowers on my grave and mourn me as you mourn your husband."

"Mourn?" She reached for her wine and sipped it, looking thoughtful. "No, I do not mourn his loss. There was always you between us."

"To take your love was one thing; to steal your will a different matter entirely. I'm sorry I intruded on your life so long ago, then left you so thoughtlessly."

Her laughter had barely changed. "You came to apologize after all these years?"

"No, Sylvia. I came to say good-bye."

Although she'd expected this would be the outcome of their meeting, the thought was not a happy one. She sat up and motioned to a second wineglass. He shook his head. It was a temptation, but tonight even a taste would be too much. He would need his senses sharper than they had ever been before. "I suppose good-bye is for the best," she began. "It's certainly . . ."

"You don't understand," he said with soft persistence. "I

want you to pray for me and mourn me. I intend to die this day."

She gripped her glass with both hands, afraid it would fall, as she stared at him standing by the fire . . . tall; lean; his face unmarred, unlined, beautiful. "You don't mean that," she whispered. "You're playing games with me."

"No, Sylvia, and, belatedly, your will shall become your own once more."

"I wish you hadn't come at all," she muttered, and finished in a voice harsh and old in its anger. "I never would have wanted to know."

"But you would know, anyway. You share a part of me and you will feel it when I die. I wanted you to be prepared."

"Prepared! When I have watched myself age and said, 'He does not change'; when I think of my death and say, 'He will not die, he will remember me'; and so I will achieve that kind of immortality. And now you say you will die and, worse, that you intend to die. Life is a gift, Kavil. What have you done with yours?"

He refused to be baited, knowing how fast his kindness could depart, and so he answered with the simple truth. "As surely as if I had possessed a plan, I destroyed it."

She wagged a finger at him, the way she did when she used to lecture Lydia, certain her words would be as ineffective. "Then you are a fool, worse than a fool, for you will not learn from your mistakes and so become wise. Is there no room in your mind for self-forgiveness?"

He leaned his hands on the mantel and watched the flames burn like the Austra furnaces at Moulins the night he poured the first sheets of red-and-gold glass. "Forgive? I suppose I could forgive," he said bitterly, "if only I could forget." He turned to face Sylvia, his shadow falling over her. "Isn't it ironic how you who live such a brief time forget your childhoods, forget whole months of years gone by, even forget part of what you did yesterday or last week, while we who live centuries are condemned to recall perfectly every detail of our lives? Such a curse assures lives of great rectitude or unrelenting despair. No, Sylvia, once deeds are done, they cannot be altered. It is too late to forgive."

In impotent anger she flung her wineglass at him, but he stepped out of its path and it shattered in the fire, the thick red liquid hissing on the hot coals. "No, Sylvia," he repeated, "it is good-bye." He moved toward the door.

It would be best if he left, he knew. Already he could feel his will failing, the facade of gentility beginning to crack, but he turned to listen when she said, "Wait, we never had a proper farewell."

"And you wish one now?" He walked toward her, his voice scornful of its own seductiveness. "Shall I kiss you? Shall we lay together? Shall we—"

"Can you merely tell me that I have had your love?" she interrupted, her voice more pitiful than angry.

"Very well, for what little warmth it has given you, you have had my love." He bowed low before her, a gaudy imitation of a courtly gesture, and reached for her hand to impart an almost-noble kiss. She pulled it away, and as she did, he caught the thought. "Of course he is more kind," he said cynically. "He could well afford the chivalry. After all, you gave him your granddaughter, didn't you . . . both her body and her soul?"

Sylvia's look was one of contempt. "I am thankful she never knew you."

"She shall. I intend to meet her this night, and then we'll see if she possesses the proper qualities to join the family. And now it is good-bye, Sylvia." He brushed her mind and kissed her reluctant lips once, with sincere tenderness, and departed into the night.

She reached for the wineglass and looked down into its clear depths, which captured the firelight, wondering how the sorrow would feel when it came and how she would survive the hollowness that would follow. She prayed fervently for the impossible . . . that the past could be remade.

## III

The sounds of the storm intensified, then dulled. The candles flickered in the brief, invasive draft. Absorbed in his prayers, O'Maera did not hear his killer return until a hand lightly brushed his shoulder and a harsh voice contradicted the gentleness of that touch. "Come, it is late, and I can wait no longer."

O'Maera crossed himself and looked up into shimmering, dark slashes, eyes crystallized by a resolve to complete what must be done. Though he had given O'Maera a choice, Charles had already known the decision, and no less than death would be required on this night.

O'Maera had shed the ceremonial outer garments and stood humbly attired in the white linen alb, his silver cross its only adornment. This simplicity imparted an aged innocence, and Charles eyed the priest with distaste. Catching a tenuous thought, he lashed out with deliberate malice. "Don't try to condone what I do tonight to yourself or to me. Were you in your twenties and this the eve of your ordination, it would make no difference. Destruction is my birthright and I claim it as I wish." He concluded with mock compassion, "I admit that when you are dead, I will feel remorse."

The priest's pulse barely quickened, and Charles sensed in O'Maera a fear of dying, though none of death. A true believer and, beneath that soft exterior, a core of steel. Charles was heartened. His brother would come. Resting his hands on his victim's shoulders, Charles watched him with calm intensity as he asked, "Have you made your peace with God?"

"I have." O'Maera stood stiffly, his labored breathing forced into near silence as he looked beyond Charles into the charged darkness. He held his head high, his hands relaxed at his sides, waiting.

The laughter was born as a chuckle, then acquired a life of its own until it was cut off abruptly. "I see you've given some thought to the manner of your death. Unfortunately, that method would be too sweet and too swift, and I have no taste for what you could give me. I need your agony, Father, and that will be your gift to me, your unwilling aid this night. Do you wish to choose another method?"

Since O'Maera had been compelled to return to Charles, he had felt as if he stood outside his body, already dead, watching a reenactment of the final scenes of his life. To speak would be to break the spell he had woven for himself, to end the passivity and thrust him too cruelly into the present. Then he would remember how much he loved life and he would struggle and he would lose. Accept, he thought, accept. And so, as he listened to his killer's words, he stood, watching the intermittent flashes of the rose floating above him, still and silent even in thought.

Charles followed O'Maera's eyes to that highest and most beautiful place in the church. "As you wish," he said, and picking up his bow and glass-tipped arrows, he led the priest down the aisle and up the steep, narrow steps to the choir loft.

# IV

Midway between midnight and dawn, the squad car appeared. It moved slowly down the hill to stand at the curb, the windshield wipers the only sign of life as its protected inhabitants waited for a lull in the storm. Once the rain slowed, Parker ran up the stairs to Helen, who stood in the dimly lit doorway waiting for him.

As he began to relay his message, Helen motioned for him to come inside, then turned to wait until Stephen opened his eyes and joined them. "I'm supposed to give this to you," Parker said quickly, pulling an envelope out of his pocket and handing it to Stephen. "Corey said I should tell you we were there, that we found them."

"I see."

Austra's eyes held a disturbing depth that made Parker nervous. He looked anxiously at the wall and found himself recalling the scene in the hotel room. He heard Helen whisper a shocked "Oh!" and he looked at her, her moist eyes beautiful in the candlelight, and sorrowful, as if she had already read Corey's message. He waited to hear the usual questions so he could provide confident replies, but there were none. Intending to soothe, he said, "We'll be right outside till morning, keeping an eye on the place."

"Really?" Stephen asked bluntly. "Both of you at once?"

"I—I don't understand," Parker said, stammering.

"Of course you do. *The Glass Key*, page 171. Forget the book tonight, Officer; your lives may depend on your watchfulness."

When Parker returned to the squad, he found O'Reilly had already pulled out both book and flashlight. He glanced over his partner's shoulder. Page 171. "Gimme that!" he ordered. Before O'Reilly could protest, Parker had snatched the book away from him and tossed it over the seat. "Tonight we pay attention." Parker rolled down the passenger window, and although the rain continued to fall, to be blown fiercely by the disorderly winds, he had a clear view of Helen's flat. "At three I'll walk around the place, then stop and make sure everyone is okay before we radio in."

"You'll wake them up," O'Reilly protested.

"If Corey wrote about only half of what we saw tonight, nobody's going to be sleeping in here."

But Corey had made his note terse and deliberately vague, the only new details a hopeful prognosis and a hospital room number. And the news that Charles would be making his calls. After Stephen read it, he handed it silently to Helen, then lay back down, his mind moving out to protect once more. Better to guard than to contemplate what he had seen in Parker's mind. He experienced a flash of rage as he considered how those hours Richard was missing had been spent and a deep sadness when he realized what savage ruthlessness now drove his brother. Embrace that sadness, Stephen thought, and let it hold back the anger. Of one thing he was certain: Tonight Charles would make a pinpoint attack on his sanity, and rage would be his most deadly weapon.

Helen contemplated the night's devastation in silence, then moved to stand beside Stephen, intending to plead as persuasively as possible for an end to this intolerable struggle. Before she could speak, however, Stephen's expression changed. He furrowed his brows, licked his lips, then shook his head as if trying to disperse a nightmare. Watching him, Helen detected the afterimage of a thought. —. . . hold you back . . . — She touched his shoulder and he returned to her.

"Let him come, Stephen. If you can hold him, hold him here."

It seemed such a rational suggestion that the intensity of his reaction disturbed her. "No! Tomorrow night, and for every night thereafter, I will find safe places for you and for Richard's children. Then I will hunt Charles in my own manner, and I will not hunt alone. I am sure that in the morning your uncle will be able to tell me precisely where I can find persons who, for a price, will not hesitate to finish this deed for me."

"And what of your future when you have finished this terrible deed?"

"It is a risk I must take. There is danger in his continued existence. He knows this far better than I."

She was about to continue the argument when Stephen added, "I have never forced your will, Helen, and I have no desire to begin now. It is apparent, however, that I have left you in ignorance far too long. You saw what Charles did to your uncle and Judy. Shall I show you the girl with the slashes on her neck, the bruises on her body, and the memory she gave to me? Would you like to view the bodies of those he killed? Then you can sit in this stormy darkness and wonder what he has planned for you . . . as I do."

As he spoke, his mind hinted at the scenes behind his words, and dread visions stalked her. "It won't be necessary." Her voice was cold and even. "I made you a promise and I will honor it." She sat in the chair beside him and ended on a softer tone. "Do what you must."

Stephen resumed his guard and, as on other nights, Helen noticed the troubling emotions brushing his mind. Eventually, she pulled her feet onto the seat of the chair and, leaning her head against its high arm, tried to sleep.

The storm had quieted though the rain still fell, when Helen, dozing fitfully, was awakened by a cry of anguish wrenched from her lover's throat. "No!" He retreated so quickly, he became disoriented. His eyes were wounded. Charles had begun his nightly assault.

"What is it?"

"It appears I am not to know for a little while." He leaned his head against bent knees, crossing his arms behind his neck. When the agony struck again, he would be prepared.

# V

The deep gloom of the choir loft was broken only by the light of four tall candles resting on the massive organ and the intermittent flaring of the rose. Charles sat next to O'Maera on one of the hard wooden benches the choir used during Mass, holding one of the priest's hands palm up. His fingers gripped comfortably, yet so tightly, that O'Maera could not have pulled away. In the oppressive night below them, St. John's brooded silently, waiting for death to walk its aisles.

Charles tilted his head and looked deeply into his victim, not certain how to proceed. At last he began, with unusual compassion, "Tonight I held a man for whom life was more important than honor, than purity. I played with that weakness and we fought the kind of battle I will soon fight with you. We fought for hours until I threatened what he valued above all else, and in an instant he was mine. Now I hold you, whom death does not trouble, and I wonder what it is you cherish most, Patrick O'Maera. Is it your love of God or the trappings of your office . . . this church, these magnificent Austra treasures that are a part of it . . . the parishioners who kneel to confess their sins and who call you Father with such reverence? I would not presume to hear your confession earlier, but I ask now, which is it?"

"B-both," O'Maera said, stammering. "Truly, it is both."

"Is it? Or did the church impart on you a certain nobility you could never have obtained elsewhere?"

"I chose my vocation because of my faith. I did not know where my order would send me. Yet I have been blessed with this church, the leadership of this parish. I suppose I have become guilty of pride."

Charles ended their contact abruptly, not wishing O'Maera to sense his self-disgust. In spite of his need, Charles wanted nothing more than to drop the priest's hand, to leave this person, this place, untouched. To come between any creature and its god was loathsome. His features sharpened as he remembered who he was, what he must do.

As they had conversed, Charles had been twirling an arrow between thumb and forefinger. Now he held it above the priest's wrist and plunged it down, severing veins but stopping short of the artery. The tip was so sharp, the pain only came when Charles pulled it out.

"It's not bleeding very hard." For the first time O'Maera shuddered, and there was a trembling in his voice as he considered how much time would pass between his final prayers and his death. He feared he would weaken or, worse, be forced to weaken. He felt the presence in his mind and his fear intensified.

—It will bleed.— With that promise, Charles repeated the act on the other wrist.

O'Maera looked apprehensively at his wounds, at the blood staining his alb. "A parish is like a family," he began tentatively, not wishing to beg. "I would hope that my death would not lead to scandal or to another's guilt."

"Humanity does assume guilt so easily, doesn't it?" Charles began in a mocking tone that quieted when he realized the priest would accept even this final indignity. "I promise you that when we are finished, your death will not look like suicide." He braced himself for what would follow, and his voice hardened once more. "Now, Patrick O'Maera, let us discuss your faith. . . ."


. . . They raise him in loneliness, setting him apart from his four brothers and sisters, preparing him for the priesthood from the day it became apparent he was the intelligent one, the scholar. "You have a vocation," they tell him in words too loving to be an order, and when the uncertainties begin, his only solace is his god. When he is eleven, he dares to stammer his doubts to his mother and, in response, she pushes him to his knees on the cold linoleum floor of their kitchen and kneels beside him. They pray, not for guidance, for his life has already been decided, but for his acceptance. And in the seminary, he is forced to face his doubts and his hate. . . .

He dances at his oldest brother's wedding, taking the girl for a walk on the long covered porch off the hall. He becomes forward, awkward with inexperience, and she runs, flushed and angry. "A seminarian!" Her words echo back shrilly and in shock, as if the kiss he had given had imparted a mortal sin. . . .

Yes, he hates and he questions. He considers other lives until acceptance becomes vocation, a desire for that pastoral life in the faith, and he forgives his parents and enters a broader family, a more perfect whole. At his sister's wedding, he performs the service with no regret. . . .

He first sees St. John's when, as a deacon, he comes to assist at Sunday Mass. As he administers communion, he must fight to stay aware of the congregation, to refrain from gaping at the splendor surrounding him. Over the years he returns, and the awe is revived. He advances well to that memorable day when he is summoned to the chancery and told this would be his congregation, his church. He does not remember the words he chooses to express his gratitude, only that he leaves in haste and seeks a private place where he can let the unseemly tears of joy fall as he thanks God for this gift.

It became his family . . . the wood, the marble, the windows were his children; the light and the music that filled it his only spouse. He had protected, had nurtured, and he would leave it greater than it had been.

It seemed petty that he should long so terribly to see the rectory windows in place, feel such sorrow at this small loss when he would die with these treasures around him and he hoped he would be alive at dawn to see that first deep glow. Through a dream in darkness, he saw Charles aim his bow and send an arrow flying across the church, hitting the small window, the single blue-clad angel that hovered above the altar. The broken glass fell silently, the power of the storm drowning out its sound. A second arrow followed, then a third, and the delicate angel was gone.

—Summon him!—

O'Maera shook his head. "What pleasure is there in destroying such beauty?"

"None. Except that is it not my right to destroy that which I have created when it pleases me no longer?" He turned, aiming now for the highest tip of the rose. —Summon him!—

Hearing no reply, Charles looked back to O'Maera and,

without watching its path, let the arrow fly to lodge high in the wood support for the window.

The shot caught O'Maera by surprise, and before he saw its outcome, his mind bellowed —No!— He marveled at his composure. So far he hadn't said a word.

A few miles away the first wave broke.

"You created these treasures?" O'Maera asked, astounded that his killer's revelation did not diminish the love he felt for his church.

"We created them together, my brother and I, just before he returned to Europe to reclaim his throne."

The small red pools beneath O'Maera had stopped spreading. Though his arms hung heavily at his sides, drops no longer fell from his numb fingertips. Charles raised the wounds to his lips, and they bled freely once more. "Now that you've offered me my own kingdom," O'Maera said dreamily, "will you tempt me next with bread?"

"No, but with something as natural." And he revealed Claudia, in a gossamer robe of deep red shot with gold, standing next to a Roman pool from which thick steam rose. She runs her fingers through blue-black hair, raising the disorderly ringlets from her shoulders, then letting them fall. Her robe drops to the marble floor, and stepping over it, she descends the few steps into the water.

"She was beautiful but this is no temptation, not anymore." There was a sheen of sweat on O'Maera's face, and his clothes felt sticky against his weakening body.

"Isn't it? You tell me."

. . . The vision shifts. The pool's calm waters become angry waves . . . hours of them, days of them flowing by with impossible speed. Her hair is tangled with seaweed, her face burned by the sun and the salt. She swims in circles, seeking only exhaustion, her expression frantic and guilt-filled. In her selfishness, she has killed her son. She sees the fins cutting through the water and thinks only of food. . . .

Charles panted from the anguish of reliving the consuming intensity of her final struggle. —Summon him!—

O'Maera hears her screams, feels her pain. Death is terrible. It must be denied. His acceptance began to crumble as he longed to avoid this premature end to his life. —Ste . . . — He caught himself, in time he thought, then forced speech through a painfully dry mouth. "Why didn't you tell your brother the truth about her death?"

"Because I will not share what is ultimately my guilt. Now we must finish this." He stood.

"Please, one final question." Charles nodded, but O'Maera, his vision clouded, perceived the assent only from the length of the pause. "Was that lie an act of love?"

"As you wish."

The implication was more than O'Maera could comprehend. His eyes tried to focus on his killer. He wanted to bargain, perhaps even concede. As he was about to speak, the words dissolved.

"If it comforts you, know that you die for your people as well as his." Charles gripped O'Maera firmly by the arm and pulled him to his feet. O'Maera swayed and leaned against him, feeling inexplicably light-headed from such an insignificant loss of blood. "Come, we will end this now." He spoke with the respect of a general for a noble adversary being led to the place of execution.

. . . the pernicious throbbing continues, returning him to church, and he finds it is filled with music, with chanting of a magnificence he has never imagined . . . banners are held aloft, medieval heraldry moving in the wind from the open doors . . . a gold crucifix, intricately wrought, leads the procession . . . not his church but a church larger and more elaborate, and it is dedication day, the day of the first Mass. As he studies the festively dressed congregation, he sees Stephen standing on the steps below the choir loft, bathed in the devotion that ascends like incense from the congregation below. His head is bowed, his eyes almost closed, and on his lips is the hint of a smile, shy and private. As the ceremony continues, Charles appears to stand on the step above his brother, resting a hand on Stephen's shoulder as they watch the pageantry and chant the responses softly so no one below will be aware of their presence, their difference. O'Maera feels their love, shares their rapture. —Stephen?— He does not summon, barely thinks, yet his friend hears and looks up to O'Maera, and his eyes are filled with the centuries that stand between them. . . .

# VI

The disquiet had begun as a hint, a teasing . . . perhaps as an old, deliberately distorted memory that Charles sent to torment him as he had on all these nights . . . begging, ordering, screaming —Let me come! I must have her! She is mine!— Stephen stoically endured each cry as they became more explicit: a vision slowly forming. The repeated calls, weak and reluctant, told him someone else was there . . . and it came to him: St. John's, and then Patrick not safe in his rectory but at the center of the message. Patrick, who called; Patrick, who was tormented and withstanding the pain so bravely; Patrick, who was . . .

He had fought the vision silently, not wishing to share the anguish until understanding tore through his will. He screamed.

Helen was wrenched back from fitful sleep and her pulse raced in time to his panic. "What is it?" she asked.

"I am not certain, but wake Carol and Alan. Wrap them in blankets. There is no time to dress them. We must move!"

"Where are we going?"

"I am going to St. John's. You and Richard's children are taking a drive in that squad car to any destination the police choose, so long as I do not know of it. Come."

"If you meet him?" she asked, already knowing the answer.

"I will do what I must do. But should our meeting end with my brother's blood on my hands, I will not ask that you stand beside me." His voice was already filled with the loss.

Certain she held the key to another way, Helen willed herself calm and thought only of her lover. "I will not desert you."

"And I will never be lonely." He would not hold her to that promise later, but for the first time in a millennium he thought of his own children without dread.

Soon afterward, Stephen pulled open the squad's rear door and thrust in a half-sleeping Alan. Helen followed, fighting simultaneously to grip her protective covering as it lashed in the wind, and lead Carol, who, while awake, wanted nothing more than to return to her dry and comfortable bed. Only when the three were inside did Stephen explain to an already protesting O'Reilly, "Take them anywhere you wish that is not in the direction of St. John's. While you go, radio for an ambulance. There's been an accident at that church."

O'Reilly didn't start the car. "How do you know?"

"You know your orders, now go!"

O'Reilly grimaced, turned on the ignition, and let the car roll forward a few feet before popping the clutch. He wished, after that send-off, that they were on level ground and his rear wheels deep in a puddle. He took a right at the corner, heading into town, then looked over his shoulder at Helen. Though he could see only the hint of her face and hair in the darkness, her presence excited him. "Is he right about St. John's?"

"Yes! Now, would you call?"

"Sure. Sure." He radioed in an emergency request and in turn received a demand for specifics. O'Reilly muttered something under his breath, then, "It's a secondhand report. I have no details." With that evasive finish, he signed off.

"We sure are sending in a lot of mysterious calls for ambulances tonight," Parker commented to Helen. "First for Wells and that woman, and now. . ."

"My father?" Carol leaned forward. "What happened to my father?"

"He had an accident, Carol," Helen said, gripping the girl's hand for reassurance. "The doctors say he'll be fine. Isn't that right, Frank?" Helen spoke politely, though she wanted to throttle Parker for his stupidity.

Alan leaned against Helen, asleep as if he'd never left his bed, while Carol shivered and began to complain miserably. She wanted to visit her father. When told it was impossible, she wanted to be dry, to go home. Her voice rose half an octave as she continued her complaints.

Ignoring her cousin, Helen stared into the darkness and executed a far from perfect plan. In spite of the dangers, she had to return to her apartment. She had to see Charles. Their meeting had become her obsession.

Uncertain of her capabilities, she pushed with all the power she possessed. The car skidded as O'Reilly took a sudden second right, then, in a few blocks, a third.

"You're heading back the way we came," Parker commented. "We're supposed to get out of this neighborhood, yes?" He hit the final word with sarcasm born of dislike.

"It's good that John is heading back," Helen said to Parker, her voice beautifully commanding, her use of O'Reilly's first name deliberate. "I want John to drive us home."

Though he'd been the one to make the turn, it was O'Reilly who protested. "Austra said to take you away from there, and our orders are to listen to him."

"Your orders do not include heeding insanity, John. These children are in my care, and it is dangerous to take them for a drive on a night like this. Don't you agree, Frank?"

She laid a hand on Parker's shoulder, making certain the side of it brushed his neck. "Yes, I do. We could have an accident or the car could stall. What would we do with these three then? Helen and the kids should be safe at home."

"You're right," O'Reilly said, "but when Wells finds out we disobeyed his orders, he'll—"

"He'll thank you," Helen interjected, "for keeping his children dry and secure on this terrible night. And besides, the two of you will be right outside. If I need any help, I assure you I will call." The melody of her tone implied she might call, anyway.

That possibility was enough for O'Reilly. While the cat's away, he thought, then cut off the metaphor nervously. After the slashes he'd seen on Wells, the idea seemed far too fitting.

When they returned to Helen's apartment, the rain abated. They had been gone less than ten minutes.

After sending the bewildered children back to their beds, Helen sat in the darkness and waited, though not with the blind trust that had dominated her earlier thoughts of this meeting. Had she a weapon, had she a chance of using it, she would kill Charles on sight. She wasn't amazed at the intensity of her emotion . . . only that it was undiluted hatred and that it overpowered her.

# VII

If the elements had conspired, they could not have aided Charles more. When the third storm line broke, its lethal fury matched his own, and the police car shuddered from the forceful blasts.

Parker futilely tried to scan the empty streets through the sheets of rain, the steamed windows, and the brief, clear spaces the windshield wipers made as they swept the glass. But the street was black, the house dark, and he could see nothing at all. It was a few minutes after four, a few minutes after they had agreed to check on the family and radio in. They had waited, hoping the storm would quiet, but it gave no sign it intended to be cooperative.

Thinking of Helen, O'Reilly said, "You just dried off, Frank. I'll take my turn getting soaked." He pushed open the driver's door, holding it tightly so it would not slam back against him, when a gust of wind hit from behind, jerking it fully open. As O'Reilly stood stretched, one hand on the steering wheel, the other on the door frame, the arrow—with only a whisper for an announcement—skewered him, and he fell back into the driver's seat.

"You all right, John?" Parker questioned, not sure if he ought to laugh or be concerned. In a flash of lightning, he saw the blood and the arrow and reached for his gun. As his fingers touched the holster, an arm crashed through the side window and, with a grip such as he'd never felt before, held him tightly at the back of the neck. Faster than his eyes could follow, another hand reached inside and unlocked the door. Before Parker understood he'd been attacked, his assailant sat beside him, one hand on his neck, the other holding his wrists in an unbreakable grip.

Parker tried to swing his body forward, to get some leverage with which to fight. This should have been easy, but he could not move. It was then he realized with flawless terror the impossible alien strength of his adversary.

Next to him, O'Reilly was choking, drowning as his blood filled his lungs, and the sound was horrible. But even worse was the sound in Parker's mind...of derisive, charming laughter. "You will call your station and tell them everything is fine."

"I wasn't supposed to..." Parker began, then sobbed audibly as the fingers gripping his neck squeezed, wounding nerves he'd never known existed.

"Don't assume I am naive," his captor said. "I will know if you are lying. Please make your call."

Parker's hands were freed. He thought of his gun, and again the vise on his neck tightened. This time he made no sound, though hopeless tears ran down his face. He could no longer feel his legs or the spreading stain on his uniform pants. "I will know," his attacker repeated. "Please, make your call."

Parker had no alternative. He reached for the radio, aware that his life was nearly over. He might have been more wordy with the dispatcher, less businesslike in his conversation. He longed to leave some brief good-byes or scream a warning, but he feared the pain and the extra moments would mean nothing, really. With tired resignation, he signed off.

"That was perfect," the almost human creature praised, and relaxed its hold so that Parker was able to face it for the first time. In a spattering of lightning, he saw the beauty of that tightly muscular face, and those huge nocturnal eyes, and that beauty was more terrible than any ugliness might have been. As his expression changed to one of wonder, he heard the sound of his spine snapping.

# VIII

The demons played outside the church that night, their renewed wails masking the soft, serious sounds within. Stephen walked through the desecrated church as the windows flashed raucously in the storm; his sensitive eyes searching, his mind seeking the source of the agony searing his senses. Nearing the altar, he detected in the church's intricate acoustics the faint, familiar wheeze of labored lungs, and a sound even more intimate: a steady drip too thick for rain. He breathed deeply, and from that breath he knew.

He faced the back of the church and lifted his eyes to the great rose window, now hidden with the night. In a burst of light, he saw the silhouette suspended like a spider at the center of its web . . . a human replication of the death of Christ.

For an instant he denied his senses, then ran to the choir loft above which O'Maera hung. The pain and the rage stripped Stephen clean, and it was something *other*, something more than he that ripped and clawed with powerful hands until he freed his friend from that profane position and lowered him from the great rose window that had become his cross.

With the weight of his body no longer constricting his chest, O'Maera's breathing eased, and his eyes fluttered open, first unfocused, then, with determination, attempting to fix on the face of the person holding him. "Stephen?" he asked with despair.

"Yes, Patrick, I am here."

"I must have called you. . . . I didn't want to call you, but dear Lord, I was so weak." He spoke in a ragged voice, while Stephen fought back the fury threatening his control.

"No, Patrick. You could not have resisted him. He shares my gifts." And, Stephen reflected bitterly, the reality of this act had not been necessary.

"Helen . . . he told me he would meet Helen tonight. You must not stay here." He tried to grip Stephen's hand and cried out as his pierced wrists responded only with stabs of pain.

Stephen ran a cool, moist hand over his friend's forehead. "Shhh, Patrick, I knew. He won't find her." Ripping off the hem of the alb, Stephen began binding O'Maera's wrists, wishing the priest was younger and healthier. Unless the ambulance arrived within minutes, his friend would die, and in this storm, such speed would require a miracle.

"I'm going to move you, Patrick. There's help coming, and if you're just inside the church door, it will save some time later."

"Don't, laddie . . . I saw my death, it embraced me." His

breath rasped until, with a final burst of strength, he continued, "I . . . must tell you . . . Do . . ."

—Don't try to speak. Think the words and I will hear.—

—Do not give in to temptation. The price is too great.— And the thinnest shadow of an idea.—He pays now.—

—Is it sealed or can you tell me?—

—Sealed—O'Maera trembled. Stephen was no believer, and he prepared for an assault on his dying mind.

—No, Patrick, I will not take it from you, and I will remember your advice.—He stilled his thoughts and for a long while there was only the music as he had sung it so long ago . . . its beauty deadening sorrow as he devoured the pain and labored to conceal his brother's act; his hands moving mechanically, detached from his soul.

As O'Maera lapsed into final unconsciousness, Stephen detected a message suppressed until the end.—He said my death is for you.—And Stephen swayed with O'Maera in his arms, unwilling to relinquish what little remained of his humanity until his human friend had died. Softly, with that control he still possessed, he touched O'Maera one final time.—Do you wish me with you now?—

The answer returned, resigned and brave.—Help those who yet live.—

Still Stephen waited until that final broken breath. Then the facade burst as Stephen's shriek of denial crashed off the stone walls and the glass. And from the darkness he heard the echo of another's torment . . . the assault continuing. Enraged, he leapt over his friend's body and with open hands shattered the resurrection at the center of the profaned rose. He followed his arms through, and when his feet touched the ground, he was already running.

# Chapter Twenty-Three

## I

IF THE HUGE tree in front of the Wells' home had fought another half hour, it would have survived intact that last and most vicious of the storm fronts, but it had no way of knowing calm was so near, and it was exhausted. First one limb, then another, began to crack in this final furious gale.

Not certain what violent trick the weather was now playing, Helen roused Carol and Alan and sent them before her down the back stairs. "Is it a tornado?" Carol asked, her voice shaking.

"No, but the wind may be dangerous and we'll all be safer in the cellar. Now hurry!"

"But it's so dark!" Alan protested, clutching the handrail and forcing his feet to move in spite of his fear.

Helen's eyes had grown perceptive in the darkness, and in her quick action to ensure everyone's safety, she'd forgotten the obvious. After walking them to the windowless coal cellar, she returned to her apartment for a candle.

The wind rushing through the open front door had extinguished the tiny flames, though two of the wicks still glowed in the oppressive darkness. As Helen reached out for one, a powerful hand circled her wrist.

With a startled cry she lashed out, then tried to pull away and found that, for all her newborn strength, she was helpless. Gripping her shoulders, Charles whirled her to face him and, as she boldly met his eyes, he touched her thoughts.

He was all she'd expected and so much more! She felt his

mind crawl over hers, then, powerful and demanding, penetrate to study her resolve, her will, her desires. It seemed they faced each other for hours while she, proud of what she was and would become, made no attempt to hide. His satisfaction was obvious when he broke the silence and told her bluntly, "So you tricked them and came back, did you? I knew you would. You have insight of your own, and as I expected, you are stubborn enough to trust it. An admirable trait or a curse . . . we shall learn which it is before this new day is over."

All the words she had so carefully planned to say were forgotten as she returned his stare and listened to that bewitching voice. Releasing his hold, he pushed her down to the sofa. "Stay here, granddaughter. When I am certain we will not be disturbed, I will return for you."

"No! No, you can't!" she pleaded in a frantic whisper, and gripped his wrist. "I will help you but you must leave them alone! They haven't . . ."

His mind stole her words once more, and his look was one of undiluted scorn. "You have already helped me far more than you realize. All I require is your presence. You have nothing with which to bargain." He pulled his arm away, and his form, no more than a deeper shadow in the deadly night, disappeared in the direction of the back stairs.

"My God," Helen groaned, then bit the side of her index finger to keep from screaming out a warning, because warning her cousins would do them no good at all.

In the dusty cellar, Carol and Alan sat on two cement blocks, huddled together in dark, fearful misery as they waited for Helen. When long, terrible minutes had passed and she still hadn't returned, Alan began to shiver and Carol wrapped her arms around him. "She'll be back soon," she said, trying to sound confident and older.

"It isn't just that!" Alan began to sob. There were footsteps in his mind that sounded like those he heard at night. Only now he understood the difference . . . these were real and there were no words to make them disappear. He clutched his sister tightly, terrified she would be plucked away from him and he would be left alone and blind to wonder how she had been punished.

Carol held him, peering into the blackness surrounding her

as if somewhere in it lurked the courage she needed to walk through the cluttered basement and up those steep stairs to her cousin's apartment. She had visions of windows blown in, roofs coming down, Helen injured and bleeding. These broad, horrible thoughts overrode her private fear of darkness and the small things that thrived on darkness which she was sure were now creeping toward both of them.

She had begun to tell Alan she must go back upstairs when they heard an unexpected voice say softly, "I have to come to keep my promise, Alan."

As Carol flinched, Alan yelled "No!" and broke away from her to run in the direction from which these words had come. He tripped on the uneven floor and fell hard, skinning both arms, then sprang back to his feet to run forward and beat small, ineffective fists against Charles's chest. "Don't you touch her!" he ordered with all the ferocity a six-year-old boy on the edge of hysteria could muster. "I take it back! Just go away!"

His scream was more surprise than fear as he was scooped up like a kitten and held at arm's length so his blows fell on air. "I'd expected you to say this."

That sugary reply, the brief burst of sinister laughter, and Alan's second, more terrified, wail made Carol leap to her feet, weak-kneed with terror yet ready to rush in defense her little brother.

"It's too late for both of you, Carol. You see, you both have to be out of the way tonight and very, very quiet . . ."

When Helen had made her decision to return and wait for Charles, she'd gambled that her cousins would be asleep when Charles came and she would have time to reason with him. Now it appeared she had been tragically naive.

She tried to extend, to know what Charles was doing, but she could not tame her emotions to obtain the necessary control. She tried to listen, but angry winds destroyed all other noises. Rushing to the kitchen, she pulled a boning knife from the drawer and, holding it behind her back, moved quickly down the stairs. On the landing, she sensed the presence of another in her mind and fought for calm, refusing to think of the weapon she carried.

Her negation was enough.—Give it to me.—He stood on

the top step to the basement, holding out his hand.

She moved back a step, barely able to resist his control.

—Give it to me!—

Somewhere was a thought she would not allow to form—she regretted Stephen had never forced her will. She imagined how it would feel to submit.

—Very good. Now give it to me.—

Helen slumped against the wall and moved her arm slowly out from behind her. Then, in a single burst of almost alien speed, she slashed her weapon sideways, aimed for his heart. She cried out as her wrist was caught and the weapon clattered uselessly to the ground. Then she waited bravely for the ensuing attack and her own destruction.

Charles merely glanced at the tear in his shirt, though his brows shot up in amazement and he looked approvingly at her. "Sad that I anticipated the move. Still, in another month I doubt I would have needed Stephen. But come, let us go somewhere more comfortable to wait for our kinsman."

Exposed for the first time to a fully commanding power, Helen began to obey, then stiffened. "What did you do to my cousins?" she demanded.

"What I had to do." With that laconic answer he reached for her, but she sprang back to grip the handrail.

For a moment he studied her in frank amusement, then his look grew grim once more. "You must learn to lose your concern with fragile humanity. What's done is already done, and besides, you ought to be more interested in my plans for you. Now come!"

She raised her chin in defiance and held the rail more tightly.

He shrugged. "Very well, I don't have time to argue." Rearranging the bow and sheaf of arrows, he pulled her to him and flung her over one shoulder, then carried her up the stairs, following the same path Stephen had taken on their first night together.

After he deposited her on Stephen's low bed, he ignored her cries, her pleas that he stop and, with open palms, beat the glass from the wine-colored window, leaving an empty hole in which only pieces of the more durable leading remained as a reminder of what had been destroyed.

Although only its beauty had been alive, each blow to the

rainbow-filled window brought Helen pain. She wrenched forward, her hand flying to her neck to clench that small piece of cobalt glass as she took what comfort she could from the happy memories that room still held. Some minutes after the blows had stopped, she raised her head to see Charles watching her keenly, one finger rubbing her chin. "Very pretty," he commented with a lewd smile, and she flushed.

He reached down and pried her fingers off the blue stone, snapping the chain and holding it beyond her reach. "An Austra trinket! And tell me, Granddaughter, how does it feel to clutch something inanimate yet so pure . . . permeated with all of the potency of a land on whose soil you have never walked?"

He gripped her chin and turned her face up to his, staring intently at her eyes, blue-black in the darkness, fearful yet passionate in their rage. And he admired her . . . how she sat with her hands frozen at her sides, refusing to submit by ineffective struggles to the power he wielded over her. "My granddaughter," he whispered proudly, "that attack on the stairs was no brave concern for your charges. You would kill me if you could, wouldn't you?" He saw her assent, the delight it would bring. "Would that your uncle could find your strength."

Her uncle? It took her a moment to realize he meant Stephen, not Dick, and she found herself studying Charles with greater calm and growing disbelief. He moved back, held out his arms, and gave her a merry bow. "Stephen's age doesn't bother you but my youth does. You'll get used to the timelessness eventually, and there are familial compensations. Sometime ask Stephen to draw you a family tree. It most resembles the Gordian knot."

He sat beside her and pushed her down on her back, one hand brushing her neck while the other moved down her legs in a manner oddly clinical. When his examination was complete, he looked at her first in surprise, then, in response to her thoughts, licentiously. He chuckled at her revulsion.

"It wouldn't be that odious, but I have neither the time nor the inclination. I do, however, apologize for what I must take. Judging from your strength and your heritage, I doubt you will remain where I place you unless you are restrained, and so I restrain you."

Helen screamed once as the too-familiar paralysis de-

scended on her legs, then, angry at her show of weakness, she
glared at him and pushed herself into a sitting position. She
had been a fool and she was trapped, but even now, whatever
he had planned for her, she planned to fight.

"You are so close to perfect, yet kept so ignorant." He
knelt behind her, wrapping his arms around, making it impossible to struggle. "Now, Granddaughter, let me keep my promise and show you eternity."

She fought his mental onslaught until she was blind from
the pain, then submitted to his power. The images flowed
past, an obscene movie played at a dangerous speed. . . .

. . . They hunt for men and women, human beings, creatures of more diverse uses . . . their kind and hers beginning
the unspoken warfare that stems from the dawn of civilization
. . . the victims wear skins, later rough woven rags, while their
hunters are naked, impervious to shame, to cold or to
mercy. . . .

The scenes were too sharp, the deaths too real. Helen
struggled to pull her body forward, gagging, certain she was
about to be sick and despising her weakness, but he only
gripped her more tightly, forcing her back against his chest,
and whispered, "Artistic. I suppose in one sense we always
were. Look closely, for this is how the legends were born in a
past before my past . . . fact not superstition!"

. . . A tiny, damp cell cages a creature reduced to less than
an animal but still far more than human . . . she paces with the
victim, frantic, ravenous, waiting for the planned destruction,
the attempt to bring life to a finality it could not comprehend. . . .

"A brief scene from a far more recent retaliation."

Tears ran down her cheeks. "Tell me. Did he live?" She
guessed at the sex, for she could determine nothing from how
she had felt, what she had seen.

Bitterness seeped into her.—I'm here now.—And, to her
silent query—We hide until we can hide no longer and then
. . . usually . . . we survive and we kill. Here is still more recent history.—

. . . Three children, the youngest a toddler, the oldest
Carol's age, in chains in the middle of a dusty town square.
With no madman to lead them, the townsfolk, uncertain and
guilty, bring water and food but the water gives no sustenance

and the food is useless and from dawn to dusk they burn.

One day of sunlight is endured and nearly forgotten as night falls and the body grows in strength and renews . . . two, three, five! They shade one another as best they can. Six. The youngest screams, draws the crowd. The oldest covers his mouth with her hand, pulling him to her. Seven. The hunger is unbearable, not confined but breathing in every nerve, every demanding cell. Eight. The youngest lays dying and, at the first light of dawn, with the innocent instincts of children they devour him, knowing which must get the greater share so both may live.

Darkness. Quiet. The eldest washes the dirt off her face with the water, smooths back her hair, strips off her rags, and, tapping powers formed prematurely in need, lures the jailer away from his sleep and into her deadly arms . . .

"Rachel is a wonder with children and the oldest of our women, for she vows she will have no children of her own."

. . . If they had caught her as she ran, they would have known what she was but her leg orders *stop* long before they near. Unsuspecting, they find her and drag her, flaccid as any woman, from her hiding place and rip off her clothes to search so thoroughly for the devil's mark. Seeing only perfection, they are aroused and, panicked, she cannot quench their rising lust. She tries to bolt but too many hands reach for her. Fighting, screaming, they pin her down, pounding her face and chest, gripping her legs, wrenching them apart.

Helen fought the penetrations wildly, beating her head against Charles's chest, clawing at his hands with her nails, screaming, "This is monstrous, let me go!" in a language she had never spoken. Then she became the males . . . kneeling between her straining legs, running calloused hands down her thighs, feeling the pain as she received more pleasure from the torment than the act.

"The desire! Feel it, Granddaughter; feel it and understand how exposed the magnetism will make you to those attacks. Now do you comprehend why you must be able to run?"

. . . Satiated, no longer ignorant, they debate the demon's destruction and, ignored, she takes that one chance to escape, to live with a memory that will never dull with time. . . .

Then he showed her how those attackers died. The exquisite satisfaction Helen received from their torture disgusted her.

"Austra vengeance is remarkably appropriate, don't you think? And here is another page of our history."

. . . When madness infects so many they are impossible to control, so he achieves the only advantage he can and the fires are set at dusk rather than dawn. But the hours pass too quickly and his people do not come. His life is his own to preserve.

What sorcerer has spun these bonds that hold him in such a tenacious grasp? Push back concern, for they are but ropes and the stake is wood and both will burn while he, like the Phoenix, will rise from the ashes for revenge, for night has come and he is powerful.

Helen moves within him, immense as deepest winter, a glacier to hold back insatiable heat.

. . . They burn him and his lover first, back to back in common bonds. Torches fall and smoke is of pine and ash, thick with life and decay. It stings his eyes and makes him oddly dizzy as he battles the impossible ropes. The woman, her voice frantic from approaching pain, cries out, "You're cutting me!" And he remembers her mortality and the one act remaining between them.

—I'm hungry, love.—His thought so gentle, she understands and turns her head, stretching back her neck so he can glut on her before the flames reach. Her blood pulses down his throat, warm and rich with life ended, the taste cloying with terror.—I will remember. I will not be consumed and I will avenge.—He revels in their scent, the lust of the crowd so thick, it drowns the smoke. The destruction will be their own, for he cannot die and he will kill. . . .

Trapped within him, Helen trembled. "There is nothing, nothing but the cold!"

An arm pinned her tightly, a hand covered her mouth. —And there is heat.—

. . . The fire hisses a warning, then roars, blasts against flesh that fights its attack and nerves that survive to show no mercy. The screams rise up and up with the smoke, seeking madness—that tantalizing relief!—while with instinctive control, his legs push out to break the ropes as they weaken in the flames. With feet black and cracked, he pushes against the stake and, as his hair ignites, he breaks free to roll naked and smoldering to the feet of his gaping executioner. His skin creeps slowly as it repairs, and when sight returns, he notices first the throng, frozen only in disbelief. He stands, his fingers curled, waiting to slash the first who try to toss him back, and sensing his weakness, his prey closes in. . . .

Helen snarls with his triumph, feeling the first touch of family.

. . . The arrows fly one, two, three, cutting down the rashest of adversaries, while he, a victim no longer, reaches out with bleeding fingers and with one deft squeeze paralyzes, then flings a new sacrifice into the flames. The pain hammers her, the screams claw at her. She laughs. . . .

And his glory, her glory, in the killing began.

. . . Men and women, all but the smallest children, slaughtered quickly, then more slowly; and last and most mercifully, the next intended victims who have witnessed their deliverance and cannot be allowed to live.

She kneels, her face buried in another's life, too greedy to breathe. Someone pulls her to her feet.—Can you run, little brother?—

The lives he had taken expand, filling him.—Always!—

And swift, silent, bloody as great cats following a gorging, the victors depart, leaving their carnage to rot with the coming sun, for they do not bury what is not their own. . . .

"The roots of Austra vengeance lay firmly in denial. Remember this and remember, half-human, to always guard your thoughts. Only I can tell you this, for only I know fear . . . as I know that flames can kill and that I am a coward."

. . . Night after night he builds the fires, watching the flames burn, greedy and beautiful, moving closer, always closer, until he walks through them, letting them tear at his flesh while he feels no pain. . . .

"And what did he gain but another talent to hide, and one day, perhaps, a painless death? Your lover, my brother, you do him no justice by thinking of him as any more, or less, than he is."

The visions stopped. She found her calm. "The scenes were so old," she protested weakly.

"It's been less than forty years since they flung my son to

the waves. I was saddened most by my surprise." And scenes, briefer, no less horrid, continued.

. . . captivity, floggings, more elaborate tortures, times when inexplicably the victims refuse to die . . .

Permeating all was the constant secrecy that made them vulnerable while imparting the only protection from the envy, the hate, the ensuing merciless destruction of their private world.

In her exhaustion, a strange lucidity possessed her. "Why did you take these thoughts? Why did you wish to know?"

"They cannot be hidden from me. They are my sustenance."

And from his consummate misery, she understood the morality Stephen had tried so often to explain: You become what you choose to take. She protested one last time: "This is not our world! Our world is different!"

Though she meant something else, he showed her the fire storm of Hamburg, of London, of Berlin . . . Auschwitz . . . Hiroshima! The deaths, the deaths, the countless deaths. Mountains of knotted corpses . . . the near past and the future . . .

He stole her voice when she tried to scream, he held her down when she tried to fight, and he showed her the women who were lost, choosing to be lost rather than returning to live in this pernicious human world.

His thoughts pounded her. —Do you want that future? Do you want that time? Do you want to be a part of eternity? Do you?

"I am merciful, Granddaughter," he hissed while she searched for some anchor as she drifted too close to madness. She found it in Stephen.

As he returned her to this room, her self, his words rushed like an avalanche sweeping away even love. "Do you know what you are destined to become? You will have the blood of the Austras and the reproductive ability of humanity. You can have children, as many as you wish, and live. With Stephen as your mate, you will breed true, and your children will possess the power of Stephen's mind, your own mind. At last the most magnificent of the Austras can assume his most important responsibility without that terrible loss. Had my brother despised you, he would have treated you no differently than he did in his love."

"Nooooo . . ."

The word trailed off into a low, desolate moan. He released her and she rolled away to face the wall, to fight the implications of the words and visions. She ignored Charles, now moving away from her until she sensed the concerned touch and heard the voice, her lover's voice demand, "What have you done to her?"

Helen looked toward the doorway, aware for the first time that the storm had passed, and through the webbed hole that had once held wonder came the bright glow of the sunrise. Its rays enhanced the lines of Stephen's face, taut and beautiful in its anger. But what had once fascinated now horrified, and at the sound of a language she had thought beautiful, she pressed her hands against her ears and struggled not to hear.

In response to her inaudible scream, Stephen's rage intensified. "What horrors have you shown!"

Charles responded with more quiet anger, heavy with contempt. "You've been living a romantic fantasy. I merely gave her the facts and showed her the world as it was, is, and ever shall be. Even you would not have allowed her to choose our life in ignorance. And today she must choose."

Stephen moved a step closer to his brother, and Charles raised his bow, pointing it at Helen's heart. "Don't move, Granddaughter. Don't even think of moving." He looked triumphantly at Stephen. "Well, little brother, you were going to stand between us. Dare you attempt it now?"

Eyeing the weapon with disgust, Stephen replied, "You know what she is. You will not harm her." His tone and words were meant to reassure, but now they brought no comfort to Helen. For a moment she was unsure which brother she hated more and, in response, Stephen's resolve weakened.

The bow did not waver, though Charles appeared thoughtful. "I suppose I should not shoot. She is, after all, my own flesh and blood . . . and yours, too, eh? But you see, her death will only be one more despicable deed among the many I have committed on this night. You stand there enraged at the loss of your friend. Consider how you will feel when this arrow pierces her heart. You will attack me then, Stephen. Find the will to attack me now. I will shoot her or I will drop this bow when I feel your hands on my throat. Sense my pulse, Stephen. She is ten beats from death."

There was silence. Stephen's protective instincts surged to override his love. Helen had disobeyed, had betrayed him and placed him in this self-destructive dilemma. He wanted nothing more than to turn and leave this room and let her face whatever fate Charles wished . . . yet he could not. Quickly, he tried another approach.

—Seek to hold me, brother, and I will not wait to shoot.—

—Don't do this!— Helen told Stephen, even as her eyes were trapped by the gleaming tip of the arrow, even as she felt the pain radiating from the place it would strike. She prayed for time, for her lover, but while she obeyed Charles and did not move away, she raised her hand slowly, intending to make one final valiant attempt to deflect death as it flew to her.

Her futile bravery, her sacrifice, and ultimately his love forced Stephen's decision but his body, obeying only survival, began to turn. With the swiftness of thought, he heard the promise Charles made both of them.—If you leave, I will take her as I did Dick Wells, and after I am done with her soul I will destroy her body more painfully than I did that naive priest's. I promise you, Stephen, that you will feel the large and the small of her torment. When it is over, you may face the family, but, little brother, what of yourself?—

Stephen shuddered then, with a low growl of rage, whirled to make the only move he believed left him. He sprang.

It was a ruthless attack, one only another of his blood could repel, and the defense was deadly. Whatever doubts Stephen had concerning his ability to complete this attack became irrelevant as Charles, in one fluid motion, swung and fired his weapon. The arrow passed through Stephen's shoulder, hurling him around. He grabbed the half-open door to keep from falling and this pause, barely perceived by Helen, allowed Charles to send a second arrow flying to slam into Stephen's back, severing an artery and impaling him to the door frame. As Stephen's moved to push his body free, a third arrow struck lower, piercing a chamber of his heart, then imbedding in the wood below the first. Stephen slumped, waiting for the arrow that never came. Through the pain of the wounds his body already fought, he felt the destructive rays of the sun. His instincts dominated, his heart stopped, and he died.

Helen grabbed wildly for Charles but he'd moved beyond her reach. "He was giving you only what you wanted, and for that you killed him, you killed him, you killed . . ." She screamed the words over and over, seeking some way to make them comprehensible.

But Charles did not hear her cries. All the hate, all the rage . . . his own and what he had stolen . . . was depleted in that instant. He fell to his knees, curled his body forward, and with a long, low moan consumed the agony pervading this room. How could he have done this? Where had he found the will to stop? He looked up, his eyes trapped by the sight of the blood flowing bright red from his brother's shoulder, darker from the chest, the growing puddle at Stephen's feet measuring his grisly triumph. As Helen's screams subsided, he dared to hope, and when at last he turned to her, his eyes were compassionate, his voice low and comforting. "No, I could not kill him, though you and time may do it for me. However this ends, I will return for you." Forcing his eyes to meet the painful sunrise, he added, seemingly to himself, "I think it's going to be a beautiful day."

He walked to the doorway, then stopped to gaze sadly at his brother's face, white and still as it leaned toward the light. He touched Stephen's cheek in a gesture of love, of good-bye, then, without a word, left Helen to wrestle with insanity.

Charles had lied, Helen knew. Stephen was dead. Nothing could be wounded as he had been and survive. Was this terrible destruction the end her instincts had foretold? Were these deceptive feelings the powers she must learn to trust? Human doubts, human emotions of alien intensity swirled through her mind, fleeing before they could be grasped. As she sat and stared at her lover, only two thoughts touched her and remained . . . the hideous evil of the act Charles had committed and how right, how perfectly right, it was to be a part of Stephen's world.

Her decision was made. She would take her chances that Charles was wrong and the future would be preferable to that violent past. Words that were intended to be a cruel revelation now imparted to her only hope. She would go to her new family and they would accept her if not for who she was, then for the children she could give them. And she would live in spite of the sorrow and the guilt and the knowledge that her personal future would never be as happy as this last summer from her past had been.

As the first rays of sunlight brushed her hair, Helen remembered the dancing rainbows that had altered the dawn so soothingly in this room, which had once known love. "Stephen," she called repeatedly while she mourned him. Then her eyes grew wide and she gasped in joyful and horrified relief when he slowly raised his unscathed arm and, placing his palm against the wall, pushed.

The arrow stakes remained imbedded in the wood, though the ends moved a few inches into his back, briefly increasing the flow of blood. There was now a small space between his body and the door frame. He pushed again.

Was that his pain scalding her shoulder and her side? Was that his heart, three-chambered, beating with human speed, wildly struggling to maintain the life inexorably departing? "Oh, love," she whispered, and tried to go to him, only to find her legs were still not her own. Pulling herself with her hands, she moved closer to where he battled in silent agony.

As she neared him, the terror began, the warning becoming louder . . . feeding her fears until she sensed herself falling into a helpless shock that would render the rest of her body as useless as her legs. As she fought the rising emotion, she sensed within it a fast flutter, a draining strength and, on the edge of submission, she understood. She had seen her death, her slow destruction. But her knowledge broke the spell he could barely cast. Forcing herself forward, she sat beneath him, her cotton skirt absorbing the blood. "Stephen, you fool!" She fought back the wild laughter. "How empty eternity would seem without you!"

If she could somehow reach them, she could pull out the arrows, but there was nothing to support her except the wall and door frame. Careful not to lean against Stephen, her fingers gripped the bloody molding and she tried to use what small strength her legs still possessed and stand. She fell and tried again, succeeding in balancing herself on her knees. Holding tightly to each side of the doorway, she began to inch slowly upward.—No—he warned.—Go away before I kill you.—

"And where will I go? Please, I am responsible for this. I

can't watch you die, then live with the memory. I must help you."

His need conquered.—This is not the way. Grab my legs and pull.—His useful hand, she saw, was pressed flat against the top of the frame, and as he pushed with quick jerks, she added her weight until the thick shafts snapped.

His fall jarred the ends of the stakes, opening the wound his body battled so skillfully, and beneath him, the stains spread. Pull the arrows. Did he say it or did she think it? No matter, it made sense. Gritting her teeth, trying not to think of the pain this must cause him, she fought for an effective grip on the wood, finally wrapping her skirt around them and wrenching them free.

And still the blood flowed, dripping from him to the floor, drying in the light. She collected as much of the freshest as she could and, using a cupped palm, held it to his lips.—Too late. The sun.—She looked down at the offering, black and lifeless, and understood how time would kill him. Reaching behind her, she pulled the thin sheets off the bed and shaded him with those and her body, then, measuring the distance to the darkness down the hall, she frantically wondered . . .

# II

Holding each other for comfort, Carol and Alan sat in silence, certain that to move or speak would bring the punishment they had been vividly shown if they disobeyed. They were thankful for the stone wall at their back; the wind that muffled other sounds; and the thick wood door between them and their jailer, who might be present nearby. As time passed, Alan gradually relaxed into great sobs of misery.

"Shhh." Carol held him tightly and whispered, "Alan, what's wrong?"

"Don't touch me. I don't deserve it when I've been so bad. I'm the one who told him to come."

"Alan, why?"

He described the meeting and ended with words nearly impossible to understand. "He said he would hurt you, get even for me. He told me . . . oh, Carol!" With that he began to cry harder. In fear that he would be heard, and harmed, she wrapped her arms around him and pulled his face to her chest to muffle the sound. He sniffed and finished, "I didn't mean it. I didn't want to do it, but it sounded so good for a second . . . I'm . . . I'm sorry." The apology was more a broken breath than a whisper. He knew how useless the words were now.

Carol hugged her brother. "It's okay. He didn't do anything." She held him while his crying subsided, and they sat, holding hands in silence, until the storm rolled away and the screams began.

They screamed themselves as each received a vivid vision of what was occurring next door. Through her fright, Carol heard a voice, her own voice, speak to her and tell her what she had to do. In spite of the warnings, in spite of the bloody fate that would be theirs if they disobeyed, she trusted that voice as she would a parent or an adult friend. Unwrapping her brother's clinging arms, she stood and calmly announced, "We're getting out of here. We have to help."

Though cold tremors threatened to destroy all brave intentions, Carol groped her way to the door and pushed optimistically against it, but the bar was in place on the outside. "Oh, hell," she swore, and might have cried. But then she remembered the cold air shaft.

She slipped into the shaft, her eyes tearing from the square of daylight above her. Pressing her bare feet against the narrower sides, she climbed easily to the top, then hooked her fingers through one edge of the grate while she pushed against the loose corner. Though the thin metal moved, she could not bend it back.

Returning to the cellar, she told her brother, "We need something I can use like a crowbar." They searched the cellar and found only two rotten wooden slats. Alan remembered the old coal-furnace tools, stored on a shelf somewhere in the rafters. Carol lifted him up, and brushing away spiders and things that crawled faster and must not be named, Alan groped blindly until he reached too far forward and fell out of his sister's arms.

Carol made him sit in a corner while she stood on stacked cement blocks and tried again. On the fourth attempt, she was rewarded with the dusty ledge. She sneezed as she extracted the metal bar that had been used to tend the coal fires. It was awkwardly long and heavy but otherwise an ideal tool for their escape.

Carol slid the bar up the return, then walked up the sides and gripped the cover. Alan ducked in under her and handed up the bar. One hand, sweaty from her efforts, closed around it, but she lost her grip and it fell, its pointed tip opening a ragged cut on Alan's temple. Though she could not see the damage, she heard the blow and his painful cry and winced.

"Hand it up," she ordered, and prayed as she waited for the bar to brush her legs. When it did, she held it more tightly and waited for him to move away before she began her work.

She maneuvered the bar through the loose corner, then pried, moved the bar and pried again. Room opened for her head and shoulders, and, despite the sharp metal pieces that ripped her clothes and raked her back, she pushed, then pulled, her way through. Quickly, she picked up the phone but found the line was still dead. Giving way to one brief exclamation of panic, she held the bar in front of her and rushed down the stairs to rescue her brother.

A startled, weak cry greeted her as she swung open the cellar door, and in the dim light now leaking in from the basement windows she saw the blood running down her brother's face. Guiding him upstairs to Helen's apartment, she laid him down on the sofa and patted his arm. "You'll be all right. I'll be back in a minute."

She hoped she'd be back, she reminded herself as she walked through Stephen's unlocked front door and up the stairs. At each step, the silence spoke more eloquently to her fears than any whimpers of suffering or screams of terror ever could have done. When she reached the top, she paused before turning the doorknob, half hoping it would be locked.

Instead the door swung open to reveal an empty workroom, an empty living room, and, she discovered as she tiptoed through the flat, an empty kitchen. It was there that she heard them . . . the soft sounds, as of a small animal in pain. For one selfish moment Carol lamented that she was so brave. Then, forcing herself forward, she peered around the corner and down the hallway that led to the bedroom.

Helen had heard the footsteps before they entered the apartment, and had she been rational, she would have known

them for a child's, but she had moved to touch a different
reality, one that threatened to slip through her fingers like
water, like blood. When she looked up at Carol, her eyes were
wild, primitive, half blind.

Carol stepped back, her fists covering her mouth, then
blurted, "Helen! Helen, look! Don't you know me?"

The face was not her enemy's. The voice did not belong to
him, and so, with a loving caress, Helen unwound her mind
from the other's and reached out to draw her cousin to her.
"Oh, Carol! I thought you'd been killed."

Carol did not hear the words. She was staring at Stephen's
back; at the blood, the holes. He had gotten nearly through the
doorway. Now he lay still, summoning from hidden places the
strength to continue. "Is he dead?" Carol whispered, turning
dull, shocked eyes to Helen.

"No." As she said this, Helen felt a further lightening of
despair. "And he will not die, especially now that you're here.
We must move him out of the light."

Carol didn't question that strange need or Helen's helplessness. Instead she pulled and Helen pushed, and they inched
Stephen through the doorway, three red streaks recording their
progress into the shadows. After Carol shut the bedroom door,
Stephen shuddered and began pulling himself toward the multicolored living room, his fingers digging into the wood floor
like claws.

Hearing whispered orders in her mind, Carol looked questioningly at Helen, who nodded in agreement and rushed forward to lower the dark shades on the unprotected north
windows, then into the kitchen for a bottle of lukewarm water
from the refrigerator. She handed it to Helen and stood above
Stephen, staring down at his face: white, luminous as new
snow in the moonlight, his hair every color that flowed
through the windows. Trapped by her concern and this bewitching beauty, she began to kneel.

A child's presence, such a temptation! Yet so unsafe and so
much a friend. Stephen struggled to remain conscious, to consider other hopes, aware of how dangerous he was becoming
as need trampled control. Already he was so weak, so hungry,
and she so magnificently alive!

He rolled partially to his side, one hand reaching up to
Carol, motioning her to come closer. As he touched her

shoulder, he glanced beyond her to Helen and pulled back, laying flat once more, hugging the floor. —Go!—Carol heard this and other orders as well and, with one last fascinated look at Stephen, she obeyed, leaving and pulling the main door shut behind her.

Helen sat beside her lover, wondering how he could still live. He was stiff, his skin white, his wounds no longer bleeding, she was certain, only because his body had no blood left to give. When she touched him to push back the hair matted to his forehead, she shuddered at how cold he had become. Gently, she rolled him onto his back, and ripping off a portion of the hem of her ruined skirt, she soaked it in the cloudy water, cleansed the wounds, and finally laid the cloth over the most dangerous of the holes. Cradling his head in her lap, she poured a small trickle of water into his mouth. Some went down. Heartened, she tried again, and now he drank with greater ease. "More?" He responded with a faint shake of his head.

Seeing the improvement in him, she could bear to ask, "Stephen, will you leave me?"

—No!...I need time...I need...—He slammed his mind shut to her, but through his weakness she detected his unfinished thought and understood why she hadn't considered the obvious before.

But even now she could not hide from him.—Leave me. It is death for you to stay. Let time heal and it will be safer for you to come to me—A lie, but with her gone he could summon an unknown victim. Now, as his mind extended, it found only her...her scent, her blood, her life.—Get out!—he ordered with what power remained.—I need time.—

Time! They had no time. Charles said he would return and they must be ready. Lying beside Stephen, she used the cobalt stone to open a deep gash on her neck and, like a mother guiding an infant, she pulled his head up toward the wound. His hands rose, trying to push her away, but she was the strong one now. His efforts to disobey weakened him, her vitality tempted him, and he surrendered to her greater power and drank. As the life force grew within him, his arms lifted once more, this time to circle her body, to press this cherished victim more tightly to him.

At first the sensation was pleasant, reminding Helen of

their nights together. Later he held her too close and his teeth grated against the wound, opening it further. When at last, in a belated struggle for her own life, she tried to push him away, she had no strength. Too late she understood his warnings and wondered, with dwindling concern, if she would survive.

# Chapter Twenty-Four

## I

ALAN LAY ASLEEP where Carol had left him, a great purple welt growing around the cut on his forehead. He rolled over, sobbing as the wound brushed the sofa back. Knowing only one way to help him, Carol went to the silent refrigerator and returned with a few remaining pieces of ice wrapped in a towel. After wedging the ice against the lump, she sank wearily to the floor next to her brother and cried out as she felt the slashes across her back. Then, so sleepy, so exhausted from effort and fright, she let her eyes drift shut and she slept.

The loud pounding at the screen door woke her. With her shoulders held stiff, she opened it to admit Larson and Walker. "Is Stephen Austra here?" She shook her head. "Is Helen here?"

"They're both gone. There's just my brother and me."

"What happened to him?" Larson asked, noticing the ice bag.

"He fell . . . on the stairs when we ran to the basement." Carol began inventing details she hoped would make her story more believable and keep the police from asking anything else.

While Carol was talking to Larson, Walker had searched the empty rooms, sure the girl was not telling the entire truth. Returning to the living room, he swore when he saw Carol's back, then hastily toned down his language. "Geez, what happened to you?"

"I fell too." It was becoming easy to lie. "We'll both be okay."

"Sure you will, sweetheart," Walker said, "just as soon as you get to a hospital." When he picked Alan up, the boy didn't stir. "We'd better move it," he told his partner.

"I don't want to go," Carol protested.

"Don't worry." Larson took her hand. "We'll drive you to Elmbrook and after you're treated, you can see your dad."

And that was how Carol found herself standing at the side of her father's bed, staring intently . . . first at the blood (that unpleasant reminder) dripping into his arm, then at her father, who lay so pale and still, so much like Stephen. She wanted to throw herself on the bed and wake her father and hug him, but Corey, remembering Dick's fearful reaction to just the touch of his hand, held her back. "Call his name, honey, until he wakes up."

She did, and when Dick's eyes opened, they darted in fear, then filled with relief as he saw his daughter. He held out his arms and she yelped when he hugged her.

"What's the matter?" Dick asked. In reply, Carol told him the same story she'd told the two officers.

"Is Alan all right?"

"He's downstairs getting X-rayed." Larson said. "He has a concussion and they want to keep him in for observation."

Dick hadn't believed more than a few words of Carol's story. "Let me see your back," he said. She turned and raised the hospital-issue shirt, and Dick stared in horror at the two long slashes, then held his fingers up to them as he tried to decide.

Corey looked as well and shook his head. "Too far apart," he commented.

"Excuse me," Larson interrupted with an odd glance at both men. "I'm not just here playing kid delivery service. We've got a big problem on our hands. I'm sorry to have to talk to you both in your hospital beds but—"

Dick cut in. "Should my daughter leave?"

"I think so."

Once Carol had gone, Larson began. "This morning around four forty-five a train collided with Squad Ninety-four near Seventieth and Lorain, making one hell of an explosion.

The train conductor and engineer are both in the hospital and lucky to be alive. Parker and O'Reilly are dead. It took us over an hour before we were even able to ID the car." Then Larson addressed Cory. "I suppose you'll want to see the bodies, but there . . . ah, isn't going to be much." Though he'd known both men well, Larson went on evenly, giving Corey details before turning his attention back to Dick. "The last report from them came in at four A.M., stating they were parked in front of your house and that everything was A-okay."

Dick and Corey exchanged a quick, sad glance. Charles had made his calls.

Leaning back in apparent weariness, Dick sighed. "I'll talk to my daughter, and when the phones come back up, I'll call you if she has anything to add."

Larson caught Corey's eye and the two of them left together. After sending Carol back inside, Larson pulled out a pack of cigarettes and, ignoring a nurse's disapproving look, offered one to Corey. Only after they'd shared a match and walked some distance down the hall did he continue with his bad news. "I wasn't sure how much I should say to Wells, but those kids were home alone. There was no sign of Dick's niece—or of Stephen Austra."

"They'll show up. Dick can talk to them later, or I will."

"There's more. We got an earlier call from O'Reilly. He requested an ambulance be sent to St. John's. It arrived too late to save the pastor. The attendants found the body in the choir loft beneath the round window. The wind apparently destroyed the center brace and the upper sections fell in on him." He described the scene, O'Maera's broken leg, multiple cuts and bandaged wrists, as well as the blood discovered at the center of the window. "We can't tell if this was a murder, an accident, or a suicide. Were Wells and the priest friends?"

"Close. I'll give him the bad news and stop by St. John's later to take a look. I planned to check out soon and go back to work, anyway. Send me a car, an automatic, as soon as you can, then call my office around four. I'll probably have plenty of questions and maybe a few answers for you."

Larson rapped on Corey's cast. "I see why you're out of commission, but what's Dick doing here, anyway?"

"He was attacked by his alien monster, but keep it to yourself, okay?"

Corey's chuckle was meant to make the truth sound like an evasive joke, but Larson answered seriously. "I thought so, but I'm learning. If anybody asks, he had an accident."

Cory didn't know how much more bad news his friend could take but he neēdn't have worried. When he returned to their room and saw Dick's face, he knew nothing he could tell would be worse than the story Dick had heard when Carol cracked under pressure. After sending the girl downstairs to look in on her brother, the two friends pieced together the night's events. "It's over, Cor, isn't it?" Dick said despondently. "Our secrecy was blown to bits with that squad car."

"I gave you my word, partner."

"We've always gone out on a limb for each other, but I can't hold you to any promise now, Cor."

"You're not asking, I'm doing. Hell, those two died in the line of duty. The families collect the pension and insurance either way."

With luck there might be an ally left to appreciate this risk. "I'm going home," Dick decided.

"You don't like being on the list of wounded in action; you want your name at the head of the death column, right? Let me go instead, partner. St. John's will wait."

"No! Even assuming Carol exaggerated, Stephen is wounded and dangerous. Walk in there, Cor, and you'll just look like lunch. Me? I'll be all right. After all, they all know me . . . damned intimately." He swung his feet over the side of the bed, then sat up and gripped the headboard as the room danced around him.

"I've got an idea, partner. Let's speed up your IV, and while we're waiting for your tank to fill, you and me and that stupid contraption you're strung out on can walk across the hall and peek in on Judy. When my car shows, I'll drop you off at home." Dick stood, his body shaking, and thankfully gripped the arm Corey offered. With each step he fought the renewed dizziness, finally deciding he might be able to function . . . just barely.

Judy lay awake and managed a wan smile as Dick kissed her cheek. They began an awkward, uncertain conversation. A few times Corey saw Dick look at Judy in sharp expectation, as if he were waiting to give or receive some terrible confession. But none was forthcoming. They had lapsed into a self-conscious silence when breakfast arrived and they sat with trays perched on their laps, comparing opinions on the wretchedness of the food until, with no warning, Judy flung hers off the bed, rolled into a fetal position, and began to scream.

Dick reached out to try to calm her but she kicked him away, hysteria giving her an abundance of strength. He staggered, knocking his blood pack off its hook to splatter on the white tile floor. Rage flooded back, and before the nurse arrived with Judy's sedative, Dick had pulled his IV and gone to his room to dress. His service revolver felt oppressively heavy but the weight reassured him. Nothing would give him greater pleasure than the opportunity to fire it.

## II

Stephen held Helen's life locked to his will as he battled without weapons or words the faceless, formless, brilliant adversary, Death. And he was losing.

He had known when he awakened that his arms would be wrapped around a corpse, and in his need he could have accepted any victim but this one he so loved. For a moment, as she had done with him, he mourned her death, then touched and felt that most important piece of life, that almost alien soul still clinging to its body. He did all he could . . . searched for her, called to her, begged her, then drew her mind close to his, forcing himself to remain calm, knowing she would not survive the hours until his blood could save her.

Before he began that last great gamble and released her to search for the only one capable of helping him, the shadow of his brother fell across them where they lay. Charles waited until Stephen looked up at him before speaking. "So you did not die, after all, Stephen." He sounded as if the outcome had been certain.

Stephen slowly released Helen, and his expression and

voice were devoid of all emotions save sorrow. "Are you here to bait me, Charles? To give me your bow and tell me to shoot you out of anger for your part in this tragedy?" He ran his fingers over Helen's hair, then brushed the ragged, bloodless hole in her neck. "I can't unless I am prepared to accept suicide as well. Do what you will, Charles; destroy the world to destroy yourself. I'm beyond caring "

Charles appeared not to have heard. He knelt beside Helen and studied her face. "How beautiful! And to think I did not have to witness the agony of her birth." His eyes reflected the past . . . of Claudia, of Marie, of others from centuries before.

"She's dying. She forced me to feed on her and now I cannot help her. So whatever fate you had planned for her, Charles, will have to be abandoned, unless . . ." He anticipated the response and did not finish.

"Unless I save the child?"

Stephen's head jerked up and he clutched his brother's arm. He had expected only a scornful refusal, and when he heard these hopeful words, he questioned if the figure before him were real or merely another vision from this seemingly endless nightmare. Something warm and wet coated his fingers, and he saw they were covered with his brother's blood.

Charles displayed the deep, dripping wounds on his wrists. "Of course I will save her. There is enough blood left, just enough. But while I act the role of mother, you must be father and midwife and allow me my choice. This is the price for my aid . . . that almost peaceful death."

"You knew she would do this!" Stephen was astonished at the danger of the game Charles had played. As hope returned, so did anger. The only real threat had been to himself.

Charles responded to both words and thought. "This was no gamble, Stephen. You would have found someone. We always do. As to her sacrifice, did you ever really doubt it?" He looked away. "I suppose you would; sacrifice is not a usual family trait. Still, you surprised me when you sprang, and I'm thankful you did. I was not certain I possessed the resolve to shoot you in the back."

If Stephen made any reply, Charles did not hear it. He stared first at his brother's windows, then at his own creation. There was something about the sculpture's hind legs that had always troubled him. If he had some paper, he could draw a correction, and then . . .

Even through creativity, instincts struck. Charles shook his head sadly and turned back to his brother. "You grow into sacrifice, though I hope you never need to understand. As for me, now that my life is nearly over, I admit that I still long for time. But I am brutally rational. Will you help me now?"

Here was the tragedy Stephen had sensed and never fully seen. He stared at his blood-covered fingers but the blood meant nothing now, save for the life it would give and the one it would end. He searched and found no guilt, no denial; only unyielding sorrow. "Very well, Charles. I will aid you, though I don't understand what you wish me to do."

"The father's role is easy. The midwife's . . ." Charles shook his head too quickly, the gesture a shudder. "I learned their secret in the worst of circumstances. If necessary, I will tell it to you. Now come, this light is too healthy for my taste, and she does not need it yet."

They moved to the darkest corner of the workroom close to the top of the stairs. Charles stretched out beside Helen, cradling her head on an arm. Then he ripped open the already closing wound on his free wrist and held it to her mouth. The blood trickled slowly down her cheek, darkening her pale hair. "I'm sorry to deny you your one night of such unique and splendid passion, but a parent's embrace is so much more fitting for this creation than that of a lover. Still, it makes me feel incestuous. How stupid . . . how very human." Brushing Helen's cheek with his fingers, he coaxed, "Come infant, nurse." She choked and he jerked her head back, forcing her to swallow. Afterward she sucked, first weakly, and finally, as her lover had done to her, instinctively with growing strength, the motion of her face and neck the only sign that she lived.

Charles noted Stephen's expression. "You never could have killed me," he said.

"I was prepared to try, and in that moment I believe I would have succeeded."

Charles sighed. "Perhaps. I thank you for the attempt."

"I did not act for you, Charles," Stephen replied with remarkable calm.

"I know, but no matter. I could not allow you to destroy yourself for her or for me; not if there was some other, better way. Had I known she was here before I came to you at St. John's, there might not be this pile of inconvenient corpses between that night and the present."

"Inconvenient!" With manifest control, Stephen forced back the rage. What had been done could not be undone, and anger would only leave a sadder memory.

"Agnosticism is but one more protective instinct, little brother. For my own part, I believe the priest is with God, and I pray he intercedes for me. If there is no forgiveness in the afterlife, I want no part of it."

Charles touched his lips to Helen's temple in a kiss. "Her pulse is even but weak. We have a little time." His expression became one of intense paternal pride. "I suppose you were too occupied to notice how firmly she chose our life. Not through some silly notion of endless romance, but in the throes of despair with her eyes wide open to all the consequences of being one of us. You gave her the good, I showed her the terrible, and still she wants it. I knew she would. She is mine, and now I will make her strong, Stephen, the way our women make their children strong.

"You've never fathered children, so you do not know how, after the attendants are gone and all that is left is the father, the corpse of the mother and the newborns, you can look at the babes and see which was responsible for its mother's death. With us it was you, little brother—not I, born a few minutes earlier; not Claudia, ripped from our dead mother's womb—but you who pushed into life on the back of mother's soul." He glanced down at Helen. "I pray she received only my strength and none of my weakness; I would not want her tainted with any part of what I have become."

Understanding came to Stephen surprisingly late. "You planned this end over forty years ago, didn't you?"

"Yes, but I had not intended to wait for Helen. I had hoped to bring this beautiful infant's mother to you, and it would have ended with you and I and Lydia working peacefully together. This act, you will agree, requires trust; I'm not sure you would have given it even before we met at St. John's."

Stephen's look questioned but Charles continued quickly. "I never thanked you for sending Claudia to me. She would not admit it but I knew she had not wished to leave your arms."

"Her time approached and I would not be the father. We agreed, Charles, and she loved us both. We did not speak of her death, of course, but we thought new lives would add some happiness to yours."

"They would have." And there was nothing, nothing he had desired more than to raise them, to love them . . . but to know them would have been to destroy them, or worse.

To Stephen the sentence seemed incomplete. Perhaps the words recalled memories too painful to resurrect. He sat on the other side of Helen and reached across her, resting his hand on his brother as if his touch had the power to heal. "It was tragic she died so terribly after possessing such strength."

"Yes, she had strength." Could it have been Stephen instead of himself lying here now, dying for that sin? Never, Charles decided, for Stephen respected his weaknesses while Charles only laughed at his own until, in retaliation, they attacked and overpowered him. For an instant he thought of destroying the lie but love overrode that sudden surge of useless envy.

Charles pulled his eyes away before his expression revealed too much and looked down at Helen. "And she has strength and she will need it. Tell me, have your experts set the date yet?"

"They have."

"And are they trembling as they contemplate their projection?" He looked back at Stephen with a wry smile. "Of course you've promised them protection with that magnificent paternalism that stems from having seen both sides of slavery. The question is, little brother, can you deliver it?"

"I will try."

"You may succeed. I always thought I'd hold out until the end. That last desperate scream of humanity would make an exotic final feast." He sensed the question returning to Stephen's mind and continued quickly. "No, little brother, don't ask. I am far too weary. I believe I'll only miss being there when you explain to the family the manner of my death. Better yet, refuse to explain. Give them a mystery to occupy their endless time." He brushed his hand over Helen's neck, that deep wound now no more than a recent scar. As her body grew in strength, his own will weakened.

He touched her mind, pristine instinct in an empty shell,

that almost human soul wandering in the vast space between life and death. "Her body changes and she has grown confused. We must find her and you must bring her back. When it is done, treat me as you would one of our women, and do for this child as I did for Ann Marie in that final act of creation."

Stephen stretched out on the other side of Helen, still holding his brother's shoulder. "I will, and I know she will understand."

Helen's teeth dug deeper, finding the artery. As she bit it through, Charles lowered his head to the bare wood floor and thought of how he, with the promise of eternity, now measured his life in minutes, and then . . . then perhaps he would forget or discover something even more wonderful, though forgetfulness would be enough. "I'll say good-bye now, little brother, and again on a different plane."

"Very well. Good-bye." Stephen's eyes were dry, beyond tears. He closed them, merged with his brother this last time, and slipped into Helen's mind . . .

. . . and searched for her soul. Across that empty plain, into the dark, narrow vortex that stretched beyond imagining in the warm, red dark . . . and where the hollow ended was the light and the hum, low and pulsing . . . familiar, mesmerizing, but they fought and held above it.

It seemed she had always been in this place, featureless, helpless, alone . . . her body would not call to her, Death would not claim her. She had traveled beyond choice, beyond concern for past or present, as she waited for some future to beckon. When it came, she moved toward it until, hearing the cry, that voice from her past, she paused. Confused and uncertain, she held out insubstantial arms, beseeching him,— Come to me . . . come to me . . . to me.—

Love responded,—Come back to me—but she had no form, no direction. She drifted to and fro, seaweed in a gossamer ocean so brilliant white that, had she eyes, she would have been blind.—Come back to me—love called.—Do not leave me . . . come back . . . come back—

So similar to the words he'd used. So much a hope, so much a condemnation, a love that strong.—Go farther, little brother . . . go to her, bring her back . . . I will hold the way.—

A hesitation, then one final fusing as the trust flowed between them. Tendrils—smoky, incorporeal—joined and

lengthened. He ignored all instincts and moved closer, farther
. . . closer than he'd ever dared before, almost through . . .

—Come back to me!—

She tried to obey but direction was gone, and she waited
for her love's touch, her love's strength . . . and he found her
and held her with his thoughts and, as their souls merged, the
other drew them into life. . . .

In another place, a place of objects. In a front hallway. A
storm door opened. A screen door slammed.

—NO!!!—

Dick stopped and stared. In front of him he saw fear. He
drew his gun and waited.

. . . threads, tenuous threads, joining, waiting . . . .uncertain
except for the one who stood away.—Come, little brother.—

Heeding the command, he held her and pulled, and his grip
on life was more tenacious than on Death. They broke free!

She struggled, caught a breath of air, and fought, her arms
and legs lashing out; fiercely needing to live, unaware she had
just been saved. Released, she crouched, panting as the power
flowed through her, devouring humanity, wondering and
watching, half terrified, as body and soul reunited in a new
harmony. There was the sound of loss and gain, the unavoidable wail . . . the sound of birth. . . .

And the brothers remained together in that formless place,
locked in a farewell wordless beyond time . . . and afterward
one stayed back to feel the approach and turn at last to look on
Death.

And Death met her almost perfect conquest. Her counte-
nance, her brilliant beauty bewitched, and he hungered for her
as thousands had for him . . . here is perfection, more powerful, more glorious then he. A wild joy overpowered him and
he pursued, devoted, while she ran, growing brighter, ever
brighter, dazzling as the stars. In the instant he reached for
her, he began to struggle, began to weaken as, stronger than
his will, stronger than his soul, stronger than Death, his body
pulled him back. . . .

—You cannot deny me, little brother . . . let me go . . . me
go . . . It's just a shell, only a shell, yet it binds me and draws
me back. Give me your hands . . . mine are dead . . . lend me
yours. Touch me, little brother . . . touch me . . . touch . . . —

—Yes!—Stephen placed his knees below his brother's

shoulders, lowered his head, forehead meeting forehead; took a deep breath and tensed. This was the correct posture for a final ritual. He remembered . . . from the moment of his birth he remembered!

—Now?—

—Now!—

His hands left his control to grasp his brother's neck and squeeze. As his head pushed down, he heard a snap.

It ended as he remembered, with low, fading laughter. . . .

Stephen dropped his brother and rose, stretching arms wide, throwing back his head. His elemental lamentation moved up and out, spreading beyond the walls and ceiling to the air and the sky . . . an excruciating shriek of loss.

And throughout the world the family paused, wondered, and began their private mourning.

From his place at the foot of the stairs, Dick pointed his gun at the form filling the doorway, uncertain who stood above him. He looked to Helen for some sign, but she crouched at the feet of the survivor, appearing dazed until, noticing the body beside her, her lower-pitched cry joined the other.

Dick moved back a step, his body shaking, but whether it was from relief or weakness he did not know. As the victor's arms rose, he saw the three holes in the blood-coated shirt and knew it was Stephen who had survived.

He should have put his gun away then but he didn't. Instead, his hands still unsteady from the night's struggles, he pointed it at his ally. For a moment the only thing preventing him from firing was fear as he thought of whose death Stephen lamented. They were the same . . . their concerns, their codes, so inhuman. "Caring is a luxury. . . . I savored the terror that sweetened his blood. . . . Desire, Richard . . . hours . . ." Damn him! Damn her! "Be thankful we are friends. . . ."

A self-disgust more terrible than any he had felt in all those hours with Charles hit him with physical intensity. He began to lower the weapon when behind him he heard the screen door open, the ensuing human scream.

Her father had found her downstairs in a room with Alan.

Without waiting for Corey or arranging a release, he'd commandeered the first cab to arrive at Elmbrook and dropped her off at her aunt's. As the cab pulled away, Carol knew she must get there ahead of her father. She had a job to do; no one must enter that flat. No one! She ran.

She opened the screen door and saw she'd returned too late, saw her father... saw his gun drawn and pointed at Stephen, now so altered... heard that earsplitting wail. The night, the morning... now this! She screamed.

At the sound Dick jumped, his hands moved, his fingers instinctively squeezed, and the bullet did not miss. Looking up, Dick saw Stephen, blood dripping from a new wound, his lips pulled back in a snarl, his eyes smoldering with rage.

How many shots could he fire? Dick began to aim, then, horrified at the temptation, dropped the gun as if the handle were red-hot. "Get back to Billy's!" he ordered, and thrust Carol through the door.

Acting on some remembered knowledge, he locked his hands behind his back, stared at the ceiling, thought only of surrender, and prayed. He listened for Stephen's descent, prepared to count the steps to his own death, but Stephen, when he came, did not bother with the stairs. A shadow rolled over him and through him, and he spoke in Stephen's language in a familiar, dreadful voice impossible for him to achieve. As the presence in him vanished, he collapsed.

An echo returned him to consciousness, his own voice repeating word for word the thoughts being planted in his mind. "No, Sergeant, everything's all right. I had an accident. No one was hurt.... Of course, I'll have the gun checked over tomorrow morning...." His body even managed to dredge up a convincing caricature of a smile as he closed Stephen's lower door.

But he bore no ill will toward his neighbor, no anger for how thoroughly he was being manipulated. In the instant when he had held his gun on the man—yes, damn it, the man—that was his friend and thought, *Dare I risk it*? he realized the just concern Stephen had for the future of his people.

Dick turned from the door and saw Stephen watching him intently from the top of the stairs. Understanding passed between them and Stephen released him and, without waiting to see which way he would go, moved out of the doorway.

Dick began to ascend the stairs . . . one step, two, three, then stopped and slid weakly down to lean against the wall. He could continue. He did not wish to continue. His aid would be needed but it could wait. Inexplicably, he mourned. He lost track of time as he sat there, perhaps he even slept, and he only knew it was later when he finished the climb.

Upstairs, there was no sign of a body, or blood, or of any struggle. Helen lay sleeping, curled in a comfortable ball on the end of the sofa. Stephen's back was to Dick, his body silhouetted by the warm-toned glass as he leaned on outstretched arms against the autumn window. He had been recalling how Helen's presence had been all that had stopped him from destroying this man's daughter a few short hours ago in his voracious need for life. He meditated on this because it was the hardest thing to consider . . . far worse than the deaths because those were over and could not be undone, while his nature would hold him forever separate.

But there were times when, in spite of impossible odds, the distance between their worlds was bridged. "After what was done to you, what you knew about me, you trusted me?" The words were heavy with sadness and surprise.

"The alternatives were worse."

"Dying with the sin or living with the memory?"

Dick nodded, then saw Stephen wasn't facing him and remembered that that, too, made no difference. "Your brother told me what to do. I guess he even left the right words with me."

Stephen turned. "I've learned restraint with age. Perhaps your stance alone would have made me pause. Thank you, Richard, for surviving." He looked at Helen. "For giving me one other priceless thing to balance the loss."

"My life?"

"Your friendship."

This conversation had become too intense, too intimate for Dick. He walked around the table to look down at Helen. She was covered with caked blood—on her clothes, in her hair, a thin line running down one cheek—yet her sleep was as unconcerned as a small child's. "Will she be all right?" he asked.

"I believe so. She made her choice, and now she must learn to live as one of us in your world. I doubt her tranquil years here will make the lessons easier, though, perhaps, easier to bear."

Emotion charged this room, as real as the colors that permeated the air...a relaxation, a feeling they had been cleansed as the city had been washed free of debris by the rain. Yet the problems were far from over. There would be a multitude of questions, of deaths to resolve, and, somewhere, a corpse to destroy. Still, Dick would not break the serenity of this moment with such troubling, concrete words.

Instead, his eyes roamed the room, sweeping nervously past the crystal sculpture, then returning to lock on it. This had been him not so long ago, trapped by a passion beyond human in that narrow space between pleasure and pain. He heard movement behind him and turned slowly, uncertain of what to expect.

Helen was stretching and sitting up, and when she opened her eyes and looked at him, all his concern for her future vanished.

These were not the eyes of his niece; they were not Stephen's ancient, commanding eyes, but rather the eyes of an infant—unfathomable and utterly pure—and she looked at him the way a person blind from birth must stare at the first human face he sees when given the gift of sight. He felt her mind move through his and held his breath, waiting for her to speak. But all he received was compassion so intense, tears should have followed.

A whispered thought meant only for him.—She cares for you and so she shares your pain.—

So many questions answered so easily. Sitting down beside Helen, Dick wrapped his arms around her shoulders. "We're all going to be fine," he told her, then looked up at Stephen and silently renewed, with a fierce new resolve, his agreement to do everything necessary to make certain those words stayed true.

As he sat in that quiet room, Dick found he wanted to apologize, as if he were personally responsible for what had happened here today. He would have begun, but he could not find the words to explain.

—Don't search for them.—Even the thought was muted, and they sat without speaking until the ringing of the phone shattered the silence.

# III

That evening movers arrived to transfer crates and cartons and most of the furniture from Stephen's apartment to La-Guardia for a private flight to Chavez. Their activity went unnoticed among the neighborhood talk of the strange accidents that had claimed three lives during the height of the storm.

Four afternoons later a thronged St. John's said good-bye to its pastor, who had died in a futile and, many parishioners agreed, foolhardy attempt to stop the storm's destruction of the rose window. The Good Samaritan who had come to his aid had bound his wrists and arranged for an ambulance that never came.

Dick and the children attended the service. Helen and Sylvia stayed away, mourning an additional loss in private. Stephen Austra visited Judy.

She let him enter her untidy apartment with a reluctant politeness that stemmed from being certain she could not keep him out. It was mid-afternoon, yet she was still wrapped in a thick, comforting chenille bathrobe. She had not left these rooms since she'd been released from the hospital two days earlier, and this morning it had been an effort even to comb her hair. When Dick phoned, she would not speak to him.

Stephen leaned against the closed door and crossed his arms. As she had been with him at their last meeting, he was blunt. "I came to ask you when you intend to live."

"When I can forget."

Judy had meant these words to sound bitter. But he responded simply. "Would you like to forget?"

"No." Her whisper had the intensity of a scream.

"Then you never intend to live."

"It isn't like that." She spoke softly and, as she did, leaned against the back of the chair and stared at some indefinite spot on the floor between her feet and his. Aware of how fearful her stance had become, she glared at him as she continued. "I

371

was responsible for what happened to Dick . . . to both of us. Three people died because of me. I have to learn to live with that guilt."

"And?" he continued mercilessly, knowing she was lying.

Pushing herself upright, she walked to within a few inches of him and, startled at her anger, lashed back. "And I wish it had never happened . . . and I know there is no one who will understand this sorrow, this wrenching loss. He didn't rape me. I wanted him. I want him now, and I hate you both for killing him!" Her fists were white-knuckled and she wanted to pound them against him.

In reply, Stephen took one of her hands, uncurled the fingers, and enclosed them with his own. "I killed him myself. I did it only because he knew he must die. But had he ever said stop, I would have saved him. Now he is dead and you are alive."

In response to Stephen's sorrow, her eyes began to fill with tears, but she blinked them back. "That knowledge won't help. . . . It doesn't explain how I feel."

And what would? That Charles had seduced her, had used her only as a means to his end? It would be the truth, but to say it would only add one more obscenity to the many this woman had endured. Instead, he replied, "When any creature lives as long as my brother lived, it is natural to mourn. When he took you as he did, even though his motive was not to give pleasure, you received it, and it is right for you to wish to remember. It is good you have this strength."

She took a small, decisive step and leaned her body against his, though neither of them raised their arms. "But you exist . . ." she began.

"Judy, if I thought my loving you would ease your sorrow, I would not hesitate, but it would only add the hurt of one more parting."

She rested her head on his shoulder. "Then I don't know what to do."

"Why not begin by yielding to one very human luxury." He stepped back and slowly raised her palms and kissed them in gratitude for that which only she could give. "Now cry," he said, and pulled her against him. As their minds linked, her tears released them both.